Daughter
OF THE
Otherworld

Also by Shauna Lawless

The Gael Song Series

Novels

The Children of Gods and Fighting Men

The Words of Kings and Prophets

The Land of the Living and the Dead

Novellas

Dreams of Fire

Dreams of Sorrow

Dreams of Chaos

Gael Song: Era II

Novels

Daughter of the Otherworld

Daughter of the Otherworld

SHAUNA LAWLESS

GAEL SONG: ERA II, BOOK I

An Ad Astra Book

First published in the UK in 2025 by Head of Zeus,
part of Bloomsbury Publishing Plc

Copyright © Shauna Lawless, 2025

The moral right of Shauna Lawless to be identified
as the author of this work has been asserted in accordance with
the Copyright, Designs and Patents Act of 1988.

All rights reserved. No part of this publication may be: i) reproduced or transmitted in any form, electronic or mechanical, including photocopying, recording or by means of any information storage or retrieval system without prior permission in writing from the publishers; or ii) used or reproduced in any way for the training, development or operation of artificial intelligence (AI) technologies, including generative AI technologies. The rights holders expressly reserve this publication from the text and data mining exception as per Article 4(3) of the Digital Single Market Directive (EU) 2019/790.

This is a work of fiction. All characters, organizations, and events portrayed in this novel are either products of the author's imagination or are used fictitiously.

9 7 5 3 1 2 4 6 8

A catalogue record for this book is available from the British Library.

ISBN (HB): 9781035911295; ISBN (BROKEN BINDING HB): 9781035924141;
ISBN (XTPB): 9781035911264; ISBN (EBOOK): 9781035911271

Cover design: Susan Burghart
Map design: Jamie Whyte

Printed and bound in Great Britain by
CPI Group (UK) Ltd, Croydon CR0 4YY

Bloomsbury Publishing Plc
50 Bedford Square, London, WC1B 3DP, UK
Bloomsbury Publishing Ireland Limited,
29 Earlsfort Terrace, Dublin 2, D02 AY28, Ireland

HEAD OF ZEUS LTD
5–8 Hardwick Street
London, EC1R 4RG

To find out more about our authors and books
visit www.headofzeus.com

For product safety related questions contact productsafety@bloomsbury.com

For my family

Characters

The Descendants of the Tuatha Dé Danann

Isolde (Is-old-a) – Daughter of Fódla the Descendant and Murchad son of Brian Boru, sister to Aoife and Tairdelbach.

Broccan (Brock-an) – A warrior, son of Rónnat, cousin to Isolde.

Fódla (Foe-la) – A healer, mother of Aoife and Isolde, now deceased.

Aoife (Ee-fa) – Daughter of Tomas and Fódla. Born giftless, now deceased.

Rónnat (Roe-nat) – A witch, sister of Fódla and mother of Broccan, now deceased.

Colmon (Cole-mun) – A warrior, cousin of Fódla and Rónnat.

Affraic (Af-frik) – A healer, mother of Báine and Étaín, grandmother of Neasa.

Báine (Bawn-yeh) – A witch, daughter of Affraic.

Étaín (Ay-teen) – A witch, daughter of Affraic, mother to Neasa, now deceased.

Shae (Shay) – A harpist, uncle to Gisela.

Méabh (Mayve) – A cupbearer.

Gisela (Giz-ella) – A harpist, niece of Shae.

Senna (Senn-a) – A witch.

Siobhan (Shiv-awn) – A healer.

Tomas (To-mass) – Leader of the Descendants of the Tuatha Dé Danann, father of Aoife. A druid, now deceased.

Echna (Eek-na) – A druid, now deceased.
Neasa (Nee-sa) – A healer, granddaughter of Affraic. Taken by the Fomorians.

The Fomorians

Gormflaith (Gorm-la), known as Alys (Al-iss) – Fomorian, sister to Máelmórda, mother to Sitric, Donnchad and Godfrey (deceased).
Máelmórda (Mal-mor-da) – Fomorian, brother to Gormflaith, father to Cecile.
Donnchad (Dunn-a-kha), known as Donn (Don) – Fomorian, son of Gormflaith and Brian Boru, father to Angelo, half-brother to Murchad.
Angus (Eng-yus), known as Angelo (An-je-lo) – Fomorian, son of Donnchad.
Cecile (Sess-eel) – A Fomorian, daughter of Máelmórda and Neasa the Descendant.
Olaf Tryggvasson (O-lav Trig-vass-on) – A former king of Norway. Not a Fomorian, but kept captive in bird form by Gormflaith.

The Kingdom Of Dublin

Asculv (Ask-ulv) – King of Dublin.
Eric (Err-ick) – Wealthy trader.
Hálfdan (Helf-den) – A trader.
Håkon (Hoe-kon) – An orphaned boy.
Sitric (Sit-rik), known as Sitric Silkbeard – King of Dublin, son of Gormflaith and Amlav of Dublin.
Godfrey (God-free) – Son of Gormflaith and Olaf, brought up by Sitric as his own son, now deceased.
Edysis (Ed-yah-sis) – Daughter of Sitric and his first wife Onguen, now deceased.

The Kingdom of Connacht

King Ruaidrí Ó Conchúir (Rou-a-ree O'Connor) – King of Connacht, married to Gráinne, father to Róisín and Conchobar.

Queen Gráinne (Graw-ne-yeh) – Wife of King Ruaidrí.

Róisín (Ro-sheen) – Daughter of King Ruaidrí and Queen Gráinne.

Conchobar (Kru-hur) – Son of King Ruaidrí and Queen Gráinne.

Cathal (Ka-hul) – Younger brother of King Ruaidrí.

Cuan (Koo-an) – Son of Bardán, nephew of King Ruaidrí, nephew of King Godred of the Isles.

Bardán (Bar-dawn) – Brother of King Ruaidrí, father of Cuan.

Osán (Oss-awn) – Friend of Bardán.

Fearghus (Fer-a-gus) – A warrior of Connacht.

Scolaí (Scull-lee) – A warrior of Connacht.

Blinne (Blin-yeh) – A woman of Connacht, a distant relative of King Ruaidrí.

Tóla (Toe-la) – King Ruaidrí's brehon.

The Kingdom of Leinster

King Diarmait Mac Murchadha (Deer-mit Mac Murrough) – King of Leinster.

Domhnall (Doe-nall) – Son of King Diarmait.

Énna (Ay-nah) – Son of King Diarmait.

Eva (Eve-a) – Daughter of King Diarmait.

Connor (Conn-er) – Son of King Diarmait.

Riagáin (Ree-awn) – Translator for King Diarmait.

Caomhán (Keev-awn) – Son of Domhnall.

Olcán (Ul-cawn) – Son of King Diarmait's foster brother.

The Kingdom of Ulaid

King Magnus mac Duinn Sléibe (Mag-nus Mac Donlevy) – King of Ulaid.
Nuala (Noo-la) – Granddaughter of King Maghnus.
Dáirinn (Dawr-inn) – Granddaughter of King Maghnus.
Moncha (Muncha) – Granddaughter of King Maghnus.
Naoise (Nee-sha) – Stablemaster.

The Kingdom of Bréifne

Tigernán Ua Ruairc (Tier-nawn O'Rourke) – King of Bréifne.
Derbhfhorgaill (Derv-al) – Former Wife of King Tiernan.

Rathlin Island

Móirne (Morn-yeh) – A friend of Isolde, sister to Síoda.
Síoda (Shee-da) – Younger sister of Móirne.

The Anglo-Normans

Richard de Clare/Strongbow – Contested Earl of Pembroke, Lord of Striguil, an Anglo-Norman knight.
Robert FitzStephen – An Anglo-Norman knight.
Maurice de Prendergast – A Flemish knight.
Meilyr FitzHenry (My-lear) – An Anglo-Norman knight.
Hervey de Montmorency – An Anglo-Norman knight.
Miles FitzDavid – An Anglo-Norman knight.
Gerald FitzStephen – An Anglo-Norman knight.
Raymond FitzGerald, known as Le Gros – An Anglo-Norman knight.
David FitzWilliam – An Anglo-Norman knight.

The Kingdom of the Isles

King Godred (God-red) – King of the Isles, uncle to Cuan.
Ragnall (Rag-nall) – Son of King Godred.
Olaf (O-lav) – Son of King Godred.
Bjorn (Be-orn) – Friend of Cuan.

Animals

Sleipnir – Cuan's horse.
Bruce – Maurice de Prendergast's hunting dog.

I shall not see a world that will be dear to me,
Summer without flowers,
Kine without milk,
Men without valour, captures without a king,
Woods without mast, seas without produce,
Wrong judgements of old men,
Every man a betrayer, every boy a reaver,
And the queen of the cowslip and clover will be
the only one to save us,
Two daughters she will have,
One to pass through death
The other to destroy fire.

BEFORE

PROLOGUE

Donnchad

Dublin, 1064

Fifty years after the Battle of Clontarf

Only three days ago, I had answered to many names. Donnchad, son of Brian Boru. King of the Dál gCais. King of Munster.

The latter two were gone now. Stripped from me by my nephew, Toir, whose army snapped at my heels.

Riding hard, day and night, it was the sight of Dublin's walls that became my first comfort – the only time my sense of dread had eased at all since Toir had taken the dun at Killaloe from me. For fifty years, I'd held my father's kingdom, but it seemed that the days of Donnchad Uí Brian ruling Munster were over. With the loss of my kingship, my safety had eroded. It wasn't just Toir who followed me, but also Broccan, a warrior Descendant of the Tuatha Dé Danann.

It was Broccan who scared me the most. With no mortals to shield me and get in his way, he would come for me and rip my body apart. That was the truth. That was what awaited me. If Toir's army didn't find me first, Broccan would be sure to finish me off. I could only imagine that the devil would take my soul.

I brought fire to my left hand for a moment. The flames danced there. Fomorian was another name I owned, a name no one could take. *With my fire-magic, I could burn it all.* Not just the forest I rode through, but everything. Dublin. Munster. Tara. I could burn all those who had failed me. I could wait here for Toir to reach me and destroy him before he even set foot on the grass. With my other hand, I reached for the water of the River Liffey. This was my other gift. My strength. With fire and water to dance at my command, few could challenge me. Broccan, yes. A Descendant with the warrior gift could destroy me. But not Toir. Not his mortal army.

Perhaps, if I had been alone, I might have stood my ground. I might have thought death at the hands of Broccan worth it, if I could raze this land first.

But I was not alone. My son, Angus, rode in front of me. No. I could not let Broccan kill him. And so, I let the flame in my hand recede, rode on to the gates of Dublin and waited for Sitric's men to allow me inside.

My brother did not greet me at the doors of his fortress as he usually did, cup of wine in hand, ready with a slap on the back, or else some insult to explain why he could not favour my kingdom over another. This time a warrior took me to my brother's bedroom. A bedroom that smelled of death and rot.

"Is that you, Donnchad?" The body lying under thick furs moved a little as I entered.

"Brother." I moved to his bedside. Angus stood by the door, then moved to his knees and crawled into the corner of the room.

"He's yours?" Sitric asked from his bed, though it wasn't a true question. Anyone with eyes in their head could see he was mine.

"He looks like our mother."

"He does."

Sitric sighed, his eyelids closing a moment longer than was usual. "You are here because Toir has finally ousted you from your kingdom. Is that right?"

I nodded.

"I cannot help you, Donnchad. I am dying."

He did not say this looking for sympathy, so I gave him none. Only the truth. "Yes, brother. I see that you are."

"I've decided I wish to go to Sláine when I die."

"Not Valhalla?"

Sitric shook his head. "When my brother Gluniairn died, there was a big meeting in this very hall. He was murdered, still in his prime, and no one knew how he wanted to be buried. He was pagan his whole life, but he had converted. Not a true conversion. He merely wanted to trade with the Christian princes and kings across the water." Sitric closed his eyes again, a small smile growing on his lips. "You don't remember him, you are too young, but oh, Gluniairn was tough. *Iron knee*, they called him. A frightening man in many ways, but what a man. What a king. I was in shock when he died. My mother manipulated the funeral, of course. Had him buried as a Christian just so it would appease King Sechnall of Meath."

"You think now it was not the burial Gluniairn wanted?"

"Not think. I *know* it wasn't… but wise men learn from the mistakes of others, and so everyone here knows what *I* want. I've decided, though I miss my brothers, it is my wife and my children that I wish to see in my afterlife. Edysis, my daughter… you remember her, don't you? She will be there. Sláine had her baptised, even though I did not care for the Christ faith at the time."

My brother, his skin sunken and almost grey, smiled as he pictured those dead and gone before him. His daughter, Edysis. I remembered her. A wild girl with an infectious laugh. I remembered Sláine, my half-sister, too. Cold and clever, she had been, much like our father.

"This is a wise choice, brother."

"Perhaps. If heaven awaits, yes. God knows I have paid enough gold and silver to these priests for indulgences that my salvation must be assured, though there are many who will say I do not deserve it."

I nodded, for I could not think of anything to say. Besides, judgements on salvation and who deserved it were not mine to give. Whatever awaited my brother, it would come for him soon. Death hovered in this room. It was a smell that permeated everything. I could taste it in my mouth. Sitric had days left. If that.

"I am glad you have come here, Donnchad. I knew you would. I just hoped I would still be alive when Toir made his move."

"Toir has been very persistent... And in the end... In the end, the people loved him more than me."

"To be king is one thing. To stay king is another." Sitric glanced at the door where light and the sound of distant voices drifted through. "My sons and grandsons will find Dublin hard to hold. The Irish kings see the prize that Dublin is and will try to take it once I go. I pray that they are strong enough to resist. War flows through their veins. Not fire."

He spoke the last two words quietly. His eyes, heavy and red, were still sharp enough to take me in. We had not spoken of my fire-magic. *Ever.* Mother had told me she concealed it from him as she had from all mortals, and yet, I could see in those heavy-lidded eyes that he knew the truth of what she was. Of what I was.

"Even fire doesn't save you in the end, brother."

He grunted, shivering a little as he pulled his blanket closer. "Where will you go?"

"Away from this land. That is why I came here. Someone is following me. Someone who wants to kill me. Which ship in the longphort could bear me and my son away today?"

"There's a ship of monks. They leave for Rome. At midday. To pray for my soul."

"They will take me?"

Sitric nodded. "The ship is owned by a man called Cnut. Tell him you are my brother."

I took his hand in mine and kissed it. "Thank you, Sitric. We argued often, but thank you for this."

Unexpectedly, Sitric gripped my hand tight, crushing my fingers together. "I don't do it just for you. I do it for my children and the children that will come after them."

"What?"

"When you see my mother, tell her I have told my children about her. Tell her they have told their own children to never let her into this city. Tell her that kin-slayers and those who murder the children of Sitric are not welcome within these walls. The priests have cursed her name, so have the Valkyries. If she comes back here, she will die. Tell her that."

Sitric coughed and let go of my hand. Blood and bile poured onto the pillow as he lurched forward. Quickly, two of the female slaves who'd been working in the feasting hall came running in to turn Sitric over. I thought of telling him that our mother would be dead by now, for she had left Ireland fifty years ago and had been old by mortal years even then. But the time for lies was over. Just as he seemed to know about our fire, he also knew we did not age in the same way as he did. Lying on the bed, white-haired and withered, he looked every bit a man in his tenth decade. I was in my sixties, but still looked in my prime. The evidence of my Fomorian nature was written upon my face, and I would not ruin my last words with Sitric by lying to him.

Instead, I stood. Inched backward. "Goodbye, Sitric."

"Goodbye, Donnchad," he wheezed as the women gently set his head back onto his pillow. "And do not come back here either. Go. Take your poison to a land that can suffer it. We can bear it no longer here."

He coughed, his lungs rattling, and the slave girls, once again, tried to comfort him.

"Come, Angus." I walked out of Sitric's room and into the feasting hall. Sitric's grandsons sat there drinking. All of them save for one was dark-haired like Sitric, me, and my mother. The other's hair was flaxen, eyes of the palest blue. They all watched me as I walked past them, smirking and laughing. I said nothing. It was all well and good for them to laugh now at the king who was, but my brother was right. When Sitric died, the Irish kings would gather like wolves around a fresh carcass. Soon, it would be *them* without a kingdom.

★

I spotted the monks as soon as I made it to the longphort. Glancing around me, I searched for signs of Broccan. The panic inside me, however, had lessened. I was close to the sea now. Close to the water that danced to my command. If he attacked me here, I would win.

"You are going to Rome?" I asked the men tending to the ship, speaking the language my half-brother Sitric had taught me in my youth. "Who here is Cnut?"

"I am," a man answered, tall and balding. He pointed at the monks who were already clambering into the ship. "They bring gifts from Dublin to give to the holy Pope so he will pray for the soul of King Sitric. What business is it of yours?"

"Sitric is my brother. He told me you could take me and my son with you."

"We are leaving now," Cnut said, frowning. "Where are your provisions?"

I reached into my leather bag and took out a golden cup, embedded with jewels, that my father had given me. Cnut's eyes widened, then narrowed. He knew it was too much and wondered why I offered it.

"I must pray for my soul," I said. "What use is wealth if we are not welcomed into the Kingdom of Heaven. Sitric understands this, and it is why he said I can go with you. Ask him yourself if you wish."

Cnut glanced at my son, who stared up at him with his large golden eyes. Then Cnut turned his gaze to the fortress. Sitric's priest stood on the steps there, watching the two of us, and nodded.

"Very well." Cnut gestured for us to go aboard. "We have enough for two more."

Smiling, I lifted Angus onto the ship, before the man could change his mind, and sat beside the monks.

Cnut began to bark out his commands. The sails were to be readied. Someone was to bring in another barrel of water. His men should take out their oars. His instructions fulfilled, the rope attaching the ship to the longphort was let loose, and the men holding the oars pushed the ship into the Irish Sea.

I glanced at the beach as we drifted out, the ship, for now, staying close to the shoreline. All was quiet, but then I saw him. A man galloping toward Dublin. His long golden hair blew out behind him, and I could see the red scars along his face.

It was Broccan. Warrior Descendant of the Tuatha Dé Danann and my eternal enemy. For I had killed many aside from my father that day in Clontarf and he'd sworn vengeance upon me.

"Hurry," I said to Cnut. "Move further out."

Broccan rode closer, his head already turned to the sea, spear in hand. He could smell us. Smell the fire-magic that Angus had practised using so recently. I didn't put it past him to try to reach us still. My water-magic might be strong enough to hold him back, but on a ship like this, I could not use my fire-magic, for it would burn and Angus could not swim. If he reached us, our lives were over.

"Further out, Cnut," I shouted.

Cnut gave me a knowing smile as he moved the steering board and turned the ship out to sea. He understood now why I had offered him so much. He understood that I was not leaving but escaping. Cnut did not know Broccan was a Descendant. Fomorians and Descendants of the Tuatha Dé Danann were a secret to the mortals of Ireland, though anyone could see that the man riding along the beach was a killer.

Using my water-magic, I urged the currents to push the ship out to sea. *Faster. Faster.* The wind blew into the sails and the ship sped forward, piercing the waves. The longphort and the beach grew smaller. As did Broccan. He stared after me as the ship sailed away. That had been close, so very close. But no other ship could bring him after us this day, and so, for now, I was safe. And Rome was to be my sanctuary.

★

Gold. Silver. Men talk of such things in Ireland with a glazed look in their eyes. They want it, desire it. Rarity and beauty. Two things combined.

I wish these men, all of them, could see Rome. See the churches. See that, in some lands, gold and silver and beauty was everywhere. Not rare at all. In Rome, statues of emperors and angels stood side by side. Power and the divine together.

It truly was a place of plenty. From prince to priest, the men dressed so decadently that the Irish queens would burn with envy, and I saw so much unclothed flesh that I felt as if I were inside of a dream.

Exhaustion tugged at me as I walked. Though I was dressed in my own silks and furs, I smelled more of salt and sea than man. It had been a hard voyage. If the swell of the waves was not ravaging me, it was the blaze of the sun above. I did not complain. Could not. Every lurch of the ship had brought me further away from Broccan.

Despite my fatigue, I felt oddly at peace as I walked about in this strange land. Not scared to be only in the company of my seven-year-old son and no warriors at my side. I had time. Time to be alone. But solitude had to wait. There was someone I had to see first.

My walk to the Lateran Palace was short but illuminating. Now I was closer to His Holiness, so were others. Here my eyes still feasted, but my other senses died a death. *Urine. Shit. Sweat.* Rome was like a battlefield where no one was fighting. Or perhaps they were fighting, not for thrones and crowns, but merely to live under the shadow of angels and not catch their gaze while they sinned.

Angus pinched my hand as he stared at these same statues, the ones made of marble that stood along the pathway to the Lateran Palace and shook his head. He did not want to enter.

"Stay here," I said. "Hide. And no fire."

My son didn't need to be told twice, and I watched as he ran down an alleyway. My own flesh and blood, and I let him go, though I knew the risk. If Broccan had followed us, I had to assume he would kill Angus, too.

So why did I not run? Why did I not grab Angus and flee? The question ran through my mind, over and over. I should run now. I should run and never stop, but Sitric's final words wouldn't leave me. His words of heaven and hell.

Of choosing where to go when you died.

Where did men who killed their own fathers go? What about men who had tried to kill their mother? My sins didn't end there. I had ordered the killing of my half-brother Tadc, too. Ordered thousands of men to die fighting for me. If I were to go to heaven, only God's closest servant could forgive me.

I took out my crucifix, the golden one that had once belonged to my father, laid it against the fur trim of my tunic and made for the doors. The men standing guard, the very same ones who pushed beggars and paupers away, stood aside to let me in. And inside I went. Toward the infallible.

Pope Alexander II stared at me as I came into the church. He stared at my silver and gold and jewels, unimpressed, though my fur did hold his gaze a little longer.

"What do you wish of me, my son?"

"I wish to confess my sins."

This man, so finely dressed in silk, made the sign of the cross and beckoned for me to come closer. "Tell me them."

"I killed my father. My half-brother, too. I tried to kill my mother by putting a blade in her stomach. As king, I have killed at least fifty others with my own hand, hundreds have been killed at my request, and many more have died because I sent them out to fight in my name."

"Such is war," the Pope said, licking his lips. "Such is life as a king. But to murder your father and brother, to try to kill your mother, these are grievous sins indeed. Mortal sins."

"Yes. I know." I removed the golden crucifix from around my

neck and the rings from my fingers, then held them out for the Pope to take.

"To be granted an indulgence for such sins, it will cost a great deal. What do you have to offer me? It must be more than this."

I lowered my head and looked at the worn leather of my shoes. What more could I give a man of God? "I would give you all the souls of Ireland," I said. "If you would grant me papal aid to retake my kingdom, your warriors to defeat my foes who haunt my steps, we could save thousands of souls."

"I already have the souls of your kingdom. Ireland has converted."

"No, I fear you do not have them. The Irish kingdoms live in the old ways still. I see it now so clearly. The angels… they watch Ireland and despair. Men there still have many wives. They divorce. They listen to the old laws, not the laws of Christ. If you were to give me assistance, I would go back and show them the light I have witnessed here."

The Pope leaned forward, took the gold crucifix from my hand and rubbed it between his fingers. "If I could give you help, my son, I would. Alas, there are wars beyond this land I must see to first. Barbastro. It is all I see. The Moors there are our enemy, you must understand, and I have no time to spare on a war with those who call themselves my children. It is for the bishops there to tend to their flocks. But I do hear your plight, my son. I will record it so that those who come after me will know of Ireland and the sin that festers there. One day, when the time is right, my servants will visit your land and decide what must be done."

I bit my lip as I pushed the rings he would not take back onto my fingers. It would not do to show my disappointment. "And what of my forgiveness?"

"I absolve you of your venial sins, my child. As Christ forgave Barabas, I forgive you of these. I cannot, however, forgive your mortal sins with such a trivial gift. Come back to me when you have more to offer, and we shall speak again."

★

I was no longer a king. Now no longer a man, for how can one be a man with such a sentence hanging around his neck? Hell. It was a noose, and with every day that passed, I would feel that noose tightening.

I made my way outside of the palace, pushing past the beggars and whores grabbing at me, their eyes glittering with the gold and silver I wore on my fingers, until I reached the alleyway where I had left my son. Perhaps gold and silver was not so commonplace here as I first thought.

"Angus, we must go," I called out.

I stared at the gloom of the alleyway for a while. No child came forward.

"Angus!" I pushed through a crowd of children throwing dice and strode into the alleyway. The putrid smell here was unlike anything I'd encountered before. Rats ran over my feet and along the streets. Not in ones and twos but in groups of ten and twenty. "Angus!"

"You must be more careful, Donnchad. Children are precious. Those with fire, even more so."

I looked to my right. There was my mother, her hand wrapped around my son, the two of them sitting on some steps that led to the upper floor of a house. *Sitric was right.* She was alive. Alive, and more beautiful than ever.

"Are you here to kill me?" I asked.

"Why should I kill you when you bring me such a gift?" She smiled down at Angus, squeezing his hand tight. He gazed up at her, and very slowly, he smiled back. "Killing is so final, is it not, and there is much you can do for me, Donnchad. Many ways that you can make up for what happened at Clontarf."

I ran my hand over my beard, thinking of an excuse for what I had done, then stopped myself. There was no point. "How did you find me?" was the question I asked instead.

"I dreamed of you, but I also dream of another. Broccan of the Tuatha Dé Danann is only half a day away from Rome. He means to take your life."

"You lie. He could not have caught up with me so quickly."

"I do not lie. This is why I am here. I might have let him kill you. Indeed, I was not sure what I would do when I reached you. But I cannot let him kill Angus, and I suppose you are my son. If you value your life, you must come with me."

"All my possessions are in the inn. Everything."

"All replaceable. Your life and that of your son are not. Come," she said, standing. Her long dark curls ran to her waist, and even in this place of dirt and gloom, she appeared as pure as any of the angels outside the palace. "We must stay ahead of Broccan."

"How can we?"

"We must get ahead of him so he can no longer catch our scent." She stared me over. "Give the beggars your cloak. Take one of their ragged ones in return. You are a king no longer but a vagabond, roaming for scraps."

"My fur is valuable. We can trade it for—"

"No more. Now it is only a marker, a way for Broccan to discover our whereabouts when he is too far away to smell us. Think of how easily you can recall the men who guarded the Pope. Now think of all the beggars you passed on the streets and of how you cannot remember a single one of their faces."

I did as she asked and stripped away my finery, while she transformed herself into an old woman, indistinct and sexless. That was her stolen gift. Witch-magic. While I controlled the water, she could change her image or the image of anyone she touched. She reached out then, touched my hair, and my black curls turned grey and white. The skin around my eyes sagged, my back hunched over.

"That is much better. You both will need new names, too. Mine is Alys." She stared at me. "Yours can be Donato. And you." She winked at my son. "You can be Angelo." Holding hands, my mother and son moved further into the alleyway, disappearing into the squalid gloom. Disrobed of my kingdom, my finery, my face, and now my name, I followed.

I pushed away my feelings of guilt and fury and loss. There was a lesson here, a lesson in my mother's reappearance and apparent forgiveness. Survive. Live. There will always be another chance to take back what was yours. And I meant to take it all back. Time was all I needed, and fortunately, I had that on my side.

Broccan

Sahara Desert, 1152

The sun burned so hot that the air danced. Hazed and rippled. The sand at my feet glistened almost white, though the dunes beyond the haze were darker, deeper, full of reds and oranges and the colour of fire.

The people of this land said that the ghosts of the desert showed false pictures within this dance. They showed you beautiful strangers, lovers of times past, sumptuous feasts and rivers. Anything your heart desired. Anything that might lure you toward them so they could steal your soul and ride with it to the afterlife that had forsaken them.

I liked to listen to tales like this.

I had travelled far and wide over the last one hundred years, and it always intrigued me to hear the similarities between mankind's stories. While new religions rose and crashed against each other, creating conflict and war between their followers, I found the older ways held more wisdom. Men and women spoke of them with smiles upon their faces.

"Broccan, do you wish to continue?" my guide, Ziri, asked. I could tell from his tone that he hoped I would say no. His gaze flickered toward the haze. Whatever he saw there, he did not wish to go any closer.

"Does anyone live out here?" I asked.

"No. It is impossible. Only nomads pass through, but they are from this land and know the desert more than they know themselves. No one else can survive here."

"Are you sure?"

"The desert is cruel. Too cruel, and cruellest most of all to those who do not understand it."

His eyes roved to my pale skin and blue eyes. *You do not belong here*, he was trying to tell me. The desert was death, especially to an outsider like me. If I were to walk toward the haze, toward the faces I saw shimmering there, I would die with only ghosts to watch me pass over. And yet, I could sense my quarry out there. The Fomorians were close. I knew it.

"Another day, Ziri." I mounted my camel and urged it forward. "Just one more. I promise."

Ziri frowned, but nodded, and he shouted at his two nephews to hurry packing up the tents. He did not ask me what I needed out there, and I could not have told him if he had. I could not tell him that the Fomorians who had murdered those I loved most in the world were out there somewhere. I'd had their scent in Tripoli only two moons ago. I knew that Máelmórda had taken a bride from the family of a local warlord there. But before I arrived, they had already moved on and left this young bride behind, their scent vanishing with the wind.

This had happened to me many times now, to have them almost in my reach only for them to escape. For them to move on, change their appearance and their names, and each time, my search had to begin anew. I would not let that happen again. I knew they were hiding in this desert somewhere. I could smell them.

That night, in my tent, I could not sleep. I saw the faces of Gormflaith, Máelmórda and Donnchad when I closed my eyes. They were not ghosts in this vision, but flesh and blood, and still, I could not reach them, could not touch them.

This vision only made me want to have my Fomorian foes under my sword all the more. *Somehow, they knew when I approached.* Báine had spoken of the gifts of witches once, saying that Gormflaith, who had stolen the witch gift, might dream of us, might see us when she lay sleeping. I had scorned this idea, or at least been arrogant enough to think my warrior gift could overcome such dreams. Now I was not so sure… And yet, I could not turn from this path until I had each of them under my blade.

I wished now that I had killed Donnchad while he was king in Munster. That I had pierced his heart with my sword and watched his last breath leave his body. I could see this vision so clearly in my mind. *My sword in his heart. His blood, red and hot, spilling at my feet.*

Affraic had stayed my hand. Told me to wait for the other kings and princes of Munster to oust him. *You will cause a war if you kill the king*, she had said. *Donnchad's supporters will blame Toir. Toir will know it is not him and blame the Eóganacht clan. You must let the mortals push him from his position of power, and only then can you have him. Otherwise, you will only create more dead souls for us to mourn.*

It took many years, but oust him they did. Donnchad and his son fled to Dublin, took a ship to Rome, and then disappeared.

I'd been following his trail ever since. I knew he and his son had met up with his mother, Gormflaith, in Rome. Then his uncle, Máelmórda, in Frankia. Recently, I had caught the scent of another Fomorian, and the five of them wove their way across the world, always, somehow, keeping ahead of me.

Shivering, I pulled my blanket over my shoulder. It was cold now, for the desert was cruel at night too. As the sun burned in the daytime, the moon froze in the night, and I lay there, wondering where the Fomorians could be. *Gormflaith, did she see me? Did she laugh in her dreams, knowing she had thwarted me once again?*

Suddenly, the wind grew, and the quietness of the night was shattered by Ziri and his nephews shouting.

"A storm!" they called out. "A storm is coming!"

I already knew these desert storms were deadly. It was not only the furious wind that killed, but the sand that rose into the air, blinding and suffocating all in its path. I didn't move. My tent was secured, and I was safer here than outside. I merely listened to the edges of my tent buzzing like a swarm of bees as the wind rattled against it.

"Broccan!" Ziri came crashing inside. "Into my tent. Quickly. The storm coming is the worst I've ever seen. It will bury you on this side of the dune. Come. Now."

I shoved my belongings into my bag and ran after Ziri. Sand spun in the air, a wall of it. The wind was so strong that I could no longer see my guide. I kept running, following his scent, and using my warrior strength to push through.

Broccan.

A voice I had not heard in many years spoke. A voice in the wind that swirled around me.

"Mother?" I fell to my knees. It couldn't be. My mother was dead. She had died in my arms over one hundred years ago.

Broccan.

"Yes," I shouted, knowing it *was* her. That somehow, she'd found a way to speak on the wind that had always whispered to her. The sand under my hands shook and fell away, as if it were a monster, opening its mouth to consume me, but still, I could not move.

The wind hissed in my ear. *You must return. You must find her.*

"Who?"

Isolde. She needs you, Broccan. The fire will come for her.

My mother spoke of my cousin. Fódla's baby who had been taken to the otherworld.

"I waited on Rathlin for many years. She didn't… She never came." Coughing, I pressed my scarf over my mouth. The air was vanishing, and my lungs burned. I wanted to tell her that Affraic and I had both waited for Isolde to come through the otherworld to Rathlin Island. *For years and years.* That was why I had been late to discover that Donnchad had left Killaloe, for I had spent my time guarding the hawthorn tree and awaiting her arrival. But I couldn't get the words out. Couldn't tell her that Affraic had stopped waiting too. We had given up hope.

The wind pushed me lower to the ground, the sand slicing at my face and hands. I needed to stand, to get to Ziri's tent. Using all my strength, I tried to rise, only for the wind to push me back down.

It is time for you to go home. To the hawthorn tree. The magic of the warrior land on Rathlin will keep her safe, but you must protect her, teach her. The fire will come for her, come for you. She must be strong enough to destroy it.

The storm lifted as my mother's voice trailed away. As suddenly as it had come, it departed. The sand fell to the ground like snow, the wind abated, and I gazed upward at the sky. At the stars.

My journey home took many months, and I listened to the people I passed with interest. The world had changed since my search for the Fomorians had begun. God was everywhere, it seemed, and wars were being waged in his name. As I rode west, fighting men rode east. From these men's mouths, I heard the songs of death. The Pope had sent them, these men said. The Crusade, this war was called. God's war.

I did not see any god with them when I rode past, and instead my thoughts moved to Ireland. It is a strange thing to be away from your homeland. To feel you might be a stranger in a place that once was all you knew. I wondered what she would make of me when I set foot upon her soil.

This question filled my mind as I travelled. These months were filled with storms and droughts. The land rose and fell. The waves of the sea swelled and crashed, but soon the salt wind of the far west blew against my skin and the Kingdom of Ulaid came into view.

In my dreams I had pictured grey skies, green grass and white-tipped waves, but somehow my dreams had become muted, for what I saw before me was so full of colour that I felt I could burst.

Yet, I could not stop. I could not pause to walk through the trees and mountains and let new memories form. Instead, I bought a small rowboat along the northern coast and rowed to Rathlin Island. My heart thudded as I stepped upon the beach. If Ireland was my homeland, then Rathlin Island was my home. Long ago, when my aunt Fódla was still alive and I a boy, we had lived here. Colmon, too. Our cousin. A mighty warrior. He had taught me all he knew, trained me. *Loved me.* The swell of joy in my heart abated then and a wave of melancholy replaced it.

Banishing bitter memories was not so easy to do here as when I was trekking across the desert. Flashes of my boyhood came now, unbidden. It was the shape of the rocks, the smell of wildflowers in the air, and soon, flashes of the battle at Clontarf played over in my mind.

Tairdelbach drowning, Donnchad pulling him under the water using his stolen cupbearer gift. Donnchad using his Fomorian fire to burn my body. Catching up to Fódla and Murchad only to find them both dead. Isolde, still a baby, taken by the roots of the hawthorn tree into the otherworld.

Quieter memories came to me too as I reached Colmon's ráth. I pictured my aunt sitting by the fire, telling me stories. Her long red hair hung over her shoulder, returning my smile when I smiled at her. How I wished I could see Fódla once more.

Putting my head down, I strode to the hawthorn tree that grew at the edge of Colmon's land. The tree upon which my mother had cast her spell. *After one hundred and thirty-eight years, had Isolde finally come through?* Surely it could not be. Time moved differently in the otherworld, but this seemed like too much. Too long.

Silence greeted me as I reached the foot of the tree. Stillness. And I started to laugh. The baby I'd hoped to see was not there. Never had been. I would have smelled traces of her if she had… and most likely, she would never come. Exhausted, I sat down and leaned against the trunk.

Perhaps my sanity was in doubt. Perhaps the ghosts of the Tripoli desert, knowing they could not kill me, had played a trick instead.

I ran my hands through my hair, long and unkempt. My beard now reached my stomach. A beggar man, I looked to be. They avoided me, the mortals I passed. They saw the dullness in my eyes that told them I was alive, but not living. No man was more dangerous than that. But why was I like this? Why could I not move on? Affraic and the other Descendants had. They did not hunt the Fomorians who had killed all their kin and friends. They lived in Seir Keiran, an abandoned monastery, and went about their lives as if nothing had happened. As if they were happy, or at least, as if it were possible to try.

I closed my eyes and wrapped my cloak about myself. I would sleep here tonight. Tomorrow, I would leave. *But where would I go?*

The last thing Affraic told me was the desire for revenge in my heart had to fade before I could heal. I had perhaps two hundred more years to live. Should I continue my search for the Fomorians? Or should I search for peace instead, feel a lover's hands upon my body, see desire in someone's eyes. Return it? I closed my eyes and imagined how this love would look. Was it possible? I didn't know. I was so tired. So very tired.

It was a low wail that woke me.

I opened my eyes and rolled onto my front. On the opposite side of the tree, there was a baby, wrapped in swaddling, which I recognised as the embroidered fabric of one of Fódla's dresses. Strands of red hair poked out from underneath the cloth. Soil smudged against her cheek. She breathed softly as I picked her up, her soft eyelashes fluttering with the sunlight, then closing.

I pressed her cold hands against my chest, then took her inside the house. Quickly, I lit the fire. Using my warrior strength and speed, it wasn't long before the house was secure and the fire roaring. I'd need to buy a goat in the morning from one of the farmers on the island, for she was a newborn babe still, and would need milk to drink.

After setting up the bed, I placed her on the mattress. That was when I felt something hard underneath the fabric of her mother's dress. Peeling it away, I found two items. A knife and a silver pendant. *Isolde* was the name engraved upon the latter. I set them under the bed and tucked a blanket around Isolde before she grew cold and wakened. I watched her as I did this, the slow rise and fall of her chest. The delicate mouth and tiny fingers.

"I will look after you, Isolde," I whispered. "I promise you that. I will look after you always."

NOW

Spring 1169

Isolde

Rathlin Island

I ran, legs stretching along the sandy beach.
Móirne kept pace for the first half of our race but slowed well before we reached the inlet where the river water drained into the sea.

Laughing, I spun around, arms raised in the air.

Móirne rolled her eyes but laughed too, or at least half laughed between her gasps for air. "I don't know why… I bother… racing you. You always win."

"I don't race to win. Neither should you."

"If not to… win, then why?"

I stopped spinning, squinting in the direction of the southern bay where the fishermen of the island moored their boats. "Do you ever see the old fisherwomen waiting on the shore for their husbands to return? Some of them hobble, so stiff they are. But do you know, when they were young, I bet they ran too."

Móirne scratched the side of her head, frowning. "And?"

"How did they slow down so much, do you think? At what age do you think they went from running with the wind, to not wanting to run, to not being able to? I don't want that to ever happen to me. I want to run always."

I spun around again, fighting with my hair to keep it from blowing against my face so I could see what Móirne made of this statement, but she'd already stopped listening. Today, my ramblings were set aside in favour of examining the pebbles and small rocks that littered the sand. She rubbed her fingers over one that was smooth, thin and black. Not like the usual rocks on the beach which were dark grey or tawny. Perhaps it was from somewhere far away. Somewhere that my cousin Broccan had visited when he was younger.

"How many times?" Móirne asked as she picked it up.

"I'd say four."

She flicked it into the air, caught it deftly between her fingers and threw it into the sea, skimming it along the waves. Two times it bounced. Three. Then it sunk into the waves.

Móirne stared after it, shaking her head, but quickly began to search for another skimming stone that might yield a better result.

"Isolde!"

Broccan's voice rang out in the air, and I gave my friend an apologetic smile. "I'd better be off."

Móirne picked up two more stones, good ones, and put them in her pocket. "I need to go anyway. My mother needs me to help with the cooking this evening. We've guests coming to visit. A cousin from the mainland."

"Are you going fishing again tomorrow?"

Móirne shook her head, a shadow seeming to fall over her eyes.

"What's wrong?" I asked. "Is Síoda sick again?"

"No. Not that." Móirne took a step closer. "I've been looking for a way to tell you all day. We are leaving the island. In a few weeks."

My mouth turned dry as I took in her news. Indeed, it took me so long to form words in my mouth that Móirne had fixed her shawl about her shoulders twice before I spoke. "Leaving? For good?"

Móirne nodded.

"All of you?"

Another nod.

"To go where?"

"My mother's cousin from the mainland. He's coming to help us move over. He says his brother-in-law has a nephew who wishes to marry. Mother thinks we might suit each other."

I frowned at this. Móirne had never spoken about wanting to

marry before. "How would your mother know that? Has she ever met him?"

Móirne sighed as she opened her mouth, but the words on her tongue drifted away, or perhaps she found them as difficult to form as I. Instead, she rubbed one of the stones she'd picked up, moved it between her hands and threw it over the waves. Three times it bounced, then a fourth time, before disappearing into the sea. "I suppose... I realised," Móirne said slowly, "that I don't want to be alone, and there is no one here. Just old men and their old fisher-wives."

"It's not so bad as that. The Ó'Neill family live on the other side of the island. So do the Ó'Baoills. And traders come here from time to time."

"Everyone you talk about is either old or married." She pointed at the mainland beyond the waves. "All the young men go there, and they never come back here once they've left. And why would they come back? There is nothing to come back to. No people. No king even, to look after us. The land is so poor it can barely sustain our sheep. It is hopeless here, Isolde. I didn't see that when I was younger. Now it's all I see."

"And now it's you who will never come back. All for a man you've never met. What if you don't like him?"

Móirne reached out her hand to hold mine. "I am sorry to be parted from you, Isolde, and I know you don't understand, but I was not made to run forever. Not like you. I'm eighteen now. I wouldn't mind having my own children to mind instead of my sister. I wouldn't mind slowing down if I had somewhere to call my own. And so, this man, I don't know him, and I might not like him, but I know I can't stay here any longer. Mother knows it too."

I forced a smile. Nodded. Even though I didn't understand how she could want this. I was seventeen, almost as old as her, and I couldn't imagine moving far away to marry a man I didn't know. It was a simple life here, yes, but it was safe. Wars plagued the mainland, Broccan said. Kings always fighting and at each other's throats. Priests and monks telling the people how to live. To exist in such a place required a mask, he had told me. And you could not be free if you could not show your true face. I struggled a moment, thinking how best to convey this to my friend.

"Are you sure, Móirne? It is dange... There is so much fighting. What if you—"

"I'm sure." She gave a firm nod of her head, and her fingers rubbed over my hands, holding them tight for a moment. "Now, tell me this. What will you do tomorrow?"

"I don't know."

"Fishing again?"

"No. Not fishing."

She looked at me with such pity, I couldn't bear it. Grasping, I tried to think of something that she might regret missing out on. "I was thinking of looking for puffin eggs on the west side of the island. Broccan said he'd spotted a few nests there."

Móirne, who'd always enjoyed searching for puffin nests, smiled, but the regret I thought I'd see was absent. Instead, she ran to the basket of fish that she'd set down before we'd begun our race and set three of the mackerel we had caught that morning into my empty one. "This is your half."

"Yes. Thanks, Móirne."

"No. Thank you, Isolde, for being my friend. I was lonely before I found you. What a shock it was to find another girl my age living on this island, and what fun we've had together. I'll never forget you."

"I'll never forget you either, Móirne. I will visit you before you leave... if your mother will let me."

"She will let you. She'll have no choice."

Móirne's mother would be so happy they were leaving that she'd put up with me, was the truth behind those words. *The girl who lives on the cursed land will bring us ill-fortune*, I'd heard her say to Móirne once when we were younger, and she blessed herself whenever I knocked their door. I hadn't minded. I had been lonely too, and even though Móirne had spun to a different song to mine, she'd been good company. *A friend.*

Móirne waved, then made her way back along the beach and over to the cliff path that led to her father's land. My walk was not nearly so far, just past the river, then up the stone pathway.

I should have been home before now, and I prepared myself for a scolding from Broccan. I even began to scold myself. It was wrong of me to take the whole day to go fishing with Móirne, especially when there was so much to do at this time of year. Tending to the sheep, the goats, the garden too. Collecting seaweed, cleaning the bedding, the floor. Chopping firewood. Collecting honey from the beehive. I had promised only last week that I'd be more of a help to him, and already I had fallen into my old ways. I guessed it wouldn't be so hard to stick to my word once Móirne left. Or was that a lie? My love of this land didn't seem to be dependent on another, and yet, the thought of *always* being alone in my exploration didn't fill me with any joy. Perhaps I could convince Broccan to come exploring with me as he had done when I was younger. This thought lifted my spirits as I ran toward the house.

"Isolde," Broccan said as I approached. "You go too far these days. How many times must I remind you to stay inside our boundary? If you want to fish, you can do it along the beach here."

"Yes, Broccan," I said. "I'm sorry. Móirne said a shoal of mackerel had come into the bay." I lifted the three mackerel out of my basket, proof that my exploits had not been completely wasted.

Broccan gave me a half-hearted smile, but did not look angry, so I sat on the grass beside him. "I'm sorry I wander, but I can't help it. The sun was shining, and I wanted to run. The winter we've just had felt so long, and this was the first bit of heat I've felt on my face since—"

"Last summer?" Broccan finished.

"Well, yes. And that was so long ago."

Broccan laughed at this.

"Not that it matters anymore," I added. "Móirne and her family are leaving the island."

"Oh?"

"Móirne says her mother's cousin is related to someone who has a nephew or a brother... I can't remember who exactly... but he needs a wife. Móirne's mother has suggested Móirne as a suitable match, and so off they are all going."

Broccan leaned back on his elbows and gave a soft grunt. "Is Móirne upset?"

"No. Not at all. Isn't that odd, don't you think? Móirne has never even spoken about wanting to be married, and now she's quite happy to be going away to marry someone she's never met."

"It is strange, but it is the way of things. If you want a family, children, then you must find a partner somehow. On an island such as this, there are few opportunities. I am not surprised they are leaving. Móirne's father has been unwell for a while now, and this land is difficult to farm. A home inland, and with Móirne married to a younger man, will make things easier for them."

Broccan was right – he always was. Still, I did not like it. I did not like that my only friend was leaving. I did not like that she was taking such a gamble with her happiness.

"Should you like to get married, do you think?"

Wide-eyed, I turned my head to see if Broccan was being serious or not.

"Not an arranged match," he added. "One of your choosing."

"I don't know." I shrugged. "I don't know anyone I would like to marry. And I like it here. Why would I want to leave Rathlin for a stranger?" I pointed to the sea, wild and crashing, then at the sun shining above us. "Look how beautiful this land is, and yet, it changes all the time. I love the wind, the wildness of the storms. This morning it rained, but look at how brightly the sun shines now. Look how yellow it makes the flowers on the gorse. Even that crow perched on the hawthorn tree looks beautiful today."

Broccan pushed himself up, lifting his chin as if noticing for the first time himself that the cold winds had finally faded. Sometimes it seemed as if he did not like the spring, though I couldn't understand why. Spring was my favourite season. A season of new life and change.

"It will be summer soon," I added, hoping this would cheer him. "It will be so warm we won't need to light the fire every day."

Broccan nodded, and he rubbed the scars along his face. He said that these old burns on his skin didn't hurt anymore, and yet his smile faded when his hands brushed over them. It happened often these days, this smile that slid away. Usually when he thought I wasn't looking, but sometimes when I was, as if he forgot I was here. Or perhaps he did know and still couldn't help himself.

"Broccan." I cleared my throat. "Is there something wrong?"

"No. It's just you remind me of someone, you being so fond of running away and not doing what you are told."

I grinned but couldn't bring myself to laughter, for though it was said to make me laugh, sadness tinged his voice. I had noticed it before, of course, but never said so. But perhaps today, because I was sad too, I couldn't remain silent.

"Why aren't you telling me the truth?"

My cousin stared at me then, his smile returning. "Nothing is wrong."

"I'm not a child anymore. I know when you are lying." I ran my fingers through my hair, now a little uncertain as to whether I should have challenged him or not. "You always say I can talk to you, but you can talk to me too, you know."

"I know I can, Isolde. There is nothing wrong. If I am a little quiet, it's because I must tell you that I will leave the island for a time. A couple of weeks at most."

"Why?" Plucking a dandelion from the grass, I threw it at him. "Don't tell me you are bored of this island too?"

"No." Broccan snorted. "I need to trade some of our goods, and I want to buy a few more chickens to make sure we have enough to see us over the next winter."

"Can I come?"

Broccan shook his head. "I need you to look after our land. We cannot leave it vacant. We could return to find all our possessions and animals gone."

Scowling, I picked another dandelion. This day was going from bad to worse. First Móirne was leaving and now Broccan wanted to go to the mainland without me.

"There should be enough food for you, and you can fish along this beach if you need more. I promise to be as quick as I can."

"Yes, Broccan."

"And most of all, I need you to promise that you won't leave the boundary of my land. Not even for Móirne."

"What? But I promised her that I would see her before she goes."

"I'll be back before that happens. Don't worry."

Knowing he couldn't be turned, for he never could when it came to my safety, I reached out to collect Broccan's empty cup that lay on the grass beside him.

Broccan waved my hand away. "No. We can wash up later."

"Why? Is there something else I should do? Will I collect more sea—"

"No. Let's train."

"Really?" I scrambled to my feet before he could change his mind, and ran to put on the old bull-hide armour he had given me.

Broccan chuckled at my enthusiasm. "What weapon today?"

"Sword."

"You pick that every time," he said.

"It's better than a spear."

"Not always."

"If you wanted me to practise with a spear, why did you give me the choice?"

Broccan held up his hands and threw the wooden sword he'd carved for me in the air. I jumped, caught it and ran to the far side of the training square.

"Now, answer me this," he said. "What do you do when you are outnumbered, Isolde?"

"You run," I answered.

"What do you do when your enemies have the advantage? Do you stay and fight?"

"No. You must destroy their advantage first."

"What do you do if you cannot run and cannot fight?"

"You wait and you watch and prepare yourself for the battle to come."

Broccan nodded. "I want you to give me all you've got this time," he said, taking hold of his sword, and slashing it through the air. "Will your body to hit harder. To move faster. Yes?"

Without waiting for him to ready himself, I charged forward, thrusting my sword toward Broccan's arm. He turned and parried, pushing me back with a counter-strike. Circling him, I switched sword hand and moved forward, hoping to slice his thigh before he moved out of the way.

Quickly, he shifted back, well before the blunt tip of my sword got anywhere near his leg. We moved closer, slower, each waiting for an opportunity to strike.

Broccan didn't speak to me about his past, but I knew he had fought in battles over on the Irish mainland. Many of them. He trained me often, but still I found him impossible to beat. Every time I progressed, grew, or built up any strength, he seemed to move faster, grow stronger.

This time, however, I was determined to catch him. This time, *my sword* would be the fastest.

Moving forward, just the way he told me, I charged, twisting my body at the last moment, to strike his side. Once again, he met me, then began to move forward with blows of his own. Now it was my turn to defend, to move, to shield.

I twisted and turned, strike after strike. I hadn't been able to land a blow on him, but he couldn't land one on me either. That was until I moved so far back that my heel hit the boundary of the fighting circle, and his sword pressed against my shoulder.

Sighing, I acknowledged his win. How could he always predict my next move? I tried to move faster, I did, but no matter how fast I moved, he always got there first.

"You fought well," he said, "but still not fast enough."

"I am sorry, but I will win soon," I returned. "I'm getting faster.

Móirne says so. Besides, you'll slow down one of these days. How old are you again?"

"*J'ai trente-huit ans*," he replied in Norman French.

"Thirty-eight? *Tu es un vieil homme*," I returned, grinning, and wiping the sweat from my brow.

"I'm an old man... Yes, I suppose I am, but you need to inflect your vowels more to impress the Norman lords. If they can't understand you, you'll have to try to converse in Latin."

"*Senex es.*"

"Good. If they don't know Latin, you could always try the old Saxon English."

"*Thu eart ealda.*"

Broccan nodded and set down his sword, but somehow the smile had slipped from his face as I had spoken. Knowing I'd pronounced the last word incorrectly, I thought of something else to please him. "Do you want me to say it in Arabic too? Or should I say it in Norse French again? My vowels..."

My cousin shook his head. "No. There is no need to tell me I am an old man in another way. I know it already, and your Norse French is fine." He gestured to the fire. "Why don't you light it while I clean the fish. We can steam them for dinner."

Setting my sword back into the hold, I nodded and did what he asked. He smiled at me as I walked away, but once again that strange look moved over his face. A look not only of sadness, I realised, but also of regret... or frustration.

There were secrets inside him. I'd known that for some time, but today, this realisation crashed over me. What were they? Why did they make him sad?

Why wouldn't he confide in me and tell me what they were?

Isolde

Rathlin Island

When I woke the next day, Broccan was already gone from the house. I put on my shawl and boots and walked outside, glad to see that it was another fine day. Suddenly, a terrible thought came to me: Broccan was not on the island. He had gone without saying goodbye, and I was all alone.

Broccan wouldn't have gone without telling me, would he? I ran down the stone path that led to the beach to look over the sea. No. Our rowboat was still there, dragged up over to the rocks so that the high tide couldn't pull it out.

Where was he, then? It was unusual for him to be up before me, even more unusual for me not to waken on hearing him move about the house.

I was strolling back toward the ráth, thinking he might have risen early to see if he could trade with the other families on Rathlin before attempting the journey south, when I saw him standing by the hawthorn tree that stood at the far edge of our land.

I was about to walk toward him when something caught my eye. A crow. A crow was on his arm. What a strange sight. It pecked at something on his sleeve, quiet and docile, then flew away.

"A tame crow?" I shouted as I watched it soar into the sky. "Where did you find it?"

Broccan stared at me, though he didn't speak until I reached him. "What are you doing up so early?"

"I could ask you the same. But don't change the subject. The crow. How did you get it to land on your arm like that?"

"It must have been tired," he answered, watching as it flew

toward the mainland. "It was hungry, either way. I picked a worm up from the grass for it to eat, and it gobbled it up quicker than you eat your stew after a day of swimming in the sea."

"Móirne's mother says crows are bad luck. That they bring ill-tidings."

"There can be some truth to that, I suppose." Broccan, usually so quick to dismiss things that Móirne's mother said, surprised me with his answer.

"Why do you say that?"

"When we talk of luck, we talk of old stories that have been forgotten. We know something to be true, something that has been passed down from generation to generation, but we can no longer remember what it is. Feelings endure when words are long lost. Fear. Rage. Anger. Yes, we always remember those things."

"Do you know the truth behind why people say crows are unlucky? Or have you forgotten too?" I squinted up at him, so bright was the sun as it rose above the horizon.

"Hundreds of years ago, it was the Tuatha Dé Danann who ruled Ireland, and they sent messages to each other using crows. I suppose, when you send messages to others, they are often ones that give bad news. They are messages of death or war. And so, the people remember the fear of seeing the crows and the messages they brought, even though they begin to forget the Tuatha Dé Danann. That's what I was told, anyway."

"Did my mother tell you that?"

"Aye."

"Did she believe in all the old stories? Like you do?"

"Yes, she did."

"What about my father?"

"He believed in the new faith… but he also believed in the wisdom of your mother. Do not worry so much about which one is right and which one is wrong. There can be wisdom in both."

I stared up at him, hoping he'd tell me more of my mother and father. Sometimes, on a good day, he would tell me about them. About my gentle mother. About my father, who had taught him the meaning of courage. Just as I was about to ask, Broccan nodded in the direction of the sea. "The tide is in. Time for me to go."

"I thought, when I woke, you'd left without saying goodbye."

Broccan frowned. "I'd never do that. Indeed, I'm hesitant to go myself. I'd much rather stay here with you, but it's best to trade now. I'll get a better price for the tools I've made than if I go after Beltane."

Opening his arms, he pulled me into a hug. "Be careful, Isolde. Don't do anything dangerous. No climbing trees or swimming if the sea is rough. And most of all, don't leave the boundary of my land. I'm trusting you to keep it safe."

"Yes, Broccan."

He set one of his arms around my shoulder and the two of us walked side by side toward the beach.

"I'll miss you," I said as we reached the little rowboat.

"I'll miss you too, Isolde."

"Will you tell me more about my mother and father when you return? I want to know who they really were."

I blurted it out, knowing I'd regret not asking for the whole two weeks Broccan was away if I didn't.

"Yes. I promise I will." He steadied the boat with his hand, the waves now nudging it back and forth as they broke over the sand. "I've let my own sadness get in the way of talking about them. I'll mend my ways when I return."

Relieved that he had complied so easily, I waved goodbye as he pushed the boat deeper into the sea and hauled himself inside. "Keep safe, Isolde," he shouted as he sat down and picked up the oars. "I won't be long. Promise."

That night, I threw a few logs onto the fire and sat on my chair. The days were lengthening and there was some heat to the sun, but the air was still cold and sharp, once it set. On evenings such as this, I loved nothing more than to sit and listen to Broccan tell me tales of magic, of the old religion that the priests didn't like. Sometimes we composed songs together and I would sing to him.

With him gone, though it was only to be two weeks, I felt odd. The silence of our house overwhelmed me, and even the warm fire and a thick blanket did not comfort.

If only I could have gone with him.

I loved it here, I did. It was my home, but it would have been such an adventure to travel to the mainland with him. What did the people there have to say? How did they go about their lives? What would the land look like? Broccan had told me that, on the mainland, the forests were thick and dense and full of flowers and plants that didn't grow here, and that there were mountains so high that it took whole days to climb them.

I took my frustration out on another stick, which I snapped in half before throwing it into the firepit. I knew I had to stay. It was silly to think it could be any other way. Someone had to tend to the animals and keep the house.

"Isolde!" A knock at the door followed. "Isolde. It's me. Móirne."

I kicked off my blanket and rushed to the door. My friend was standing outside, a grin on her face. I'd invited her to my house many times, though she rarely came. I thought perhaps the scars on Broccan's face scared her, or perhaps her mother's tales about our land being cursed did. Either way, she did not look frightened now.

"What is it, Móirne?"

"My father paid for a seanchaí to come over from the mainland. He's telling us stories this evening. Everyone is coming. Even the Ó'Neills and the Ó'Baoills."

She spun around and took hold of my hand. "Come on."

"I can't," I said. "Broccan told me to stay here while he was away."

"Sure, it's only on the beach. If we walk fast, it won't take long to get there."

I gazed into the distance. A thick plume of smoke was rising close to where the men kept their boats. I could picture it. A gathering of the islanders around a fire, listening to stories of legends and heroes.

"I made a promise. I cannot."

Móirne placed her hands on her hips. "Please, Isolde. I'll be leaving soon." The giddiness of her smile slipped then. Her eyes narrowed. "We've sneaked off before and Broccan never found out. He's hardly going to know if he isn't here. It's not like we're doing anything dangerous."

"It's because he isn't here that I cannot go. If something happens… I…" Pausing a moment, I rubbed my arm. Something felt wrong tonight. I didn't know why. Perhaps it was the remnants of my earlier thoughts, the part of me that felt aggrieved at being left here alone.

Móirne sighed. "I'd better get back then. I don't want to miss it."

"Sorry, Móirne. Truly."

"I understand. I'll see you when Broccan returns?"

"Yes."

I wished I could go with her as she walked away. As she moved along the path, the worry inside me edged away. A flash of anger filled me instead. *Why shouldn't I go?* Who was on the island who would take our land or animals at this time of night? If Broccan wanted to leave without me, then why couldn't I see my friends?

"Wait! I'll walk with you along the beach for a bit."

Without waiting for Móirne to reply, I ran to catch up with her. She gave me a sly grin and linked her arm into mine.

"It is kind of your father to pay for a seanchaí to come over."

"It's his way of saying goodbye to his friends."

"Are you still sure about going?"

Móirne nodded.

"Won't you miss this, though?" I pointed ahead at the fire in the distance and the dark silhouettes of her friends and family who stood beside it.

"There will be festivals on the mainland. My mother's cousin says the O'Neill king there has one every feast day. I'll miss you and the other families who live here, but when I look out across the sea, I know my future is there. So much so that if I could leave tomorrow, I would."

I held in the remainder of my arguments. Móirne had made her decision. It wasn't for me to change it… and somehow, her words had stung. *If I could leave tomorrow, I would.* Just like that. So easily could she be parted from everyone she knew.

As we reached the boundary of Broccan's land, I came to a stop. "There. I'd better return home now."

Móirne pressed her lips together. "Now it's my turn to ask if you are sure."

The fire burned so brightly in the distance that my eyes were drawn to it. The people of Rathlin were standing around it, laughing and talking to each other with an ease I hadn't seen before. But it was more than that. It was the fire itself. The shapes inside it.

"Why don't you just come for a while? It will be fun."

Standing on the very edge of Broccan's land, I hesitated.

"Do you remember, the other day on the beach… You said you were afraid one day of no longer being able to run, and you wondered when that happened to the old fisher-wives?"

I nodded.

"This is how. They grew afraid."

I stared at my friend as the wind blew through her hair. Móirne, usually so quiet and in her own world, suddenly seemed older. Wiser. And she was right. It was fear holding me back.

Nodding, I linked my arm back into hers and followed her along the beach.

By the time we reached the fire, the people of Rathlin had begun to sit. Using boulders and fallen logs as chairs, they waited for the storytelling to begin. The seanchaí was an old man, short with long white hair. He smiled at the children. Whispered jokes so that they laughed while their parents passed around cups of ale. Finally, even this stopped, and the talking ebbed away.

I felt the gaze of some of the islanders on me then. *The cursed girl*, they called me. *The cursed girl who lived on the cursed land.* I felt them edge their bodies away from me, even though, to Móirne, they smiled and reached out to hold her hand. I stayed back, while Móirne went to sit with her family, and sat on a boulder that was a little apart from the others. Broccan had told me to be respectful to the other islanders. They had their superstitions about our land, and there was no telling them otherwise. This was why Móirne's friendship had meant so much to me. She had played with me, even when others had told her not to. *And now she was leaving.*

The seanchaí held up his hand, waiting until there was complete silence. Slowly, he looked around the crowd, the light of the fire casting shadows around every edge and line of his face. When he came to me, he paused, held out his finger, and pointed. "Are you of the Tuatha Dé Danann?"

Startled by the directness of his gaze, I shook my head.

The seanchaí laughed at the expression on my face and of those who had turned to stare at me.

"Before the Northmen came, red hair was a sign of the Tuatha Dé Danann. Did you not know that?" He pursed his lips, as if lamenting the loss of our knowledge. "We know from our histories that the sons of Miled banished the Tuatha Dé Danann to the otherworld… but I have heard stories that not all of them left our land. I've heard they come up from the otherworld using the hawthorn trees, and they watch us. Sometimes, they walk among us and play tricks on us."

Móirne's mother, who sat beside her two daughters, made the sign of the cross and tightened her shawl over her shoulders. Síoda, Móirne's sister, snuggled into her mother's side, her eyes wide with wonder. Síoda had a strange weakness in her lungs and found even walking difficult. It was wonderful to see her so animated for a change.

"I've heard tales of an old woman with long white hair," the seanchaí continued. "It is said she claims the bodies of the dead for herself and brings them to the otherworld with her."

"We must pray that she never comes here," Móirne's mother said.

"Indeed, you should," the seanchaí answered. "If the sons of Miled banished the Tuatha Dé Danann underground, we must pray to the Lord that they stay there." He paused then, took a long drink. "Have any of you children heard of the Morrígan. A fearful prophetess of the Tuatha Dé Danann, she is. A goddess of war and death. For even the mighty Cú Chulainn could not escape the death she foresaw for him."

"Tell us of Cú Chulainn!" Móirne's father shouted. "Tell us of the war between the warriors of Ulaid and Queen Medb."

"A fine choice." The seanchaí chuckled as he took a sip of his ale. "A fine choice indeed."

The story began in earnest then. I'd heard of the war between the men of Ulaid and Queen Medb of Connacht before. Broccan had told it to me, though I did not mind hearing it again. Everyone enjoyed it, even Móirne's mother, though she blessed herself every time the Morrígan made an appearance.

Once the tale was over, the people of Rathlin made their way home. Tired after so long a day, I waved a goodbye to Móirne, promising to visit as soon as Broccan returned.

Starlight guided me to Broccan's house, though I could have walked it blindfold, and a sense of relief washed over me as I passed the boundary to Broccan's land. I almost laughed at this. When I was younger, I took great delight in sneaking away. What had happened to make me so fearful? The laughter on my lips faded. No, it wasn't fear that had held me back tonight. It was my word. I had made a promise to Broccan that I wouldn't leave... and I had broken it. Well, I wouldn't break it again.

Resolved to keep to my promises from now on, I hurried home.

Usually when I was out past sunset, I would look up at the stars and wonder about all the people who lived underneath them. I would examine the starlit clouds and the colours they cast, trying to guess what weather would come to us the following day. But tonight, even though the sky was clear, it was the hawthorn tree that commanded my attention. *A link to the otherworld*, the seanchaí had said.

I did not like the hawthorn tree. There was something about the twisted branches and gnarled roots that disturbed me, but tonight, I walked over to it and touched the rough bark. It felt so cold. Cold like the dreams I'd had when I was younger, of being trapped and alone in the dark. The hairs on my arms rose as I thought this, and whispers I did not understand seemed to float in the breeze.

A strange feeling came to me then. A tightening. A knowing that something was wrong. A sense that everything was about to change.

Quickly, I pulled my hand away. *What a fool I was to be frightened by the words of the seanchaí.* Broccan would laugh when I told him, and he'd be right to do so. If he was ever to consider me an adult, I had to start behaving like one. That was what was wrong. Móirne, only a year older than me, was to be married soon, while I, Isolde, was afraid of a memory of a dream.

Gormflaith

Paris

The land around me was green and damp. Not Paris where my body lay. No. This land was inside of my dream.

Nothing was clear, not yet, but I knew this place; remembered it like a sickness. Feeling the sharp coldness in the wind, the salt within it, I opened my arms and let the Irish air wash over me. What else can one do when a plague arrives but accept it?

In the distance, the grey sea swelled up and down. Beside me, the gorse and leaves shivered, frost-tipped. It was spring – of course it was spring – but the sun had set, and the winds that blew in from the north made it feel like winter. Oh, I remembered this wind. Its hardness. Its bite.

"Báine," a man said. "Talk to me. Tell me what has happened."

A woman sitting by a fire shrugged. She smelled of bird and wore no clothing. A witch she was. A powerful one. Her long dark hair covered her bare skin, but already she began to shiver, the fire not enough to banish the coldness of the air. "I told you everything yesterday. Shae is ageing. There is nothing left to say."

Broccan removed, then held out his cloak for Báine to take. "Why did no one come sooner to tell me?"

I crouched down in the grass and crawled until my body was completely shielded by the trunk of an alder tree. The Descendants of the Tuatha Dé Danann had not worked out I could see them in my dreams, but I suspected they would sense me if I was not careful. I could not get too close, lest even in this dreamish half-haze, these two Descendants might smell me. A warrior and a witch. No, that would never do.

"It only began at the start of last winter," the witch said as she wrapped the cloak around herself. "It has progressed more quickly than anyone imagined. I don't know how long he has left. That's why I've come to tell you now, so that if you wish, you may say goodbye."

The man walked closer to the witch. He had pale skin, though it was scarred and red along his left side. I knew this man very well. Broccan, nephew of Fódla. I had watched when my son, Donnchad, had burned him with his fire-magic. I'd then endured him chasing me and my family for nearly a century, using my dreams to see when he came close, so we could move on before he reached us. That last time, in Tripoli, he'd come close. So very close to catching us... and then, all of a sudden, he had disappeared.

In these dreams, he had walked the land alone. Bereft of kin and company. He'd followed us wherever we went. Constantinople, Rome, Paris, Venice, Tripoli. Never had I seen him in Ireland. What could have brought him back? This witch, perhaps? Her presence was intriguing, for I thought we had killed all the other Descendants during the Battle of Fennit Island. And she mentioned others. How many? How many Descendants had escaped us?

Now these were secrets worth knowing.

I lifted my head a little higher, trying my best to hear over the moan of the wind as it soared through the leaves.

"That is not the only news you brought, Báine," Broccan said. "If what you say is true, there is someone else I need to see."

"Yes. I know. Age is a terrible thing, even for a Descendant. One by one, it is picking us off, and aside from Isolde, there are none to take our place. Soon, she will be alone in this world. The last Descendant."

Isolde, the last Descendant. Who was this? Inching a little closer, ever so slowly and quietly, I muffled the sound of my breathing with my hair. I had to know more. I had to hear everything.

The witch looked at Broccan, the tightness in her jaw loosening a little. "What did you tell Isolde? Why does she think you've left the island?"

"She thinks I'm away trading goods... but I cannot lie like this any longer. To keep our knowledge from her when she was a child was fine. But Isolde is seventeen now. Eighteen, once the summer ends."

"She's still not presented with a gift?"

"I've seen no evidence of any, but that was why I asked you to stay for the day and watch her. What did you think? Isolde interrupted us before you could say much."

"A day is not long enough to know someone, but I must confess, I saw no gift." The witch ran her hands through her hair, her lips pressing into a thin line. "I find it so hard to believe that Isolde could be giftless. The prophecy… it has all come true so far. Why not this last part?"

"You should come to Rathlin as yourself and stay for a while. If you tested her, if the others tested her too, we would know for certain. Either way, I cannot keep the truth from her any longer."

"Are you sure you wish to tell Isolde everything? If she has no gift, what can she do with such knowledge?" Báine moved away from the fire, holding the cloak tight as she shivered. "It would only be an unkindness. All that grief, all that anger and injustice, it would tear her apart."

"The truth is always best. I know it will be hard for her, but…"

"Hard? If what happened is too much for you to bear, how can you expect her to carry the weight of it?" She reached out and gently touched the scars on Broccan's face.

Flinching, he pulled back, and a flash of red ran along his cheeks. "Why are you so set against me telling her, Báine? You are telling me lies too, keeping things from me, I think. I can smell this on you."

Báine barely moved and did not react to Broccan's rising temper. "We all decided to keep the truth from Isolde so she could have her childhood, her innocence. I know that it cannot last for much longer. And you are right. We must test her. If she is giftless, we will know it by the end of the year… and then we can decide on what to tell her."

This seemed to placate Broccan for a moment, but then the same irate look reappeared in his eyes.

"Are any of you looking for them?" His voice rose, a flash of rage erupting within his words. "The Fomorians are out there. Five now, no longer just three. Is that why you do not come to Rathlin? At least then I could understand your absence."

"I have no desire to search for the Fomorians, Broccan. That is why

I did not join you in your search all those years ago. We stay in the monastery because it is our home, and we've made lives for ourselves there. The land of a warrior is not a home for the rest of us. It is you who should have come to live with us."

The warrior shook his head. "Go on then. Fly home. I will see you there in a week or so." He made his way over to a horse and pulled himself up into the saddle.

"Broccan," Báine said, throwing the cloak to him. Her voice was soft.

"What?" he answered, his voice soft now too.

"Travel safe. War is brewing and the clans are gathering. The roads will be dangerous."

Broccan nodded as the woman transformed into a crow and flew into the air.

Broccan stared after her until she became merged with the darkness of the sky, then pulled his hood over his face. Pausing just a moment, he sniffed the air.

I woke from the dream, heart pounding, glad that my French stone walls had replaced the wildness of the Irish forest.

I'd not had a dream like this in many years. What was it? Fourteen, fifteen? No, it was longer. Eighteen years.

It wasn't through lack of trying. Every night, I'd told my dreams to search for Broccan as I always did, to see how close he was to us. But these last years, he had completely disappeared from my sight... as if he were dead. Perhaps he was dead, I'd thought. *Hoped.* Perhaps the desert of Tripoli had taken him, though I'd heard no reports of his death from the nomads who had taken us in.

Either way, my dreams could not find him. Nor had they found any other Descendants. My witch-dreams had fallen into darkness. Instead, I saw things I did not want to see. Not visions of the present, but rather memories of the past. Edysis screaming. Ethla choking. Olaf betraying. The birthing of a son who I'd had to give away. *Godfrey.*

As much as those memories pained me in my dreams, I bore them because it meant we were safe. Memories of those long dead, painful though they might be, were nothing to the fear of knowing Broccan was close. I saw his eyes when I watched him in my dreams. Beheld his anger. His rage. I knew that if he found us, he would kill us, rip us apart, limb from limb. This fear had driven us around the world. Always running and escaping. That was until eighteen years ago when he had vanished. Since then, we'd been at rest.

But these days of rest were now over. Broccan was alive. He had merely returned home for a time. Other Descendants were alive too. I replayed the conversation he'd had with the witch, Báine, over and over. This girl, Isolde… could she be *Fódla's* daughter? How interesting that she might be alive after all these years. *Alive, and giftless. And apparently so young.*

Could it really be her? When Tomas had told me the roots of the hawthorn tree had taken her, I had filled with rage. Decades he told me it might be for her to travel through the otherworld and return to the mortal realm. However, if she was only seventeen, it had taken much longer than that. Over one hundred and thirty years. The part of myself that had lived with the mortals said this was too long, that life could not endure outside of our realm for so many years. But I was not mortal. I was Fomorian, and though I did not know all the mysteries of our kind, or those of the Tuatha Dé Danann, I knew enough to never underestimate their power.

Only once morning broke did I get up and peer out through my bedroom door. One of the serving girls, Jehanne, was already arranging the cushions and seating area, as well as feeding my pet dove.

I walked out of my room, and Jehanne jumped upon hearing my footsteps. A sweet thing, she curtseyed, still smiling even as I sat against the cushions that she had just plumped.

"I will bring you breakfast right away, mistress."

"No," I said. "First tell Phillippe to find my brother and sons. Tell them I need them at once."

Jehanne scurried off to find her elder brother, another servant we kept, to do my bidding. I walked outside. After a dream filled with cold and damp, the dry morning heat felt glorious against my skin. I walked along the pathway to the edge of our garden, letting the hem of my dress brush against the cobblestone path. The view from here was spectacular. In Paris, it wasn't the sea or mountains stretching out before me, but rather a city full of thousands of people. A different sort of wonder. It reminded me a little of Dublin, except time had moved onward. Stone had replaced wood. Roman architecture had made its way west and as such, some of the buildings were beautiful rather than merely serviceable. There were not only churches but places of learning here. Places of fashion and entertainment. It was a fine city. Perhaps the greatest of this century.

Rome, of course, had once been the greatest city of all, but conflict ruled it now. The great families set the houses of other great families on fire, and they used strange machines to pull their rivals' towers down. Dissent, corruption and jealousy were everywhere in that city, which had been fortunate for us, for Rome had been good to us on two separate occasions. But alas, we could never stay anywhere for long. After our escape at Tripoli, we had ventured to Paris. Here, a new power was forming. A new empire.

We were not rich, nor related to any of the great Frankish families, but we had enough wealth to be tolerated by those in power and by those who wished to be. Máelmórda, for all his faults, could be amusing. Donnchad was handsome. I was beautiful. So was Cecile. In truth, the Frankish nobles looked for little else when seeking company. *Where were we from? Where did our wealth derive? What did we want?* No, no, no, these were not questions we wanted to answer. For now, we did not need to. We kept to ourselves, did not move beyond our station. Our house was far enough away from the beggars and the river sludge of the Seine that I could smell the sweetness of the spring roses in my garden, but not so close to the palaces of the aristocracy that we needed to watch for knives in our backs. I'd had one of those in my stomach before. I did not want to feel such pain again.

Recently, Máelmórda had suggested moving, said that we had lingered too long, even without Broccan chasing us. Other cities had risen in the last few years. Florence. Orleans. Venice. A fresh start. But so far, we had stayed. It was long enough that I'd begun to age us all using my witch-magic, giving us wrinkles and greying hair. I guessed this was the real reason Máelmórda wanted to leave, for he was vain enough to dislike this intensely.

Phillippe coming into the garden pulled me from my reverie.

"Has my son arrived yet?" I asked him.

"No, mistress," he said. "It's your brother."

Máelmórda came into the garden a few minutes later and nudged my shoulder as he came to a stop beside me.

"I thought Donnchad was with you," I said.

Máelmórda took out a pear and a knife from his pocket and sliced the fruit in half. "No, not last night."

"What about Angelo? Dare I ask where he is? It's been weeks since I've laid eyes upon him."

Máelmórda shrugged again. He'd assured me on many occasions that Angelo was somewhere in the city. He needed to be free for a while. To roam. *To be a man.* I took this to mean he was ensconced in one of the many brothels that the city had to offer. For a man who did not speak, I imagined there were few other ways to experience pleasure in a city such as this.

"I do hope you've told him to be careful," I added.

This drew another shrug from my brother. "Come inside," he said. "The wind has turned and is blowing over the river. The smell is insufferable."

"You don't smell so nice yourself," I said as I followed him into the house and closed the door behind us.

Máelmórda sniffed his armpit but otherwise seemed unperturbed by my comment. I supposed, if he chose to drink in the whorehouses, then he would smell of the cheap wine they drank there. My house, clean and smelling of the flowers I grew in my garden, was a sanctuary indeed.

"Cecile. Where is she?"

This time, it was I who shrugged.

"Cecile!" Máelmórda walked toward the bedrooms at the back of the house. "Daughter!"

My niece came out of her room and smiled at her father, wrapping her arms around him, not seeming to notice the odour of his shirt. Máelmórda laughed at something she said and walked with her into the seating area.

I continued to pace by the doors, waiting for Donnchad. Thankfully, it didn't take long for him to appear. Just long enough for Máelmórda to finish a glass of wine and pour himself another.

Once the three of them were fed, I returned to the living quarters and dismissed the servants. I gave them messages. Things I needed them to do in the city so they would leave us be for the next couple of hours. Phillippe was to try to find Angelo again. Jehanne was to get some bread and beef for the night's dinner.

"What is it?" Máelmórda asked, at last noting the serious expression on my face. "Has Broccan found our scent again? I told you we've lingered here too long."

"No. He's no longer following us, though I did have a dream about him last night. He's in Ireland. Living on an island called Rathlin, though I've never heard of it."

"Given up, has he?" Máelmórda asked, leaning back into the cushions, the relief palpable in his voice.

"Not quite. He spoke to another Descendant. A witch called Báine. They spoke of a young girl who has not yet come into her gift. A girl called Isolde. I believe she is related to Fódla."

I searched for Máelmórda's gaze when I said this. His eyes lifted to meet mine. He remembered then. He remembered the reason I had wanted to kill this child all those years ago. The prophecy that Ethla had told me as she lay dying was that *a granddaughter of words* would be the one to kill me. I'd discovered that it was the daughter of Murchad, the son of my then husband, Brian Boru, and that Descendant, Fódla. I'd nearly found this girl as a babe, for I had chased Fódla after the Battle of Clontarf… but she and her witch-sister had used their magic to conceal her from me. The roots of a giant hawthorn tree had dragged the baby underground and carried her away. Ever since, this prophecy had haunted me. A whisper always in the back of my mind.

As the morning had passed, I'd become more and more convinced that Fódla's daughter was the girl that Broccan and the witch were talking about. Now I was certain. Who else would Broccan be guarding so fiercely? *Who else could have pulled him away from us when he almost had us in his grasp?* It could only be this girl, this girl who'd been prophesied to kill me.

"What of it?" Máelmórda finally said as he picked at the figs in the bowl beside him. "They can stay in Ireland. We can stay here."

Donnchad shook his head. "We must return to Ireland. When this girl is grown, Broccan will come and look for us again. Better to attack now while he doesn't expect it."

"If you are so eager to fight him," my brother said, "why didn't you do it when he was looking for us?"

Donnchad scowled. "There was never a right time. When Angelo was young, we needed to protect him. When Cecile was born, we had to do the same for her. Then, when he nearly had us at Tripoli, we were so far from water, it… I… I might have lost. And you, uncle, were quite clear that you didn't want to fight him either, despite the fact you have the warrior gift."

"It was you who burned him and killed his friend. Why should I risk my own life for you?"

There. *That* was the reason I'd fled from Broccan rather than fight him. He was powerful, but we were powerful too. If we worked together, we might have killed him, and yet I could not trust my son and brother to fight with me. My son was unpredictable, my brother was a coward. The first might sacrifice me to kill Broccan, the second might sacrifice me to save himself. They were my kin, and we had lived together for many years, but deep down, I would never trust them. Not completely.

"Enough." I held up my hand before their bickering escalated into a row. "It is time for us to leave Paris in any case. Where should we go? Donnchad says Ireland. What do the rest of you think?"

Máelmórda sighed. "Venice."

"No. Ireland," Donnchad said.

"Why?" Máelmórda asked. "Why return after all these years?"

Donnchad folded his arms. "I've always wanted to return. For me, it was only a question of the right time. If Mother has had a dream in which Broccan is weak, we should make our move."

"Return for what?" Máelmórda asked, sitting a little straighter. "Our claim to the kingship of Ireland by legitimate means is gone. As for Broccan, we can escape from him as we did before. Why risk ourselves unnecessarily?"

"What do you want to do, aunt?" It was my niece, Cecile, who spoke. Giving me an inquisitive smile, she fixed her gaze upon me.

I pondered this question as I took a drink of wine. *What did I want to do?*

I thought of how much I had endured in my lifetime. My time in Ireland was as a nightmare to me now. To return was almost unthinkable. And yet, Donnchad was right. If we didn't find Broccan, one day he would look for us again, and this daughter of Fódla, the one who was prophesied to kill me, she might come with him. We had to kill her first. Now. While Broccan said she had no power, and while he could be distracted by protecting someone under his care. But as I thought on this, I realised I could not be the one to do everything this time. It was not me who should bend and bow and suffer. After all I had done for this wretched family of mine, it was their turn to save me. I just had to convince them it was in their best interest to do it.

"I think we should go to Ireland," I said. "We should kill Broccan and Isolde and destroy any other Descendant we find." I glanced at Donnchad, knowing that he was my best chance. "If you wish to seek power, once that is done, I will help you."

Máelmórda stared back at me, lips pursed together. He didn't like that I had promised to help my son over him. This was good. His jealousy might be the only thing to shake him off that seat and set down his wine.

"I will go, aunt."

I stared at Cecile, looking to see if humour lined her words, but her gaze was in earnest. Pleased that she had sided with me, I smiled. However, Cecile was not who I needed at my side. My niece was of little use. Her fire-magic was weak, and still she struggled to conjure it. It was only that Máelmórda was so taken with her, so relieved that finally he'd produced a child with any gift at all, that I'd agreed to let him bring her with us when we left Venice. She was a sweet girl, yes, but what use was that in times such as this?

"No, Cecile," Máelmórda said, sitting up. "It is not safe, especially not if Gormflaith has seen another Descendant in her dreams. If anyone goes to Ireland, it will be Donnchad, Angelo and me."

"You cannot protect me always, Father," she answered. "I will go. I'm determined. Paris has been a wonderful home for us, but soon, Aunt Gormflaith will need to age me again so I can fit in… and I grow tired of the company we have here. It is time to move on."

My brother stared at his daughter, then kissed her hand. He could not say no to her – it was a terrible weakness in him, and in that, I supposed, I had found my use for Cecile.

"Then it is decided," Donnchad said. "We will return to Ireland."

"You think I will return and fight to make you king?" Máelmórda snorted. "Never."

"You can be king too," Donnchad answered. "We can split the land into five provinces and each rule over one."

"Are you sure?" I asked, though I had to admit this was a clever idea. A way to ensure all of us were invested in his plan to regain the kingship. Still, as always with Donnchad, I didn't quite believe him. "It sounds very noble, but last time you pursued the kingship, you tried to kill me. If you want my help, you must convince me of your sincerity."

"I was a boy last time," Donnchad said. "I thought I understood, but I didn't. There are five of us now. Only what, three of them, according to your dream? Broccan, Isolde and the witch. Do you think there are more?"

Ah, now this was a question. Should I tell them the truth? Tell them the witch in my dream had said other Descendants lived still, somehow escaping the Battle of Fennit Island? Or would that make him less eager to return to Ireland and kill the girl?

"If there are, they cannot be very strong, otherwise they would have hunted us alongside Broccan."

Donnchad gave a curt nod. "Then it is time to return. It will be a relief to kill Broccan and know he no longer haunts my steps. I will kill him, Mother, and the girl and the witch, and any other Descendant I come across. You have my word." He opened the palm of his hand and let a ball of fire grow there. A promise made with fire. That was interesting. Unexpected.

"Will I try to find Angelo and tell him our decision?" Cecile said. "Or perhaps I should go to the festival with Marie like I promised?"

"Go to the festival, my love," Máelmórda said. "I shall find Angelo later."

Cecile nodded, and with a kiss for each of her father's cheeks, she walked outside of the house and along the steps to Marie's house, which was situated closer to the city. My brother watched after her, until Cecile had reached Marie's house, and together they walked into the city.

Once she moved out of sight, Máelmórda stood to go after her. He always did. Paris was a dangerous city – even more so for beautiful women.

"No, I will go, uncle," Donnchad said. "I'll see that she is safe. I'm meeting some friends at the festival anyway."

Máelmórda, already five glasses of wine down, sat, his eyes beginning to close. My brother was a fool, always had been. If he hadn't been in such a hurry to satiate his own lusts, he might have noticed it in Donnchad as he walked down the hill after his cousin. For Cecile was beautiful. So very beautiful.

"Careful, sister," Máelmórda said as he stretched his legs over the chair and kicked off his boots. "He's still a snake, that one."

"If he kills this girl for me, I don't care."

Máelmórda shrugged.

"It should be you offering to kill her. You know the prophecy. You know the stakes."

"Seeing as Donnchad is so keen to play the hero, I thought I should let him."

Rolling onto his side, my brother promptly fell asleep.

Later that afternoon, I walked outside to find Angelo standing in the garden, staring out over the city as I had done that morning. He was tall and slender, and while he had dark hair like me, he wore it short as was the fashion in Paris. It gave him a haunted look, and yet, when he smiled, the women couldn't help but watch him.

"Hello, my love. Thank you for coming here," I said as I moved to stand beside him. "I had a dream this morning. Broccan is in Ireland. He stopped chasing us because the girl, Fódla's daughter, is alive. Do you remember what I told you about her?"

Angelo nodded.

"I think we should go to Ireland. Once this girl is grown, Broccan will begin his search for us again. But I feel the time for running and hiding is over. Now you and Cecile are older, we should bring the fight to them."

Angelo picked up a stick and drew the outline of Ireland on the soil. Once this was done, he handed me the stick.

He wanted to know where they were.

"In the dream, he mentioned an island. Rathlin." I ran the stick over the southern coast of Munster, the west coast of Connacht, and then the north coast of Ulaid. "There are islands here, here and here. But I've never heard the name Rathlin before."

Angelo walked inside and opened the bird cage. The dove's wings flapped as Angelo caught him.

I knew what Angelo wanted, and indeed, it made sense. Using my gift, I changed the dove into a golden eagle, giving him long, powerful wings to speed his journey north. "Olaf," I whispered into the bird's ear, "find Rathlin Island. See if you can discover Broccan and the child of Fódla and Murchad. We will sail to England as soon as we can. Once you know more, come and find us."

The eagle flapped its wings and flew into the sky.

By the time Olaf flew beyond sight, Angelo had written something in the soil.

Le Serpent de Mer. Demain matin. Bristol.

I took a breath. "*The Serpent of the Sea* leaves for Bristol tomorrow morning?"

He nodded.

"Then go and pay for our passage and find Donnchad and Cecile. Tell them to come home at once. We leave at first light."

Angelo threw away the stick and made his way into the city. A good boy, Angelo. Devoted to me. Simple of mind, a healer had once told me, but that was no bad thing. It meant he did as he was told, which was more than I could say for the others.

While I watched him leave, I half thought about calling him back. Leaving Paris in the morning was a rash decision. I could have pondered and plotted. Let Donnchad and Máelmórda argue some more. But I couldn't wait. The girl had to die. Now. While she was weak.

Like a shadow, the prophecy had hung over me all these years. It was another reason I had always run from Broccan. I was sick of it. Sick to my stomach at the thought that I, Gormflaith, should be frightened and cowed before another.

No more. Now that Donnchad had agreed to do my bidding, it was time to move before he could change his mind. It was time for me to regain my purpose. For I had been a queen once. In time, I would be a queen again.

Broccan

The road to Seir Kieran

The use of my warrior gift did not give me the joy I once believed it would.

When I was a boy, I imagined myself on horseback, a sword in one hand and a spear in the other and thought how glorious it would be.

Of course, as with all boyish dreams, this was not reality. Swords and spears meant war. Death. And I was sick of both those things. Sick of giving it. Sick of receiving it.

Time heals all, I'd been told. But that wasn't true, at least for me. There was an emptiness inside of me still. Isolde had stopped this hollow void from growing and taking me over, but she was not with me now. Her laugh and her smile were absent, and I felt this loss keenly after six days of travelling alone.

As I journeyed, I tried to move my thoughts away from self-pity and melancholy. I needed to get better at controlling this. Isolde saw these emotions at times when they broke through, and I had resolved to hide them deeper. I did not want my sadness to become her sadness.

Today, distraction had come easier than usual, though I did not like the cause. I sensed a rising danger. The danger felt distant, the feeling fleeting, and I could not know for certain what it was... and yet, the conflict in Leinster that Báine had warned me of *was* being spoken of by the mortals. Perhaps this was it, this building threat. Mortal conflicts had a habit of brewing for years, only for there to be an explosion of violence.

I began to listen when I rode past the women cleaning their

clothes by the river. I listened as I rode past the men herding cattle with their sons. Leinster warred against Bréifne and Connacht, these people said. They spoke names I had not heard before. There was a banished king called Diarmait Mac Murchadha who'd fled to England to recruit an army to help retake his land. I heard of a King Tigernán of Bréifne whose wife had been stolen by King Diarmait, which had caused the feud in the first place.

Letting the gossip wash over me, I tried all the while not to worry. Even if there was a war here, it could not affect Isolde. Life on the island was a slow life, but a safe one. Made even safer by the spells on my land that prevented my enemies from entering. The real danger was Isolde leaving my land while I was away. She had promised not to, but she had left without permission before. Sometimes, her friend Móirne would call for her and they would sneak off together, Isolde thinking I didn't know.

Of course I knew.

I didn't mind. She needed to have some freedom, and the innocence of their activities made me laugh. Nothing like what Tairdelbach and I were up to when we were young. They skimmed stones against the waves. Ran along the beach, laughing as they ran away from the breaking waves, or else they would lie on the grass and talk.

And I trusted Isolde. I did. However, now that I was not there, and my warrior gift was warning me of a growing threat, an uneasiness swirled inside of me. *Perhaps I shouldn't have left her? I hadn't left her before.* Seeing Colmon and Shae was important, yes, but nothing was more important than Isolde and her safety. What if she swam in the sea and a storm blew in? What if a sickness on the mainland blew over and she caught it? What if the Fomorians came to Ireland while I was away? What if I couldn't get back to her in time?

As these scenarios, each worse than the one before it, played in my mind, I closed my eyes and breathed. I had sensed no trace of danger when I left the island. I wouldn't be away long. Only seven days there and then seven days back, and Isolde was tough.

Tougher than even she realised, and she would be safe... so long as she didn't stray from my land. *And she had promised me she wouldn't.*

I pushed my horse a little harder, wanting to make sure I reached Seir Kieran before darkness fell. If I reached the monastery in good time, I could speak to Affraic tonight, which in turn meant I could leave early tomorrow morning.

Luck was on my side. My horse, purchased cheaply because of her age, had more stamina than expected, and just before the sun lowered below the horizon, I arrived at Seir Kieran. By the gate, I dismounted and walked my horse into the monastery grounds. The mortal men and women who lived within the monastery, mostly escaped slaves or those cast out by family, were still working in the gardens, though beginning to talk of making their way home before it got dark.

Seir Kieran was a lovely place, and I felt a little calmer as I walked through the grounds. A place of peace and tranquillity for those who needed it, the fertile soil inside the walls was plentiful, Affraic and Siobhan's healing gift allowing the plants, root vegetables and herbs to grow without infection or blight. There were apple trees too. Bee hives. Pigs, chickens and goats.

There was no fighting within the confines of the monastery land, either. Gisela sang each morning and evening. Her harpist gift gave peace to the hearts of the mortals who lived here when times were hard. Happiness when times were good. Solace during times of loss. Healing to those who had suffered. Báine and Étaín used their witch gift to make sure that roving armies stayed away from the land, conjuring rain and winds to render the monastery a less desirable destination to those looking for easy pickings.

"Evening, Broccan."

Affraic was the first to spot me. She grinned as I walked toward her. I returned her smile, but then I noticed something. Strands of grey in her hair, visible only when the wind blew. In a mortal, this wouldn't signify much, but in a Descendant, this meant only one thing. She was ageing. Dying.

"We've been expecting you," she said as I reached her. She patted the nose of my horse, then asked one of the mortal laymen tidying away their tools to take the horse to the stable.

"Báine arrived home safely?" I asked once the man had left.

"Yes. Of course. A little over four days ago. Let me tell you, it took her a wee while to warm up." Affraic linked her arm into mine and led me inside. "Those winds in the north are harsher than here."

"Where's Shae?"

"He's sleeping in his rooms, or else writing down some songs for Gisela. I'll take you to see Colmon first."

"And what of you?" I brushed her hair with my hand as we walked, my fingers lingering on the grey strands I'd noticed outside.

"Ah, enough. I'm old." She flicked her hair out of my hand. "The oldest one here, in truth. It's my turn."

"I am still sorry to see it."

Affraic nodded, though didn't say any more as she led me to the room of my old mentor.

Colmon was my mother's cousin. Bound by blood and memory, there was no one I loved more in this living world than Colmon, other than Isolde. *How I wished I could talk with him.*

Affraic opened the door to his room and stepped aside to let me pass her. I took the seat beside him and took hold of his hand. "I am here, Colmon," I said. "It's Broccan."

Colmon didn't answer. He didn't move. Just as I knew he wouldn't. He was in a coma of sorts, Affraic said. The potion of death Tomas had given him on Fennit Island had killed him and the antidote given by Echna had come too late for him to waken properly. We had saved him from death but had not been able to give him life.

I took his hand in mine and noticed the grey hair in one of his braids. "So, it's true. Colmon is ageing. Three of you at the same time."

Affraic nodded.

I squeezed Colmon's hand a little harder. When I first heard that he had not woken, I had feared for him. Wept. That raw pain had ebbed away the first time I'd sat with him. I had felt no pain from him when I touched his hand. He was sleeping. Dreaming. I believed he had no awareness of time or that he was locked inside himself.

Perhaps this dream state was not so very bad, to be away from this existence of ours. If he was awake, what would I say to him other than burden him with my problems? Now that I was here, seeing the white hairs glistening between the black, I decided that Colmon's death was not something to be sad about. After one hundred and fifty years, he would finally be reunited with those he loved. This strange half-life over.

Affraic sat on the seat opposite mine and ran her fingers over Colmon's hair. "When we came here after the attack on Fennit Island, there were nine of us. Now that Echna and Étaín are gone, there are only seven. In a couple of years, another three of us will have passed over to the otherworld. Our lives are long, but the Descendants of the Tuatha Dé Danann do not live forever. Our time is almost over."

"What of Isolde? What will become of her if we are all gone?" I asked.

"You told Báine that she has not presented with any gift. If that is the case, a mortal life awaits her."

"That's not what my mother saw."

"Perhaps... perhaps her passage under the tree... the time it took for her to reach us.... maybe it altered the prophecy. Or maybe the prophecy is wrong, after all. Rónnat's mind was broken by the end. Who knows what she truly saw."

I contemplated this. My mother's mind had wandered often, but that last time I'd spoken to her on her crannog, she'd been so certain. And her voice on the wind in Tripoli telling me to find and protect Isolde... how could that be false, for I had found Isolde by the tree, just as she had told me?

"No, Affraic. It cannot be wrong. Isolde is the one who the prophecy spoke of. I know we all thought her gift would show of its own accord, but perhaps that won't happen for her. I've been watching, testing her when I can. She's not a warrior, though I have taught her to fight as best I can. However, the gift of a witch. A druid. Weapon-maker. Harpist. Healer. I do not know these gifts so well. They are more subtle. You should come and test her. There must be something I am missing."

"Those gifts usually reveal themselves long before the age of seventeen. You yourself were only a young boy. Suddenly you could run so fast no one could see you, and you became stronger than a grown man. It's not something that can happen to you and not be noticed."

"You truly think she has no gift?"

Affraic took a deep breath. "Before she died, I spoke with Fódla. She said she believed that as a babe in the womb, Isolde had summoned a hailstorm to help them escape. Afterward, she said Isolde went quiet. Fódla feared Isolde had burned herself out. Perhaps the gift she was born with has left her?"

"Isolde summoned a hailstorm? That is a witch gift. A strong one. If you knew this, why did you not tell me?"

"I did not want to sway your opinion of Isolde. Make you see things that weren't there or ignore what was."

I felt my temper rising, bubbling upward like an avalanche. Trying to bite it down, I clasped my hands tight together. What was done was done. These old Descendants, they had lived so long keeping their secrets, they still could not bring themselves to tell me everything. "You should come with me to Rathlin when I return," I said, once I trusted my voice to sound calm. "Leave Meabh here to care for Colmon. Gisela to care for Shae. But you, Báine and Siobhan could come with me. You could test her."

"I will come with you to Rathlin tomorrow." Affraic leaned back in the chair and pushed her hair away from her face. "I'll ask the others to come once Shae has passed over. They will not want to leave him until that happens."

"And then we will tell Isolde the truth?"

Affraic took a sharp intake of breath. "You must think on that, Broccan. You know Isolde. Can she understand what this means?

How will she bear it when she knows that those who killed her parents are still alive in this world, and that without a gift, she can do nothing about it? I know you think withholding the truth is wrong. When we lived on Fennit Island, we kept our secrets, didn't we? And I know that is why you think we do not wish to tell Isolde of her past, but it is not. It is for her own happiness. To take on all our history, our grief? It would be an unkindness to her." She pressed my hand then. "Let me come to Rathlin. Together, we will test her, and I will talk with her and see what her heart truly desires."

"She wishes to stay on the island. That is what I wish too. It is safe there for her."

"Maybe that's true now. That is because you are with her, and she loves you. But she is a child no longer. She might wish to have a family of her own in a few years. You don't know how her mind will change as the years go by. If you insist on telling her the truth, it might change her in ways you can't imagine. Damage her, even."

Affraic stood, her expression wearied by our conversation. Usually so serene, I could see the strain she carried, and so I said nothing more.

"I will leave you to speak with Colmon," she said. "Find me afterward in the feasting hall. Siobhan has made a stew for supper."

I took Colmon's hand in mine once Affraic closed the door behind her. "How are you, old friend?" I asked. His face, which I watched so closely, remained expressionless. Unresponsive.

"I am selfish, I think, to want you to waken, but I wish you could see Isolde and know her. She is very like her mother. More impetuous, though. More impulsive. She would make you laugh." Pressing his hand against my forehead, I took a long breath.

"What should I do, Colmon? What if she wants to leave the island as Affraic says she might? It is not safe. And yet… if she is mortal… then she must be allowed to live her life. Is this the pain you had when I left Rathlin? I didn't understand it at the time. I thought I was a man, but really, I was still a boy. I see that now.

"Isolde, she is young. Sweet. I want her to be herself and not have to mould herself into something other people want her to be. Perhaps it is naïve of me to think this can be so… but I must not talk to you only of my problems. You are ageing, my friend. Soon you will be with Fódla and my mother. Murchad and Tairdelbach, too. You must tell them that I think of them often, and that one day, it will be an honour for me to join them."

I only left Colmon so I could go to Shae's room. It would be best to see him tonight, so I could leave at first light.

Shae lay on his bed, his eyes half-closed when I entered. While Affraic's and Colmon's hair was streaked with grey, his was completely white. His cheeks were sunken too, and his chin and nose were covered with thin red veins.

"Ah, Broccan." He blinked sleepily, then held out his hand to hold mine. It was weak and thin. Fading just like the rest of him.

"Oh, don't look at me like that," he said, smiling as I sat on the edge of his bed. "It's my time, and I must confess I look forward to seeing my friends who have passed before me."

"How old are you, Shae? I've never asked before."

"Four hundred and twelve. Much too long to be alive, really."

I nodded. Yes, this was a long time to live. I was not half this age, and I could not think of living double what I already had.

"Enough about me. How are you, Broccan?"

"I am well. Isolde keeps me on my toes."

"I am sure she does. Children have a habit of doing that, but she won't be a child for much longer."

"That's true. I feel it now more than ever. She seemed to be a child for an age. All of a sudden, she seems so grown up."

When I next glanced at Shae, he was staring at me. A low hum vibrated in the back of his throat. He was trying to calm me down. Some of my pain eased. Some. But not all.

"I can feel the sadness within you, Broccan. If you would let me sing to you, I could alleviate your pain while you are here."

I shook my head.

"You miss Fódla, we all do. And I know you lost people you loved at Clontarf, but you cannot pretend not to feel and push everything down. Believe me, that way your sadness will tear you apart."

My chest ached as he said this. The pain of losing Fódla and Murchad had been difficult to bear. My mother too. And Tairdelbach. I had loved him. I would have followed him anywhere. I would have died for him, and yet he was the one who had lost his life at Clontarf. I thought of him then, when the two of us were alone and talking. The way he laughed. So loud and confident, and I remembered the secrets we had shared. I had loved him, yes… and I had never asked him how he felt in return. Tears rushed to my eyes and my throat felt so thick I could hardly breathe. Shae's hum had changed, I realised. Instead of trying to ease my pain, he wanted me to feel it. He wanted me to feel what I was trying so hard to bury.

"Don't," I whispered.

Shae stopped and the pain eased a little. The rawness subsided.

"You are right, Shae." My chin quivered as I spoke, and I took a moment to compose myself. "Sometimes I feel as if I cannot take what happened. That this failure of mine was too much, and I hate myself with every fibre of my being."

"It is not your fault, Broccan," Shae said, his hand reaching for mine. "We have our gifts, but it is not always in our power to defeat the evil in the hearts of others."

His voice had turned soft as he spoke. There was a melody in it, and I found the ache in my heart easing again and the pain subsiding further.

"I told you I didn't need your help."

"Ah," Shae said. "When you are old, you can do whatever you want. You are hardly going to shout at an old man like me, are you?" He winked, lips twitching, but this small use of his gift had tired him, and he sunk deeper into the pillows that propped him up.

"You do not need to worry about me, Shae. As long as Isolde is well, I am well."

"Then return home, Broccan. Believe me when I say that I'm happy to be leaving this land for the otherworld. When I pass, I don't want you to shed any tears, rather rejoice that I am with friends. And I know Colmon would say the same. No tears for him, either."

I nodded as I stood, feeling more at ease than I had in a long time.

The next morning, I rose early, said my goodbyes and made my way outside. Affraic was already standing beside her horse and walking it slowly around the gardens. Her mare was beautiful. Tawny and muscular, her mane shone in the morning's light. Affraic gestured at another horse being led toward us by one of the children. This one black and white but just as bonny.

"I thought I'd put that old mare of yours to pasture. She felt about ready to keel over when I tended to her last night."

I ran my hand over my new horse's nose and hauled myself onto her back. "Will they know their way back? We won't be able to get them across to Rathlin on my boat."

"They will find their way home, yes. I've trained them well."

"Then how will you return home?"

"Oh, I don't mind walking, or perhaps, if I'm lucky, I can buy another old nag who can bear me here before keeling over from exhaustion." Affraic grinned as she mounted her horse.

A coldness swept over me then. The fear I had felt on the way here, it surged within me again. "Come, Affraic," I said, pushing my horse forward. "Let us move quickly. I long to be home and see Isolde."

Isolde

Rathlin Island

I waited on the sand as the rowboat approached, letting the water rush over my toes as the waves came ashore. I knew it was Broccan, even from a distance. But who was this woman in the boat beside him? I couldn't account for it. He rarely spoke about his life before he came to live on the island. There was certainly no one who he'd kept up any contact with.

Impatient to greet Broccan's friend, I lifted my skirt and ran into the sea to help steady the boat so they could disembark without getting wet. Broccan smiled as our eyes met, but before I could speak, he jumped out, took hold of the woman's hand and helped her overboard.

Now I could see her up close, her beauty was apparent. Long brown hair and deep brown eyes. Elegant.

"Good morning, Isolde," she said, once she steadied herself.

Surprised by the familiarity of her greeting, I let go of the rowboat. "How do you know my name?"

A wave crashed in, and the rowboat swung around, knocking the back of my legs. I stumbled forward. Quickly, I pivoted, just in time to catch the rowboat before the waves pushed it again. Broccan ran to help me. "I have it now," he said as he hauled it out of the sea and dragged it up onto the sand.

I waded out of the water, realising that I'd soaked my skirt when I'd fallen forward.

"Oh, no," I said to the woman, wincing at my own clumsiness. "I should have been more careful."

"Not at all. I should have waited until you had moored the boat until I started speaking. I distracted you."

I waved away her apology but held her gaze, the question of how she knew me still lingering between us.

"My name is Affraic, and I visited you once when you were a baby," she said. "Many years ago."

"How can that be?" I replied. "You look so young."

"Ah, not so young." Affraic pulled back her brown hair to reveal a few strands of grey and white along her temple. "And my legs are not as good as they once were. They click when I jump and run. That's the problem with growing old. It's not loss of beauty, but the tiredness in your mind, and the pain in your joints."

I gave a sympathetic nod, but really there weren't so many grey hairs, so for all her talk of fatigue, she couldn't be that old. Móirne's mother was only thirty-nine, and already half her hair was grey and white. "Tell me, how is it that you met me as a baby?"

"I knew your mother."

My mouth opened. *She knew my mother.* This was wonderful.

Affraic laughed at my obvious delight. "I met Broccan while he was trading on the mainland. I asked him to bring me here so that I could see you again."

"Yes," Broccan said on rejoining us. "I thought you'd enjoy a guest, Isolde."

"Of course." My smile widened. Aside from Broccan, I'd never met anyone who knew my mother. This was perhaps the greatest surprise Broccan could have given me on his return.

Affraic took my hand in hers and we began to walk away from the shore. I wished now that I hadn't run into the sea to help. My wet skirts clung to my shins and a thin layer of sand had caked along the hem.

"I'm very excited to see you again, Isolde," Affraic said. "I have to say, *you* do look much older. You're a woman now. A baby no longer." She bit her lip, her eyes shining as they took in my face.

"And so very like your mother. Your father's eyes though, and his height, for you are a little taller than me."

"You knew my mother *and* father?"

"I didn't know your father well, no. But your mother… I was her friend for many years."

I tightened my grip on her hand and led her up the path toward our ráth. "Tell me something about my mother. Her favourite colour, perhaps. Broccan says he doesn't know."

"Oh, I'd say it was the colours red and yellow. At least it was when I first knew her, though it could have changed. Don't you think favourites alter over the course of your life?"

"I think that is the way of it for many people."

"But not for you?"

I contemplated this question. People changed often, didn't they? And sometimes with no warning. Móirne had grown tired of her home, a home she had once professed to love. I found myself looking out over the empty sea and the empty beach, all signs of the seanchaí's fire gone. Had my love for this place diminished too? Was I such a fickle creature? I couldn't tell. I couldn't tell if the feelings surging up inside me were telling me to leave this place too… or perhaps to hide myself away.

"I do not know, Affraic. Lately, I feel that I do not know myself as well as I once did."

"Ah," she nodded. "Then you really are getting older. The certainty of childhood has its benefits, but we cannot stay there forever."

I had never thought about growing up in this way, and yet now it seemed so obvious. This woman who knew my mother was certainly wise. I felt that when she spoke. She didn't blurt out her thoughts like I did. Everything was so measured, so calm.

"Come," I said, noticing that she shivered as the wind blew in. "Let me put on some broth for you and Broccan. You must be tired after such a long journey."

★

Affraic, Broccan and I ate well that afternoon. Feeling strange within my own skin, I listened to them talking while I cleared everything away. I couldn't account for my sudden shyness. On the occasions Móirne had come to visit, I'd speak to her with enthusiasm, barely stopping to breathe at times, but that exuberance had disappeared today. Instead, I watched Broccan and Affraic. Affraic's appearance had given me many questions to ponder. Had she really just happened to see Broccan while he was trading? That seemed unlikely. Perhaps Broccan had sought her out?

I searched for signs of attraction between them but found none. They spoke slowly, dispassionately. Their gazes didn't linger on each other, and they spoke of insignificant things, like the passing of the seasons and the snow drifts that lingered on the mainland. Nothing of love, nothing of old memories. The conversation felt stilted and this seemed the oddest thing of all. It was almost as if they barely knew each other. But how could that be if Affraic knew my mother so well and my mother had raised Broccan?

I brought over a cup of milk for each of them, now that they had finished eating. Deciding I'd listened long enough, I began to ask my questions.

"Which way did you travel, Broccan? Did you stay in Ulaid, or did you go as far as Bréifne?"

"No, not that far," Broccan answered. "There is talk of war and the clans are gathering. I thought it best to stay close to the north. The northern kings are staying out of it for now."

"A war?" I sat down beside him. "Why? What's happened?"

"Who knows, Isolde. Greed. Power. Land. So many wars are unjust; there is often no real reason. The kings fight and then there is peace and then they fight again. Leave them to it, I say. We are better off here, away from all of that. Aren't we?"

"Yes, of course. But… what is this one about? How do you know if it's just or not if you don't know the cause?" I turned to Affraic. "What do you—"

"Isolde," Broccan interrupted, "what care do you have for kings you have never met?"

"I don't care about the kings. I care about Móirne, who is moving to the mainland. I want to make sure she's safe. And besides... wasn't my father a warrior? If every war is unjust, then why do you speak so well of him?" I turned to Affraic. "You knew my father. What would he have thought of the war on the mainland?"

Affraic reached forward to hold my hand. "I did not know your father well, but I know that if he'd had his way, there would be no wars. He always did his best to avoid them."

"What wars were these?"

Broccan lowered his gaze, avoiding mine, and that look of sadness I knew so well flooded his features.

Oh, I had done it again. Upset him when I didn't mean to. I'd gone from being silent to asking question after question, and in front of someone who Broccan had not seen in a long time. My curiosity, it had just got the better of me. "I am sorry. It's just, I like to hear about my mother and father."

"And I am happy to talk about them." Affraic stood. "Why don't you come for a walk with me? Broccan mentioned the puffins have already arrived. I should like to see them. We don't have them where I live."

"Yes, I should like that."

Broccan nodded. "I'll clear up today, Isolde. You go with Affraic. We can talk more when you return."

Affraic swept out of the house, and I followed. Giving Broccan a final glance as I crossed the threshold, I saw his expression held no trace of the sadness I'd seen earlier.

"Go on," he said, waving me away, but with a smile upon his face. "Enjoy your walk."

I led Affraic toward the rocks along the west coast of the island. She smiled as we walked, looked about her with interest, and asked me a few questions about the strange birds that flew here from the north. I answered, but all the while thought of Broccan. He was keeping something from me. I knew this. Well, I would keep my questions to myself while Affraic was here, but once she left, I would pull him out of his silence and make him talk of what he kept from me. He had promised, after all, on that day he left Rathlin for the mainland.

"There aren't that many puffins," Affraic said as we reached the rocks the birds nested upon.

"Not yet, though there are more than usual for this time of year. By this time next week, these rocks will be covered."

"Do you like watching them?"

"Yes." I smiled. "It's wonderful to watch the birds nest, and then for the eggs to turn to something living. Ever since I can remember, I've come here to watch the nesting. Even as a little girl."

"Do you know what game I played when I was a little girl?" Affraic asked.

I raised an eyebrow.

"Me and my sister were always racing, especially along rocks like these. My father called my sister a mountain goat, because she rarely lost her footing. He called me a baby hare because I was so quick."

"Sea rocks are sharp," I said. "You must have cut your legs and hands to pieces."

"Yes, I suppose we did sometimes." She laughed and pointed at one of the larger rocks that jutted upward, a foot or two taller than the others. "Come on," she shouted. "Let's race to that one. You aren't going to let an old woman like me win, are you?"

This sudden burst of energy from Affraic made me grin, and I ran after her. A race was a race, after all. Affraic scrambled over the rocks, but just as I had warned her, they were sharp, and she slid down one of them, the molluscs and lichen cutting into her hand and wrist as she tried to stop herself from slipping further.

I came to a stop and ran back to her. She winced as she held up her left hand, which was covered in scrapes and a long cut that ran from her palm to forearm.

"Alas," she said. "I couldn't turn my foot in time. I'm not a leveret any longer. I'm too old."

Scrambling onto the rock beside hers, I held out my hand. "Let me help you up."

Taking her grip on my offered hand, I pulled her up, and we made our way back onto the path.

"Is it bad?" I asked.

She released her right hand, which she'd been holding with her left, and showed me the large gash. With the release of pressure, thick blood ran from the cut and dripped onto the grass.

"If you can push the skin together," she said, "I've some loose fabric in my pocket. I'll bandage it up as best as I can."

I did as she asked and held the gash tight.

"Do you know," she said as she rummaged around. "When I cut myself as a child, my mother would hold her hand over it and imagine that the wound healed itself. She believed that those wishes would help the cut to mend."

"Did you ever believe it worked?" I asked.

"I did. Why don't we try it now? It's never a bad thing to wish for good things to happen." She peered up at me, wincing a little as I held the cut tight. "For old times' sake."

There was something about this story that rang false to my ear. I couldn't say why, only that something inside me spoke the word *lie*. But perhaps it wasn't the falseness that niggled. Maybe it was because it seemed such a silly thing to ask. I might have appeared childish earlier when I was asking so many questions, but I was *seventeen*. "I'm a little old to believe such things, Affraic. If we could simply wish for cuts to heal, then no one would die from wounds and injuries, would they?"

"Such cynicism," she said, tutting. "Try. If only to make an old woman happy. What harm can it do?"

She closed her eyes, pressing her other hand, now holding the fabric bandages, over mine.

I closed my eyes as she asked, for I didn't want to be rude. Besides, even if it was odd, what harm could well-wishes do? In my mind, I imagined the wound healing, the skin knitting together and the scars disappearing.

"Have you done it?" she asked. "Has it healed over in your mind?"

"Yes."

"Then open your eyes."

I opened my eyes and lifted my hand away. As soon as I released the pressure on the skin, blood poured from the wound.

I gave her a sympathetic smile as I reached for the fabric she'd taken out. "It's a good story. I'm sure, when your mother did that, it distracted you while she cleaned the wound out."

"Ah," Affraic said, giving me a small smile in return as I wound the fabric over her arm. "I think you might be on to something." Without another word, she tied off the bandage and then pulled down her sleeve.

I ran my hands over my hair, staring more deeply at Affraic as she did this. I was right, wasn't I? It had been a childish sort of memory that she'd brought up. I couldn't quite account for it… unless she had meant it as a way to talk about mothers.

"What is wrong, Isolde?" she asked. "You've gone pale. Was it the blood?"

"What was my mother like?"

"Oh." Affraic bit her lip. "Your mother, Fódla, was very kind. Beautiful, with the same thick red hair as you. Thoughtful. Brave, too, though I don't think that would be the first thing others would have said about her. But she was. In a quieter way, I suppose. Brave in her mind rather than with a sword. She spoke the truth, and that is the bravest thing of all, for it can turn people against you."

"Is that what happened to her?"

"At times, though it didn't stop her."

"Was she as wise as you?"

"Not many people are as wise as me, though perhaps that is arrogant of me to say so."

"I wish I was wise," I said.

"You are."

"No. I'm not at all. I don't know anything. I can speak five languages, and I know the names of all the kingdoms in Ireland and those beyond the sea, but I am not wise."

"You are still young. Wisdom is something that must be learned, often through hard lessons."

"Tell me more about Mother," I said. "What was she like, truly? Not just nice words and compliments. I want to know everything. What was she like at my age?"

Affraic smiled. "When she was younger, she was sweet like you. Naïve, I think. She fell in love with a man who took advantage of her nature. She couldn't see it for herself for many years."

"Who was he?"

"A man called Tomas. He manipulated, he deceived, and told lies to everyone around him. Your mother loved him very much, but she saw through him in the end and was able to break away. That was when she met your father."

The truth hurt, even though I had asked for it. I had built up my parents to be these beautiful beings. Like angels. Always smiling. Always happy. To hear of my mother's suffering, it rendered her for the first time as someone flesh and blood.

Affraic stared around the island, the sharp north wind blowing her hair forward. She reached out her hand and pulled it back, then turned into the wind so her hair blew out behind her. "Life is short, Isolde. I feel that more now than ever. Decisions are hard to make at times and they can bind you. You must take care to remember that. You will have to decide how you want to live soon. To do that, you must be honest with yourself."

"I don't understand."

"This island is beautiful, but do you truly wish to live here forever?"

"I don't know. I think so. Yes. Broccan is here. I would not leave him."

"But if he was to leave, what would you do?"

"Broccan doesn't want to leave. He hates the outside world."

Affraic twisted her lips, but her expression cleared. Deep in thought, she did not want me to know what she was thinking.

"Come," she said. "Let's gather some eggs. I'll make us something special tonight, and while we walk, I'll tell you a little more of your mother." She pointed at a patch of wildflowers up ahead. "Is that cowslip over there? Yes, I think it is. Your mother used to make the most beautiful headdresses from them. I can show you if you like."

That night, Broccan and Affraic went to bed after dinner. It was earlier than usual, but then Broccan must have been exhausted after rowing from Ulaid to the island. As such, I did not have a chance to ask him questions about my mother and father as I had intended. Affraic's conversation played over and over in my mind instead. Someone had been unkind to my mother? A man called Tomas. Did Broccan know him? If so, why had he never spoken of him?

Deciding that I would ask him my questions in the morning, I doused the cooking fire, made my way into the house, and collapsed into bed. However, despite my fatigue, sleep wouldn't come. I tossed and turned, only ever seeming to fall into a half-sleep, where the sounds of the waves crashing onto the shore played over and over in my mind. A wolf appeared sometimes in my daze. A wolf with blue eyes that watched me. Once I chased it, and it ran into its den where I could not follow.

I couldn't tell what hour of the night it was when I woke from this half-sleep, only that it was voices that had roused me. I prised open my eyelids and glanced at the empty beds inside the house. At first, I closed my eyes, wishing myself to fall back into a slumber, but then voices sounded again. It was Broccan and Affraic. They spoke in whispers, but every so often their voices would rise. Anger and frustration within these words. Silently, I pushed away my blanket and crept to the door, which was ever so slightly ajar. I peered through the gap. The fire was alight again, crackling as Broccan threw more sticks upon it. Affraic stood at his side, arms wrapped around her chest.

Broccan shook his head. His cheeks were flushed, jaw clenched. "Are you sure?"

"She is not a healer, and I cannot see that anything else presented today," Affraic said, her voice soft, lower. She sounded older now, perhaps deserving of the grey hairs she had showed me. "I think Gisela should come next. The harpist gift is more subtle."

"Isolde has a beautiful voice," Broccan said, "but not one that dampens or emboldens emotions. I don't believe she's a harpist."

"The stronger gifts. The warrior, the witch, the cupbearer, they would have surfaced of their own accord by now." Affraic rubbed her hands over her mouth. "If only Echna was still alive. He could have tested her to see if she is a druid. That is a subtle gift too."

"Isolde is no druid. Besides, what use would that gift be against the Fomorians?"

"Perhaps her gift burned out, as I suggested at Seir Kieran. Perhaps the gift she should have had is gone?"

I pulled my head back a little, knowing that I was listening to something I shouldn't. Part of me wanted to return to my bed, but another part, stronger than the first, wanted to hear. To spy felt intrusive… but they had said my name. Even though I didn't understand their meaning, they were speaking about me. I leaned forward, pressing my eye to the gap in the door.

"No," Broccan said in answer to a question from Affraic that I had not heard.

"You must think about it. When she was born, I suggested you both come to Seir Kieran, and you dismissed it because you felt Isolde was safer here with you. We agreed that was right and that she should have her childhood without the fear of attack. And the rest of us left you here, alone, because we knew a movement of strangers to this isolated island would be noted and we didn't want that either. But now I'm here… now that I've spoken to Isolde, I think it is best you both come with me."

"No."

"Don't you think that would be better for her? To be around

more people instead of isolated on this island with no one her own age? To be around others who knew her mother. Isolde is so curious about her."

Broccan lowered his head. "There are protections on this island that are not there in Seir Kieran. I will not give them up."

Affraic grunted. "Isolde already knows something is wrong. She knows she's being tested but doesn't understand what for, and she will be eighteen by the end of the summer. If she is not what we thought, we must let her go. She must be able to live a life and live a full one of her own choosing. You are afraid for her. I understand that. And I can see she is like a daughter to you, but you must do as I say. She will resent you if you don't."

This conversation made no sense to me. All this talk of druids and gifts and Fomorians. It was like something from one of the stories Broccan had told me. Only it wasn't a happy story. I had failed him somehow. *Done something wrong.* Hardly daring to breathe, I watched my cousin as Affraic's words of warning played over his mind. He looked wretched. Sad. Sadder than I had ever seen him.

He threw a stick into the fire, the flames casting the sharp edges of Broccan's face into shadow. "It is not as safe there as it is here. What if *they* come for her?"

Affraic sighed. "Isolde is almost a woman, Broccan. No, not almost. Is. You treat her like a child. Following her when she is outside the boundary, working yourself to the bone so she never feels the slightest pang of hunger or a chill on a cold night."

"And so I should leave her to them? To those monsters? Never."

"They may not come for her. You do not know…"

"The fact they rode after Fódla and demanded to have her baby means they know the prophecy. Tomas must have told them. They will come for her again. I feel it in my bones. When my mother last spoke to me on the wind, she told me to protect Isolde. I promised that I would."

"They haven't returned to Ireland since Clontarf. If they knew she was here, don't you think they'd have tried by now?"

Broccan shook his head. "All I know is that she is in danger and that she must be protected."

Danger? Why was I in danger? Part of me wanted to run out and demand that he tell me, but I couldn't move. It was as if my feet were stuck to the floor.

"The monastery is a good place," Affraic said. "There are other mortals there, and if she is giftless, she can make a life for herself. Here, there is no future for her. No future for you either."

Broccan stiffened at that. "I'm not worried about my own future."

"But you long to leave, don't you? To look for them again. I see you look over at the mainland, at the sea. Even now, your heart longs to find them. To find Donnchad." Affraic gathered her shawl about her shoulders and moved closer to Broccan. "If you are so desperate to find these Fomorians, you can search for them again. Isolde will be safe with us."

Broccan lifted his head to meet her gaze. At first, I thought he was going to say no, but then that word disappeared from his eyes, and I realised he wanted to say yes. *He wanted to leave me.*

Quietly, I forced myself to step away from the door, not wanting to see the relief shining in his eyes.

Isolde

Rathlin Island

I woke the next morning, almost convinced that I'd dreamed the conversation between Affraic and Broccan. I walked outside to look at the fire, already believing that it would be dead and cold. Crouching down, I touched the sticks and felt the soft heat still upon them.

It was true then. Someone... No, not someone. *Monsters* wanted me. They wanted to hurt me. I couldn't understand why. Running over their conversation, I could make little sense of it. They spoke of healers, harpists, druids, Fomorians – all words from the old legends that Broccan had told me before bed. This wasn't a story though. They had been too afraid for that.

And there was something wrong with me.

That was clear. And Broccan did not want to stay here anymore. Not because he loved someone else, but because he hated them. I couldn't believe such hate existed within him, but there was no disputing it. I'd put the sadness I'd seen in Broccan's eyes over the years down to something that had happened in his past. But it wasn't true. It wasn't his past that was the problem. It was the present. *It was me.* He had stayed here to protect me, but this duty had become a prison for him. How blind I had been not to realise this earlier. I'd spent so long searching outward for his problems, that I had forgotten to look in.

As soon as the sun rose over the horizon, I put on my cloak. I needed time to think. Without saying farewell, I walked to the beach then up the steep path that led to the cliffs. There was a small goat path there that ran alongside the cliff face. If you walked far enough, the path wound around a lough and then a forest which led to Móirne's house. Broccan didn't like me walking up here, but today, I didn't care.

Today, I decided I would do as I wanted. It was wild, once I moved onto the goat path. I walked as close as I dared to the edge. The drop below was hundreds of feet, and the waves crashed upward, bashing against the cliff face itself as well as the jagged rocks and boulders that littered the bay. This morning, the wildness matched my mood. The tempest outside me matching the one happening within made me feel less alone.

"Isolde!"

It was Broccan shouting my name. He must have woken and noticed that I'd left without saying so.

"Isolde! Wait."

I didn't slow my pace, but soon enough, I heard Broccan's footsteps crunching against the bracken and loose rocks behind me.

"Are you going fishing?" Broccan asked. "It's safer to walk along the beach. Gusts—"

"Gusts and sudden winds can blow in. I know." I kept walking.

"Why did you leave without saying goodbye? Affraic might have wanted to walk with you."

"I'm sure she'll be fine."

Broccan caught up and ran to stand in front of me, about to scold me for my lack of manners, but I was in no mood for such a reprimand.

"Firstly," I snapped, "you don't need to worry about me. I know how to look after myself. Secondly, Affraic hardly wishes to walk with me again. And lastly…" I paused to take a breath. "If you want to leave, you should go with her. I'll stay here."

Broccan frowned. "Why would you say that?"

A burst of the anger and anxiety that swam in my stomach bubbled upward, and I pushed past him, continuing along the path.

"Isolde, what is it?" Broccan ran again to catch up, walking beside me, a bemused smile on his face. "Whatever it is, you can tell me. Is it Móirne leaving?"

"What is wrong with me?" This time I couldn't hold my temper. "Nothing is wrong with me. You are the one who is unhappy. Why didn't you tell me that I was holding you back?"

The smile dropped from Broccan's face. "You aren't. Why would you think that?"

"I heard you and Affraic talking last night. I'm in danger, you said. Then Affraic said that you should leave, and I should go somewhere with her. And you wanted it. I could see it in your eyes."

"That's not true."

"Then what do you want? I don't understand much of what you said, but I know you've been keeping things from me. That's very clear. Are you going to tell me what it is? Who is after me? Why are they?"

Broccan ran his hands through his beard. "Come back to the house. I will explain everything."

"No. Explain it to me here."

"It would be better with Affraic there…"

"No. If you won't tell me now, then go." I pushed him away, both my hands banging against his chest. "You don't want to be here, so go. I don't need you anymore."

"Isolde."

"Thank you for all you have done for me. I release you from your burden. Go anywhere in this world that you want. You are free and I can look after myself. These people you wish to find, go find them." I pulled my cloak around my body, the wind blowing so hard that I could feel it tugging me closer to the cliff edge. "In fact, when I return to the ráth, I'd like you to be gone. There. I've made the decision for you. No need to feel guilty now."

I held his gaze to make sure he saw the seriousness in my expression. Another frown flitted across his face, and his hands rubbed his forehead. "I'm not leaving, Isolde."

"Then I shall be the one to go. First thing in the morning."

"You can't go."

I ignored him and continued along the path. *I could go. And I would.*

Broccan ran after me. "Please, listen to me, Isolde. The secrets I have kept were to keep you from pain."

"And that's worked so well."

"Stop." He moved in front of me. "Please stop."

"No. You should get out of my way."

He bit his lip, then straightened. "Make me."

"What?"

"Make me get out of your way."

With my temper so riled up, I pushed into him without a second thought. But he did not move. My anger growing, I pushed against him again. As with the last time, he didn't move, not even an inch. Frustrated, I rained blow upon blow on his chest, until I could do so no more. Panting, I took a step back.

"You want me to move?" he asked. "Now I will."

He ran then, over to the edge of the forest and back, so fast my eyes had difficulty following him against the green of the bracken and leaves. My eyes couldn't comprehend it at first. I wasn't sure if it was an illusion or the sun hitting my eyes. But when he returned, he held out a bunch of bluebells which grew along the edge of the forest and set them in my hand. These were real enough.

"I don't understand."

"I…" he began. "I am a Descendant of the Tuatha Dé Danann. Affraic is as well. The stories I have told you in the evenings are the legends of our ancestors. The people of Ireland do not believe in them anymore. Not really. Our legends have become tall tales told by storytellers and poets to entertain and amuse, but the Tuatha Dé Danann are true. We are true."

Dropping the bluebells, I went to move past him. "Don't lie to me, Broccan. I'm not a child anymore."

"I know it is hard to believe. Your mind works against it, but believe your eyes. Believe your heart." He bent down and picked up one of the bluebells I dropped and spun it between his fingers. "I have the gift of a warrior. Affraic is a healer."

"No." I shook my head. "She fell yesterday and cut her arm."

"Come. Let me show you."

I stood my ground.

"Please, Isolde. Please, just trust me this last time."

Reluctantly, I followed him back to the house. I wished I could say no. This, all of this, was hurting me more than I could bear. The question of why he had wanted to leave me was bad enough, but now that question was replaced with others. *How had he run so fast? What would Affraic show me?*

Affraic was standing outside the house, cooking a fish stew over the fire.

"She heard us speaking last night," Broccan said as we approached. "Show her your arm."

Affraic, without hesitation, came closer and unwrapped the bandage. I waited for the long red cut to be revealed, but instead, her skin was perfect. Not even a trace of a scar.

The disbelief that had pounded through me began to wane, though some part of my mind still struggled to accept it. It was madness what he was telling me. And yet, the way he had just moved... so fast I couldn't see him. Affraic's cut had vanished, and I had felt the blood pouring from the wound there myself only yesterday.

"Were my mother and father Descendants also?"

"Your mother was. She was a healer like Affraic. Your father was a mortal."

My hands ran to my cheeks, brushing away the tears that trailed down them, some of the hurt I'd felt earlier seeping away. Broccan gave me a small smile as he spoke, the anguish on his face when we argued beginning to leave.

"And what am I? What gift do I have?"

The smile on Broccan's face faded as quickly as it had arrived. "That is the thing, Isolde. That's what I was talking to Affraic about. We... We don't think you have one."

Isolde

Rathlin Island

Large waves crashed against the cliffs. I watched from the beach below as the sea hurled itself against the grey rocks, white sea-spray flying upward only to fall back into the grey swell a few moments later. The newly arrived puffins flew overhead, the wind and waves too strong for them on this side of the island. Many of them gave up and flew back to their rocks on the west side of the island, with only some of the braver ones deciding to dive into the sea to catch some fish.

I usually enjoyed watching the waves and the birds flying overhead. There was something soothing about watching the chaos of nature from afar. But today, that solace didn't come. I thought about returning to the house a few times but could not. It was not solace I needed. It was solitude.

Solitude, however, could not last forever, and soon, the familiar outline of Broccan came into view. I shifted along the rocks to make room for him beside me.

"I'm sorry, Isolde," Broccan said as he sat. "I wish I had told you earlier. I just didn't know how."

"There is no need to apologise." All the anger had gone from me. Now I felt cold. Detached. "I asked for the truth, and you gave it to me."

"Yes… but there are ways of giving the truth, and I have done this poorly. I wanted to tell you earlier, but… Well, these excuses don't matter now."

"Be at peace, Broccan." I looked up at him and reached out to hold his hand. "I wasn't ready before. It took me until now to realise that things were not quite right. You've made life so wonderful. So easy. If anything, you've been too good to me."

"I have tried to make this life a beautiful one for you, Isolde, and I mean for it to stay that way. I want you to know that whatever you decide to do, we will do it." Broccan wrapped his arm around me and pulled me close. "And I will tell you the truth from this day forth. I promise. The time for secrets is over."

"My truth is, I don't know what I want. It is a strange thing to think you are one person for your whole life only to realise none of that is true. Even stranger to realise that your cousin is something from the legends of old. A warrior. Just like Cú Chulainn." I smiled up at him as I said this, which made him smile in return. I was glad, for I did not want him to continue to chastise himself.

"I do understand your pain, Isolde. Your mother, Fódla, lied to me when I was young about my gift, too. She did not tell me that she and my mother were Descendants of the Tuatha Dé Danann because she assumed I was mortal like my father. She lied because she did not want to tell me about a world I could never belong to. When I found out I had a gift, I was so confused."

"If you hated being lied to so much, then why did you lie to me."

"Because the truth I must tell you, it is a hard one. I delayed and delayed, thinking the conversation would follow naturally when your gift presented."

"And it hasn't."

Broccan shook his head. "Not as far as I can tell. Affraic thinks some of the other Descendants should test you. Gifts can be subtle sometimes."

"You are disappointed, though. I can tell."

"No. To be giftless is no bad thing. Your father was mortal and one of the greatest men I've ever known. And you, already, are one of the greatest women. I'm anything but disappointed."

"Affraic is. I heard it in her voice last night. Tell me why. She spoke of a prophecy too, and I know it's somehow linked. She thought I was meant to do something, and now I cannot."

Broccan's lips twitched, but he did not falter. "There is a prophecy, yes. It was foretold many hundreds of years ago by the Morrígan that a woman would have two children. One would conquer death, and one would conquer fire. My mother believed this woman was your mother and that you are the child who would conquer fire."

This new piece of news made my heart thud against my chest. "Conquer fire? What does that mean?"

"It means destroy the Fomorians. Our enemy."

"The ones you want to find?"

"Yes."

"Why? What did they do that they deserve such a fate?"

"Many terrible things." Broccan put his head in his hands. "I don't know how to tell you this, and this is why I've kept so much from you. It will hurt you, Isolde, to hear this truth."

I tightened my hold on his hand, and gently, I placed my other hand on top of his. "Tell me, Broccan. I am not a child you need to protect any longer. Please. Not knowing is worse than anything you might say."

"These Fomorians killed your father. You also had a brother on your father's side, called Tairdelbach. He was my greatest friend, and I loved him more than life itself. They killed him too. They killed many of our kind when they sailed to Fennit Island, which was once our home, and drowned all the Descendants who tried to escape."

So much death. So much pain. I found it hard to comprehend.

"Is… Fennit Island where my mother died?"

"No. A Descendant druid called Tomas befriended the Fomorians, and it was he who killed your mother." Broccan took a deep breath, and for once, that sadness I saw so often sweep across his face settled there. *Tomas.* Affraic had told me of him yesterday. She had told me that my mother had once loved him and that he had betrayed her. A wave of anger flooded through me as I thought of this.

"How could my mother ever have loved this man?"

"It is not always easy to see the evil in the hearts of others, Isolde. To some men and women, power is a calling and they will do anything to hold it, and the greatest strength of the wicked is their ability to hide their true nature. When Tomas was in control, he could conceal his desires, but when he lost his seat at the Descendants' council, he conspired with his enemies rather than lose his influence. He craved the return of his power so much that he brought his enemy into the home of his own people and helped the Fomorians massacre them."

"And that's why you want to kill the Fomorians?"

"Yes and no." His voice broke then, and his tongue ran across his teeth. "There is vengeance in my heart. I cannot deny it. But the real reason I searched for them was because I couldn't bear that this burden, this burden of destroying them, would one day be upon you. I failed you, Isolde."

The anguish in his voice gave true meaning to the prophecy. *I was supposed to kill these Fomorians. I was supposed to destroy these beings who had killed so many of my own kind...* and Broccan was terrified for me. This was why he'd wanted me to have a powerful gift. This was why Affraic was disappointed.

"I don't... I can't..." My heart pounded, as I spoke, so hard I could hardly make out my own words. How was I supposed to destroy these Fomorians when I had no power to do so? I wanted to run. I wanted to run until I couldn't breathe. It was only the bitter tears streaming down Broccan's cheeks that stayed me. This was the pain I had always seen lurking in his eyes, and now, I had to let his story unfold so that, for once, I could understand it. His pain needed to become my pain as well.

"Start from the beginning, Broccan. Tell me everything."

A long story unfolded – one of Descendants and Fomorians and mortals fighting among each other. A tale of how three Fomorians conspired against King Brian Boru so that Máelmórda, a Fomorian himself, could be High King, and of how they turned on my father and mother when they tried to escape.

I let Broccan speak without interruption, though many things did not make sense to me. It was only once he finished that I began to piece together my life with that of my ancestors.

"So, my mother gave me to a hawthorn tree, and it took me… over one hundred and thirty years to reach here?"

"Time in the otherworld is not the same as it is here. My mother, Rónnat, knew the spells to make this happen."

"And my aunt, your mother, she is dead?"

"Yes, though somehow part of her exists in this realm still. I heard her voice on the wind when I was in Tripoli. It was she who told me to come here and find you."

"And she is the one who told you about the prophecy and this is why everyone believes I will be the one to defeat the Fomorians?"

"My mother was ignored for most of her life," Broccan said by way of answer. "But in the end, everything she had said turned out to be true. She says that you will be the one to conquer fire… and I believe her."

I couldn't conceive of this being true. I had never struck someone in anger before. Never even had to.

"But Affraic thinks she might be mistaken?" I gazed at Broccan, hoping that she was right.

Broccan's gaze hardened. Pity rather than sadness marked his expression now. "I wish more than anything my mother was wrong. This prophecy has placed a terrible responsibility upon you, and yet, I believe my mother to be right. You have power in you somewhere; we just don't know what it is. Gifts do not always present as we expect. That is what happened to your sister, Aoife."

Yes. I had a sister.

"She is the one who conquered death?"

"Yes. And it was only in death that we understood she could move between the land of the living and the land of the dead when the veil weakens."

I stared out over the shoaly sand and once again at the waves crashing up onto the cliffs. If this island could no longer give me solace, what was left? Had this land been forever spoiled by Broccan's revelations? The house we lived in – I had so many memories there. I couldn't bear for that to be tarnished, and yet, somehow, it was.

"We are safe here, yes?"

"Inside the boundary of my land, we are. There are old spells on this land that keep my enemies away. That is why the mortals do not like it. They say the land is cursed because there is something within the spells that makes them want to leave it."

Móirne's mother calling me *the cursed girl* suddenly made more sense, and I found myself more forgiving of her suspicious nature. She was right, after all. This prophecy… It felt like a curse to me.

Broccan leaned back and took a breath. "We can stay here forever if that is your wish." He stared at me, waiting for my answer, but I still didn't know what I wanted. *Did I want to stay here now? Could I?*

"You and Affraic argued last night about where it is best for me to live. Affraic mentioned a monastery at Seir Kieran. She said more Descendants lived there."

"Yes. There are seven Descendants living there. Shae and Gisela, our harpists. Báine, who is Affraic's daughter and a witch. Meabh, a cupbearer. Siobhan is a healer like Affraic. Another, the warrior called Colmon, is there, but he has not woken since the Battle of Fennit Island."

"And they all knew my mother?"

Broccan nodded.

"Then let's go there. This has been my home, but I do not wish it to become my prison, and that is how it feels today. I feel if I don't move away, I'll become too afraid to ever leave. Does that make sense?"

"The protections we have here will fall away once we leave the island. Are you sure?"

"Yes. I want to speak to the other Descendants, so I can learn more about my mother and your mother too. Also, once we arrive in Seir Kieran, you will be free to go."

Broccan ran his hands through his hair. I watched his expression as he did this, wanting to see the truth on his face before he spoke.

"No, Isolde. I cannot be anywhere but by your side. I will never leave you."

"You must, Broccan. Not for vengeance. Not for me. For yourself. You talk of me living, but you must live, too. Please do that. You cannot stay with me out of duty for the rest of your life."

"I have happiness with you."

"That is not enough. You and I both know it isn't." I stood then. "No more about it now. Let's return to the ráth and plan our journey into Leinster, with Affraic. That's my decision."

Broccan stood and linked his arm into mine, and together, we made our way back to the house.

Affraic was sitting by the table when we returned to the ráth, leaning back in a chair and drinking a cup of warmed milk beside the fire. I could see her curiosity when we walked inside, but she didn't speak.

"I have decided that I wish for Broccan and I to go to Seir Kieran," I said.

Affraic's eyes widened, and a grin spread over her lips. "We should all like that very much. How long do you think it would take you to be ready?"

"Not long," Broccan answered. "I will need to give the animals away to people on the island so they can tend to them. We will need to gather provisions, too. A few days."

"And I should like to say goodbye to Móirne before she leaves."

Affraic nodded. "Then I shall stay on the island until then so that I can accompany you to the monastery." She kissed my cheek and then Broccan's. "I might go and visit the islanders now and stay with them for a few days. That will allow you both to pack up in peace."

"There is no need to do that, Affraic," I said.

"Yes, there is. You will want time alone to say goodbye to your home. Besides, there are people on Rathlin I should like to help."

"Oh, please go to Síoda," I said. "Móirne's sister. She gets a strange sickness that comes and goes, and she can hardly walk she gets so tired."

"Of course I'll go to her. Móirne's house will be my first call."

Affraic pulled on her cloak, gave us both a wave of farewell, and left.

"Do you think she will be alright on her own?" I asked Broccan as I watched her walk away.

"It is a fool that spurns the help of a healer," Broccan answered. "She'll be well fed and watered and looked after as she makes her way around the families of the island, believe me."

That evening, Broccan and I washed our clothes and packed away our belongings. As we did this, Broccan pulled out his furs from the wooden box he kept at the bottom of his bed. He also pulled out a parcel wrapped in leather.

"I've kept this hidden away, but I wanted to give them to you now." Opening the leather binding, he took out two blades. One was a short knife with a wooden handle. The other was a sword. Not a training sword, but one made of steel that was both sharp and deadly.

"The sword belonged to your brother, Tairdelbach. You should have it now."

I took it from Broccan. The sword was heavy, though it was smaller than the one Broccan had. "While we are travelling, we can train with it. It's longer than your training sword. That will take some getting used to."

The knife was less impressive, but I took it next.

"Your mother gave this to you before she died. It came with you through the otherworld."

"Does it have magic?"

"Yes. The knife is called *Fragarach*. If you point it at the throat of another, they cannot lie."

He held something else in hand. Something small and shiny. "This necklace came through with you too."

I set the sword and knife down on the table and reached out to take it. It looked to be a silver pendant with strange markings scratched over it. "It says my name."

Broccan nodded.

I put it around my neck and grinned at Broccan. "Thank you for keeping them safe for me."

Taking the sword and knife, I secured them against my belt. I felt more ready now. More like I could face what was to come.

"What do you think is going to happen when we leave?"

Broccan folded up the leather wrapping. His hair hung over his cheeks and he became very still for a moment. "The Fomorians are out there, Isolde. You need to know that."

I glanced in the direction of the sea. "Do you think they've been there this whole time? Waiting for an opportunity to catch me?"

Broccan shook his head. "I've never smelled them or sensed them since I've been on the island. Not once. However, I think that cannot last forever. I will take you wherever you wish, Isolde, but we must be careful. Fire moves quickly, and when it comes, it is hard to put out."

Gormflaith

Bristol

*A*n eagle soared overhead. Golden were his wings and the sea beneath him was rough and white-tipped. Grey-blue and cold. The eagle moved lower, his eyes locked on the island in the distance.
Rathlin? I asked.
Yes, I felt Olaf reply. Rathlin.
Olaf flew low over the island. There were people working on their fishing boats on the shore. They were withered, these people. Their skins aged by wind and sea and sun. Some had already pushed their small boats into the sea, their nets at the ready. Others emptied their lines, already having caught what they needed for the day. Beyond the beach, two men, one old, the other young, seemed to be separating the lambs from their mothers and bundling them into wooden pens.
Nothing of interest was here, and Olaf flew away from the beach and up over the cliffs. There was a ráth in the distance, a small one situated between the cliff and a forest. Olaf flew downward, landing on a tree that grew beside it.
A beautiful woman stood by the front of the house, speaking to an older woman and a young girl. The older woman hugged the beautiful one and gave her an embroidered scarf while the little girl picked some flowers.
The beautiful woman smiled. Oh, yes, she was beautiful, with long, dark hair and brown eyes. She reached forward to accept the scarf and then the handful of wildflowers the little girl had picked.
With a wave of farewell, she left the mother and young girl and walked west. She walked through the forest and past a lough, making her way toward an area of grassland, full of rocks and bog-meadow

weeds. Olaf followed her, flying overhead, when suddenly she disappeared. Completely.

Where had she gone? Olaf flew lower, but now only the grass was visible below him. Nothing else. Not even a footprint.

"Find her, Olaf," I said. "Find her and then come to me. We are nearly in England now."

Olaf soared back into the sky. Searching. Searching.

"Gormflaith, wake up."

I heard the words, but didn't react, hoping that the speaker would give up and let me drift back into my dream. I wanted to see the woman again, to find out where she had gone, but a sharp flick to the side of my head disabused me of this notion. As I moved, a stale taste swelled in the back of my mouth from drinking the last of our wine last night. Adding to my discomfort, the air was damp and my clothes even damper from a night sailing through fog and sea-spray. Oh, the irony of being simultaneously so thirsty and so wet.

"Wake, you fool."

I pushed away the hand prodding my side.

No. I couldn't fully waken. Not yet. Quickly, I ran over the dream. A Descendant woman. She was somewhere on Rathlin. Who was it? Fódla's daughter? Or another of these wretched Descendants? Those brown eyes reminded me of Fódla, though she didn't resemble her in any other way. I tucked these thoughts away for a time when I had peace to dwell on them and finally lifted my head from the wooden bench.

"That's it, up you get," Máelmórda said, smirking as he leaned over me.

As I pushed myself up, I opened my eyes and glanced at the sea. How I wished I could drink it. The sea was a curse, so it was. Water that was undrinkable. What spiteful prick of a god thought to make it so.

"How's the head?" Máelmórda asked.

"I'm sure it's not half as bad as yours."

"I'm sure it's every bit as bad." He tilted his head to the front of the boat and pointed east. "But I have the antidote for the both of us."

Sitting up straighter, I followed the line of his finger. *Ah. Land.* The English coastline had given me heart once before. Máelmórda, Olaf and I had sailed to Wessex after the loss at Clontarf and our banishment by Sitric. After so much loss, so much failure, I had found comfort in a new land. Some parts of England were better than others, that was true. The Romans had discovered that for themselves, taking over the south and leaving the north to its own care.

I hoped it was further improved since I was last here, and I had every expectation that it might be. The Normans had invaded not long after I'd left England, bringing with them a new wave of people. All that fighting between Wessex and Northumbria and the Vikings. All those eyes on the north, when really, the English should have been watching the south. From the look of the port we sailed into, I could tell it was not London. They had said when we left, they were making for Bristol, and I hoped they hadn't changed their minds. Gods, I hoped it wasn't York, or even worse, Orkney. It would still be a shithole, without a doubt.

"Are you sure about this?" Máelmórda asked, as our ship turned toward the port. "It's not too late to ask the men to take us to Constantinople. They say they sail there next, once they've traded their goods."

"No. We were in Constantinople forty years ago. Someone might recognise us." I tugged at my black curls, ran my finger over my smooth and plump skin. Glad that once again, I could banish my grey hair and wrinkles. Finally, I could be myself. "Besides, we are not running away anymore. Remember?"

"You come here because you believe this girl Broccan looks after will be the one to kill you. I understand why you would want her dead, but why run toward her when we can run away? If Broccan could not find us in all his years of trying, why do you think she can?"

"I want to kill her now because she is weak. No gift has presented yet, they said in the dream. Now is the time to strike."

"Even more reason to leave this place. If she has no gift, then how could she ever hope to kill you? Fomorian and a witch, you'd out-scheme her without breaking sweat. She is no threat to you. Broccan, however, is, and it is he we are moving closer to as well as her." He looked out at the grey clouds and the wind-battered shoreline. "Why be here at all when we don't have to? Look at it. It's fucking miserable."

This was true. I'd pondered this decision myself during the seven days it had taken to cross the sea. Why throw myself in harm's way when I didn't need to? We couldn't go to Constantinople just yet, but we could go to Lisbon or Granada, or any small provincial town, and live as we wished. And yet... *And yet...* My dream of Broccan had changed everything. I could not live in fear anymore. I was a Fomorian. Twice a queen, once of Dublin, then of Munster. We had not lived the last one hundred and fifty years or so of our lives as we should have. We'd been running. Hiding. Crawling through sand and swamp.

Broccan, a warrior Descendant of the Tuatha Dé Danann, had frightened us. Angelo and then Cecile were not ready for such an attack. He would kill us all. I was sure of it. But in that last dream, I had not seen someone strong and mighty as he had seemed in my dreams before. This time, I had seen a broken man. Broken by us. *It was he who was afraid.*

"Ireland is our home, Máelmórda. *It's ours.* It is time for us to take it. Once, this was the only thing you wanted."

Máelmórda shrugged, though his eyes shifted to the west. We couldn't see Ireland from here, it was too far away, but we were closer to our homeland now than any time since we'd left it. My brother could feel it, I knew that. But did he *yearn* for it? Did he remember that once he'd been King of Leinster with the High Kingship within his grasp? Was that why he wanted to leave already? Did being here remind him of the land that had almost been his but that he'd now lost the ambition to take?

His hand moved to the leather purse I had hidden in the pocket of my dress. I let him feel the silver arm-rings and Frankish coins there. It was lighter than it had ever been, for we had enjoyed ourselves in Paris, and now we were left with very little after paying for the passage here. All manner of possessions had been left behind. Paintings. Furniture. Silk dresses and tunics that were much too fine for the part we must play here. We'd bought woollen clothing at the port at Rouen, so here we were. Poor. Friendless. Starting from the bottom. Usually, the first thing we did was find someone suitable for me or Máelmórda to marry, but this time, we had to hold back. We had to work out the lie of the land first.

"Well, we are here now, brother. Let us make the best of it. We shall see what can be done when we reach land."

My brother, oddly silent, moved to the prow of the ship, while I huddled against some of the other passengers. A girl with short brown hair and hazel eyes frowned as I sat beside her. Her eyes were wet with tears, and the man beside her, head bowed, didn't stir. For the first few days of the voyage, he'd emptied his stomach over and over into the sea. Now all he could do was lie in a heap, eyes closed, hands clasped in perpetual prayer.

The man who owned the ship, usually laughing and smiling, was serious today. He shouted at his men, told them to check and then recheck their ropes. Soon, the sails were pulled down, and the oars taken out. The currents didn't seem too strong here, but it was always best to be cautious.

"Is this Bristol?" I asked him as he passed me by.

"It is," he replied. "It's the only port in England where I can get away with selling them." He nodded at the man and woman I'd taken a seat next to, then at the group of women from Iberia who sat at the far end of the ship.

"They don't allow slavery anywhere else?"

He shook his head. "Bristol is the last port that doesn't check. This close to Wales, we can still get away with it. I suppose it doesn't matter. I can go to Dublin next. They always take what I can't sell here."

The feeling of ground beneath my feet after a seven-day voyage at sea was indescribable. My legs ached, my head throbbed, but still I felt nothing but joy as I walked along the wooden longphort. I made sure to lift my skirts to avoid the mud and sludge. I was poor now. I had to remember that. It would be me washing out the stains this time, not a serving girl. The port town and market of Bristol was well-constructed, I had to concede. More organised than Dublin, with the streets laid out neatly and the houses of a similar size and build, rather than built on top of each other and sprawling onto the road.

Máelmórda, Donnchad, Angelo and Cecile walked behind me, each of them taking in the market that loomed ahead of us. Máelmórda and Donnchad's faces bore little emotion. Neither did Angelo's, although his face was never animated. But Cecile, she was amusing to watch. After a life of luxury and warmth in Paris and before that, Bologna, the English landscape was new to her. The greyness. The wind. The rain. The damp. The squalid little houses and stalls. There was no grandeur here. No splendour. No music or poetry.

"Will we go there?" Cecile asked. She looked a little more hopeful as she spoke, for there was a castle in the distance, tall and made of stone. This was something the Normans had brought with them from the south. Something she could understand.

"Not yet." I looked at my brother. "Wait here."

Walking downriver, it didn't take long to find the washer-women we'd passed on the way up the Avon. The smell of piss was overwhelming here, with buckets of excrement from the city being poured into the river to be washed out into the sea. There were boys too, washing new leather hides in pots of dog faeces, but no one here seemed to notice the stench as they went about their work.

One of the washerwomen, an old lady with a broad nose and long chin, gave me a wary eye as I came closer. *Ah, perfect.*

"Pardon me. Who has the care of this castle?"

"That would be William FitzRobert, Earl of Gloucester."

"Do you know if there is any work to be had?"

I spoke to her in the Saxon language, knowing that an old woman like this would not know the tongue the new lords had brought over from Normandy with them.

"What sort of work?" she asked, giving me a good look over.

"I've worked as a lady's maid before," I answered, putting a stop to a probable suggestion that I washed clothes with her. "Is the lord here looking for any maids, or perhaps he has wives and daughters that I might tend to?"

"You come at a bad time," she answered. "He had guests for the whole of last month where he might have taken you on, but they are leaving in two days. Heading into Wales, or so I'm told. Though why they'd want to go there is beyond me."

I let disappointment cloud my features.

"It's not a bad thing, I tell you. The castle grounds are full of Norman men who are marching for war. A young woman like you might find yourself in trouble, for they drink us dry, and the drink gives men like that wicked thoughts. Even worse, they've had Irishmen in their company, although thanks be to God, they have gone now. The Irish are always trouble. Even worse than the Scots." Her nose wrinkled.

"Irish? What were they here for? A wedding?"

"No. Something was said about an Irish king losing his land and wanting the English lords to help him reclaim it. Rough-looking, the Irish king was, with a beard down to his waist." She made the sign of the cross as she said this and then began to knead the fabric against her washer rack while another woman poured fresh river water into her bucket.

The woman's attention waned as her work beckoned. I smiled, gave her my thanks, then made my way back to my family.

"What did you discover?" Máelmórda asked.

"There are warriors here. They are marching to Wales in two days. Something about helping an Irish king retake his kingdom."

This, for all his earlier lack of enthusiasm, held his interest.

"Come then," he said, holding out his arm for Cecile to take. "A castle this size is bound to have a good market. Now we're on dry land, my appetite has returned."

We walked away from the longphort and toward the castle grounds. The line of huts and shacks soon made way for a moat that had been cut around the motte and bailey, and a drawbridge led us into the castle grounds, where the main fortress stood. High-walled and well-constructed. Grand, though not ostentatious. More impressive than I had anticipated.

There were many buildings within the castle grounds, including a church, taverns, houses and a forge. Some market stalls, too, though only those that traded in finer goods. The stalls that traded in food and wool lay outside the walls and on the other side of where a small tributary river and moat had merged. Another drawbridge allowed the people to cross back and forth with ease.

Máelmórda and Donnchad moved toward one of the taverns. It wouldn't take them long to discover why the Norman warriors were here. Angelo followed them but didn't remain in their company. He walked toward the forge instead, fingers roving around the swords on display.

"What shall we do, aunt?" Cecile asked.

"We must discover what is going on and who is in charge."

"Very well." She took a step to the right, moving toward the second drawbridge that led to the other market.

I grabbed her arm. "Not so fast. You are a beautiful young woman and a stranger in this land. You must not wander about alone, and you must no longer call me aunt." I looked her over. She'd inherited her mother's sweet smile, but her father's dark curls. We could be sisters. Cecile was a fine name, French, for she'd been born in France, which suited us. It was my name that needed to change. Gormflaith wouldn't do here. One of my previous names, Alys, however, would do very well. "From now on, I am Alys. I'm your elder sister. I am twenty-two. You are twenty, and we have travelled here with our brothers. Understand? If anyone asks you anything else about yourself, change the topic of conversation. We must wait until we hear back from Máelmórda and Donnchad before we form a more detailed history of ourselves. We don't want to say we are from a province that is unpopular with the men here."

Cecile nodded.

She moved to stand beside Angelo, who was slowly deliberating what knife to buy with the few coins he had left. She smiled at the right people, listened, and followed after her cousin, her eyes already on the jewels on display on one of the few market stalls permitted inside the city walls.

While Cecile had Angelo to watch over her, I moved over to another of the taverns, feigning interest in a shrine that had been erected between it and the church. Several warriors stood outside this tavern. *Knights*, they called themselves. Their chain-mail gleamed in the midday sun. These men were not farmers rounded up from the fields. They were fighters, all of whom spoke a strange type of French, which meant they must be Anglo-Norman. I did not make eye contact with them. Instead, I blessed myself and pressed my hands together in prayer, and from this position, I watched the men as they drank their ale.

Most men liked to watch women. But warriors watched us in a different way. I'd come to notice that over my lifetime. With death so close and always dancing around them, they saw us through a different lens to the men who sowed and reaped and made, men who do not acknowledge the passing of time. And within this warrior class, there were three types of man.

The first type liked to use women as tools for pleasure. Passion existed for them but not love. Never love. There was no room in their hearts for that.

The second revered women. They worshipped us because we gave life, and they gave death, and they were fascinated by both. Madonna and Jezabelle. They loved us in equal measure.

It was the third type of warrior I sought today. The one who hoped to live. The one who hoped for a future the other two dared not even dream of. This man sought a woman, not to bed and not to pray to or worship, but to love and hold and to hold him in return. A woman whom he dreamed of returning to.

To attract this man, you could not be too alluring. He seeks a secret type of beauty that will unlock only for him. Whores and harlots, he gives to the first two types of men, while he continues to watch.

Several of the men looked over as I prayed. A few of them muttered lewd things under their breath, telling their friends about all the things they would do to me if they had me for the evening. I stepped away after a while, blessed myself, while touching the foot of the statue depicting a saint I had never heard of. I lowered my gaze then, turning my back on the men, to let them know I had heard their crude words and did not approve.

As I'd hoped, one of the men followed me. But which type was it? The first, second or third?

"*Excusez-moi*," he said. He spoke French well, not the bastardised Saxon French the Anglo-Normans spoke. More like the French spoken in Paris.

"What do you want?" I answered. "Have you come to insult me further?"

"No. I've come to apologise for my friends' behaviour."

I gave a curt nod, glanced up at him for only a second, then looked away.

"You are from France," he said. "My grandmother was from Caen. Where are you from?"

Giving him a hint of a smile, I turned to walk away. "I cannot be telling so much about myself to strangers I do not know."

"Then at least tell me your name?" he called after me.

I didn't answer.

"I am David FitzWilliam."

Stilling for just a moment, I bowed my head to acknowledge I had heard his name, then kept walking.

★

That evening, Donnchad and Angelo, Cecile and I set up a camp outside the town walls, while Máelmórda remained in the tavern. We lit a fire and sat around it, eating the food Cecile had purchased earlier. There were other people camped out in the field alongside us. Settlers from all over England who had come to trade in the market, but not rich enough to have a house.

I didn't speak to my kin, though I was aware of them. Cecile sang a song. Angelo was sleeping. Donnchad sharpened his sword.

As usual, they left me to make all the decisions. *What to do. What to do.*

I couldn't decide. Olaf. I needed Olaf to tell me what he'd seen. I couldn't think of anything beyond Fódla's girl and Ethla's prophecy that she would kill me.

"Sister."

Lost in thought, I had not noticed Máelmórda returning. He sat beside me, a serious expression on his face. Less drunk than I expected.

"What have you discovered, brother?"

"Many things."

"Tell me."

"The men here are led by a Raymond FitzGerald, but he is not in charge of the army. That is another man called Richard de Clare. Strongbow, they call him. He isn't here, though. He's in his castle in Chepstow. That is where the warriors are marching to next."

"Why? Where do they wish to fight?"

He cleared his throat. "Leinster."

"Your old kingdom?" I was surprised. I had imagined any invasion would centre on the Viking ports. Dublin, Wexford and Waterford were prizes to be sure, trading towns full of wealth. What could the endless forests and mountains of Leinster offer in comparison?

"It seems that my great-great-grandson, Diarmait Mac

Murchadha, has lost his kingdom, and Strongbow has agreed to send an army over to help him. In return, King Diarmait has offered his daughter's hand in marriage to Strongbow, and the kingship of Leinster when he dies."

"Then this Richard de Clare is a fool," I said. "Kingdoms in Ireland don't pass through the female line. He's risking his men and spending his coin for nothing."

"But lands and titles do pass through the female line in other places. Look at Jerusalem, León and Provence. Maybe it doesn't even matter. Maybe Richard de Clare will go over to fight for Diarmait while intending to take Ireland for himself, irrelevant of any claim Diarmait's daughter gives him. Just as William the Bastard took England, he intends to take Ireland. You mark my words, sister. Change is on the horizon."

"That is interesting. Chaos is good for us."

"Not if another intends to make himself king. Did you see the warriors' armour? Their weapons? We cannot defeat these men, as well as the Irish."

"Ah, brother. As always you have too little imagination."

He rolled his eyes upon me saying this, but didn't argue any longer. "What do we do now?" he asked instead.

"We wait for Olaf."

I stood then and walked toward the city.

"Where are you going?"

"To buy some wine. I need something to keep me going until then."

Máelmórda flipped me a coin from his own purse. "Make sure it's good. The ale I drank earlier was the stuff of nightmares."

The castle drawbridges were still open, for it was not yet night, and there were still people drinking around the taverns, with one or two market stalls open for trading. I ventured toward one selling honied ale.

The man called David was still sitting with his friends outside the tavern. More inebriated than earlier, they laughed raucously as they downed their drink. Holding a cup of watery ale in hand, David walked toward me and held out his cup so that I could take a sip. I shook my head, refusing the offer. By the gods, it looked to be foul stuff, just as Máelmórda had warned me. After being spoiled by the wine in Paris, it would take some time to get used to the muck they brewed in a land where the grape did not grow.

"Your family has left you?" he asked.

"No. We are encamped outside the walls for tonight. My brother gave me some coin for wine, but I cannot find any."

"I'm afraid we have drunk the city dry of wine, but I must tell you, it is not safe to walk around at night alone. Your husband should be with you."

"I have no husband. The men you saw me with are my brothers, but I assure you, I can take care of myself."

"If you were my sister, I wouldn't let you out of my sight. You are uncommonly beautiful."

I stood, lowered my eyes, though stepped a little closer. "You are kind, but you jest with me, sir."

"No. I do not jest."

There was such an earnest look in his eye when he said this, I almost smiled. But that wouldn't do. I frowned instead, and this time stepped away.

"If you have come to warn me about the vices of men, you should not try to seduce me in the same breath. Because I tell you now, I will not be seduced. I am not like the other women here. I came to buy from the market. That is all."

David's cheeks flushed red. "I had no intention of insulting you. I apologise. What was your name again?"

"I didn't tell you my name."

He smiled at this. "Why not?"

"You are a knight. I am merely the daughter of a trader. If not a seduction, what else would a man like you want with me?"

"I would marry you."

"I'm sure your lord would disagree. I am not a suitable match."

"My lord sends me to war. He will not say no."

He moved to kiss my hand, and I let him. I had to play the chaste card this evening, so I smiled and pushed him away as if my desire was so strong that I might no longer be able to trust myself around him.

Chivalrous enough to respect my decision, he watched me as I walked away.

Goodbye, I thought.

Goodbye, my husband-to-be.

Gormflaith

Bristol

It was still dark when Olaf landed on the ground beside me.

"Hello, Olaf," I whispered. Even though I was tired, I stroked his feathers and stood, eager to hear what he'd discovered. "Come, let's go to the forest and I can change you."

The golden eagle launched himself into the air, and I walked toward the forest behind our campsite, where we could speak to each other away from prying eyes and ears.

As soon as I was ensconced in the foliage, I came to a stop and waited for Olaf to find me. He landed on a boulder not long after and ruffled his feathers, while I used my gift to change him. On transforming, these feathers faded, and a broken and ruined man appeared. Scarred. Shattered. The wounds of Svein Forkbeard had never faded. Oh, and time had punished him too.

Over the last one hundred and fifty years, I'd kept Olaf mostly in bird form and so he had not aged the way other mortals did, but still, his body had changed. His hair had greyed in the years since he betrayed me. His skin was lined and sagging.

Using my gift, I changed his form again. This time to the Olaf I had once fallen in love with. The man with smooth skin, ice-blue eyes, blond hair, muscled thighs and arms. The tattoos over his chest and neck, including the snake that ran along his hand, turned darker, the greens and blues bright rather than pale and faded. Handsome, he was. Young. It made his love for me easier to bear when it came in this form.

He kneeled before me. His hands reaching for mine. I let him hold them, knowing it would give him pleasure. It was best to reward him from time to time, otherwise the love potion I'd given him would cause his passion to turn to desperation. He would beg and plead and beg and plead, telling me that he would kill himself if I could give him no favour. *There was nothing in this life more irksome than that.*

"Tell me how I can prove myself to you," he said, kissing the same part of my hand that David had touched yesterday.

"You prove yourself to me over and over, Olaf. What would I do without you?"

He stared at me, his eyes, oh so clear and the palest blue, drinking me in.

"Tell me about the island."

"Rathlin is an island north of Ulaid, but there is an area of land within this island that I cannot see. I cannot land on the grass there, nor see anyone when I fly above it."

"Yes, I saw a woman walk inside this land while watching you in my dreams, Olaf. She must be a Descendant."

"Yes, you are right, my love, as always, for later that day, I saw Broccan himself with a young woman. There is a house, a little back from the cliff face and close to the forest. The young woman who walked with Broccan is friends with someone who lives in this house. After their visit, they returned to their land, and they disappeared from sight again."

"Did you recognise this young woman with Broccan?"

"I have never seen her before, but… she had long red hair… and bore more than a passing resemblance to Fódla."

I was right. Broccan had returned to Ireland to look after Fódla's daughter, and I had found her. *The girl from the prophecy.* After all these years of living in fear, finally I knew for certain where she was. Getting to her, however, would not be easy. I thought on the rest of Olaf's words. Why could he not see anything within this land or enter it? A spell, perhaps? Old magic of the Descendants designed to keep their enemies away.

"That is good, Olaf. Well done."

"What do you want to do, Gormflaith?" He reached for my waist, his finger pressing against my skin.

"It's Alys now," I snapped, pushing him away.

He fell to his knees and bowed his head. Low. "Sorry, Alys. I'm sorry for offending you. I didn't—"

"Do not worry, Olaf," I soothed. "I was just thinking that I must tell the others what you have discovered."

"Don't trust them, Gorm... Alys." He reached for my hand again, pulled at it. "Don't trust any of them. They mean to hurt you once they have used you again. All of them. Máelmórda, Donnchad, Angelo and Cecile. I can see it in their eyes when they look at you."

Smiling, I kneeled beside him. Hope sprung into his eyes that, perhaps, this day I might love him. Give myself to him. Body and soul. Disappointment followed as feathers sprouted along his wrist. Seconds later, he was a bird again. "Sorry, Olaf," I said. "I understand your thoughts. That is why I need you like this. So you can watch over them for me. If they talk of betraying me, you must tell me. Can you do that?"

The eagle propelled himself into the air. Yes, was the answer in this gesture. For what else can a man in love do other than obey his heart?

I returned to the campsite then. The sun had risen now and Máelmórda was stretching. Glancing at me through half-opened eyes, he yawned.

"Some warrior you are," I said. "If you wake up and I'm gone, you should be looking for me."

Máelmórda shrugged. "I could tell you were fine, and I have no desire to walk in on you and your new lover."

"I wasn't with him." I pointed upward.

Máelmórda opened his eyes properly this time and dragged himself into a sitting position. "Ah. Olaf is back."

"I thought warriors were meant to have superior senses. Didn't you hear him arrive?"

"It's hard to hear anything when you're asleep."

"You" – I shoved a finger in his belly – "have become lazy. I need more from you. Now, more than ever."

This woke Máelmórda up. "Why? What's he found?"

"Wake the others. No point in having to repeat everything."

Once everyone was awake, I told them what Olaf had relayed to me. We had found this daughter of Fódla. She was within our grasp, and Rathlin was only four to five days away if we could persuade someone to sail us there.

"You want us to kill this girl?" Máelmórda asked. "Not to focus on how to ingratiate ourselves with the knights who go to war for Leinster?"

"The girl represents a risk to my life, but the truth is, all Descendants are a risk to all of us. Olaf saw three of them on Rathlin. I think we should strike, but…" I paused. "It is not for me to put myself on the line to do this. It's your turn." I pointed at the three men before me. All Fomorians. One also a warrior. One also a cupbearer. "Which of you will go?"

Donnchad was the first to step forward. "I will, Mother. Broccan has too long followed my steps. I will kill him and the girl he protects, as well as the other Descendant who is with him. I want you to know that I also do this for you. It will be my apology for what happened at Clontarf."

"You have apologised before, Donnchad, and I accepted it, though I never understood why you betrayed me."

"I was angry."

I stared at him when he said this. He stared back, daring me to look deeper into his soul.

"What had I done to make you so angry? I birthed you, raised you, trained you in the use of your fire-magic. I found a Descendant for you to steal a gift from. What had I done that was so very bad?"

"Nothing, Mother. Back then, I didn't understand all that you sacrificed to keep me safe. This is why I ask you to give me this chance to show you how sorry I am."

"Broccan is a skilled warrior, and you ran from him once before. Does he no longer frighten you?"

"No. He frightens me, but still, I will fight him."

I found some pity in my heart then. For he meant to go, even if I doubted the sincerity of his apology. "Why are you afraid, Donnchad? You nearly killed him the last time you fought."

"Only because he tried to save Tairdelbach."

Yes, this was true. I remembered. I remembered Broccan screaming as Donnchad's cupbearer-magic pulled Tairdelbach under the water. I had used my witch-magic to try to hold Broccan in place, and oh, how he had struggled. Like a wild animal, he'd used every ounce of his strength to reach his friend without thought or care for himself.

"This time, he will try to save the girl," I said. "She is giftless. Just like a mortal. You will have the same advantage again."

Donnchad nodded. "Yes. And this time, I will have Angelo with me."

Angelo?

Angelo lifted his gaze to stare at Donnchad. This move surprised him too, though quickly he stood to stand at his father's side. What was Donnchad doing? While they were not close, Donnchad did love his son. I knew that. Why choose him over Máelmórda? Máelmórda was the warrior.

"If I kill Broccan," Donnchad said, seeing the question in my eye, "don't you think it would be a waste to not take his gift? Angelo doesn't have one yet."

This idea made sense, yes, but I wasn't sure I liked it. The main problem was that Broccan might win and kill the two of them – turning our advantage of five Fomorians back to three. And of course, for this even to be possible, I would have to relinquish control of the knife of immortality.

"You doubt my intentions?" Donnchad asked when I didn't reply.

"Trust is easy to give in times of peace. It's harder now. But you are my son, and when I rescued you in Rome all those years ago, it was because I decided to give you another chance." I reached into my dress lining and pulled out the white knife. The knife of immortality. The blade that could kill a Descendant and remove their gift. "You remember what happens? Angelo must use his fire-magic to take the gift once the Descendant dies. Afterward, he will be unwell. Perilously so. You nearly died when you took your gift from the cupbearer."

"I remember."

Donnchad reached out to take the knife.

"Don't betray my trust again, Donnchad," I said as I released the knife into his care. "I won't be so forgiving again."

He nodded. "Thank you, Mother."

"And before you go, I need you both to know this." I gestured for Angelo to come closer. This grandson of mine – I knew there was more to him than he wanted to show. Though he never talked, and thus was easily dismissed by Máelmórda, and even his own father, there was greatness within him. I felt this now more than ever. I wanted to protect him, and yet, he needed to prove himself. He could not be the forever child I'd allowed him to be in Paris.

"If you get close, Broccan will be able to sense the Fomorian blood that surges through your body. If you use your fire-magic, he will smell you. He will be keeping watch for you, too, so you must watch him first. Wait for him or the girl to move outside of their land and then strike. Patience, always."

Taking out my purse, I opened the leather bindings. We had some gold and silver left, but not much. Still, this was more important than anything else. We could make wealth again, take it. A chance to kill this girl while so unprotected was worth everything I had. "Use this to pay someone at the port to sail you to Rathlin."

Máelmórda stood. "Good luck, Donnchad. Good luck, Angelo."

"You are not going with them?" I asked.

My brother shook his head. "Who will protect you and Cecile if I go?"

His eyes hardened as he spoke. He didn't want me to challenge his cowardice, for that's what this was. He was afraid to meet another with the warrior gift, I could sense it. Smell it fermenting alongside the ale in his sweat.

"I'll go into the city and buy some food for Donnchad and Angelo." Cecile tapped the coins she had in her pocket from yesterday and walked toward the walls of Bristol.

"Come, Angelo," Donnchad said, "let's go to the longphort and see who might be willing to take us north."

I sat down once they left. Stared into the fire. Cecile had asked me the day before we left Paris. *What do you want?* I still wasn't sure. I stared at the castle, at the stone walls that were all but impenetrable. Then I thought of the knights who walked through the market and the washerwomen wringing out their clothes by the river. This world we lived in, so many lives were possible. Which one did I want? To be left alone? To be a queen? Or was there another possibility open to me?

Máelmórda sat beside me, watching his daughter until she disappeared from sight. "I'll go back into the taverns and listen. See what else I can learn."

"So eager for more ale? I don't know how you drink it when it smells of piss."

He shrugged, but walked ahead, anyway. I let him go, hoping he knew to behave himself around the knights who, no doubt, would have their eyes on the same women my brother meant to pursue.

I reached out with my fire-magic to stoke the fire and wrapped myself in my cloak. Sinking into the grass, I closed my eyes.

"Where is she?" Máelmórda screamed.

I opened my eyes, his shouts startling me out of my sleep. "Where is who?"

"Cecile!"

"I don't know. She went to buy food for Donnchad and Angelo. Didn't she come back?"

"You know she didn't."

"No, I don't. I've been sleeping. Could she be with one of the knights?"

"No. Of course she isn't."

"Then I don't know. Can't you smell her?"

"Her scent is everywhere. All over the campsite, all over the markets and town, which doesn't help me work out where she is now." He kicked the log I was sitting on, some of his warrior strength going into it, and I hurried to my feet. "Ask him to find her. Do it now."

We walked into the forest where I'd left Olaf. He might not be there now, but I knew when he flew that he kept a watchful eye on me and would come to the forest if he noticed I had gone there. As expected, the eagle landed on a tree branch next to where I stood a short while after. "Find Cecile," I said to him.

Olaf opened his wings and flew into the darkening sky.

"She's fine," I said to my brother. "I know you can't bear to think of her with other men, but she's a woman now. Not a child."

"I know, but it's different here. In Paris, people knew her. They knew she was connected. Had status. Here… the men… they don't know that."

"She is Fomorian, brother. A weak one, but fire still dances to her song. She will be more than a match for any who might try to hurt her."

He grunted but still stared at the town gates through the trees as if willing her to walk out of them. Minutes passed. Then a few more. "I'm going to look again."

"No, wait." I pointed up at the sky. "Look. Olaf returns already. See, I told you she couldn't be far away."

The bird landed on my arm. Olaf, careful as always to land gently and not tear at my skin, rubbed his beak over my left hand. Ah, that meant Donnchad. I knew then exactly what had happened.

"She's left with Donnchad and Angelo."

Máelmórda flung the knife he'd been spinning in his hand into a tree. He threw it so hard the sapling trunk split in two. "This is your fault."

"How so?"

"That son of yours is pursuing my daughter. I noticed it yesterday, and I spoke to him about it. He told me he'd leave her alone, but as always, he lies, and now he's somehow convinced Cecile to follow him."

"You only noticed yesterday?"

His mouth dropped at this, and his eyes flickered as he roved over old memories, combing over things previously thought to be innocent, to see when Donnchad's infatuation had started.

"He cannot be with her."

"Why not? If we want there to be more Fomorians, a match between Donnchad and Cecile is the best way."

"He cannot because I say he cannot. Cecile is my daughter."

"Ah," I shrugged. "But now she has gone after him. It's not your choice any longer."

"She doesn't love him, you fool. She's gone because she wants to be part of this…" He brought fire to his hands and watched as it faded away. "It is not safe for her to go. You know it isn't. Her gift isn't strong enough."

"Yes, she's weak. We all know it. And yet, if there is another Descendant there, she has a chance to gain a gift too."

"Don't speak nonsense." Spittle formed along my brother's lips and his cheeks flushed red. "She will not survive the taking of a Descendant's gift. And Broccan is there. A warrior. He'll kill her."

Máelmórda pulled his knife out of the tree and marched out of the forest.

"Where are you going?" I called after him.

"To find another ship. If Cecile has sailed off with Donnchad, I must follow. I do not trust your son to save her if it comes to it."

"So, you'll leave me by myself?"

"If anyone can look after themselves, it is you." He gave me a nod of farewell. "I will see you soon, sister. Do what you can to better our position, and I will do the same."

"And you have coin, do you?" I smiled as I said this, knowing that my brother had hoarded away some of his gold when we'd left Paris rather than give it to me as the others had done. "You must really love Cecile to spend it." I pressed my lips together. "She isn't worth your life, you know. She's too weak."

"She's my daughter, Gormflaith. After all those years you spent helping Sitric, I'd expect you to understand why I must go." Storming off, he didn't even glance my way to say goodbye. Why did he always have to be such a hateful bastard.

"Brother," I called after him, "don't come back if you don't kill Fódla's girl for me."

This made him pause.

"I mean it. I don't want to see you or hear from you ever again if you fail me."

He nodded, and with that, he ran toward the port.

I held out my hand, and Olaf flew onto the soil. "I am going to transform you," I said. "You must go with Máelmórda. Say that I sent you to him to help him and make sure you reach Rathlin in time to be of assistance to Donnchad and Angelo. The four of you together might pull this off."

Olaf transformed before my eyes. From eagle to old man to a young one.

"I will find you clothes. Wait here."

Shivering, Olaf shook his head. "Your brother is right. You should not be alone."

"I can take care of myself in a town of mortals. It is my kin that I do not trust. Not completely. That's why you must go. I need you there, so when they come back, I will know if they really killed the girl. It is foretold she will kill me, Olaf. Her death is the most important thing. You are the only one I trust to tell me the truth. Will you do this for me?"

Olaf nodded.

"Good. Now wait here. I won't be long."

Walking out of the forest, I took out the final piece of jewellery that I had sewed into the lining of my cloak, so I could buy Olaf a set of good clothes.

There. Fate had now decided what I was. A pauper. No better than the washerwoman I had spoken to yesterday.

Queen I might have been once. Queen I might be again. For now, however, I was a nobody. This thought would once have made my heart sink, but as I marched toward the marketplace, I found myself not sad at all. Not even a little… for I didn't intend to remain a nobody for long.

Isolde

Rathlin Island

I watched the sea between the island and the mainland. It was clear this morning, all life existing below the waves rather than atop. This was the usual way of things. The fishing boats from Rathlin never strayed too far, and fishing boats from the mainland rarely sailed in our direction, either. The currents were too strong, and there were better places to fish along the coast of the mainland.

As such, it was easy to spot when someone was making the crossing from Ulaid to Rathlin. I'd come to the beach every day to watch the sea since Broccan had told me about my past. These Fomorians who wanted me, they were out there somewhere. New emotions moved over me. Fear. Rage. Sadness. With such inner turmoil, somehow I'd expected everything on the outside to change and feel different, too. For the waves to be bigger. The wind to be stronger. The truth was, nothing had changed at all.

That could not be for much longer, though. Any day now, Broccan, Affraic and I would leave Rathlin. Soon it would be us sitting in a fishing boat and rowing toward the mainland, a blot on the mass of blue. That was why I came here so often. To memorise this view. To remember the sea as it truly was before I became a part of it.

A strange sensation flooded my stomach on thinking this. The hairs on my arms stood up. *Something didn't feel right. Not as it should be.*

I felt it as surely as the rain when it fell upon my skin. But on looking out over the sea again, I didn't know why I should feel this way. Perhaps it was merely that the feeling of safety had been eroded? I was a child no longer. The veil of certainty had gone forever, and with that, everything I'd ever known was about to be ripped away.

"Isolde!"

I turned to find Móirne walking hand in hand with her younger sister, Síoda. I waved and ran over to them. The feeling of fear faded on seeing them. Joy replaced it, for it was wonderful to see Síoda so strong that she could walk here. The path down to the beach was steep. Even worse, the path between the cliffs and forest stayed close to the edge for a while – perilous to someone unsteady on their feet if a sudden gust blew in. It was hard to imagine that, only a week ago, Síoda had struggled to make it from her house to the seanchaí's fire.

"You look well, Síoda," I said.

She smiled but hid behind Móirne's legs as I approached.

"She's a little shy," Móirne explained.

I crouched down. "Don't be afraid, little one. No one will harm you here."

"That's what I said. The curse that the other islanders talk of, it's only an old story, isn't that right, Síoda?" Móirne laughed and hugged her sister tight. "In any case, she's not so shy that she didn't want to come and give Affraic this."

Síoda held out her hand and gave me a small bunch of wildflowers tied together with a ribbon.

"This is for Affraic?"

"Yes." Síoda nodded, her cheeks flushing pink. "To say thank you."

"Affraic will love this. You can come up to the house and give them to her yourself if you like."

Móirne took hold of her sister's hand. "She can't. That's the other reason we're here. We are leaving today. All our possessions are over on the mainland now, and my father has finally sold the last of our cattle. My mother's cousin is sailing here today to bring us over."

My smile faded, though I tried to hide it, for I was leaving myself now. Our time on this island was over for all three of us. "I wish you well, Móirne. I wish all the happiness in the world to you and your family."

"Thank you, Isolde. Will you come to wave us off?"

"Of course. After breakfast, I'll come to your house."

Móirne nodded, took hold of her sister's hand, and the two of them walked back along the beach toward their home. I almost ran after them. There were so many things to say to Móirne that I didn't want to leave unsaid. I wanted her to know how much her friendship had meant to me. I wanted to explain that we were leaving too, so that if she ever did come back, she would not be upset when she couldn't find me. But once again, a strange feeling came over me. It was not that something wasn't right, or at least not only that. This time, there was sadness within it too.

Once they had made their way up the steep path and onto the cliff, I walked to the ráth. Broccan sat outside the house, cleaning his sword and knife, while Affraic was adding some herbs to the fish I'd caught yesterday. They both watched me as I approached, and I couldn't help but note that there was a tension in the way they moved. Too slow. Too silent.

"What is it?" I asked.

"We were thinking…" Broccan began, pausing to wipe his mouth. "That we should hold off travelling to Seir Kieran."

"Why?"

Broccan set down his knife. Affraic stopped stirring.

"The truth, this time," I said. "You promised there would be no more secrets."

"Yes." He gestured for me to come closer. "The warrior gift is unusual, Isolde. You know I always worry about you, but these last two days, I've had terrible feelings. More than the usual fear or anxiety. I believe it is my warrior gift alerting me to something I do not yet understand."

Affraic stared at Broccan as he spoke, face drawn. "I agree with

Broccan's decision. If his gift suggests danger approaches, we must be cautious. If I don't return soon, Báine will come looking for me. Perhaps we should wait until then. It would be better to travel with a warrior and a witch."

Instead of worry, relief flooded through me. This meant I had more time to stay on Rathlin. More time to walk over it before I left. The tightness in my stomach eased. "If that is what you want, I'm happy to wait."

"You're taking this better than I expected," Broccan said, the tension in his eyes lifting a little.

"Well, I must confess, it will be nice to have a few more weeks here, and I can see you are worried. I do not like that." I paused. "What do you think it could be?"

Broccan shrugged. "When I was on the mainland, there was much talk of war. They say that Normans from Wales are going to come to Leinster to fight for King Diarmait Mac Murchadha. They say that High King Ruaidrí O'Conchúir is gathering his men at Tara. Bréifne joins him, as does Dublin. It's most likely that. Seir Kieran is within Leinster. If there is war between Diarmait and Ruaidrí, it may prove difficult to reach."

"We have chosen a bad time to leave the island, I fear," Affraic added.

"Yes," Broccan agreed. "Part of me fears we should have left already, but another part tells me to stay within the boundary of my land. Perhaps I should sail across to the mainland tomorrow and see what the people are saying." Broccan set down his cleaning cloth and came closer. "Are you sure you want to leave, Isolde?"

Broccan had asked without emotion, but I knew from the way he looked at me that he already knew my answer. He held out his arms and enveloped me inside his embrace. "Whatever you want, we will do."

The dilemma of leaving played with me again. I wasn't as certain as when I first said I wished to leave. I felt ill sometimes when I thought of not being here, but I did not want to submit to a fear of the unknown, either. And I did want to speak to other Descendants, especially the ones who were fading, so I could ask them about my mother and family before they passed.

"Affraic is right," I said. "It's time to go."

"Then we will. We can always return if you wish."

Yes, we could always return.

But it would not be the same, would it?

"Tomorrow, I'll see what the people say. Depending on what they tell me, we can either decide to leave or wait for Báine. Now that's settled, what do you wish to do, Isolde?" Broccan asked, pushing some lightness into his voice. "We can train a little, if you like."

"Maybe later. I wanted to see Móirne before she goes."

"She leaves today?" Affraic asked.

"Yes. She walked along the beach this morning with Síoda to tell me. And…" I took the bunch of flowers from my pocket. "Síoda wanted to give you these, Affraic."

"How lovely of—"

"No, Isolde," Broccan said, cutting across Affraic. "I think you should stay here today."

"What?"

"I don't want you to leave my land."

"But Móirne is leaving. If you are afraid, come with me to her house."

"I'm not afraid. I just want to keep you safe."

Frustration brewed inside of me. If the Fomorians were out there, then he would always feel like this. I was not leaving this island, only to find myself hidden away behind the walls of Seir Kieran. It was unfair that he asked this of me, but the worry in his eyes was so strong that I couldn't bring myself to argue. That he was this worried compounded the feelings I'd had this morning. There was still fear within me, I realised. A fear of a people I'd never met but who wanted to kill me. A fear of leaving behind all I had ever known.

"Then I shall watch them leave from the clifftop. I want to make sure they reach the mainland. Don't worry. I won't go beyond the boundary."

I left without another word.

I didn't often venture to the cliffs. One hundred feet high, the wind was harsh here and the surrounding land barren save for the rough bracken and grass. Today, however, it was the best place to go, for it would give me a good view of Móirne and her family making their journey across the sea.

Indeed, I could already see a small sailboat making the crossing over from the mainland. There were five people inside. Probably all cousins of Móirne's mother, coming to help them across. The waves were usually ferocious along the coast here. In my lifetime, two Viking longboats had been pulled under by the currents, and according to Broccan, many other wrecks lay beneath the white-grey surface. Today, however, was a good day for making the crossing. The waves were not as fierce as they sometimes were.

"I'll miss you, Móirne," I said to the wind. "I hope you will be happy."

My eyes stayed on the rowboat as it came closer. One of them was a woman, for I could see her long, dark hair blowing in the wind. The men all wore thick cloaks, except for one who wore only a tunic, though it was he who was in charge of the sail ropes and steering board. I leaned out over the cliff, watching until they disappeared behind the cliffs as they sailed into the cove.

I imagined them greeting Móirne. Perhaps one of them was Móirne's new husband. Would he kiss her? Would she be happy if he did? I found myself wanting to watch them for longer. To see Móirne in their company and make sure she was happy.

Was that so very wrong?

Broccan was afraid, yes, but if I just moved a little further along the cliff path, I would be able to see them on the beach.

I took a step outside the boundary. Then another. Then I walked another fifty feet to where the cliff jutted out. Sitting on the grass there, I looked down at the beach. The boat was already pulled up. The man wearing the tunic had stayed with it, but the others were already gone.

Well, they'd be back soon. All I had to do was wait.

Picking at the daisies, I watched the birds flying in the sky, and the waves crashing below me. Occasionally, I glanced down at the boat, but still no one had come back.

Suddenly, a wave of nausea came over me, and a terrible smell filled my nose. I stood, moved away from the cliff and looked into the forest. Where was that smell coming from? It was like… something burning.

A man… There was a man there. Thin with short black hair, he weaved through the trees. Just as I noticed him, he seemed to notice me and walked closer until he moved out beyond the treeline. His big golden eyes stared at me.

"Good day," I said, taking another step back. Was this one of Móirne's cousins? I didn't know him from the island or recognise him as one of the fishermen who sometimes traded with us. The hairs on my arms stood up and the nausea intensified so much that I thought I would be sick.

The man smiled and held out his hand, gesturing for me to come to him. He was handsome, yes, but there was something odd about him too. The way he stared. The silence that lingered.

I ran then, ran back inside the boundary of Broccan's land.

As I ran, I heard him following.

Speeding up, I sprinted until I reached the cliff path. When I looked behind me, the man had stopped. Just like Broccan had explained, the boundary kept people away. *His enemies away.* The man stayed there for a moment, then walked back into the forest.

Half sprinting, half skidding down the rocky path that led to the beach, it was here Broccan found me, and he wrapped his arms around me.

"There is a man on the cliffs. He's gone now, but I swear he was there."

"Did you move outside the boundary?"

"Yes. Only a little. I'm sorry."

"Did he touch you?" Broccan asked.

"No, but he tried to follow me. When he couldn't move past the boundary, he returned to the forest."

Broccan began to shake. I took hold of his hand, cursing myself that I had broken my promise. "I'm sorry I moved outside the boundary. I just wanted to see Móirne leaving."

"That's not what's wrong. I can smell them, Isolde. Smell *him*." He squeezed my hand tight. "The Fomorians have found us. They know we are here."

"That man, he was a Fomorian?"

Broccan nodded. "Come, we must get Affraic."

Without another word, he pulled me along until we reached the house. I couldn't speak, so fast did we run, but my mind was a mess. That man… he wanted to kill me? If I had gone to him as he wanted, perhaps I would already be dead.

"Affraic," Broccan called out as we reached the house. He skidded to a stop, then put his finger to his lips. "Quick," he whispered to me. "You need to leave."

Affraic came out of the house, more herbs on a plate that she'd readied for the stew, though she quickly set it down.

"The Fomorians are on the island," Broccan spoke low this time, his voice cracking as he ran his hands through his hair. "I can smell them. Four of them. Another is with them too. A mortal. I don't know how they have found us… but they have."

Affraic stared at Broccan, but then her gaze focused on something in the distance. "Look, Broccan. Smoke. They are setting the island on fire."

Broccan

Rathlin Island

Affraic was right. A thin plume of smoke rose into the sky. Within a few moments, it grew thicker and darker. Not a natural fire that took its time to spread, but one so hot that even the dampest of grass burned on first touch.

"That's close to Móirne's house," Isolde said. "We have to help them." She ran to me and pulled at my arm. "Broccan. We should go to them."

"Wait." I pressed my finger to my lips. "Máelmórda has the warrior gift. He can hear us if we speak too loudly. Let me listen."

Isolde frowned but stopped speaking. Affraic came to us, wrapping her arms around Isolde.

I closed my eyes, using my gift to hear what was being said far away. Yes, they were at Móirne's house. I could hear her mother screaming. Móirne and her sister were crying, and I caught the scent of blood in the air, thick and hot. They had already killed Móirne's father.

"Broccan," Máelmórda shouted. "Where are you? Come to us. You used to chase us. Now we are here, ready to fight. You'd better come here. Otherwise, these friends of yours will suffer in your stead."

Affraic and Isolde stared at the smoke, their ears not good enough to hear Máelmórda and his taunts.

Quickly, I took hold of Isolde's hand and began to run, but not toward Móirne's house as she expected. Instead, I pulled her into our own house. Grabbing a leather bag, I began to stuff it with food and spare clothes. Affraic rushed in after us.

"What are you doing, Broccan?" she asked.

"You and Isolde need to leave. I don't know how they found us here, but they have. It's me. Somehow, they can tell where I am. It was the same as when I was chasing them. They always knew when I was coming. Always they had left just before I arrived. You both must leave here and get away from me." I threw the bag at Affraic, who caught it. "Once you get to the mainland, buy horses and ride as fast as you can to Seir Kieran."

Without listening to any further words of protest, I pulled up the woven cloth covering the floor, then dug up the soil underneath. It didn't take long for me to reach the small wooden box I had hidden there. "I've some coin and gold in here that you can use to trade." I opened the lid and handed the pouch inside to Isolde.

"You are asking me to leave you? Well, I won't." She pushed the pouch back into my hands. "And I don't understand. You said your land was safe. Even if the Fomorians are here, they can't reach us. Can they?"

I stood, trying to block out the sobs of Móirne's mother as she wept for her dead husband. *I had brought this upon them.* Their whole family would suffer and grieve because of me.

"They can't come inside my land, Isolde, but already... already they try to draw me out."

How could I explain this to her? How could I say that if she remained on this island, the Fomorians would bring Móirne to the border of our land? Síoda, too. And that the Fomorians would cut their throats, and Isolde would hear her friends scream as they died. For that was what awaited her friends now. Death and fire. But I had promised her no more lies. If she was to escape these Fomorians, she needed to know who they were.

"Isolde, they will use things you care about against you. What will you do when they bring the islanders to the boundary of my land and kill them one by one? Will you be content to stay here then?"

She wrapped her hands around her mouth, eyes widening in horror.

"Already they've killed Móirne's father. They will kill Móirne, her mother and Síoda, unless I go to fight them." I looked outside the door once more. The sky was already black with smoke. "If I go to them now and fight them, they will forget about you and the other islanders for a while. This will give you a chance to escape. The beach is on my land. It means you can get the boat out without them noticing."

"No. We are not leaving you behind!"

"You must." I gave the pouch to Affraic and held her hand as I folded her fingers around it. "I have a chance of winning, but if I don't, they will come after you. You must get across the sea as quickly as possible. If Donnchad survives, he will be able to use his gift to pull the boat under."

"No." Isolde came toward me, her eyes and cheeks wet with tears. "Come with us. I cannot leave without you."

Gently, I held her tight. "I cannot. If I cross with you, and they follow, Donnchad will use his cupbearer gift. I could not save Tairdelbach from him. Do not make me watch him do the same to you." I ran my hand over the back of her hair, then pulled away. "You have taught me to live again, Isolde. I don't want you to worry about me. I am strong and I will defeat them. If I can't…"

"Don't say that."

"If I can't, you must live. Do you hear me? You must live. Go to Seir Kieran. Go now. I cannot fight as I must if I am worried about you."

Affraic came to me, wrapping her arms around Isolde again, and pulled her away. "Come," she said. "To the beach."

I stared at Isolde one last time. She stared right back, eyes as fierce as mine. As fierce as her father's had once been. As Tairdelbach's had been too. *I didn't want to leave her either, but I had to.* Turning my gaze to Affraic, I focused on what I had to say. Isolde might not understand, but Affraic did. She knew as well as I the danger we were in.

"Go. Go now. Use the sail. You need to get across quickly."

"I don't want to leave you," Isolde said, her voice hoarse and tight.

"I don't want to leave you either, but I must. Go. Both of you, and don't ever look back."

Before Isolde could plead with me again, I sprinted along the path that led to Móirne's house, using every bit of my gift to speed me along. The panic that had been building strangely subsided. After days of confusion, I now knew what was wrong. The Fomorians were here, and I would face them.

And they were in danger now. They had come here, unafraid, or so Máelmórda had said. This would be their undoing. Fomorians were arrogant. I knew this from our legends. They might think that four of them would defeat me easily, but this was not the case. I was a warrior Descendant trained by Colmon of the Tuatha Dé Danann and Murchad mac Brian. Before the day was over, they would regret having come here.

Máelmórda wasn't far away now. I could smell him. Donnchad was with him, too. But not Gormflaith. The other two Fomorians I had caught the scent of while chasing them were here, but standing a little behind Donnchad. These two would be weaker. Younger. Less practised. The mortal who had come to the island was hauling their boat along the sand of the beach, less than a mile away from Móirne's house.

I pushed my muscles harder, then began to slow as I reached the forest. I needed a plan, for Máelmórda had the warrior gift, too. He would hear me long before any mortal would, and thus it would be unlikely I could surprise them.

I stopped. Listened. The fire was spreading over the island as the wind swept it along the gorse and bracken. The Fomorians were moving, trailing Móirne and her family with them. Moving toward the cliffs. Toward the waves that Donnchad could control.

Now. I had to fight them now. Before they reached the cliffs and saw Isolde and Affraic escaping across the sea. Pulling out my sword, I hurried toward them.

As I ran out of the forest, I made out the four Fomorians.

Máelmórda stepped forward first, a sword in one hand, a shield in the other, but even with a blade so sharp, it was not he who caught my eye.

It was the man behind him.

The one who had killed Tairdelbach.

Donnchad.

Smiling, fire spun between his hands.

Isolde

Rathlin Island

Affraic hoisted the leather bag Broccan had packed onto her shoulder. "Come on, Isolde. Quickly."

I stared at her, watching the panic in her eyes as she scrambled to fasten her cloak about her shoulders.

"I can't go with you, Affraic."

"You must." She stared up at the sky and the darkness growing there, lips quivering. Quickly, however, she composed herself and took my hands in hers. "Look at that, Isolde. That is the power of the Fomorians. Destruction is all they know. We must go. We must do as Broccan says."

"No." I pulled my hands away. "He wants me to leave because he loves me. He wants to keep me safe, no matter the cost to himself... but why should I live at the expense of all else? To what end? To be hunted down by these Fomorians. I don't want that. I'd rather make a stand here."

"They're too strong, Isolde."

"I'm not a Descendant, you mean. I'm not this girl from the prophecy who is supposed to destroy them. I know this. But Broccan has taught me to fight with the sword and spear. I would rather fight them as a mortal than flee."

I ran outside and put on the bull-hide armour Broccan had given me. My new sword, the one that had once belonged to my brother, Tairdelbach, was lying under my bed. I pushed it into my belt and put Fragarach, the small wooden knife, there too. In my hand, I took a firm grip of my spear.

"Do not go," Affraic pleaded. "Broccan will not be able to fight if he worries about you. He is the warrior. That is his gift. Let him use it."

"And what of the islanders? What of their fate?"

"We cannot help them, Isolde. They are beyond our reach."

I hated that she said this, but as I looked out at the horizon, it was hard to have hope. Most of the island to the east of Broccan's boundary was burning now. The Ó Baoills' land was completely lost to the flames, and the forest by Móirne's house was beginning to catch too. The orange flicker of flames danced along the treetops, and already the smell of the burning wood and bracken was overpowering. Ash blew in the wind and the sky above us turned dark. Soon it would be as night.

Affraic took hold of both my arms. Tight this time. "Broccan asked you to leave, Isolde. We must. Have faith that he will win and meet us after."

I tried to pull my arms away, to follow Broccan, but found instead that I could not move at all. My mind and body were fighting each other, fear and love, despair and hope. Every part of me was at war, as if I could not make sense of all the things that were happening. The secrets that Broccan had kept from me were like a shadow, and this shadow had pulled me into a paralysis that I could not break from. *They wanted me, these Fomorians. They had come for me. No one else. If they found me, I would burn.*

Affraic took this opportunity to move, and she half pulled, half dragged me to the beach. Broccan's sailboat was kept not far from the path, though it had been pulled up onto the dry sand so the tide could not take it out. Affraic only released hold of me once we reached it. In one swift movement, she threw the bag inside and began to shove the boat forward with her shoulder.

Isolde.

I turned. The voice had been slight, but I had heard it. A voice in the wind.

Isolde. To the cliffs. Save us from the fire.

Affraic stopped pushing the boat and stared at me. "What's wrong?"

"Did you hear that? It... It must be Móirne. She's calling for me to save her."

"It's a trick. It must be."

"No. It's not."

"Of course it is. The Fomorians have her. If you go to Móirne, you will only put yourself in danger. Listen to me, Isolde. Help me with the boat."

I dropped my spear, clasped hold of the side of the boat, and dragged it into the sea. While Affraic steadied it, I hoisted up the sail mast. Affraic jumped in and held out her hand to me.

Isolde. Save us from the fire. All of us.

"Get into the boat, Isolde." Affraic stretched out her hand a little more.

"Sorry, Affraic. I cannot." I tightened the sail rope, and the boat lurched forward into the waves as the sail filled with wind. "Tell the others what has happened, Affraic, but I'm not going with you. This is my home."

Turning, I picked up my spear and sprinted along the beach until I reached the path that led to the cliffs. Now I'd made my decision, my stride widened, and I pushed myself hard as I made my way onto the cliff path.

The voice I'd heard... it had to be Móirne's. The wind was strong here and could carry a voice for miles. I sprinted past the lough and through the forest until Móirne's house loomed ahead. As I'd noticed from Broccan's house, the fire was beginning to take hold of the forest here, but it had not yet spread to the sparse bracken and grass that grew along the cliff side. I slowed then, keeping low, and inched closer to the cliff edge where the air was still clean enough to breathe.

Movement ahead caught my eye. It was Broccan. He was standing between Móirne's house and the forest's edge. Four Fomorians, all standing by the door of Móirne's house, were watching him. Broccan drew his sword. The three Fomorian men responded by drawing theirs.

As I crept closer, I studied these enemies of mine. Two of the male Fomorians had long, dark hair, thick and curled to their shoulders. The third was the Fomorian who had found me by the cliffs. Slighter than the other two and a little taller, he kept his hair short, while the woman was beautiful with long, straight black hair that ran to her waist. She stood back from the fray. One of the Fomorians with the thick curled hair stood in front of her to shield her from Broccan. This action showed that she was the weakest of them. The weak link in their pack.

"Bring the women out," one of the Fomorian men shouted.

The female Fomorian did as he commanded and brought out Móirne, Síoda and their mother. Still sobbing and shaking, their eyes widened as they took in the fire growing around them. "We will burn!" Móirne's mother sobbed. "Devils. All of you are devils."

"Let them go," Broccan shouted. "I am here to fight you. So fight."

"Where is the girl?" one of the other Fomorians asked.

"Why do you want to fight her when I am here?" Broccan returned.

I crept closer again as the Fomorians continued to taunt Broccan, my spear tight in my hand. The fire burned hot to my side as it consumed the wood and leaves of the forest. The sound was immense as the branches cracked with the heat, like a roll of thunder that never ended, and I knew that neither Broccan nor the Fomorian warrior would be able to hear me as I crept closer. Moving the spear into the correct position, I sped up, feeling the weight of the wood in my hand. Then I threw it. It pierced the Fomorian woman in the leg. She screamed and fell to the ground, releasing her grip on my friend.

"Run, Móirne," I screamed. "Run!"

Móirne, catching my eye for a moment, grabbed hold of Síoda and ran. The cliff behind her father's house was dangerous, but she knew all the ways to climb down, the same as me. Her mother, screaming, dashed after her, and the three of them disappeared behind a wall of smoke.

Broccan took the opportunity to attack. He blurred as he

moved past one of the Fomorian men, and I could see when he came to a stop that his blade was red with blood. This Fomorian spun around, blurring in the same way as Broccan had, and then the two of them began to fight in earnest. Their swords hazing along with their bodies.

"Run, Isolde!" Broccan called. "Back to my land!"

This time, I would do as he asked, but I would bring some of these Fomorians with me. We would see how quickly Broccan could defeat this warrior when he didn't have three others to worry about.

Pulling out my sword, I locked eyes with the young man who had found me by the cliffs, then with the woman who clutched at her leg. "Are you both cowards? Watching a fight rather than joining in?"

The man threw his hands forward and a bolt of fire flew toward me. I swerved to the side, the edge of it grazing my shoulder instead of striking me full on. Ignoring the pain, I ran until I reached the part of the forest not yet aflame, then weaved through the trees, where they'd find it harder to use their fire to hit me.

"After her," one of the Fomorians shouted. "Angelo. Cecile. Don't let her get away."

I didn't turn to see if they were following. The fire was catching, and I had to outrun it. If I could just make it to Broccan's land, then I could escape the fire and the Fomorians, but still give Broccan time to finish off the two who'd remained to fight him.

"Isolde!" It was Affraic. She came running toward me from the opposite direction.

Holding out my hand, I took hers in mine. "What are you doing here?"

"I couldn't leave you any more than you could leave Broccan."

"Don't stop, Affraic," I panted. "Two of them are following me. We need to get back to Broccan's land."

Keeping a tight hold of Affraic's hand, together we sprinted along the forest path. Fire sped along the ground, catching roots and leaves, moving faster than Affraic and me. But we were nearly at the end of the path. Nearly at the lough, and then it wasn't far until we reached the boundary.

As I turned to look behind me, the fire was almost upon us. Ash and smoke and smoulder dust rose into the air, flying high into the sky, which was also now full of birds fleeing their nests. Everything was running. From the smallest sparrow to the largest deer. Everything knew that to survive it had to leave this forest.

But Broccan, he was still there. He had not run.

I glanced backward again, looking for him. Where was he? Still fighting? I thought he would have caught up with us by now.

Affraic tumbled suddenly. Falling out of my grip, she thudded to the ground.

Without stopping, I reached for Affraic's arm and dragged her back onto her feet. "Just a little bit further."

Affraic nodded and did her best to keep at a pace with me. We were nearly there. The end of the forest was in sight. If we could move beyond the trees, we would be out of the smoke, and then it would be easier to breathe.

"Get down!" Affraic, who had glanced behind us, screamed as a fireball flew our way. The two of us dived to the ground and watched as the fireball crashed into a tree directly ahead of us. I looked behind me as I scrambled to my feet. A Fomorian was there. The Fomorian with short hair who'd found me earlier. He pulled out a sword from his belt, long and sharp, and the fire seemed to glow around him as he came closer.

Where was Broccan? Where was he?

I turned, but my path was blocked. Fire soared along the ground, encircling us, and the flames grew so high I could no longer see anything outside of it. Not even the tops of the trees. Not even the Fomorian. Nothing. Affraic and I could not escape. We were trapped.

"I'm sorry, Affraic."

I stared at her, crying with both anger and sadness. I had come to help Broccan, knowing that I might die, but I had not wanted this for her.

Affraic, exhausted, held me tight. "Do not despair, Isolde. Death is not something to fear." She ran her hands over her hair, searching for the white strands. "See. No tears for me. My time is close at hand no matter what, and this is the greatest truth. We all die in the end. How we die is important. Nothing else."

The circle of fire around us split, and the Fomorian came inside. He moved toward Affraic and placed his blade under her chin. Blowing along his hand, a flame built up on his skin, then crawled along the sword until the flame reached the very tip.

Affraic screamed as the metal burned her flesh.

I screamed too and pulled her away.

The Fomorian's golden eyes glowed as he spun his sword in his hand, smiling as he did so. His eyes left Affraic. Now he stared at me.

How dare he hurt Affraic. How dare these Fomorians come here and kill my friends and destroy my home. They hated us just for existing. Just for breathing.

"Get away from us!"

As the scream left my mouth, a great wind blew up around me, so hard and fast that a branch from a nearby tree snapped and crashed on top of him. He fell forward, gasping for breath, though fire still burned inside of his hand.

Rain, then hailstones, fell from the sky. Not white, but dark and black as they mixed with the ash and smoke. The flame on the Fomorian's hand died, and he screamed as the hailstones thudded against him. He screamed until he could do nothing more than huddle into a ball on the grass.

The hailstones sliced my skin too, and blood streamed from my head, chest and arm. Affraic held my hand, and I felt her gift flow into me, but for every cut she healed, another one opened. Holding each other, we ran. The circle of fire around us had disappeared, and we raced until we reached the lough. Affraic stumbled on the damp stones, and she sagged against me, the strength gone from her legs. And not a wonder. Now we were out of the storm, I could see the burn on her chin, as well as several welts from the hailstorm over her face and hands. By healing me, she had neglected herself.

"Heal yourself, Affraic," I said, pulling my arm away. "Quickly. Broccan's land is close."

Affraic shook her head as she splashed herself with the lough water. "Let me finish healing you first." She pressed her hand against the burn on my arm, but it did not disappear. "It's my gift," she said. "It's weakening now that I've started to age." Frowning, she glanced back at the forest. The hailstorm still blew around it, but it was fading, or else the fire was devouring it. "You did that, Isolde," she hushed. "I know it was you because you did this once before."

I shook my head. This couldn't be me.

"When your mother was pregnant with you, she was attacked by a witch called Gobnat. She said you used your gift from within her womb to summon a hailstorm. I thought when no gift had presented that perhaps you had burned your gift away, overextended yourself, but it's not true. You have magic within you, Isolde. You are powerful, just as the prophecy foretold."

I stared at my hands and turned them over. How had I done this? I couldn't have. Broccan had been so certain that I had no gift. I stared up at the sky, at the fire burning the trees. Broccan was still there. *What if it was true?* What if I could summon the hail again? *What if I could save him?*

Conjuring the same rage as before, I tried to summon the wind and the hail... but nothing happened. Instead, my head ached, and a wave of nausea came over me. Leaning forward, I vomited a thick, black fluid onto the ground.

"You need training," Affraic said. "To overuse our gift when we don't understand it is to risk ourselves. Do you understand?"

"But I need to save us."

"You can't. Not this time."

The fire behind us edged closer, the heat of it burning my skin. Smoke filled the sky in every direction now and I couldn't see the path that led to the hawthorn tree, though I still knew how to get there. It wasn't far. "Come on, Affraic. We can make it."

I tried to move, but my legs wouldn't stop shaking, and a strange tiredness swept over me. There was a voice too, I could barely hear it over the din of the fire. "Angelo. Angelo," the voice cried. "Where are you?"

"Wait," Affraic said, pulling me down to the ground beside her. "You're losing too much blood from the cut on your mouth." She reached forward to touch my face. "Let me heal that first. Then you will feel stronger."

"Quick..." My shaking intensified. "We have to get out of here."

Affraic pressed her hands against the cuts on my face and her finger rubbed on the broken skin around my lips. Then I felt something wet inside my mouth. Liquid on her finger. The taste of it was bitter.

"What was that?"

"I'm sorry, Isolde, but you must survive. When you wake, go to Seir Kieran. You have the witch gift. I'm sure of it. Find Báine. She will teach you to control it."

I tried to stand, but my arms and legs shook so hard I couldn't find my balance. "What's happening to me?"

"You're dying, Isolde. I have just given you the potion of death. Echna, our druid, brewed it before he died."

Confused, I stared at a small silver pendant in her hand. It was broken now. The clasp at the top was no longer there.

"Why?" I shook my head. "Why have you done this to me?"

Firmly, she took the pendant, turned it around and broke the golden clasp on the other side. She leaned over me and forced open my mouth. I tried to push her away, but my hands had lost all their strength. Carefully, she poured something else into my mouth. "The antidote," she said, though the sound of her voice had dulled. "We cannot get away from them now. It is too late, but you must live, Isolde."

"Where is... yours."

"There is only enough for one." She took my hand and pressed it to her lips. "Remember. You must go to Seir Kieran."

My vision blurred and when I tried to move, I couldn't. My body was paralysed. Locked. I felt Affraic drag me into the shallows of the lough water. She stood over me and cut open her wrist with my blade. Hot blood rushed over my stomach and chest, but then she pushed me out into the deeper water and moved away.

My vision left me, then. My hearing faded and my mind drifted toward a brightness that I had never seen in life. In the distance, as if very far away, I heard screams. Then I heard nothing at all.

Donnchad

Rathlin Island

My uncle was a man of many qualities. I'll not have it said otherwise.

But a coward, he would always be.

I knew it even as a boy. I would know it still when I was a ghost.

He began his fight with Broccan better than I might have supposed, but I knew he could never win. Not if he fought this fight one hundred times over could he ever be victorious.

Did my uncle know this himself when he drew his sword? I could not tell. Was the way he smirked at Broccan bravado, or was he a believer in his own golden-spun story? A charlatan with his eyes shut. So close did self-belief and artifice run alongside each other that only a sliver separated them, and it had been many years since my uncle had been tested.

As always, Máelmórda had acted without caution. He wouldn't watch and wait. Instead, he had to set the island alight to make a grand show.

To put fear into Broccan's heart, he had said.

Broccan is not a coward, I had answered.

But my uncle didn't listen. Would not listen to the man he knew coveted his daughter. Spite, that was his other failing, and it was a failing indeed.

I stood back, conserving my own fire as I watched the fight unfold. Máelmórda was tiring, and his fire-magic was almost spent. If he'd only saved his energy, he could be blasting Broccan with his fire any time he came close. Alas, Broccan was coming at him, closer and closer, slice after slice, and my uncle could do less and less to stop it.

The final strike was coming. Broccan had been cautious to start with, suspecting that my uncle might use his fire-magic, but of course, that caution faded when no fire-magic transpired. His caution eroded further when Murchad and Fódla's girl appeared. The fear in Broccan's heart that my uncle had wanted finally arrived, though it was too late.

And when my uncle lost, all of Broccan's rage and vengeful thoughts would turn to me.

"Now, Donnchad!" Máelmórda shouted. "Strike!"

My uncle stared at me, wild-eyed, understanding himself that he could not win now. His pride had finally eroded, and we were to work together. He had told me as much when he and Olaf caught up with us. *When I say, you will do as I ask. Then, and only then, will I talk of you courting Cecile.*

Conjuring my own fire, I blew over the grass and the flames swept along every blade like a mighty wave. The fire in my right hand grew quickest of all, and I pushed it over to where Broccan and Máelmórda fought. My uncle grinned as Broccan was forced to jump back. Step by step, the two of them danced their dance of swords and moved closer to the cliff, which was exactly where I wanted them to go. Like cattle, I herded them. So engrossed in their fight, they didn't notice. Strike. Counter-strike. Parry. Lunge. Broccan moved quicker, quicker – wanting to end this fight so he could move on to the next. *To me.*

Slowly, I took out the white blade my mother had given me. For Angelo, I had told her, knowing she would allow me to take it for him. Her pet. My mother was a clever woman, but, she didn't understand me, for I did not take the knife for Angelo. If anyone was to be having a new gift today, it would be me.

Spinning the blade in my right hand, I threw a fireball at Broccan. He dropped to the ground quickly to get out of the way. My uncle, panting, gave me a conspiratorial smile. *Fool.* A man of many qualities, but a fool, too. He should have kept a closer eye on Broccan.

A moment later, the warrior Descendant slammed the hilt of his sword against my uncle's head and disarmed him. His two swords crossed against my uncle's neck. If my uncle moved even a little, the blade would cut through his veins and bleed him dry. Broccan inched around until he stood behind Máelmórda, so that if I wanted to hurt him with my fire-magic, I would have to burn through my uncle first.

"Why?" Broccan shouted. Not at my uncle. At me. "Why did you kill Tairdelbach?"

Ah, so Broccan was a fool too.

Sighing, I lowered the knife and placed it back into my belt. I knew he'd ask me this question. Had thought about how to answer once or twice. But there was no answer. Tairdelbach had been in my way. That was all. And now, so was Broccan. *So was my uncle.*

Without waiting another moment, I summoned a fireball and hurled it at Máelmórda. The force of it pushed my uncle backward and Broccan's blade pierced the left side of his neck. So close to the edge of the cliff, Broccan could not jump out of the way as my uncle fell, and the two of them tumbled over.

Waiting until I heard the dull thud of their landing, I walked toward the edge and peered over. Both their bodies lay on the rocks below. Blood-soaked. Broccan's leg was broken, the bone piercing through his skin. His back was shattered, too. Blood spluttered from his mouth over his chin. He could not turn or move his legs.

My uncle had fared little better. The rock he'd landed on was flat and covered in seaweed and moss rather than rough and jagged like the one Broccan had fallen upon. Still, it looked as if he'd broken his arm and shoulder, and blood oozed from the slice along his neck, now swirling with the waves that sloshed over the boulders. He would bleed out soon.

"Wait there, uncle," I shouted. "I will help you."

The path down the cliff face was steep, but I had no fear of falling, so I sat on the edge and turned my body around to reach the first foothold.

"Donnchad!"

A scream in the wind. The voice was Cecile's. *She was frightened.* A sense of panic filled me. *Could this daughter of Fódla's have a gift, after all?*

I turned from the cliff face and sprinted toward my cousin. Now, who was the fool? It was me for assuming my mother's dream was right. Then for entrusting Cecile to the protection of Angelo.

Running deep into the woods, through the fire that had swept along the forest, I used my fire-magic to pull it back. I ran until I found Cecile standing by herself. The two Descendant women were close to her. One of them was floating in the water. Dead. The other was on her hands and knees by the edge of the lough, shaking so hard her teeth chattered.

"Where is Angelo?"

Cecile pointed to the tree behind her where my son was propped up against a tree. His skin was broken and swollen as if he'd been hit repeatedly on the face, and his eyes were closed over. I kneeled beside him. Oh, it was worse than I first feared. It wasn't just his face that was in a bad way, the back of his head was bleeding too.

"What happened, Cecile?"

"Angelo ran ahead. He had surrounded the Descendants with his fire-magic, but then a hailstorm appeared out of nowhere. I was able to take shelter, but Angelo was caught in the middle of it. He's got a big cut along his right leg, and he's bleeding from his ears and head. His face…" Cecile shuddered. "He's a mess."

Kneeling down, I felt for his pulse. It was there, strong enough. For now.

"Will he be alright?" Cecile asked.

"I don't know. The cut along the back of his head is serious, but there is nothing I can do about that now."

I turned my gaze to the two women. Not just the girl who had come to Broccan's aid, but another. Only a witch could summon a hailstorm, and this witch was powerful. I had to be careful.

Murchad's girl, she lay about fifty feet away, floating in the lough water. Her eyes were wide open and unblinking, and her chest unmoving. Her whole body was covered in blood and welts too. In her belt, there was a sword. Tairdelbach's sword. I hadn't thought about it before, but this girl was Tairdelbach's half-sister. My niece. Well then, Tairdelbach's sword should be mine. I waded into the water, took the sword from the girl's belt and put it in mine.

The other woman, the witch, still shaking, lifted her head and glared at me.

"How did she die?" I asked her.

"The hailstorm I conjured killed her. Just as it's killed your boy."

"My boy is alive."

"Not for long."

I stepped closer to the witch.

"Careful, Donnchad. She is powerful," Cecile said.

The witch laughed at this.

Summoning the fire to my hands, I slowly continued to walk over to her. This woman was spent. Shaking and shivering. How she had the audacity to laugh when fire danced within my hands was beyond me.

I threw a ball of fire at her leg. The witch screamed as it hit her.

"If you are so powerful, why don't you fight me?"

The witch grimaced with the pain. "I'm ageing," she said. "Not as strong as I used to be. If I were, you'd all be dead by now."

Once again, I took out the white knife my mother had given me. The knife of mortality. "Then, in exchange for the taking of my son's life, I will take yours, but before I do, I will take your gift."

The woman's eyes widened. *She knew what the knife was.* She rose up to strike me with an old blade, but so feeble was her movement that I grabbed her tight before it came anywhere close to my skin. My fire burned her arm, and she screamed as she fell back.

"Cecile, come here,"

My cousin stared at the woman, frozen.

"Cecile. Do what I say. Stab her through the heart and her gift will be yours. If you take her gift, you'll be a witch like my mother."

"I... I don't want to. I don't want to be like Gormflaith."

Oh, Cecile. So beautiful and sweet. But our life in Paris had made her soft, more like the mortal women she'd befriended than a Fomorian. If she was to be who I needed her to be, then this had to change.

Letting go of the witch, I put the knife in her hand and closed her fingers around the handle. "You will never be like Gormflaith. With this gift, you will surpass her."

Cecile watched the witch as she groaned on the grass. She felt pity for her. I understood this feeling. I'd felt it at times in my youth. I had to help her then. Help her see that pity came in many forms.

I raised my hand, summoned the water from the lough so that it pooled underneath the witch. It soaked her dress, relieved the burns on her legs as the coldness of the water touched her skin. But then I summoned my fire-magic and the water the witch sat in began to bubble and steam. The witch screamed, thrashed. She might have tried to get up, but she couldn't. The water wouldn't let her go.

"Quick," I said to Cecile, who looked at the woman, pale-faced and wide-eyed. "Before she dies, and her gift goes with her. End her misery, Cecile. She is not long for this world now, no matter what you do."

Cecile stepped forward, and I pulled away the fire. Quickly, she thrust the blade into the witch's chest.

The white mist left her body and Cecile summoned her fire. Weak as her gift was, the mist became entrapped within Cecile's fire, moved toward her and then inside her.

Cecile collapsed as soon as this happened, the white blade falling from her hand. I picked Cecile up and set her beside Angelo. Already she was shaking and sweating, as the Descendant gift took hold of her. Would she die? It was more than possible. And yet, I didn't think so. Her mother had been a Descendant, after all. Perhaps this gift would find it easier to reside within her than it had done for me, Máelmórda and my mother.

Quickly, I stood and found the knife of immortality that Cecile had dropped. Placing it into my belt, I took a deep breath. I had no more time to waste. First, I ran to the beach where we had landed. Olaf sat in our boat still, his ice-blue eyes scanning the forest for signs of movement. By all the gods, this man revolted me so much that I could scarce bear the thought of speaking with him, let alone entrusting Cecile to him. However, he was bound to my mother, and while I still found him repugnant, for now, it meant that I could trust him.

"Olaf!"

I waved him over to me. He came running, axe in his hand.

"Cecile and Angelo are in the forest. Angelo is injured. Cecile has taken a witch gift and already the fever has taken her over. Bring them both to the boat, then sail along the coast to the east. Máelmórda fell down the cliff with Broccan. If I can find him, I wish to bring his body to my mother."

"The Descendant warrior is dead?"

"Yes, I killed him. I only wish I could have done it before he took my uncle's life."

Olaf nodded, his eyes gazing at the forest behind me. "It is not burning where I left Cecile and Angelo, but hurry. I want to get us all off the island before any mortals return."

Olaf nodded and walked into the forest, leaving me to run back to the cliff. Toward Broccan, and Máelmórda.

When I reached the cliff, I glanced over.

Broccan was gone.

The waves crashing against the cliff face must have swept him away. I felt out with my water-magic but could not sense his body. He was dead, he had to be. Broken and shattered as he was. Still, an anger filled me. I hadn't just wanted him to die today. I'd needed him for much more than death. Still, not all was lost. Climbing down the jagged cliff face, it didn't take me long to reach my uncle.

"Donnchad," he whispered, blood covering his lips. "Help me." His skin was pale, his hand feebly holding on to the cut along his neck. He was so weak; he'd hardly been able to seal the wound with his fire-magic to staunch the flow of blood.

"I am no healer, uncle," I said, taking out the white knife from my pocket. The blood of the witch still covered it, and I cleaned it with my cloak.

"What… are… you doing?"

"I've always wanted to be a warrior," I answered. "To be quick and strong."

"You cannot… have more… one gift," Máelmórda stammered.

"Says who?"

"You will not… control it."

I moved a little closer. "Yes, I will."

"No, Donnchad. Don't do this."

"Hush, uncle, and do not worry. I will look after Cecile."

With that, I thrust the blade into his heart. The white mist came out of him, just as it had the time we'd killed the Descendants and stolen their gifts. Using my fire-magic, my flames wrapped around the mist and brought it to me.

The shaking and nausea began almost instantly, but before I could succumb completely, I pushed Máelmórda's body from the rock. He drifted away. The waves I'd summoned, drawing him into the sea and into the depths below.

Dragging myself onto the rock he'd lain upon, I closed my eyes and waited.

The fever came next, and it pulled me under to a place of dreams and chaos.

Tairdelbach stared at me, his hand outstretched. "Quickly. Off the beach. The tide is coming in."

Broccan stood in front of him, using his body to shield Tairdelbach from me. He knew, I realised. Knew what I was, and he hated me for it. "No," Broccan said. "He could be here to hurt you."

Tairdelbach, who had been like an older brother to me, shook his head and pushed Broccan away. "You wouldn't do that, would you, Donnchad? I know you."

But he didn't know me. He didn't care for me either.

"Why didn't you come for me?" I asked.

Tairdelbach came into the water, waded toward me. "Sitric had you in his city, Donnchad. There was no way to get to you."

Broccan followed his friend and pushed him, tried to get Tairdelbach out of the water. This angered me. Tairdelbach wouldn't leave though, not even when Broccan told him that I would kill him. Why wouldn't Tairdelbach get out of the water? Why was he so stupid?

Reaching out with my gift, I pulled him under. He stared at me as the water dragged him underneath. Those blue eyes, the same as my father's, the same as mine. I saw fear within them. Fear and pain... but not anger. Not judgement. I could only hear the roars of Broccan as he tried to pull him up, then his screams as I used my fire-magic and set his body alight.

"Donnchad." A voice in the distance shouted my name. "Donnchad. Where is Máelmórda?"

I felt a hand grab my body. I felt my body slide away from the rock and fall against something hard.

"He's gone," I managed to say. "The waves."

"What's wrong with you?" Olaf grabbed my face, pinched at the skin.

"I took Broccan's gift. The waves must have taken him too."

Olaf grunted and sat me back. The boat swayed then. Swayed as he rowed us out to sea. "Take us to my mother, Olaf," I said.

He did as I asked, or at least did not argue with me. I could speak no longer in any case. My dreams wanted me again, and I slid away from consciousness.

Water pushed against my legs. All around me I could hear the shouts of men fighting. Men dying. But against the din of battle, I could hear a voice. It was Tairdelbach. He stared at me, his hand outstretched. "Quickly. Off the beach. The tide is coming in."

His eyes opened wide as he reached out to hold me.

In this fevered dream, I wished to take his hand in mine. I felt this wish as hard as that day on the beach at Clontarf.

But once again, I could not. Once again, I watched as Tairdelbach, the only person who had ever shown me love and kindness, disappeared beneath the water.

Isolde

Rathlin Island

"Hello, Isolde."

A woman with long, grey hair stood above me, then slowly she kneeled and took my hand in hers. Behind her, I could see nothing else. It was too bright.

I was not afraid, even though the smell of burning and death filled the air, and so I focused my attention on the woman. She had large eyes and rounded cheeks that made her look younger than the long, grey hair would lead one to believe. Kindness radiated from her expression, and a garland of yellow cowslip sat on her head like a crown, shining in the bright light.

I wanted to reach out to touch her with my other hand, but I couldn't move my body, not even a finger or toe. Only my eyes seemed to work. The calmness that had held me since the woman said my name dissipated. What was wrong with me? Why couldn't I move? Over and over, I strained and struggled, but to no avail.

"Do not be afraid, Isolde," the woman said, tightening her hold on my hand. "And do not try to move. You won't be able to until you waken. Until then, you must listen to me. There is much I need to tell you."

I stopped struggling and instead tried to form words, for I had so many questions, but as with my body, neither my tongue nor lips would move.

"My name is Aoife," the woman said. "We are sisters, and I have watched over you for your whole life. I will be with you whenever I can, Isolde. Know that. I wish I could have spoken to you before now, but I cannot cross over the veil unless a death calls me."

Using all my will, I brought my voice to life, a whisper. *"Affraic?"*

Aoife looked surprised by my question, but then lowered her gaze. "Yes. It is her death that has called me. She will be in the land of the dead soon. I will collect her myself." Aoife's eyes met mine, and she shook her head. "No, you are not there. You are in the land of the living still."

"Why?"

This one word was all I managed to say, and yet, it encapsulated everything. Why had Affraic saved me? What was I?

"You are the daughter who will destroy fire, Isolde. There is great power within you. You must learn to control it or else it will destroy you. Do you understand? You must go to Seir Kieran. Colmon will explain everything."

Tears dripped down the sides of my cheeks. Tears that I could not wipe away. How could I control anything if I could not even do that.

The white light around the woman brightened, so bright that she began to disappear into it. She seemed to sense this, kneeled lower, and using her hand, gently wiped the tears away for me. "You will wake soon, Isolde. Try not to be afraid. I am with you, my sister."

She shimmered, her face fading into the light.

"Stay," I whispered. "Stay."

"I cannot. You are waking. The wind will speak to you soon. Listen to it, but do not seek it out. Promise me."

My eyes opened slowly. The light was not as bright as the one in my dreams, but still I struggled to see. Turning my head to the side, I waited for my eyes to become acclimatised to the blurred orange and yellow tones. At first, I worried that the forest fire still raged on, but as my senses awakened, I realised the heat from the air had gone and the orange light was merely the sun, filtered through a haze of whiteish smoke. It could have been as beautiful as a morning mist, save for the smell. It told the true story. The land had been burned. Burned to ash and dust.

As with the strange vision I'd had, the one with Aoife, *my sister*, kneeling beside me, my mind seemed to rouse before my body. Once again, I couldn't move – couldn't even lick my lips or swallow. This time, I tried not to panic and focused on the smallest of movements. I tried my fingers first, then my toes, then my mouth. After a few attempts, my fingers swept against my trousers and my toes brushed against the soft leather inside my shoe.

That my body was working was a welcome relief, and as my fear of being permanently locked within myself subsided, memories of what had happened flooded my mind. All of it. Affraic had given me the potion of death and the antidote. I'd felt myself die and fade away into darkness… and now I was awake.

But what had I returned to? Where were the Fomorians? Did they know I was alive?

A fresh wave of panic surged within me, and I redoubled my efforts to make my body move. Finally, I gathered enough strength to roll onto my stomach, and I felt myself sink into sludge. My body was still in the lough, I realised, though the current had carried me to the landbank on the opposite side to the path.

Trying to stand, I groaned and fell back down. Every bit of my body ached. My legs were shaking, my head throbbed, and a foul taste had gathered in my mouth. I spat on the ground and a thick black liquid splattered onto the muddy soil. The smell of it was worse than the taste, and my stomach heaved. Crawling backward, I cupped my hands and took some of the lough water into my mouth, swilled it around, then spat it out.

More memories came to me then. The look on Affraic's face as she gave me the potion of life. I had faded away so quickly, but even within the darkness, I'd heard her screaming.

Oh, Affraic, what did they do to you?

I sobbed as the sound of her screams played over and over again. They had tortured her, hadn't they? Such pain she must have felt in those final moments, and she had sacrificed herself to save me.

I wanted to find her body, to hold her, then lay her to rest… but she was not here.

Affraic will be in the land of the dead soon. I will collect her myself.

That was what Aoife had told me. These words gave me some

small comfort that Affraic's suffering was no more, and she was in the otherworld with those who had passed before her.

"Aoife." I said the name out loud, my throat thick and swollen. "Aoife. Can you hear me?"

I stared into the distance, gazing over at where the hawthorn tree stood, half expecting to see Aoife standing beside it. I didn't know why, but her absence made me cry all the harder.

"Come on, Isolde," I whispered to myself. "Get up. You need to find Broccan."

Willing myself to stand again, I made it first to my knees and then to my feet, and slowly, I made my way to the path that led to Móirne's house. It occurred to me that the Fomorians might have Broccan there and could be torturing him at this very moment.

Step by step, I walked, shaking all the while. I didn't care if they hurt me. I had to at least try to save him. The sword Broccan had given me, Tairdelbach's sword, was gone, so I took out my knife, Fragarach, and staggered along the path. Tears sprung to my eyes as I gazed at the burnt forest. The fire was out, yes, but it had razed the island. Everything was gone. Nothing moved save for the smoke drifting upward from the ground.

Móirne's house was a wreck, too, just like everything else. The thatch and wooden posts were burned to ash; only the rocks that made the ráth wall showed that once this had been a home. I walked around it, then over to the cliff edge. Broccan was not here. No sign of him at all. No sign of anyone. Even the boat that had carried the Fomorians here had gone. It dawned on me then that I could have been trapped in my death sleep for days. A week even. Parts of the island still smouldered, the heat of the fire burned deep underground, and yet, as I stared at the soil beneath my feet, I saw ants scurrying over the charred earth.

"Broccan!" I shouted his name, my voice barely more than a whisper and full of desperation. "Where are you, Broccan?"

But no one came to me. *No one.*

Broccan was gone.

I cried then. Because I knew. I knew Broccan had to be dead

for me to be alone like this. Even if he had found me and thought me dead, he would not have left my body floating in the water. He would have taken me to his land and watched over me until Aoife had come to collect my body. The reality of this broke me and I collapsed to my knees, crying so many tears that I thought I would never stop.

Feeling only half-alive, I walked to Broccan's land.

A strange line marked the boundary. Fire and destruction lay on one side. The grass was green and beautiful on the other. The hawthorn tree marked this difference more clearly than anything. Half of it was burned to a charred blackness, but the part of it within Broccan's land stood tall and proud, the leaves budding and green. I stretched out to touch the bark as I passed. "Help me," I said, though I didn't know to whom I spoke. Aoife, perhaps. Affraic. My mother and father. I did not want to think Broccan's name, but if he was dead, he was in the otherworld too.

When I reached the house, I collected what little provisions Broccan had missed. His spare knife. A washing cloth. Flint.

I didn't let myself stop, and I hurried to the beach. I had to get off the island. I had to find Seir Kieran. That was what Affraic and Aoife had told me. That was my plan now and that's all I would allow myself to think. If I stopped to question my actions, I knew I'd find a way to talk myself into remaining on the island. Or I would start crying. Or screaming. But I couldn't do any of those things. I couldn't let myself stop.

The beach was unchanged. So was the view of the mainland. Those living along the coast might have seen the fire but were untouched by it. I was glad for that – that us living on an island had stopped the fire from spreading to the thick forests across the water. I hoped Móirne and her family had made it there. I would try to look for her if I thought I could offer her any comfort… but she knew the truth of what I was now. Cursed. And I could not risk bringing the Fomorians anywhere near her again. I was alone.

Truly alone. I had to remember that. Weak as I was, shaking and shivering, I had to do what Affraic had told me to do. *Survive. Reach Seir Kieran. Learn how to use my gift.* The first step was to get off the island.

Affraic had dragged the rowboat up onto the sand, though not as far as Broccan usually did, and while I was weak and shaking, I was able to nudge it along until it reached the waves. Before I gave it a final push, I pulled out the clean clothes from Broccan's bag that Affraic had left behind. A clean pair of trousers, scarf and shirt were there. An old cloak of mine. I undressed quickly, removing my blood- and mud-soaked clothing, and scrubbed myself raw in the sea with the washing cloth. I let the sea take the stained clothes, knowing that the blood and mud would never come out, but set my bull-hide armour into the boat.

Dressing in the clean clothes, I hauled myself in, raised Broccan's sail and set the steering board into the water. I was too weak to row, but there was enough wind to carry it across. At least I hoped so.

The sail rope in hand, I sat low in the boat. My heart sank as the shoreline of Rathlin moved further and further away. Images of my mother and Broccan standing together on the beach came to me, her red hair blowing in the wind and a smile upon both their faces. Still, I did not waver in my resolve. That I was listening to both Affraic and Aoife was the only thing that kept me going and lessened my grief at leaving behind the only home I'd ever known.

When I reached the mainland, I dragged the boat up onto the beach and began to make my way toward the River Gleann Seisce. It was raining now. The wind had picked up too. Putting on my bull-hide armour and cloak, I tied Affraic's scarf over my face and hair. Face hidden and protected from the elements, I felt ready to begin my journey. But where should I go? *Which way?* Broccan had told me there was a trading market a little downstream, but that was it. The sum of my knowledge about which way to go. Deciding this, at least, was a start, I followed the river south.

In truth, I hadn't ever thought about how to get to Seir Kieran, not even when Broccan and Affraic had discussed us leaving. I had just assumed they would lead the way, and that, as always, Broccan would take care of me. Panic built up inside me. Grief too, and I struggled to breathe. To calm myself, I tried to think about what I did know. Seir Kieran was in the Kingdom of Leinster, and I knew Leinster was located along the south-east of Ireland. There were many mountains between Ulaid and Leinster and many rivers, all of which could lengthen the journey if I went the wrong way. Broccan had also told me that it took seven days on horseback for him to reach the monastery. I had no horse and nothing to trade for one. How long would it take to walk? *Double that? More?* Yes, more than double. I'd also have to stop and catch my food along the way… but I could do that. I could catch mice and hares and climb the trees to reach eggs in nests, and I was more than able to make a fire in the evening.

Feeling slightly stronger as I walked, I was relieved that it didn't take too long before a church came into view. Small and made of stone, it was situated on a hill a little to the west of the river. There were a few outhouses around the church, but no dun or larger dwelling. *That was good.* There would be a few people here to ask for directions, but not too many people all at once. Still, I was nervous and stopped for a moment to prepare. First, I fastened the bull-hide armour tighter around my chest. Then I tied back my hair and pushed it underneath my cloak and scarf. I was wearing the clothing and armour of a man, and my face was hidden save for my eyes. Broccan had always told me it was safer for men to travel alone than women, and I did not want to garner any attention. All I wanted to do here was ask for directions. Then I'd be gone.

I started walking again, head down to avoid the rain as I approached the hill. It was only then that I noticed how wide the river was becoming. Ahead of me, the river opened so much that

I could hardly see the far bank, and on this side, a wooden structure had been built to accommodate ships and boats. Several were moored there. Not only fishing boats, but longships. One of them had a prow shaped into a dragon's head. A small marketplace was visible too, with men from the longships setting their goods there for the locals to examine. Even from this distance, I could make out the gleam of steel and the shimmer of golden jewellery. The men who guarded the stalls had weapons enough of their own and watched the people inspecting the wares with watchful eyes. Others, those looking to buy the weapons, were no less formidable, and they too seemed to be searching the crowd. One of these men, a tall man with a thin face, looked up at me, eyes narrowed as I made my way to the church.

Wanting to get out of sight, I walked into the church. It was cold inside, though I was grateful to be out of the rain. It was plain too, with only a few wooden benches and a stone altar at the back. A wooden cross hung above it. No one was here, either. It was so quiet. A true quiet.

Kneeling by the altar, I clasped my hands together and closed my eyes. The silence was both soothing and terrible. Memories came to me without the distraction of birdsong and the sound of raindrops and the river. *Affraic's screams. Broccan telling me to leave him. Móirne and her mother crying.*

"*Tu es seul?*" *Are you alone?*

I turned and stared up at the man who had spoken. He was not a priest nor a monk. Indeed, he was dressed in ripped clothing and his arm was covered in blood. He spoke in the Anglo-Norman language Broccan had taught me, but I couldn't quite make myself form any words in my mouth.

"*Je suis suivi. Vous aussi,*" the man hissed.

Frowning, I shook my head. These words frightened me. *He was being followed, and so was I.* I glanced at the door. Could the Fomorians be on my trail?

"I don't understand," I replied in Anglo-Norman French. "Who is following me?"

The man grabbed my sleeve, and this time he spoke in Irish, though the form was poor. "Go to the harbour of the woman. That is where they will land. Tell the king that."

"I do not understand. I am not who you think I am."

The messenger stared at me, his forehead furrowing, then walked away. The man with the thin face who I noticed in the marketplace came into the church then and sat on one of the seats to pray. He scowled at the man who'd spoken to me as he hurried along the aisle, tutting and muttering something about being disrespectful in the house of God before clasping his hands together in prayer.

I turned away from him and kept very still, for I didn't want to walk past the man praying, nor did I want to talk more to the man who'd spoken to me. At last, another came into the church. A monk who blessed himself before lighting a candle on the altar.

"Father," I whispered, lowering my head so he could not see my face. "Can you help me?"

The monk walked over to me, speaking in a language I had never heard before. Low and guttural, it sounded a little like the Norse language Broccan had taught me, but not close enough for me to pick out any words.

"Do you have any Irish?" I asked.

The monk shook his head.

"*Pater*," I said, switching to Latin. The monk smiled this time. "*Scisne viam ad* Leinster?"

"Are you lost?" he replied in Latin.

I nodded my head.

The monk led me toward the doors of the church. He pointed to the path that continued along the west side of the lough, and described the path I should take.

This was good. I should stay along the river path and turn south when I came to the oak tree forest. Grateful that I knew at least how to start my journey, I gave him my thanks and walked in the direction he had told me.

"There are wolves. Criminals too," he called after me. "Men gathering for war. Be careful."

Once again, I gave him my thanks and continued to make my way toward the path. Wolves, criminals and armies of men. Yes. These were warnings I should keep in mind. There were no wolves on Rathlin, though I'd heard my uncle tell of huge packs living in the forests of Ireland. Fuidir too – men and women cast out of their clans. And Broccan had warned me that men were gathering for a war. That had worried him most of all.

I pulled my cloak tighter around my body and placed my hand on the hilt of my knife. The journey to Leinster would be dangerous, but I was ready for it.

Gormflaith

Chepstow

The men stopped marching once we reached the castle at Chepstow. It was a large castle, much grander than the one at Bristol, and was situated on the other side of the River Severn. Made entirely of stone, the castle was formidable indeed, a warning to the Welsh of what the Anglo-Normans were capable of and how serious they were about maintaining control of this newly conquered land.

The Normans were Viking descendants in truth, though you would not know it from the way they dressed and spoke. They'd adapted to their native country of Normandy, and once they conquered England, they had brought the stone castles they loved so much with them.

Now that I'd spent a few days marching with the retinue, I knew who the men were. Many great knights were among us, famous for their exploits in a previous war, or so David told me. Some had even fought in the Crusades. This intrigued me, this desire to fight in lands they had no connection to. What was it that drove them? Pride? Greed? Devotion to Christ?

I could not tell, for these men were a strange breed. Indeed, the whole army was different from the ones I'd previously known.

In Ireland, the king ruled his clan, but clans were also ripe with factions, infighting and backstabbing. A king could be felled at any moment, be it by a brother, uncle, cousin or son. It made mustering an army difficult, and holding it for any length of time, even harder. Lower kings could never be trusted to keep their word. Here, even though there was no king, there was organisation. A commitment to see a deed done. The men marched as if in a unit with a singular focus. Even after five days of marching, I'd not heard a single underhand comment. Not a whiff of treachery. A command had been given, and they moved without complaint.

Their armour was impressive too. Unlike the Irish, they wore steel helms upon their head. Some of these helms had pieces to cover the warrior's nose, while some were embedded with jewels. It might appear vain to so proudly wear their wealth upon their head like crowns, but they were too hardened for this to be true. No. Vanity was not their flaw. It was something else I hadn't quite worked out yet.

In truth, I hadn't had the time or peace of mind to ponder such questions. A train of wives and whores followed the army. I was not alone, it seemed, in trying to secure myself a knight or an archer. Some of these women were Norman. Others were English or Welsh. A surprising mixture of languages were spoken as we marched, and this only furthered my incredulity. How did this Strongbow inspire such loyalty among his people when they were not of the same land?

"What do you think of Chepstow?" David asked as we rode through the gates.

"It's most impressive. Grander even than you described."

David smiled and I returned it. He'd remained attentive since our departure from Bristol. He rode beside me, talking sometimes of his love for me and wish to marry, but maintaining a respectful distance. I had agreed that he might ask permission from his lord, Strongbow, though I was uncertain whether I would agree to it in the end.

David was certainly sweet and handsome. Humorous when so inclined. Not boorish or self-important. Unfortunately, he was on the lowest rung of a very complicated ladder. Bastard-born, I'd discovered from one of the whores who followed the army. Not untested in battle, but he had not fought in the English war the men called *The Anarchy*, nor in the Crusades, which bound the older members of the army together.

Experience told me to look for favour elsewhere. However, it was too late to do so. That was another odd thing about this group of men. All of them shared a devout, fervent sort of piety. Chivalry and honour were valued to the point of foolishness. They said they would rather die than break their word. And when it came to their women, purity was the quality they valued most highly. More than beauty. More than anything. While I was tolerated and respected as David's woman, I believed that whore would be my name should I try to beguile any of the other men to my side.

Strange as it was to admit... being David's woman was not so very bad. I enjoyed his conversation. I laughed at this. How old was I now? I forgot sometimes. A little over two hundred, I thought. Surely, this was too old to desire any man.

"David!" A stout man rode toward us. Raymond FitzGerald was his name, though the men called him Le Gros on account of his girth. He was an older half-cousin of David, legitimate, and seemed to be in command of the knights within his family. Two more men rode behind Le Gros. One was Robert FitzStephen, the other was Meilyr FitzHenry. These three were important men and somehow all related, though I couldn't quite work out how.

"We must go straight to the feasting hall when we arrive. Make sure to be quick."

David grinned, glad, I thought, that he had been invited to the feast. "What about Alys?" David asked.

Le Gros shrugged, unimpressed by the shy smile I gave him. "I'm sure with so many knights and archers, the kitchen maids will be happy for another to help them. When you reach the castle, speak to them and say I've asked for her to be allowed to serve. They'll know my name."

A serving wench? What a fall from grace. I could barely maintain my smile as Le Gros, Robert and Meilyr rode away. Still, it could have been worse. While the wives and daughters within the company might be allowed lodgings in the castle, it would not be so for the whores who made up the rest of the group. A bed inside the castle, even if it was in the servants' quarters, was better than wherever they'd be sleeping tonight.

"How are you, Alys?" David asked. His smile. It was so sweet. I couldn't help but stare at it. "Are you happy with Le Gros' offer? I could try to find you lodgings somewhere else."

Lowering my gaze, I gave a coy half-smile. "I am grateful for your cousin's offer of work in the castle. I cannot wait to serve your supper tonight. Thank you for your kindness."

"You do not need to thank me, Alys."

"Oh, but I do. Other men, not as good as you, might have tried to take advantage. I thank God daily for sending you to me. You are like an angel. Truly."

David laughed at this, shaking his head, but secretly pleased with my praise.

"How long shall it be until your brothers and sister catch up with you?" he asked.

"I'm not sure, though I hope it's not long."

"I hope it's not long, too. I cannot ask your brothers' permission for your hand until they arrive, and I would marry you before I leave for war. I've prayed every night that my lord will give me the permission I seek."

Not knowing how to react to this, I shielded my face with my hair, for I would not know what to say myself until Máelmórda returned. The question of if I wanted to return to Ireland depended on whether they had killed the girl. Had they done that? Was I safe? Were my brother, son and grandson alive, or had Broccan killed them? I had tried to dream of them since they left. Once I saw Máelmórda and Olaf sailing north. Next, I saw Cecile lying unconscious. But nothing else. Nothing to show me the truth of what had happened. Perhaps none of them would return to me.

"Do not worry," David said, his voice soft. "For I can see that you do. I will make any vow necessary to secure my lord's blessing."

"I cannot help but worry." Moving my horse a little closer to his, I stared around the castle. "Is your lord here?"

"Strongbow? Yes. This is his castle. He is, or at least he used to be, the Earl of Pembroke, and these lands are his."

"Used to be Earl?"

David nodded. "Strongbow and King Henry have a complicated history, and the king took the earldom from him. Richard still calls himself the Earl of Pembroke, but the king refers to him as the Lord of Striguil. While you are here, you must call him the Earl of Pembroke, but if you are ever in the court of the king, he is Lord Striguil only. Remember that."

This was a useful piece of information, but I didn't want to delve into it too much now. Instead, I moved onto something lighter. "Why do you call him Strongbow? Isn't his name Richard?"

"It is. Strongbow was his father's pet name, but his son inherited it along with the lands. His father was meant to be very good with the longbow, though I never saw him shoot myself."

I scanned the castle again. It was a fine piece of work, and the lands attached to it were considerable. If Strongbow was lord of all this, why then did he want to leave to fight in Ireland?

Our horses plodded up the path, leaving behind the townspeople and the market as we made our way to the stables. At this point, we came to a stop. David took my horse from me and gave it to one of the stable boys.

"Come, Alys," he said. "Let's go and speak to the kitchen maids about your lodgings."

Once again, he smiled, oh, so sweetly, and I followed him toward the castle, knowing that I should not enjoy the feel of his hand against mine as much as I did. Soon, I might have to let him go… but for now, I did not care. Enjoyment did not come often in life. When presented, it was always best to accept, for who knew when it would be offered again.

Isolde

Kingdom of Ulaid

I hurried along the river path for the rest of the day. I didn't like how visible I was on the open grasslands and was eager to become enveloped in the oak forest the priest had described. Wolves or not, it was safer there than by the market. From the warriors who guarded the market stalls to the strange man who'd spoken to me in the church, I felt as if I were being watched, and I did not like it. I did not like this sensation of being observed by people I did not know.

This unease faded the further I walked away from the market and church. Picking at wild garlic and dandelions for food, I kept going, and as the sky began to darken, I was glad to see that I had finally reached the forest. Three oak trees stood a little forward from the rest, like guards of some kind, waiting to ask me a question before I could pass. I could have admired them for longer, save the sun was setting and it was time to make a shelter. The wind had a bite out here in the open and the clouds above were thickening.

I quickened my pace, searching for somewhere suitable to sleep along the outskirts of the forest before it grew too dark. Now I was here, my weary bones seemed heavier than ever, each ache as I moved begging me to rest. All I needed to do was find—

"Stop. Come here," a voice shouted.

I stilled. Who had spoken? Surely not the man who had spoken to me in the church? Cursing silently, I berated myself for not being more careful. I should have hidden my tracks or run so as to reach the safety of the forest sooner. *Broccan would have berated me for leaving myself out in the open for so long.* I turned slowly, pushed my scarf back over my face and searched for whoever had spoken. But the next noise I heard wasn't from behind as I first thought. It was ahead, just at the boundary of the forest. Four men rode out from behind the trees, one of whom was the thin man with the scowl I'd noticed praying inside the church when the Norman man had run outside. *Four men. Four scowls.*

I ran my eyes over them. They were well-built. Travel weary, perhaps, but better clothed than the traders at the market or even the warriors who had guarded the goods and ships. Their horses were well-groomed and muscled. Certainly, much better bred and kept than the old mare Móirne's father used around the farm.

What do you do when you are outnumbered, Isolde?

Broccan's instructions rang out inside my mind. *Run*, I answered him, and scanned the forest. *Which was the best way to go?*

One of the men, a young redhead of a similar age to me, rode a little forward. He wore a shiny golden brooch which tied his cloak around his neck. Silken cloth, woven with five or six colours, shimmered underneath the grey fur hood. The man beside him, older, with long flaxen hair and a thick fur cloak, urged his horse forward until it stood beside the horse of the young man.

It was this man who stared at me the hardest, displeasure apparent on every feature, and he gestured with his hand for me to come closer. His other hand moved to rest on the hilt of his sword, sweeping back his cloak from his shoulder. A long red scar ran the entire length of the left side of his face, and I cursed my carelessness again. These were fighting men, a war party, just like the priest had warned me about.

"Come here, boy," the scarred man said. I knew then that it was he who had spoken earlier, only the tone of the voice was louder this time. Harsher. The thin man who had scowled at me in the church licked his lips, while the fourth man, stouter than the others with a long auburn beard, jumped from his horse and pulled his sword from its sheath.

What do you do when your enemies have the advantage? Do you stay and fight?

No. You must destroy their advantage first.

I couldn't outrun them in the open. They would catch up with me on horseback within minutes. That was their advantage. Numbers and speed. But if I could make it into the forest, I had a chance. The trees were too tightly packed for a horse to gain momentum. I knew that I was not a warrior Descendant, and I did not have Broccan's strength or his speed, but I was fast. And these men, for all their fur cloaks and fine horses, looked rather weighted down by their finery.

"I will come to you," I shouted as I raised my hands in submission.

Lowering my head, I began to walk but moved along the forest boundary until I saw a path through the forest, clear of fallen trunks or boulders. As soon as I reached it, I bolted.

My feet swallowed up the ground, jumping over branches and rocks as I went. The thud of their steps pounded behind me. I knew I couldn't afford to fall, or to veer to one side and be herded. I ran and ran until their shouts became a distant noise that faded to nothing.

My training with Broccan, the races with Móirne, these things kept me going for a long time, but soon, my already aching legs began to burn, and I knew I could not keep to the pace I needed. I pushed myself to keep going until a group of rocks, covered in gorse and bracken, appeared ahead of me. Skidding behind them, I huddled into a ball and pulled my hood over my face to dampen the sound of my breathing. I listened, but the only thing I could hear was the thump of my heartbeat.

Suddenly, a hand clasped the hood of my cloak, fingers catching my hair through the fabric. The man with the thin face spun me round and pulled out his sword.

Flinging my body to the side, I moved away from the blade and shoved my knee into his groin. He shouted as he doubled over, freeing me, but the sudden release of his grip made me fall too. Knocked off balance, I scrambled to rise, but he recovered faster and grabbed my shoulder. I reached for my mother's knife and, as he spun me round, struck him on the upper arm with it.

He roared, but the pain wasn't enough for him to let me go. Instead, he punched me in the stomach, seized my knife, and swung his other arm over my neck, putting me in a chokehold. I struggled, but with the air knocked out of me and his arm crushing my windpipe, I couldn't wrestle myself free.

"I've got him!" he called to his friends.

After a few moments, two of the men appeared, and crowded around me. The fourth, and last to arrive, was the scarred man who'd shouted at me in the clearing. I turned my face, pressing my cheek against the fabric of my scarf.

"Who are you?" the scarred man asked.

"Broccan," I replied in a low voice.

The scarred man fingered the sword at his hip. I glanced up then. His frown tightened as he looked me over. Yes, this man was a warrior. Scars covered his hands and lower arms, though all of these were white and faded. It was the scar running down his face that looked fresh. Not like Broccan's, which was from fire. This scar came from a blade. Thin and long, running from his eyebrow to his chin where it puckered. He was lucky he hadn't lost his sight, for the entire white of his left eye was filled with blood.

"What did the man in the church say to you?" he asked.

"Nothing."

"Why are you following us?"

"I'm not."

The scarred man took a step closer. "Don't lie. I double-backed on our route the last three nights and found tracks behind ours."

I shook my head. "That wasn't me. I don't have a horse."

The man with the thin face pressed his arm tighter around my neck. "Are you Norman?" he hissed in my ear.

"No."

"If you are Irish, why did you speak in Frankish and Latin to the men in the church?" the scarred man asked.

"Because they were the languages they used to speak to me."

The three men who stood in front of me looked at each other, disbelief apparent on their faces, the stout man more so than the others. "You are related to a king?" he asked.

"No."

"Then how do you know those languages?"

The man holding me pressed his arm tight around my throat again. I could hardly breathe. "Of course he's not related to a king. Look at the state of his cloak. Listen, boy, why did you run away when Cuan asked you to come to him? We're wearing the colours of the High King."

"I didn't... know... that."

"Liar."

"Is he a fuidir?" the young redhead mused. "Perhaps he is related to a king but has been banished from his clan."

The scarred man narrowed his eyes, and then his lips twitched. He grabbed me from his friend and pulled my scarf from my face. Roughly, he pulled out the tie I'd used to knot my hair. As my long hair slipped loose, my disguise fell away, and the young redhead and the man with the auburn beard began to laugh. The man who had held me moved to the side so he could see what everyone was laughing at. Roughly, he pinched my face. "Pretty," he said, smirking at his companions.

I punched him in the mouth, and he, unprepared for an assault, fell to the ground.

The stout man with the auburn hair burst out laughing. "Scolaí, you must enter the boxing at the Tailteann Fair. You stand a good chance of winning!" He held out a hand to help his friend up, but the scowling man, Scolaí, refused it. His bad grace only made his friend laugh harder.

For a moment they forgot me, and I took a step backward. Could I outrun them if I tried again and didn't stop? They were all still panting. My legs ached... but perhaps...

"Don't move," the scarred man said. The others silenced.

"Leave me alone," I snapped. "I'm on my way to see my uncle who is a monk at Seir Kieran. He won't be happy you stopped me. Indeed, you have no right to do so. I've done nothing wrong." I bit the inside of my cheek. Staring up at the sky, I tried to summon another hailstorm. I needed one to come. I needed to get away.

In two large strides, the scarred man reached me and grabbed my wrist. "I didn't say you could leave. Not yet."

"Why not?"

Through eyes that stung with tears of frustration, I glared. Why hadn't the storm come? I didn't know. I didn't even know how I summoned it before.

Purple in the face, Scolaí held out his arm. "That's right. You can't leave, girl. You've committed a crime by assaulting a king's soldier, twice." He twisted the fabric of his sleeve. "Look. You've drawn blood with your knife."

He pointed to the part of his arm where I had sliced him. He picked up my mother's knife, Fragarach, which had dropped to the ground when he'd disarmed me and flipped it over in his hand. Blood dripped along the blade, and the fabric along his arm was ripped and stained red.

"That's my knife. It was my mother's."

"It's mine now. It can go toward the honour price."

"The what?"

"The *eraic*," he snapped. "You've injured a soldier of the High King. Your clan must pay the fine and the costs of a healer, as is the law."

I paused. "But I don't have a clan."

"Of course you do. What's your family name?"

"All my family is dead except for my uncle. That's why I'm travelling to him."

"Then your uncle can pay."

"He's a monk. He won't be able to."

Scolaí sneered as he spat on the grass. "Priests and monks have more gold than all the kings of Ireland combined. He'll pay."

The young redhead strode over and inspected Scolaí's arm. "Come, Scolaí, it's not that deep."

"She drew blood, Cathal," Scolaí insisted. "The price for injuring a king's warrior is three cumal, which, unlike you, I can't afford to let go. I'm bringing her to the king's brehon. If her uncle wants her, he'll have to pay." He stared at me. "If that's even true. The man we followed was Norman, and he gave her a message. I swear to God I heard her speaking Frankish to him and then Latin to the monk. The king will be very interested to know what was said."

A silence fell over the group until the scarred man nodded. "Fearghus, bring her with us."

"No." Shaking, I tried to pull my hand free from his grip. "This is nonsense. Let me go."

"I'll tell you what," the scarred man said. "If you tell me what the Norman said to you, I'll consider it."

I paused, not knowing what to say. The man had spoken to me, though I had not understood the message. But what if I told them, and it made these men angry? "He didn't say anything."

"If you are going to lie," the scarred man said, "then I'm afraid you must come with us."

The stout man with the wolf cloak unfastened a rope from around his belt and bound my wrists. He was the oldest of the group, maybe close to thirty, though it was hard to tell. "Broccan, is it?" he asked as he tied the knot. "A strange name for a girl."

"My name's Isolde."

"Well, Isolde. I'm Fearghus." He tugged the rope and led me forward. "Where are you from? Your Gaelic sounds strange, even for a northerner."

"That's none of your concern." Tears welled in my eyes as I thought of my home. The island that I had watched burning. I didn't know why, but I didn't want to say the name of it to this man. I didn't want any of them to know anything about me. Glancing up at the sky, I searched for signs of an approaching storm. There was nothing. Just the same pale grey clouds as before. Why? Why wouldn't my gift work when I wanted it to?

Once we'd made our way back out of the forest, Fearghus made me sit by one of the large oak trees while they readied the horses.

"Leave her here, Cuan," the young redhead said to the scarred man. "She'll slow us down, and we need to be at King Magnus' ráth tomorrow, or we'll miss the hunt."

"We can't, Cathal," Cuan replied, putting his hand on the young man's shoulder. "Scolaí's made his accusation and wants to take her to the brehon."

"Do you really think he's going to get anything out of her? She must be a fuidir. What sort of woman dresses in men's clothes and armour? She's of no value to anyone."

"And what about the message the Norman gave to her?" Cuan replied. "Scolaí says he saw her and the Norman speaking. You are right, it is an odd sort of woman that roams these lands dressed like that. Perhaps she is a spy, and if that's even a possibility, we shouldn't let her go. Not until my uncle has seen her first."

I didn't like this. Any of this. I needed to find Seir Kieran, not be taken to a king's dun by a group of men I did not know or trust. Wriggling my wrists, I tried to loosen the knots, but to no avail. Fearghus had bound them tight.

Cathal kicked his foot against a tree. "I swear, if I could kill Diarmait Mac Murchadha, I would. All this talk of him bringing the Normans to our land makes me sick. Why doesn't he just go to war with us with his own men and be done with it? Why does he feel the need to invite these strangers to our land?"

"Don't get carried away, Cathal," Scolaí said. "There won't be a war. Diarmait's sixty and tired. If he's fool enough to go to war again, we'll easily drive away any Norman army he's managed to cobble together."

"Maybe," Fearghus replied. "But the King of Osraige blinded Diarmait's son. Revenge is on his mind, mark my words. I think we'll go to war no matter what King Ruaidrí does."

Scolaí shook his head then turned to stare at Cuan. "What do you think? Perhaps you have more sympathy for Diarmait than the rest of us? The blinding of a prince is a terrible thing, no?" There was a sinister edge to his question and from the shrouded looks the others gave each other, I sensed a hidden meaning lurked behind

Scolaí's words. I stopped struggling then, remembering Broccan's words once more.

What do you do if you cannot run?

You wait and you watch and prepare yourself for battle.

Cuan mounted his horse. "Yes, the blinding of a man is a terrible thing, but it doesn't give me any sympathy for Diarmait Mac Murchadha."

Scolaí snorted.

"Be quiet, Scolaí," Cathal said. "Why do you always have to argue?"

"I wasn't arguing. It's no insult to say a blind man is blind."

Cathal walked over to his horse and hoisted himself onto its back. "Come on, let's go. We need to find somewhere to camp for the night. It's going to be dark soon."

Fearghus grabbed my rope and brought me over to the large black horse Cuan sat on and tied the rope to the reins of Cuan's horse.

"This is Sleipnir," Cuan said. "Mind you don't pull too hard on the rope, or he'll let you know he doesn't like it."

Without another word, he pushed his horse into a walk, leaving me to follow behind them. The pace was brisk, and my legs already ached, but I would not show that I was tired. I would not show weakness. It was difficult, though. My legs, they began to shake, and my mouth filled with the same black fluid from this morning. I spat it out, trying to stop myself from vomiting as I did so.

As night approached, Cuan called for the men to halt. "We'll stay in the tents tonight. Over there." He pointed to a small grouping of trees in the distance.

No one argued as we made our way there. Cuan tied my rope around the branch of a tree and then helped the others erect the tent.

Once they had finished, Scolaí lit a small fire, and the others took food from their bags. Cathal offered me some stale bread and berries, but my rope remained tied to the tree, and he didn't bring me over to the fire. I pulled my cloak about me for warmth and lay tight against the trunk to shield myself from the night breeze.

They laughed around the campfire as they ate, although I couldn't make out their words. After a while, I turned my head to look away from them. The events of the last few days suddenly became too much for me and tears began to stream down the sides of my cheeks.

So many thoughts came and went as I lay there. My gift had come to me when the Fomorians chased me. It had come without me asking for it. Why then, when I needed it again, would it not work? Why were my legs still shaking? Affraic had said that it was a reaction to using my gift without knowing how to control it, but how long would this last? It was as if I could feel my strength leaching into the soil and ebbing away.

And if that continued to happen, how would I ever escape?

Closing my eyes, fatigue began to take me over. The darkness of sleep pulled me closer, and I was glad for it. For at the edges of my mind I could see fire. I could see it spreading all around me until everything was alight.

Isolde

Kingdom of Ulaid

The sky above the horizon reddened as the sun rose. Like blood seeping from a wound, it spread upward and outward, until low-hanging clouds buffered it from the blue expanse above. A red sky was an ill-omen, or so Broccan always said, but what was left to fear after all that had happened?

The night had passed by way of fitful dreams and numbing discomfort. The rope dug into my arms whenever I lay back against the tree trunk, and several times I'd had to stand to allow blood back into my fingers. For many hours, I'd given up trying to sleep. It was hopeless in any case, for every time I closed my eyes, I saw images of fire, of Broccan telling me to run, and of the Fomorian man holding out his hand for me to take. I felt the wind swirling around me, a voice upon it speaking words I could not understand, and I heard Affraic's screams. I did not want to think on such things. Could not. Instead, I turned my mind toward escape.

What do you do if you cannot run and cannot fight?

You wait and you watch and prepare yourself for the battle to come. And watch, I would. Then, as soon as the first opportunity presented, I would be gone. I just had to bide my time. Despite last night's poor sleep, my body felt better this morning, and the shaking had subsided. I was determined that the next time I ran, I'd run so fast that none of these men would catch me. Until then, I'd watch and learn about their strengths and weaknesses as Broccan had taught me.

I couldn't help but feel some regret when I thought of my gift.

Regret that it had taken so long to show. Despair that I might have helped Broccan instead of leaving him, and that I might have saved Affraic so that she'd not had to give her life to save mine. I also wished I could control my gift. If I could use it at will, I wouldn't have to wait and watch. I could simply summon another storm and leave as it rained havoc on those who held me captive.

The run of my thoughts was finally interrupted by noise coming from the tent. It was time to watch, and I cleared my mind of the painful memories that had found me.

Scolaí and Cathal were the first of the men to rise. Scolaí relit the fire and prepared the breakfast while Cathal got dressed. This surprised me. Given that Cathal was the younger of the two, I had expected him to do the more menial tasks. I found it interesting that he did not, and my gaze slid to the golden brooch on the young man's cloak. He was rich. Important. Too important to be serving others.

The other two woke shortly after, and the four of them filled their bowls with the broth Scolaí had made. Only once they'd satisfied their own appetites did they glance my way. I leaned back against the tree and stretched as if I had just woken and not been watching them all along.

"Come and have some food," Cuan said. He came over and untied the knot around the tree.

My skin was rough underneath the rope, and I rotated my wrists to push the blood back into my fingers. Cuan noted the redness, but said nothing, and waited patiently for me to stand. I did not want to eat with these men, but to escape I needed to build up my energy, so without a word of complaint, I made my way over to the fire and took a bowl of broth from Fearghus.

While I ate, Fearghus and Scolaí folded up the tents, and Cuan put out the fire. Cathal continued to eat, taking a second helping of the broth.

"How long shall it take us to reach the dun?" Cathal asked, once he finished his last spoonful.

Fearghus sniffed. "By this afternoon. Even with the girl slowing us down." He gave the young man a grin. "Don't worry. You shall make the hunt."

Cathal eyed me, a petulant look on his face, but then he sighed. "You can ride with me today. I'm lighter than the others."

Nodding, I ate my last spoonful. I could have argued and said I'd prefer to walk, but making this hunt seemed important to the young man with the golden brooch and I didn't want to antagonise him. No. I wanted them all to forget about me.

Cathal stood, washed out his bowl, and readied his horse. The others did the same.

Once Cathal was mounted, he held out his hand to pull me up.

"Can you remove the rope?" I asked, holding out my arms. "It will make riding easier."

Scolaí shoved me forward. "No chance. Up you go. And no more talk."

Like yesterday, the landscape was full of trees and rivers. The forest paths were narrow, though they appeared to be used often, and so high were the trees that I couldn't keep track of the sun.

The men did not speak to each other as we rode, aside from questions about the direction of King Magnus' dun. I feigned disinterest but absorbed all they said. Names, places, pathways and rivers. These were all their markers, and I no longer wondered why. The forests on the mainland were so thick and endless. One could get lost in there and never find a way out. I stared along the line of trees that ran as far as the eye could see. Watched as the leaves swirled with the wind. A voice seemed to whisper words within it. Low, so low I could hardly hear it.

Are you listening to me, child?

"Did you say something to me?" I asked Cathal.

The young man shook his head.

Frowning, I looked back into the forest. The wind had gone now, the air had stilled, and when I glanced upward, the sun was shining. But for all that, something within me felt ill at ease. Something was wrong. Very wrong.

"Are you sure—"

"Look! There's King Magnus' dun!" Cathal shouted.

A sense of dread filled me as we rode out of the forest. The dun stood on top of a large hill in the distance, and its high stone wall towered over the land. Even from here, it looked huge compared to any of the ráths or churches I'd seen, but it was only as we got closer that I realised how truly big it was, not to mention the three trenches dug around the lower circumference of the hill.

We dismounted at the entrance gate. Three heavyset guards greeted us and spoke with Fearghus and Cuan in a tone that implied familiarity, and they allowed us to pass while the horses were led away toward a stable within the dun grounds.

"Let me take off Isolde's rope," Fearghus said to Cuan as we passed through. "Don't have her presented to a king like a beggar."

Cuan glanced at me, his eyes catching the stains over my woollen clothes, shrugged, and walked ahead with Cathal.

Fearghus took this as a yes and began to untie the knot. Scolaí, however, ran over and clasped hold of the rope. "Don't. What if she escapes? She's been planning to ever since we caught her. Cunning, this one is. A spy, I'm convinced of it now."

"If she escapes King Magnus' dun, she'll make a better soldier of the Fianna than you or me. Look how many guards he has patrolling the boundary."

"She's a spy," Scolaí insisted. "Which means she's not to be trusted."

"I'm not a spy," I muttered, though neither of them paid me any attention.

Fearghus' face grew solemn as he stared at Scolaí, though he continued to untie the knot. "If she is a spy, she cannot escape once inside. On the other hand, if she is the niece of a monk, like she said, we should treat her accordingly."

Scolaí glowered as Fearghus finished untying the rope, though he stormed on ahead rather than argue further.

"Thank you," I whispered to Fearghus, though I was unsure as to why he was being so kind. None of the men had spoken to me as we journeyed, and I had not expected any change to my treatment once we arrived at the dun.

"There's no need to thank me. Besides, you won't try to escape, will you?"

"Of course not."

"And why would you want to? King Magnus is a generous host to his guests." He looked around the dun, a smile returning to his lips. "I bet you've never seen any dwelling so fine?"

"No, never," I answered, and this was true. As Móirne had despaired, there were no kings on Rathlin. No one to look after us. It was an island of shepherds and fishermen. These thoughts brought a fresh wave of pain as a memory of Rathlin, untarnished by the fire, came to mind.

I looked around as Fearghus urged me forward, looking at the parts of the dun that he pointed to. The stables. The feasting hall. Fearghus was right. This dun was the largest structure I'd ever seen. Rathlin had small families where a simple ráth was enough, but here, well, there were maybe as many as fifty people living inside the high stone walls. And as we walked inside, I noted at least twelve houses situated behind the stables, though Fearghus wasn't looking at them. His eyes were focused on the large feasting hall in the centre. This building was unusual and made wholly of stone. Broccan had told me of the Viking halls before, made of wood and thatch rather than the wattle ráths the Irish lived in. This, however, seemed neither Viking nor Irish. It was something new altogether.

The fort doors, made of thick oak, opened as we approached, and another guard led us inside.

I expected a building of this size to contain several rooms, but I was wrong. The fort consisted of only one space, filled with timber benches that ran along the length of it, with fires burning at each side. One table at the back was placed perpendicular to the rest, and a crowd of men and women gathered here. The chairs behind this table were ornate, with engraved crest rails and legs, though only one man sat. Dressed in fine silks, he had a lined face and long black-grey hair that hung limp over his shoulders.

"Greetings, King Magnus mac Duinn Sléibe," Cathal said.

The king greeted the men I'd travelled with by name, asked how they were, and told a young woman standing behind them to fetch some food and wine. Once the men had answered his questions, he inclined his head toward me. "Who is this?"

"This is Isolde," Cuan answered.

King Magnus motioned for another of the women standing behind him to come forward. "Granddaughter, this is our guest. Make sure she has comfortable quarters."

"Isolde is the name she has given us," Scolaí said, edging forward, "but I'm not convinced, for we found her alone in the church by the River Gleann Seisce. I think she's nothing more than a criminal or perhaps even a Norman spy, for I heard her speaking the Norman language to another at the church there. And what's more, she drew blood from me when she tried to escape. She may be a danger to your granddaughters, King Magnus."

King Magnus stood and moved to the edge of his table, frowning. "She speaks to Normans, does she?" He looked into my eyes. "Are you Norman, girl? You look too innocent to be devious, but you can never tell these days. It wouldn't be the first time Diarmait Mac Murchadha has used a woman to get his own way." His lips pressed together as he waited for my response.

"I'm not a spy," I said. "I'm from Rathlin Island. I've lived there my whole life."

The king grunted. "Then why have you left? Where's the rest of your family?"

"Dead, my king. There was a great fire on the island. I am travelling to my uncle who is a monk at Seir Kieran." The shaking returned to my hands as I said this out loud and the memory of the fire burning flashed in my mind.

"What of Scolaí's allegations? Did you truly injure him trying to escape?"

"Yes, she did," Cuan said, interrupting Scolaí, who'd been on the cusp of answering for me. "Scolaí wants to bring her to the High King to put his charge before the brehon. She says she did not know the High King's colours."

King Magnus grunted again. I wasn't sure if it was in agreement or not, and he picked up his knife, set the tip onto the wood of his plate and began to spin it around. "Tell the High King," he said, "to find out if she's a spy while questioning her, and if she's found to be Norman, I'll cut out her tongue myself. That sleekit King of Leinster seems set on inviting them into our land to fight for him, and I would do all I can to keep them away." His eyes moved from my neck to my feet and back up again.

"Shall I bring her to our rooms, Grandfather?" his granddaughter asked.

The king shook his head and turned his gaze back to Cuan. "If her character is in doubt, she cannot sleep in the fort with my kinswomen. She's already shown herself to be violent and therefore doesn't hold the status of a guest." He took a sip from the silver cup in front of him. "You can tie her up in the stables. Old Naoise stays with the horses and will ensure she's protected."

Cuan nodded.

King Magnus clapped his hands together. "Come then, let us eat and get ready to hunt. My men have tracked a herd of deer just a little north of here."

I held my head high and didn't resist as Fearghus escorted me out of the fort. Scolaí smirked as I passed him by, but giving him further pleasure through showing my misery was unthinkable, and so I didn't scowl or show any sign that I was displeased with the king's verdict. I'd slept out in the night air last night. A bed of hay was no true punishment.

The stables consisted of a large wattle-and-daub building where internal rows of wooden posts and gates separated the horses. Fearghus gestured for me to go into one of the empty stalls, took out the rope, and tied my arm to a post.

"Now, don't be any bother. King Magnus is a paranoid man with no sympathy for his enemies. Unfortunately, that's what you are to him now. Best he forgets you're here." He finished the knot tightly. "Old Naoise is honest. He won't let any harm come to you."

A tall man tended to the horses at the back of the stables and Fearghus went over to speak to him for a minute and then left.

"Fearghus," I called after him.

He stopped and met my gaze.

"How long am I going to be like this?" I held up my arms and the rope that bound them.

"We will be hunting today, maybe tomorrow too, if it goes well."

I nodded my head and, with that, Fearghus walked away.

The rest of the day passed slowly and as the sun set, the heat faded. I lay on the floor, huddling against the straw. I hugged my knees tight to keep in what little heat I had and stared at the guarded dun entrance. The warriors there changed often. Others patrolled the walls. But what about at nighttime? Would they be so zealous then in their watch? Keeping my eyes open, I watched the gate, even as the sun disappeared behind the horizon.

Escape wouldn't come easy – but it would come. I was further south than yesterday. That was good. The time of watching and waiting was almost over, and as soon as I could, I would escape. I had to.

I had to.

Gormflaith

Chepstow

The first job I was given at Chepstow was gathering water for the cooking fires. I took the bucket they gave me and trudged back and forth without complaint. I used this as an opportunity to get my bearings, to see who was important and where the guards were stationed, but in truth it was a hateful job. The skin on my fingers peeled and I'd begun to smell like the mud I trudged in. I'd have to find a way to elevate myself and soon.

On my fourth day of living as a kitchen wench, I went outside, my empty bucket in hand and walked to the river. This time, there was a man standing by the riverbank. I knew, even without him looking my way, that it was Olaf.

He was handsome when he did not realise he was in my presence. More like how he used to be. That would change as soon as he saw me, and then he'd slither on his belly if I asked him to. It made my skin crawl, and yet I could not release him or put him out of his misery. This undying devotion had its uses.

I walked toward him and sat on one of the benches that the fishermen used to gut their fish, feigning a sore ankle.

"What happened, Olaf?" I asked. "Where are the others?"

Olaf jumped on hearing my voice, then ran to my side, reaching out to hold my hands. "Broccan is dead, my love. So is the girl."

"Don't touch me." I snatched my hand away. Two women, both of whom were cleaning clams and molluscs from the riverbed, glanced over at us. "People are watching. Pretend that you are cleaning up the fish guts and try to make it look like we are not talking."

Olaf smiled despite my chastisement. Strange. Usually, a scolding was enough for him to beg for forgiveness or sulk, but not today. He had given me good news, yes, but there was something in his voice, something about the way he would not look me in the eye that let me know there was more news to follow.

"And?"

"Your brother is dead. Máelmórda died fighting the warrior, though Donnchad killed Broccan afterward."

I slumped forward. My breath left me. Máelmórda was dead?

I had sent my brother to fight Broccan and to kill the daughter of Fódla, and I knew he might die. Yet I was still somehow unprepared for this news. Tears streamed down my face, fool that I was. He had done much to hurt me, Máelmórda, but he had saved me too. He was my brother. A brother I had been raised to serve and one who had betrayed me many times, but still he had been my only family for so long.

And now he was gone.

"What of the others?"

"Donnchad killed Broccan and the other two Descendants. One was a witch. The other was Fódla's girl."

"Are you sure she is dead?"

"Yes. I saw her lying dead in the water. She had no pulse. I made sure to check."

"Then it was worth it." I took a deep breath and wiped at the wetness of my cheek. "What of Angelo? Did he take the witch gift?"

"No. Cecile did. She's still in her fevered state."

"Cecile took the gift? Not Angelo?"

"Angelo was injured in the fight and has not yet woken from his injuries."

Seething, I ran my hand through my hair. Máelmórda, as self-serving as he'd always been, at least listened to me. Donnchad, once again, had proved that he could not be trusted. Cecile was not strong enough to take a gift. She would almost certainly die, and at the most inopportune time. If we wanted to integrate ourselves into this Anglo-Norman society, marriage was a good way, and Cecile, for all her weaknesses, was beautiful enough that we might have matched her well.

"Where is my son?"

"He has only just recovered from his own fever, for he took the warrior gift from Broccan. He has purchased a horse and cart and is bringing Cecile and Angelo here. I thought I'd come on ahead to see what you thought best."

Donnchad now had the warrior gift? Two gifts. Ambitious boy. He would wear it better than Máelmórda, and yet, I did not like it. He, once again, was trying to surpass me.

"Yes. Thank you, Olaf. You did well."

Olaf bowed, a red flush rising into his cheeks.

"Tell Donnchad to meet me outside the castle kitchens when he arrives. He can tell one of the maids he is my brother, and I will come out to meet him."

I continued to rub my ankle as he walked away.

"Was he troubling you?" one of the washerwomen asked.

"Yes," I replied. "He's a chancer. Did you see him try to take my hand?"

The washerwoman nodded. "I'll tell the other girls to keep a watch out. So many strangers are coming into the city. There's bound to be a few that are best avoided."

Later that day, Donnchad came to the castle. One of the kitchen maids fetched me and I made my way outside. Moving out of earshot, we walked toward the forge. Sombre, he held out his hand to take mine. "I am sorry, Mother. Máelmórda fell."

"So I heard from Olaf. What happened?"

"He was hasty as he always is. He fought well, but his impatience was his undoing."

"And where he failed, you succeeded?"

"Yes. I have fire and water at my command, and I was able to use my gifts to push Broccan from a cliff."

"You took his warrior gift, I hear." I smiled. "Fomorian, cup-bearer and warrior. You are now formidable indeed."

"It was a risk, but I did it for us. To win back Ireland, we must be brave."

Yes, this was true. Fortune did not favour the weak. Máelmórda had never quite understood that. "What of Cecile and Angelo?"

"Cecile woke from her fever this morning. She is still fragile, but she survived. Angelo… he is not well. During the fight, the witch used her magic against him to summon a hailstorm, and it shattered the back of his skull. Time, I'm afraid, will tell if he recovers."

A slow, sinking feeling washed over me. Angelo was my grandson, the only one who I felt I had any sway over. I did not delude myself that he loved me, but he did not love anyone else either. Not even his own father. To lose him and Máelmórda would be a heavy blow indeed.

"Tell Olaf to look after them for the evening. You should go into the feasting hall. The lord here is called Strongbow, and he has gathered his knights, archers and foot soldiers. The last of them arrived this morning, which means tonight they will talk of an invasion into Ireland. You should be there to listen to what they say."

"Will you be there?"

"Of course." I showed him my hands, stained by the mixing of fruits that I had rubbed into the meat. "I'm the new kitchen maid."

That evening, I helped serve the men who had come to Strongbow's call. While I cleared away the tables and fetched new pitchers of ale or wine when requested, Donnchad sat and feasted. As it always was and always will be, the men rested while the women worked.

Strongbow sat at the top table, eating and feasting with the men who'd spoken to David earlier. Robert and Meilyr sat on his right, while Le Gros and a Flemish man called Maurice de Prendergast sat on his left. Despite David's insistence that Strongbow was a renowned fighter before he fell out of favour with King Henry II by siding with Stephen of Blois, he didn't look impressive to me. He was slender. Bald. Morose, even in laughter. He reminded me of Sitric when he was in low spirits, which was never a good comparison for any man.

Those around him, however… they were beasts of war. They longed for it. I watched the knights speak. Oh, they reminded me of Amlav. The way that their eyes gleamed at the thought of taking new lands. Brian had never been this way. He warred and he fought, but it weighed on him. Murchad was the same. Máelmórda had longed for the results of battle, but never for the battle itself.

Only Amlav had truly enjoyed the slaughter of the day, and these men, they seemed to be of his ilk. These Normans were Viking-descended. Somehow, that lust for death still flowed in their veins. Perhaps the rain of England and Ireland had watered the blood of the Vikings who had settled here.

As I cleared away, I noted a man enter the hall, dressed in the Irish fashion, with long braided hair and a long beard. I watched him as he moved along the hall and bowed as he reached Strongbow.

Strongbow leaned forward, those dull eyes sharpening. Robert, who sat beside him, stilled.

"Speak," Strongbow said.

The Irishman did, first in incomprehensible French, then once it was clear no one could follow him, he began to speak in my mother tongue. A chill ran up my spine to hear it spoken by another. I'd not heard it in some time. Angelo and Cecilia favoured the language of the countries we had found sanctuary within. Even Máelmórda and Donnchad, brought up in the Irish language, did not like to speak it. It reminded them of dark days, they said, though if anyone had endured the darkness of Ireland, it had been me.

Strongbow glanced at one of his men. "What did he say?"

The man, Hervey, I thought his name was, moved forward, but I could tell that he was already too full of wine to wrap his mind around the strange sounds the Irishman had spoken. The Irishman was asked to repeat the message.

"He has come from Diarmait Mac Murchadha," Hervey said. "He once again offers you… women… I think he says. Or it might be cattle."

Strongbow leaned back in his chair. "I have no wish for more cattle. I've no wish for more women, either." He waved the Irishman away, gesturing to a seat at one of the long tables where he might avail of food and ale.

Cautiously, I stepped forward and curtseyed low to Strongbow.

"My lord," I said. "My mother was Irish. That is not quite what the messenger said, if you beg my pardon for interrupting your feast."

Strongbow eyed me over, unsmiling, but not angry. "You are Irish?"

"No, my lord. My mother was Irish. My father was Norman, like yourselves." I made sure to speak in my best French, as if this and this alone was my native tongue.

"Who was he?"

"He was a trader, my lord. His name was Francis."

"Go on then," Strongbow said. "What did this Irishman say?"

"The message speaks on behalf of King Diarmait Mac Murchadha. The message is that if anyone wishes to have land or wealth, horses, weapons or chargers, gold or silver, he will give him very generous payments. If anyone wants pasture and livestock and a rich fief, he will satisfy him."

Strongbow glanced at his man, Hervey, who reluctantly nodded that my translation was superior to his.

"He speaks once more of land," Strongbow said. "He must be desperate."

Robert shrugged as he picked at the chicken leg on his plate. "We should go. Why not? If there is land to claim, we should take it."

"King Henry will not allow it," Strongbow answered. "Any land we take is to be in his name. He might let us fight for it. I doubt he will let us keep it."

"He might. What is Ireland to him? Besides, Diarmait gives it to you willingly. All you have to do is marry his daughter, Ava, or so he promised when you spoke before."

Strongbow pursed his lips. "Yes. That is true."

I bowed again. "I beg your pardon, my lord, but that is not how the law works in Ireland. A king does not own his land. The clan does. And in any case, a daughter cannot rule, and men cannot claim kingship through the female line. So, any marriage you make to King Diarmait's daughter will not mean you are king, nor will it make a king of any children you have together."

Strongbow threw down the meat he was holding in his hands, jaw tightening.

"There is a way to invade."

Everyone in the hall turned around to see who had spoken. The man stood and bowed to Strongbow. Donnchad. What was he doing? I had told him to listen. Not to speak.

"You are?" Strongbow asked, his small eyes narrowing.

"My name is Donatien, though people call me Donn. You just spoke to my sister, Alys."

Strongbow leaned forward. "And why would you help?" He licked his lips, his gaze hard. "I am always suspicious of those who come to me claiming they are my friend when I do not know them."

"There is nothing but the truth on my lips. I am a skilled fighter and wish to use my God-given gifts. All I wish for in return is honest payment. That's all."

This made Strongbow laugh. "Then speak, pauper. Tell me your secrets."

"Our mother was of Munster, the southern kingdom. Her grandmother said that when Brian Boru's son, Donnchad, was driven out of Ireland, he went to Rome. Donnchad begged the Pope to send an army to aid him in reclaiming his land, for the Irish had fallen back to pagan ways and they needed to be cleansed once again of their sin. The Pope refused him that day but said one day soon he'd send a force to assess the Irish conversion. I assure you it is still an ungodly country."

"You would have me go to Rome to beg an army?"

Some of the men laughed at this.

"No. You have your own men. I merely wanted to say that going to Ireland for the sake of conversion is slightly different to an invasion." Donnchad smiled. "What if you went to Ireland, not as a groom nor as a man seeking to be granted land, but as a man leading a crusade? As a man who would return Ireland to the true faith."

Strongbow leaned back in his chair, not giving anything away through his expression, but his fingers drummed softly against the table. His posture tightened. "You are ambitious, Donn. I will give you that. But I think not. I think not. King Henry would not allow it unless he was the head of the army."

Donnchad bowed his head and sat back down with the other archers and foot soldiers, while I returned to clearing the tables.

As the evening turned to night, the hall emptied. The foot soldiers and archers left for the taverns outside, where the women and whores had gathered. After I'd finished my chores, I made my way over to David and poured him a cup of wine. He did not lift his head as I did this. Did not smile or even look at me.

"Your brother spoke well earlier," he said, eyes fixed on his cup.

"He did," I replied. "I hope he can be of assistance to you."

"Oh, I am not going to Ireland. Le Gros wants us to stay put for now."

"I see."

"Robert FitzStephen and Maurice de Prendergast are going instead. Forty knights, three hundred archers and two hundred and sixty foot soldiers. It's enough that Strongbow is honouring his oaths to Diarmait, but not enough men that King Henry can claim he is launching an invasion in his own right."

"That's clever."

"Strongbow is clever."

I sat down beside him, lowering myself so as to try to catch his gaze, but it did not work. David continued to stare at the cup. "What is wrong, David? Something has upset you. Please tell me what it is."

"Strongbow has asked if your brother would go with Robert FitzStephen. He's sending his cousin Hervey with the army too, but he'd like to have someone who knows the language and customs better. While your brother is away, Strongbow has also asked for you to remain here as his guest. You have a sister too, don't you? She's to stay here also."

"That is good news, is it not? This means we can be together."

"Guest is the name you've been given, Alys. But really, you are to be held as a hostage to ensure that your brother does as Robert and Maurice ask him."

"Donn will do as they ask, I promise."

"We cannot marry, Alys. If you are a hostage, we cannot."

"Strongbow said this?"

"Yes. Afterward, we can marry, but not yet."

The reason for his ill-humour now apparent, all I could do was sit beside him and kiss his hand. "It will be a torment, my love, but if you can bear to wait for me, it will be my greatest honour to wait for you."

Slowly, David lifted his head. A slow smile building, his eyes finally met mine.

Isolde

Kingdom of Ulaid

My time in the stables passed slowly. Rather than the one or two days Fearghus had promised, it ended up being six. During this time, Naoise and his wife gave me food and allowed me to wash, but aside from that, no one came to see me.

It was a lonely existence, but I occupied myself by watching the comings and goings of the warriors. Five times a day, the eight guards at the gate would switch with another eight, and at similar intervals, fresh warriors replaced the men positioned along the dun wall. Predictable and monotonous, it was done to keep the men alert in case of an attack.

But it made escape impossible, too.

Escape, I decided, would have to wait until the men who'd found me decided to leave, but this realisation was an unpleasant one because it meant doing nothing until then. At times, this stagnation made me panic. What if the Fomorians found me and I could not run?

I had to breathe deep to stop this panic from taking me over. They weren't looking for me, I told myself. They had left my body floating in the lough water, which meant Affraic's plan had worked. They thought I was dead.

And yet... they could be in Ireland somewhere this very moment. What if their pursuit of power led them to this dun, and they saw me hiding in the shadows?

Deciding it was best to conceal my face and hair with my cloak, I hid, turning my face away from the stable boys who came in to tend to the horses. I watched and I listened instead. I slept and I ate… and I tried not to remember.

That was the hardest thing about being alone – even more so when the darkness came, and my eyes grew heavy. Flashes of the fire on Rathlin would play in my mind. Broccan's farewell. Affraic's arm reaching out to pull me into the boat.

What if I'd run faster? What if I'd discovered my gift sooner? If only Affraic and I had reached Broccan's land in time. With those questions, tears came, and once they started, it was almost impossible to stop.

On the seventh day, as I lay dozing, a horn sounded out from one of the guards who stood by the gate. "Make way for the king," another guard shouted.

Moments later, the hunting party rode in through the gate. The king rode in first, followed by Cuan and Cathal. The young redhead grinned and laughed, while Cuan's gaze flitted around the dun. Fearghus and Scolaí came in at the back of the hunting party, both deep in conversation with the other men. I hoped the hunt had tired them. That was my biggest wish. It would make escaping all the easier when we left. But as I looked over at them, I could not discover any signs of fatigue before they moved out of my line of vision. Soon after, Naoise and his stable boys led in a group of horses, sweaty and covered in mud, while the hunting party disappeared into the feasting hall.

As the day passed, the dun came alive with activity. The old stablemaster wasn't the only one who was working hard. The king's return had invigorated all the occupants. Serving boys and girls ran back and forth to the main fort carrying an endless supply of furniture and firewood. Outside, fires were lit, and the catches of the hunt were roasted upon them. The sweet smell of venison and stew filled the air.

When the sun began to set, guests of the king arrived. The stables filled with more horses while their owners walked into the feasting hall. I stared at their silk dresses, embroidered tunics, cloaks and golden jewellery which glowed orange against the dying sunlight. Who were all these people dressed so finely? Móirne would never believe it if I tried to describe the dresses and jewels to her. I had not imagined that such creations of beauty existed.

A young serving girl half ran, half stumbled into the stables. She held out a plate of hot food for Naoise but gave nothing to me. Naoise handed me his bread, and I reached up to take it.

"No," the girl said. "She is to attend the feast."

Naoise's eyes opened wide. "She can't go in looking like that."

The girl bit her lip as her gaze ran over the layer of dirt my clothing had accumulated since I'd arrived at the dun. "King Magnus said she must."

Naoise huffed, but at the girl's insistence, he untied the knot from the post and handed it over.

The girl took off and I hurried after her, stopping only once I reached the entrance of the feasting hall. The large hall was full, with every wooden bench taken up by the king's family, warriors and guests.

The girl removed the rope from around my wrist, then waved at me to hurry. Reluctantly, I followed her inside. Bitter scents of ale and sweat hit me as I ventured over the threshold, but it was the noise that struck me the most – such a din that I wanted to put my hands over my ears.

Taking a few steps, I watched. Everyone was busy talking and laughing. The king sat in his chair at the centre of the top table, and to my surprise, Cathal and Cuan sat beside him. Cathal looked flushed, his cheeks almost as red as his hair. I wondered if it was the heat or the line of eight young women who sat to his right that had caused such a reaction. These women were all extravagantly dressed, with long shining curls that hung over their shoulders. Two of them, however, wore more gems than the others. The first, a young woman with black hair, was so bedecked with jewels her whole being sparkled as the light from the candles refracted against her. The second woman had long chestnut hair which was covered with golden and silver orbs, sitting upon her head like dewdrops upon the morning grass.

"Over there." The serving girl pointed at the far left of the hall and I nodded. Lowering my head, I hurried to the space at the end of the bench. This was a good seat. Away from the front. Away from the king and his unkind eyes. When I got closer, however, I realised Fearghus and Scolaí were seated on the bench opposite mine.

Fearghus raised his hands in greeting as I sat opposite him. "You've been released from captivity." His smile faltered as he picked off a stray piece of hay that had stuck to my arm. "Didn't they let you bathe?"

"Yes, but I wasn't able to wash my clothes." I shifted my weight to the edge of the seat, noting that several empty platters of food were spread across the table. "How was the hunting?"

"Splendid," Fearghus slammed his cup on the table. "I felled a deer and a boar."

"Congratulations."

Fearghus grunted, clearly noting the dryness of my reply. "King Magnus' hunting trip went on longer than I expected. How was everything here?"

"Fine. Does this mean King Magnus has agreed I'm not a spy after all?"

"That's not for King Magnus to decide," Fearghus replied as he pierced the last bit of meat on his plate with a knife. "You've still to speak to the High King and his brehon."

"Then why am I here?"

"Young Cathal agreed to pay a surety." Fearghus waved over one of the serving girls, holding his empty cup above his head. "He insisted as you're in our company, the king should treat you like a guest, and lucky for you, King Magnus was in a good mood when the request was made. The fact he felled two deer himself might have been why."

"So, if I do anything wrong, Cathal will have to pay for it?" I asked, confused by the word surety and its implications.

Fearghus nodded.

"Then I'd better not break anything."

He sniggered. "No one's worried about the furniture."

"What else could I do wrong?"

Fearghus cleared his throat and took a drink of wine. "If you were a Norman spy, you might have sins like murder on your mind. The fine just for injuring a member of a king's family could reach one hundred cows, and believe me, King Magnus never forgets a debt." He eyed me then, as if trying to work out whether I might have such things as murder on my mind.

Licking my lips, I worked at not letting confusion cloud my features. "Cathal can rest easy. I've no intention of hurting anyone and I'm not a spy. I don't know how many times I must say so before you will believe me."

Fearghus, only half listening, roared with delight as a serving girl placed a fresh platter of sliced venison in the centre of the table.

Scolaí, who had been speaking to the man beside him, spun around to take a slice, tutting as Fearghus grabbed three and then shoved one into his mouth. "Do you have to act like a pig around your food?"

"I'm from a big family," Fearghus spat. "If you don't eat quick, you don't eat."

Deciding not to be slow to get my own food, I took two slices of meat from the platter. If I was to escape, I needed to be well-fed before we left.

Between bites, I examined my surroundings. It was a grand hall, richly furnished, but I found my eyes returning to the top table. King Magnus talked to Cuan, though he continued to gaze around the room. Occasionally, his attention drifted to the black-haired woman wearing all the jewellery, but aside from that, he seemed disinterested in the many guests who had come to attend his feast.

"Are they the king's daughters?" I whispered to Fearghus, who was picking meat off a rib bone.

He glanced at the top table. "No. They are granddaughters. All except for the woman with the black hair on his right. She's his *adaltrach*."

"His what?"

"No one on Rathlin ever had an adaltrach?"

I shook my head.

"She's a second wife. He has two."

"Oh."

Fearghus laughed at the expression of incredulity that swept across my face. "Lots of men have more than one wife. Some kings have three or four. Was there no man on Rathlin with two wives?"

"No. I think the men were all too poor for that."

I glanced up at this second wife. She was so young compared to the man she sat beside. I cleared my face of emotion. Letting Fearghus see surprise was one thing, disgust, another. I took a bite of food. "So, which one is his first wife?"

"Oh, she's in the nunnery at Clonmacnoise. Been there for a few years now."

While Fearghus picked up another slice of venison from the platter, I looked up and down the line of women again. The woman with the golden orbs in her long brown hair didn't smile as she ate, rather she scowled at the other young woman who sat beside her, especially whenever she tried to converse.

"Who is the woman with the orbs in her hair?"

"That's the king's granddaughter. Third eldest of his second son. Or maybe fourth eldest. Nuala, I think." He squinted a little but then shrugged. "They all look quite similar. It's hard to tell sometimes."

"Why does she have more jewels on her than the others?"

"She is to be married at the Tailteann games to King Tigernán Ua Ruairc of Bréifne. She's wearing her dowry. That is why King Magnus had the hunt and invited the guests today. So they can witness her wearing her finery before the marriage contract is drawn up."

"Is she going to be an adaltrach too?"

"No. King Tigernán has divorced his first wife. She's in a nunnery now, too."

I stared at Fearghus, eyes narrowed.

"Don't tell me that the men on Rathlin don't divorce their wives?"

"I've heard of it happening, but in truth, there were only three other families living there. I did think that if you were a queen, it wouldn't... Well, I didn't think a king would want to divorce his queen." I gazed up at the woman, Nuala, wearing the golden orbs, wondering what sort of life awaited her. "What did King Tigernán's first wife do that warranted a divorce?"

Fearghus pressed his forefinger against his lips. "Derbhfhorgaill deserved it well enough. If you want my advice, I wouldn't bring her up."

Intrigued, I lowered my voice. "That sounds interesting."

"It's hardly a secret, but I must say, it was shocking when it happened." Fearghus leaned forward. "She ran away with the King of Leinster, Diarmait Mac Murchadha, about fifteen years ago. She returned to Bréifne a year later, but with no honour price, and it still angers King Tigernán that he was disgraced. For not only did he feel the shame of his wife leaving him, but it was for his sworn enemy."

"The queen ran away with another king? For love?"

"Some say that, but most believe her brother told her to do it, so he could make a new alliance. She had no love for her husband either way."

"I bet the honour price was high."

"Oh, yes. One hundred ounces of gold, though King Diarmait didn't pay. It was an insult of the highest order, for it implies either King Diarmait thinks so little of King Tigernán that he doesn't have to recompense him, or else Derbhfhorgaill wasn't worth paying an honour price for."

I mulled over the information. When Affraic had visited, she mentioned the war in Leinster. It was King Diarmait she and Broccan had spoken of. Now I thought on it, the other king's name was Tigernán. Cuan had also mentioned a King Diarmait of Leinster the day they captured me. He was the king who was supposedly bringing the Norman warriors over from England. And it was all over a woman.

"King Tigernán, King Ruaidrí and King Magnus ran Diarmait Mac Murchadha out of Ireland as punishment," Fearghus continued. "If Diarmait had any sense, he would have stayed in England, but he's returned to cause trouble and has threatened to bring Norman knights over to fight for him. High King Ruaidrí should have thrown him back out by now... Perhaps he's waiting until after the Tailteann games to fight, but if I had my way, all the Leinster warriors, including King Diarmait, would be buried in the—"

Fearghus' story was interrupted by Scolaí swiping a cut of meat from my plate. Without thinking, I punched the back of his wrist, and the stolen meat flew out of his grasp and landed with a thud on the table. The men around us erupted with laughter with Fearghus laughing loudest of all.

I shouldn't have reacted, but there was no point apologising. The damage was already done. "Didn't your mother tell you it was rude to take from another's plate?" I asked.

"I'm hungry, fuidir," Scolaí snapped, "and I can take whatever I want from you."

"Take it, then." I pushed my plate toward him. "Your hands have touched it now. Who knows where they've been?"

Wine spouted out of Fearghus' mouth.

"No, thanks. Looking at your face has ruined my appetite." Scolaí swivelled around to talk to a man at the next table. Silently, I berated myself for antagonising him. The last thing I wanted was for him to pay closer attention to me.

I glanced at the top table to see if Cathal and Cuan had seen what happened, and to my surprise, Cathal was looking at me. He didn't seem angry though, rather he was pointing me out to one of the women who'd been sitting at the top table. She was standing behind the king and Cathal now and nodded her head.

I looked away, not wanting them to catch me staring, but through the corner of my eye, I saw this same woman walk toward me.

"Hello, I'm Dáirinn, granddaughter of the king," she said, when she reached me. "You're staying with me and my cousins tonight."

I stood, happy to be going somewhere other than the stables.

"There you go, Isolde," Fearghus said. "A bed at last. When we met, you were a boy; last night, a horse. When I see you tomorrow, you shall be a woman."

Dáirinn rolled her eyes, led me outside and took me into one of the buildings within the dun. It was much smaller than the feasting hall but was still large enough for there to be five beds at the back of the dwelling. The front of the house was decorated with cushions and rugs and a good fire was lit, too. But Dáirinn didn't stop there and led me into a small separate room at the back where there was a wooden tub filled with water.

Dáirinn laid out a white linen shift on the third bed and put a clean blue dress over the headboard. "This is your bed, and these are for you," she said. "I'm sorry about not doing this before the feast. We didn't know Grandfather had changed his mind about inviting you."

"You don't need to apologise."

She bowed her head and then lifted a stone using iron tongs from a steaming pot that hung over the fire. The water in the wooden tub sizzled as the stone submerged and sank to the bottom. I splashed the water, happy to feel the warmth within.

Dáirinn grinned. "There. It should be nice and warm for you. I've to go back to the feast, but I wish you a good sleep." She turned then, barely able to stop herself from running to rejoin the feast.

Now alone, I undressed and bathed in the tub. The hot stone heated the water, and I enjoyed the feeling of warm water on my skin. The grime and dirt melted away, and when I was finished, I put on the white linen shift. The bed looked so comfortable, and I was so tired, that I slipped underneath the blanket and closed my eyes.

★

I woke the next morning to the sound of hushed whispers and laughter. Six of the young girls who had attended the feast sat on the other beds, chatting and gossiping, unconcerned that I could overhear.

Rising from the bed, I picked up the blue dress, noting that my clothes were freshly washed and folded on the chair beside me. The bull-hide armour was cleaned too. Setting aside the dress, I put on my old clothes, Broccan's clothes, and armour. I couldn't wear what Dáirinn had given me, despite the fine quality of the fabric. Broccan's clothes and armour were too precious to simply discard, and it wouldn't look right to wear both together.

Only once I was ready, did I realise that Dáirinn, the girl who'd brought me here last night, was sitting on one of the cushions at the front of the room, patiently picking out some stitches from an embroidery. Her cousins sat around her, all of them now engaged in the same activity.

"Look! There they are," one of the other young women said. Every head in the room turned to look out the entrance. Two even moved their chairs to get a better view. I followed their gazes, curious to see who'd caused such a reaction, but I could only make out Scolaí, Cuan and Cathal.

"What's he like?" a slender girl with long blonde hair asked me. Her skin was so pale it seemed translucent, and the smattering of freckles over her nose and wide mouth gave her a look of simmering mischievousness. I liked her immediately.

"Moncha," Dáirinn scolded. "Don't bother our guest with stupid questions."

"It's not a stupid question," Moncha insisted, keeping her eyes on me.

"What is who like?" I asked.

"Cathal."

"No, Cuan," interrupted the teenager beside her.

"They are..." Already the women had stopped listening and my words slipped away. They were too busy arguing with each other. "Kind," I added, remembering Cathal was the reason I was sitting on a chair instead of chained to a post in the stables.

Dáirinn sighed. "None of you are marrying the brother or nephew of the High King of Ireland, so put all this nonsense out of your head."

"Who did you say they are?" I asked, sure I'd misheard.

"You've been travelling with Prince Cathal Corbdearg Ó Conchúir," Dáirinn said. "He's the youngest brother of High King Ruaidrí Ó Conchúir. And Cuan is the High King's nephew."

Strange. They said they were messengers for the High King, not that they were related to him.

"You didn't know?" Dáirinn rolled her eyes. "Sure, you can't send just anybody to invite the kings of the North to the Tailteann games, can you?"

Moncha giggled. "Imagine travelling with Cathal Ó Conchúir, Prince of Connacht, and not knowing."

"They are coming this way," one of the women hushed. "Be quiet."

I glanced out of the entrance. Cathal and Cuan were talking to each other as they strolled toward our building. Now the girls had pointed it out, I noted the similarities in their faces – the same long, straight nose, though their hair colouring was different, as were their eyes.

"Move away, Moncha," Dáirinn hissed. "They'll see you staring."

Moncha sniffed and stayed by the entrance. "I don't think I will," she said, flicking her hair to the side. "I want them to see me."

"Moncha," Dáirinn said through gritted teeth, "move away right now."

"No. If I catch their eye, they might make an offer of marriage when they see me again at the Tailteann games."

The colour in Dáirinn's cheeks turned pink. "Moncha, it's not for you to decide who to marry. They'll think you forward if they notice you there. Come away."

Moncha crossed her arms but stayed her ground. "Grandfather

gets to decide everything, but if I leave it up to him, he'll give me to some old man with one eye, like he did to Nuala."

"Nuala is marrying a king," Dáirinn muttered, "which is more than you deserve."

With these harsh words, the embroidery recommenced, but beneath the veil of productivity, I sensed everyone's attention was still with the young men, and furtive glances out the entrance were constant.

"Is Cuan a prince too?" I asked Dáirinn.

"No, you can only be a prince if your father was king, and his father, Bardán Ó Conchúir, never was."

"Don't you think Cuan is handsome, even with his scar?" Moncha asked the woman sitting beside her.

"No, the scar is ugly," was the reply.

"But it shows he's a brave warrior," Moncha insisted. "To be honest, I don't care about beauty. I'd accept anyone younger than thirty."

"Perhaps one of us will marry one of them," another of the women said, her voice filling with hope. "I'm sure Grandfather will have it on his mind at the games."

Dáirinn sighed, but as she peered outside, her eyes misted over. I found the whole conversation strange, and it reminded me of Móirne – this desire to be married, feeling so desperate that you didn't mind to whom. The girls continued to whisper among themselves. Who was the most handsome? Which would they prefer to marry if they had a choice? Something within me wanted to look at the men again. To look at them anew.

"Isolde," a voice bellowed from outside. "Come here!" I could tell by the impatient tone it was Cuan. Pushing that last thought quickly away, I said goodbye to the girls, who stared at me with an assortment of emotions ranging from sympathy to jealousy.

Cuan stood outside beside his horse, Sleipnir. Scolaí was behind them, already seated on his horse. Cuan looked annoyed. Scolaí was scowling.

"We're leaving," Cuan said. "You're riding with me."

"Where's Fearghus and Cathal?"

"They have another king to visit. You, Scolaí and I are going to visit the Uí Echach Cobo." He offered no further explanation before holding out his hand to help me up onto his horse.

Moncha came running out, my freshly washed cloak in her hands. "Here you go, Isolde. It was so lovely meeting you." She grinned as she passed it over, her gaze lingering on Cuan before she slowly walked back inside.

My smile only faded when Scolaí moved his horse beside me. He nudged me with his elbow and patted his sword. "You might have convinced Cathal and Fearghus, but you haven't convinced me. I'll be watching you, fuidir."

Gormflaith

Chepstow

It was not yet dawn, and already the castle was alive with activity. Fires were being lit, food was being prepared, the dogs were being exercised. It might seem odd to leave when so many watchful eyes could be upon me, but I often found people were less observant at such times. There was too much noise. Too much distraction.

Making my way out of the castle with my empty water bucket, I pretended I was going to the river, then veered away at the last moment and made my way into the forest.

Donnchad was waiting for me in the clearing he had described. Presumably, he too had been careful not to be spotted leaving, though I guessed with his new gift, stealth came easier to him than it did to me.

"Where are they?" I asked.

"Just a little further in."

Following his lead, I glanced around the forest. It was dark and damp and smelled of rot. I didn't like it here. Even the stench of the river was preferable to this. Hopefully, I wouldn't have to stay for long.

"How is Angelo?" I asked.

"Much better." The relief in Donnchad's voice was palpable. "I almost can't believe it, but when Cecile removed his bandages this morning, the swelling at the back of his head was much improved. Almost completely gone."

"We are Fomorians, Donnchad. Hardier than the mortals."

He gave a short grunt, but did not speak again. Not until we reached the campsite. Cecile was sitting beside the small fire, her head in her hands. Angelo was lying down on a blanket, eyeing Olaf, who was boiling a pot of water over the fire.

"How are you, Angelo?" I asked as I sat beside him. "Donnchad said you were badly hurt."

Angelo shrugged.

"Are you in pain?"

Angelo shook his head.

Pressing my fingers around his skull, I could see the huge gash, but the bone itself seemed to be intact. "You are lucky, Angelo, but now you have seen our enemy, it is a lesson to not underestimate them. Next time you find a Descendant, you will know to kill them and kill them quickly."

This garnered a smile from my grandson.

"And so, what do you need, Donnchad?" I stood. "I have no money. Nothing to give you."

"I don't need coin or possessions," Donnchad said. "I merely asked you to come here to tell you that I am bringing Angelo with me. Cecile and Olaf are to stay with you."

He said these words like a command. Raising my eyes to meet his, I stared.

"Don't you think that is best?" he asked, his tone at least slightly more questioning this time.

Well, I could ask questions too.

"I suppose that depends. How determined are you to win back Ireland?"

"I want to rule Ireland more than anything. I was unsuccessful last time, and I have no wish to repeat those failures. But... But I can only do it with your help. This is only the first wave of the attack. I need you to be ready once Strongbow himself decides to go over. I need you to get close to him."

Yes. This was a good plan. Similar to the plan I had formulated myself. Perhaps Donnchad was his mother's son, after all. "When do you go?"

"This morning. Angelo and I had better leave soon to meet up with the rest of the army."

"Then you had better join me, Cecile. Let us see if I can't find some work for you in the kitchens."

"Kitchens?" She stuck out her tongue.

For that, I didn't blame her, but beggars could not be choosers. Indeed, perhaps this might give Cecile a chance to prove her worth to me. She was pretty. It was time to see what she could do with that.

Cecile stood, brushed her skirt and limped toward me. *Oh yes, that was right. She'd been injured too.* What a shame. Being lame dampened her allure by no small amount.

"Not now, foolish girl. You can't come out of the forest with me. If we are spotted, people will wonder where you've been living. No. You must take the road with Donnchad and Angelo. Come to the castle once they meet up with the army and say you've come to stay with me while your brothers are away fighting." I turned around. "Ah, Olaf. There you are. I need you to come with me now."

Olaf peered up at me and set down the pot of water.

Taking a deep breath, I looked at both Donnchad and Angelo. "Good luck. This is our last opportunity. Do not squander it… but be brave."

Donnchad nodded. Angelo too.

Never one for goodbyes, I turned and left.

Olaf followed behind me, and I made sure we were a good distance from my family before I stopped to speak with him. The plan I'd been conjuring was the key to elevating me in status above that of kitchen maid. That might do very well for Cecile. Not for me. Six days of drudgery was more than enough.

"Olaf, once I transform you back into eagle form, I need you to pretend your wing is injured. This way, I can bring you into the castle. Once there, I shall begin to train you. You must follow my commands. Not too well at first, but as time—"

Olaf shook his head and then slammed it against the tree he stood beside. The suddenness of the violence made me scream.

"Olaf! Stop that!"

Olaf did, but he would not look at me. He wouldn't even wipe the trail of blood oozing down the side of his scalp. Oh, he was angry with me. *How annoying.* This rage toward himself happened sometimes when I didn't show him enough favour, but his anger especially flared up when I had to marry or seduce another man. At these times, his anger would also move toward the man in question too. There was a count in Venice I had courted once. Olaf had nearly gouged his eyes out. After that, I'd had to transform him into a dove and keep him inside a cage.

I would have left him that way, but sometimes I actually needed him. Times when Broccan was chasing us, and I wanted to know where he was when my dreams could not find him, I changed Olaf into eagles, falcons and hawks.

And so I had learned that to use Olaf, I had to keep him happy. From time to time, I had to give him some of this *love* that he desperately craved. Otherwise, he'd have outbursts like this and turn into an unbearable and snivelling wretch.

"Olaf," I said, sighing as I sat. "You are unhappy with me, I can see it, but how many times must I tell you that, when I seduce another man, it is only to keep us safe? Fed. In good health. It is not love."

Still, he wouldn't look at me.

"Olaf, please. Talk to me."

"Gormflaith, I cannot do this anymore." Tears filled his eyes as he said this. "I think... I *know* I would rather die than endure this anymore. I can't bear to see you with him. Kill me. Or at least let me kill myself."

"What? How can you suggest such a thing? David is nothing to me."

"That's not true. I can see it in your eyes. Hear it in your laugh. You love him. Desire him."

"This is false, Olaf. You know how it is when we move to a new country."

"No. No." His voice rose, grew harsher, and he clenched his fists.

"It isn't like the other times... but that isn't the point. How can you love me and be with another? How can you play so false?"

"You don't know how I can play false?" I couldn't help it, but my anger flared too. "It was you who taught me how to deceive. Don't you remember?"

Olaf shuddered at the harshness of my words.

"Don't you remember how you betrayed me? I sent you to recruit Svein Forkbeard to Sitric's cause and instead you killed him. Oh, I believed you wanted to help me with every bone in my body, and all the time, you were using me to get to Svein."

"I had sworn a vow to kill him... I had..."

"I know. Svein killed your mother. You swore revenge. I've heard all that before. But you destroyed everything I had worked for. I could have been Queen of Ireland, with you at my side. Instead, we've had to slither through the world as beggars and whores. It is *you* who has brought me so low. And my son. *Our* son. Our baby boy, I had to give away to Sitric. Do you understand the pain of that?"

The anger left Olaf. Contrition took its place. "I'm sorry, Gormflaith. If I could turn back time, I would not kill Svein."

"Liar."

Olaf winced. "You doubt me, Gormflaith. You doubt everything about me. Even my love for you." He moved a little closer to me, wiping his nose with his sleeve. "You think I say it and feel it only because of the love potion you gave me, but I told you then, there was no need to give it to me. I already loved you. You already had my heart."

I bowed my head. That was not true, though the poor fool could not see it. It was the love potion that held his devotion to me in place. If he had never taken it, he would not be this way. Olaf Tryggvason was a man of pride, ambition and cunning. Such a man would not be content to serve and grovel at my feet.

And even if I were soft and tempted to believe his love was true, what had happened to Cecile's mother would drive this idea from my head.

Cecile's mother, Neasa, was a healer of the Tuatha Dé Danann. Our mortal enemy, she had hated us with every bone in her body when we captured her at Fennit Island, but when Máelmórda had given her a love potion, she'd become as devoted to him as it was possible for a woman to be.

I found it cumbersome, this type of love, but Máelmórda did not hate it as I did. He was a man. Perhaps that was why. With such a fragile ego, Neasa's words of adoration soothed him when his spirits were low. When he was injured, she would heal him. He would bed her too when no one else was to be had, and finally, after almost one hundred years, Neasa fell with child.

Máelmórda was delighted. A child between the two of them would surely produce a Fomorian child, and he was right. Cecile was born with fire in her blood.

But, oh, when Neasa woke after the birthing and nursed the babe at her breast, it changed everything. When she next looked at Máelmórda, the spell within the love potion had broken. She had seen someone she loved more than Máelmórda, and that was the only thing that could break the spell apart from the antidote.

Neasa concealed her hatred for a while. For long enough to bribe a trader to sail her back to Ireland. Máelmórda had found her before she could reach the ship. He took the baby from her, slit Neasa's throat, and as she died, she cursed him, every word and every breath filled with hate.

That would not happen to Olaf, of course. We had no antidote, for over the years we had used up almost all of the potions Tomas had brewed for us, and Olaf had no living relatives who could break the spell naturally. He was mine and he would always be mine for as long as I wanted him.

"Oh, Olaf," I said, keeping my voice sweet. "I need you now more than ever."

"Do you?"

"Of course I do."

"To be your spy? Is that all you want me for?" Tears once again filled his eyes. The sadness within him was strong. The love he had for me had turned to such melancholy and self-loathing that my usual tricks would not work.

"When I am queen, who do you think I shall have at my side?"

Olaf glanced up, a spark of hope growing.

"It will be you. Always you."

Olaf reached out to touch my hand. He held it tight. So tight, I could not help but flinch.

He noticed. That fleeting spark in his eyes drained. Drained away to nothing. Taking a knife from his pocket, he pointed the tip of it at his heart, ready to thrust the blade into his body.

"No!" I screamed.

"Why should I not?" he sobbed. "I can't bear it. I can't take this life anymore. To live without your love is like living in eternal darkness."

"I do love you, Olaf. How can you not see it? See that I *must* keep you at a distance? I can't trust myself around you, Olaf, and… and I'm scared you will betray me again."

Tears came to my eyes too. Not of love or despair, but of fear. *I needed Olaf.* Fódla's girl might be dead, but my life was still in danger. He was right. Donnchad could not be trusted. And as much as I had affection for Angelo, I could not trust him either. Olaf was the one person I could rely on.

Crawling on hands and knees, I made my way over to him. I pressed my head to his feet as if he were the Pope and I was begging for forgiveness. His body was rigid. Disbelief still swam within him.

Rising slowly, I kissed his leg. "Without you, Olaf, I am nothing."

Olaf kneeled beside me, his hands moving to my waist. He kissed me gently on the neck and I pretended to like it. I wished I could enjoy it, but with Olaf there were too many memories that prevented me from escaping into a fantasy. Pretence, therefore, was all I had. I had to kiss him back and moan at his touch. I had to let him have me over and over until he was spent, and even then, I had to beg for more.

Finally, all traces of doubt had left him.

"This is my last chance for power, Olaf," I said as I lay on the grass beside him. "The very last."

"And you still want to be queen?"

"Every part of me says no except for my heart. I have no choice, Olaf. I must try." Linking my fingers through his, I kissed his hand. "Will you help me? If you won't, I can't do it. Donnchad wants it too, and I will not be able to steal it from him without you."

Olaf nodded. "This last time, I will. If you succeed, I will be at your side. But promise me this. If it doesn't happen, we will leave this land together. Go somewhere new where we can be free to enjoy each other any time we wish."

He rolled over and kissed my shoulder, and once again I feigned delight at the feel of his lips against my skin. I could imagine nothing worse than living out my years with Olaf as my companion, but for now, I smiled as if this dream of his was my dream also.

"Where would we go?" I asked. "Rome? Venice?"

"No. Somewhere quiet. A villa in the countryside. Close to the sea."

"Yes," I murmured as I stroked his hair. "Just the two of us. No one else."

His hands began to trail down the side of my breast and I made a point then of glancing up at the sky. "What time is it, Olaf?"

"Midday, I think."

Standing quickly, I pulled on my dress. "My absence will be noticed."

Olaf sighed, the pained look of longing returning to his eyes.

"Hurry. Help me with my dress."

Olaf did as I asked and then stood on the grass, waiting.

"Now, you remember the plan. It's the only way I can have you in the castle with me. You know I couldn't bear for you to be out here on your own."

Olaf nodded. Resigned, but no longer desperate.

I held out my hand, and he transformed before my eyes. This time, I made him the most beautiful eagle I had ever seen. His feathers were the colour of gold, his wings and tail long and strong.

"Hold your wing down," I said as I stroked his face. "You must appear injured. That is how I'll get you in."

Walking out of the forest, I made my way into the castle. It was a testament to how exquisite a creature Olaf was that everybody stopped to look at him as he clung to my arm. Feigning concern, I took him to the cages by the stables where Strongbow and several of his knights kept their hunting birds.

Strange as it had first appeared, this was typical conversation between these Norman knights. It was not their horses, their armour, their women, their titles. No. Hunting with these birds was their favourite pastime and the main source of their talk come the evening. *Whose bird was the most beautiful. Whose was the best trained. Which bird was most loyal.*

"What is this? A golden eagle." Le Gros, who had been checking in on his falcon, came over to me, eyes widening as he looked at Olaf.

"I found him when I went to fetch water this morning. He's injured, I think."

Le Gros came a little closer and Olaf squawked, his good wing flapping.

"Ah," Le Gros, said. "He doesn't like me, but why should he? You have enchanted him. Why don't you put him in the cage, and we can see if his wing can be mended? It would be a shame for such a magnificent beast to die."

I did as he asked, knowing that a crowd was gathering. Soon, even Strongbow himself came out.

"This woman has enchanted an eagle, Strongbow," Le Gros said, laughing.

Strongbow, not as effusive as Le Gros, gave a sharp intake of air. "You're the Irish girl."

"Yes, my lord," I said, curtseying. "I hope you do not mind my using the cage."

"Not at all."

I gave another curtsey. "Then I should be away, my lord. I have stayed away from the kitchens too long."

"Ah, well then," Strongbow said, "seeing as you have such a way with our winged friends, why don't you help old Ranulf to care for them? With so many of the men leaving with FitzStephen, I'm sure he could do with some assistance."

"Thank you, my lord."

I kept my face down as he left the courtyard. Robert FitzStephen, Maurice de Prendergast and their men were gathering in the courtyard. Getting ready to march west to where the boats would take them to Ireland. I made my way there, and it didn't take long to find Donnchad standing beside Angelo and Cecile.

I waved Cecile over to me.

"Come," I said. "I need to introduce you to someone."

I led her to the back of the castle, introducing her to the other maids and servants we passed on our way to the kitchen.

"Where have you been?" one of the cooks asked as she threw a bowl of sliced onions into a stew. "Courting that knight of yours, were you?"

"No. I was saving an eagle, but that's why I'm here. The Earl of Pembroke himself has asked that I help with the hunting birds. Don't worry, though. I've brought my sister, Cecile, to help here in my stead."

The cook snorted but came over to Cecile to feel the muscles in her arms. Her withering glance revealed her disappointment. "Here you go." She shoved a bucket into Cecile's hand. "Fetch me some water, and you'd better be quick about it."

I walked outside, quietly laughing as I watched Cecile limp toward the river. The poor girl had never done a day's work in her life, for Máelmórda had treated his daughter as if she were a princess. Now he was gone, she would soon learn what it was to be a woman with no man to keep her.

Women had to work for our desires. On hands and knees or on our backs. Cecile, for the first time in her life, was about to discover what that meant.

Isolde

Kingdom of Ulaid

Cuan's horse walked along the grass path. Scolaí's followed. They didn't speak to each other or to me, which I was more than happy about.

Escape. It was all I thought of. The chance of success, enhanced by the fact Fearghus and Cathal were not with us, was better than I'd dared hope. Running from two rather than four would be a lot easier. I mulled over the options of escaping as soon as we came to a forest I could lose myself in or waiting until they fell asleep tonight. It didn't take long to land on the latter, for Scolaí, as he had threatened, was always watching me.

There was also another reason for wanting to wait. Fragarach was in Scolaí's possession still. I found myself unable to contemplate leaving without it, and my chances of retrieving it seemed much more likely if they were both asleep.

It was late in the day when Cuan pulled his horse to a stop. He dismounted, leaving my back cold as the heat from his body and fur cloak disappeared, and led his horse over to a stream that ran across our path. Scolaí did the same.

I dismounted too, taking the pause to roll out the tension in my shoulders and the stiffness of my legs, and strolled along the edge of the stream. The blades of grass were long and thick, and I twisted them around my fingers. There were wildflowers here, too. Ones I'd never seen on Rathlin. I picked a couple, examining the petals and leaves. Already the air was warmer here. The wind not so fierce. Probably many plants were different in the south of Ulaid compared to the northern islands.

My eyes filled with tears at this realisation. The protective wall I'd built up crumbling now I'd thought of home. I missed it. More than anything, I wished I could go back, and that life could be the same as it used to be. I wished I could wake up and see Broccan by the fire, readying food for breakfast. So vivid was this image, I could see it when I blinked. How could he be dead when my memories of him were so real?

So much love had disappeared on the day of the Fomorian attack. Where had it gone? Into nothing? When your heart broke, was that what happened? Did all the love that once existed inside you dissipate into the air and leave you forever?

That Broccan might be in the otherworld with my mother gave me some comfort. If he was there, he would not be alone, but still, this comfort was not enough to numb my pain. I missed him so much that I ached. I did not like this world he had tried to warn me about. Nor did I understand myself in it.

Wiping my tears, I focused on the wildflowers between my fingers. I could do this. I could escape. I could reach Seir Kieran.

"Don't wander too far, fuidir," Scolaí shouted. He grinned as he pulled out some barley bread and cheese from his bag. He held out a cut of bread in my direction. A peace offering? Not likely, but I walked over and stretched out my hand in any case.

Scolaí smirked as I took it from him. "Are my hands not too dirty for you today? See, Cuan, she's warming to me."

Cuan exhaled loudly, a sound that couldn't decide if it wanted to be a sigh or a grunt.

"It's as well," Scolaí said, tying up his bag. As the leather fabric sealed shut, the handle of Fragarach momentarily came into view. "You're riding with me next."

"I'd rather walk."

"And slow us down?" Scolaí sneered as he mounted his horse. "I suppose if I was to be questioned as a spy by the High King, I'd want to delay it too." He leaned down, his hand reaching out to touch my hair. "I've no idea what happens to a woman spy. Perhaps

King Magnus will have his way and cut out your tongue. Even better, he might make you my fuidir to pay off the debt."

"Get off." I slapped away his hand. "You lay another finger on me, and I'll hit you again. Do you hear me?"

"Then you'll only have a larger fine to pay."

I stormed away, moving back over to the stream.

Laughing, Scolaí followed me, pushing his horse into a trot so he could move ahead of me before I reached it. His horse blocked my path as he intended, and then he held out his hand for me to take. "Come on. Up you get. It's time to get moving."

"No." Anger built up inside of me. How dare he try to stop me walking where I wanted. How dare he tell me what to do. "Get away from me."

Scolaí's horse suddenly reared, and I fell backward. The horse snorted, shook his head, and then bolted, bucking and kicking until Scolaí fell from his seat.

Cuan ran forward and took hold of the horse, whispering calming words into the horse's ear until his temper eased. "He's lost a shoe," he said, rubbing his hand along the back of the horse's front leg.

Scolaí stood, wrapped his arm over his ribs and glared at me. "You startled it."

"No, she didn't." Cuan handed him the reins. "Go back to King Magnus' dun and have his smith give him a new one."

"Why don't we all go back?" Scolaí snapped.

"It's your horse," Cuan replied, managing to keep his voice low and calm. "You go. Isolde and I will continue to the bruidean like we agreed this morning, so that I can speak to the King of the Uí Echach Cobo. If you're quick, you'll reach us tonight. If not, catch up with the others and we will meet at the border of Bréifne tomorrow."

Scolaí shook his head. "We should stay together. There are wolves in these parts."

While they argued about which way we should go, I rubbed my

head and reached for my shawl. Beside it was my knife. Crawling toward it, I picked it up.

"No chance," Scolaí spat.

Wrapping my hands around the handle, I pulled it tight to my body. "It's mine."

Cuan marched over to me and held out his hand. "It's not yours yet. Don't make me take it off you."

Reluctantly, I handed it over, though was glad to find that Cuan put it inside his bag rather than give it to Scolaí.

"The knife is part of the payment—"

"There has been no judgement yet," Cuan interrupted. "So no, the knife isn't part of anything." Cuan took the reins of his horse, and though he showed no outward signs of annoyance, I could tell his temper was rising. His movements were slower than usual. More deliberate. "The bruidean is closer, so that's where Isolde and I will go. You need to have your horse tended to, otherwise his foot could be permanently damaged. My uncle won't be happy if that happens."

Scolaí looked set to argue, but at the mention of Cuan's uncle, he scowled and mounted his horse. He offered me one last glare before kicking the horse's flank and riding back to King Magnus' dun.

I rubbed the bruise on my side, and once the thud of hooves pounding the ground dimmed, got up. Scolaí had gone.

"Are you hurt?" Cuan asked.

"No."

"Did you hit your head when you fell?"

"No."

Cuan nodded. "Then let's go. We need to make good time, otherwise it will be dark before we reach the bruidean."

Nodding, I continued along the path, and I found myself grateful that he didn't tell me to get back on the horse. I didn't want to. I wanted to keep my legs moving. Despite the bruise on my hip, this day was improving. *Now I only had to run from one.*

★

Cuan and I didn't speak as we continued our journey. Though the spring weather was making way for summer, as the sun began to set, the air turned sharp. Thick cloud had blown in from the west and a fine drizzle fell. The forest around us was thick. Perfect for an escape. Certainly easier than leaving a dwelling where other people might wake Cuan to tell him that I had gone.

"Should we make a camp?" I asked Cuan. "The rain is going to come down hard soon."

"No. There's the bruidean. Can't you see it?"

I followed the line of his finger. In the far distance, a large ráth stood on a hill. I kept my eyes fixed on it as we moved closer. I'd never seen a bruidean before, but Broccan had spoken of them, as had Móirne, though neither had actually described one. What I found was a dwelling, double in size to our ráth on Rathlin Island, with a high stone wall encircling two houses. One appeared to be a stable, the other was a large wooden fort. However, more important than the bruidean itself, were the pathways around it. Four roads, no, five, and one of those led south. Finally, the route to Seir Kieran was in sight… and Cuan was the only person I needed to slip past.

This was it. I stared at Cuan's bag. Fragarach was in there. All I had to do was wait until he was asleep, take it, then leave.

"What do you think?"

I quickly shifted my gaze back to the bruidean. "It's grander than I expected. My friend Móirne spoke of the one in Ulaid before she left to be married. She thought it was kind of the Irish kings to keep them for travellers moving in and out of their lands."

"Not kind. The greatness of a king is not measured in what he has, but in what he can afford to give away. Isn't that what they say?" Cuan said. "The kings build them because otherwise they'd be shamed. It is pride. Not kindness."

Cuan's response surprised me, but I said nothing.

"Greetings, Cuan Ó Conchúir." A tall man limped our way as

Cuan's horse reached the ráth wall. He waved and reached out to take Sleipnir's reins. "I didn't expect to see you pass this way again so soon."

"Hadn't planned on it, Eoghan," Cuan answered. "But news reached us that King Aodhan died. I've come back to invite the new King of the Uí Echach Cobo to the Tailteann games. Irial, isn't it?"

Eoghan's lips pressed into a thin line. "No, not Irial. King Aodhan's younger brother took the kingship."

"Not the son?" Cuan said, dismounting.

Eoghan shook his head. "You know how it goes."

What did that mean? *You know how it goes.*

Eoghan nudged Cuan and gave me a searching look. "Who's your friend?"

Cuan glimpsed at me for a second and then removed his bag and shield from Sleipnir. His lips curled downward, but to call it a frown wasn't right. It was hard to tell with the scar that had slackened the muscles on the left side of his face.

"Her name is Isolde. I'm taking her to my uncle," Cuan said. "Scolaí might be here soon. His horse lost a shoe. He had to return to King Magnus' dun to get it replaced."

"Very good," Eoghan said. "There's food in the pot over the fire, and there are plenty of beds and blankets inside. Help yourself. No one else is here tonight, so if you don't mind, I'll be going home after I stable your horse. It's been a long day."

"Thank you," Cuan said. "I'll see you in the morning before we leave."

Cuan patted Sleipnir as Eoghan led him away, and then walked toward the house. I hurried after him. It was an odd house, not like the usual ones with thatched roofs and wattle-and-daub walls. This was completely made of wood with a hole in the centre of the roof. Underneath this hole, there was a large fire pit with a pot of stew hanging over it. A large wooden table with two benches running along either side was placed beside it, and at the far end of the room were the beds.

"Here. Have this." Cuan set down his bag and shield, poured a ladle of stew into the two bowls, and handed one to me.

The insides of my cheeks tingled as soon as I took it, and I quickly sat on one of the benches so I could eat. As expected, it was delicious. Yes, a good dinner would go down well. For, once Cuan fell asleep, I'd be leaving. I needed this dinner to keep me going for the whole of tonight and tomorrow. Maybe even the day after too.

"So, Isolde," Cuan said as he sat. "Tell me about yourself. I know nothing about you, except you're from Rathlin Island and the niece of a monk."

I lowered my face and blew the steam from the stew. "What do you want to know?"

"Anything you want to tell."

I shrugged. "I grew up on Rathlin Island with my cousin. We tended our cattle in the day, and in the evening, we sang and told stories. A boring life to the likes of you, but I loved it all the same."

"What about your mother and father?"

"They both died when I was young." I paused. "I don't remember them."

"My mother died when I was young, too."

Though his face was expressionless, I detected something different in his voice. An emotion that lifted it from the dry flatness of his usual tone. But whether it was sadness or anger, I couldn't tell.

"You must miss her."

"Very much." He took another spoonful of the stew, and once again glanced my way. "Can you tell me what happened on Rathlin? How did the fire start?"

"I don't know. All I know is that it spread very fast."

"Your cousin wasn't able to get out in time?"

I shook my head. I didn't want to talk about Broccan with him.

Cuan took another ladle of stew from the pot and leaned over to pour it into my bowl. "You're more than old enough to be married. Were none of the men on Rathlin good enough for you?"

Good enough?

"Me not being married wasn't to do with anyone not being good enough. There were only three other families on Rathlin, and I just didn't want to marry anyone. Do you want to marry every woman you come across?"

Cuan shook his head, perhaps amused, though once again I wasn't sure. After listening to King Magnus' granddaughters, I was sure Cuan had received more than a few marriage proposals from fathers keen to marry their daughters. He was the nephew of the High King, and if the old King Magnus had a beautiful young adaltrach, I imagined Cuan could have any woman he wanted. King Magnus' granddaughters were right. He was handsome too, even with the scar… or at least he might be if he wasn't always so solemn.

"I think I've finally worked you out," Cuan said. "You want to become a nun, don't you? That's why you're travelling to your uncle. Because he's a monk and you think he'll find a place for you at the Seir Kieran nunnery." He took another ladleful of stew, this time pouring it into his own bowl. "Why do you have to go to Seir Kieran, though? Any nunnery would take you in if you wished to take your vows."

"I want… I want to be with family. That is—"

The sound of someone moving outside made me jump. I stared at the door, and Cuan rose from his seat. "Scolaí was quick," he mumbled.

A knot in my stomach tightened. I didn't want Scolaí here.

Cuan moved over to the door, then stopped and stared at me. He put his finger over his lips. "There is more than one person," he whispered.

"How many?" I whispered back.

He turned his head so that his right ear was close to the door, then held up three fingers.

Three? My heart thudded. The Fomorians. They had found me. It had to be them.

Cuan's fingers brushed the hilt of his sword, quietly removing it from the sheath. With his other hand, he took the knife from his belt.

"Don't," I hissed. "They have come for me. You should run."

Cuan frowned.

Grabbing Fragarach from Cuan's bag, I held the knife tight in my hand. "Go, Cuan. Run."

Expressionless, Cuan looked away from me, moving his gaze to the door. Slowly, he lifted the latch. With a bang, the door swung open.

Three men charged into the room, swords drawn, though the first was thrown off balance by the sudden opening, and Cuan stabbed him in the neck with his knife. Kicking his body back, Cuan shifted to the side, his sword swinging in his right hand, his bloodied knife in the other. He swung at the second of the men. This man swerved, and Cuan missed. Running back, Cuan grabbed hold of a chair. He kicked it upward, blocking the sword which hurled down at him from his attacker. The wood cracked, shattering, but the man recovered quickly and moved forward again.

I threw Fragarach. Slicing through the air, it pierced the attacker's arm. He howled with pain and fell, preventing the third man, who'd been standing in the doorway, from running forward. Cuan sprinted to our table and set down his knife in favour of his shield.

Shoving the injured man to the side, the third man, a tall man with a broken nose, rushed toward Cuan, and they began to fight while the man with Fragarach in his arm wrenched it out. Tossing it to the floor, he drew an axe from his belt and moved toward me.

Part of me was waiting still for the fire to come, but as the man came closer, I knew he wasn't a Fomorian. Not that it mattered, for he wanted to kill me all the same. I picked up my chair to hold him off as Cuan had, but before he reached me, Cuan leaped. Sliding over the table, he plunged his sword into my attacker's side, then pulled it out quickly, just in time to parry a strike from the man with the broken nose.

I stepped back from the table but couldn't take my eyes away from the dying man at my feet. Blood oozed from his body and stained the floor red.

"Leave now. I'd rather die than be taken hostage," Cuan shouted.

I looked up. He and the final warrior were now circling each other by the door. Eyes focused, their feet treading lightly.

"Have no fear, Cuan Ó Conchúir," the man replied. "We aren't looking for hostages today."

Cuan spun his shield with his hand until he got his grip, then he beat it with the hilt of his sword. Soft at first, then harder and harder.

Both men lunged forward at the same time. Cuan met his attacker, pushing back with the shield, then striking with his sword. He aimed for the warrior's neck, but his opponent was too quick and raised his own sword to meet the blow.

That's when I noticed a fourth man standing in the doorway. He stared at the fight and drew his sword, but didn't make a move to join in. Why did he wait?

"Cuan," I shouted. "The door."

My voice propelled the new warrior into motion. He rushed forward, and jumped over the table, avoiding Cuan and his assailants, and moving toward me.

I retreated to the far end of the room, then spun round just in time to avoid his fist. Panicking, I scanned the room. Fragarach was under the table, but I didn't think I could reach it. I sprinted toward it anyway, but my attacker reached me first. Grabbing my hair, he dragged me back and flung me against the wall, striking my head against a wooden post. Warm blood spilled from my forehead onto my cheeks and mouth. As I staggered to the side, his thick arm wrapped around my neck. A moment later the cold metal point of his sword pressed against my chin.

"Put down your weapon or I'll kill her," he shouted to Cuan. He dragged me forward, making sure Cuan could see where the blade's edge pointed.

Cuan swung his sword at the man in front of him. "She's a

fuidir," he said. "Kill her if you wish, but once I finish with your friend, I'm coming for you."

Struggling, I tried to move out of the man's grasp, and then I noticed that Cuan's gaze flitted to my waist. I moved my hand to where his eye had travelled, and it brushed against the hilt of a knife sticking out from the man's belt.

Slowly, I pulled the blade free and felt the weight of it against my palm.

"Perhaps I'll kill you anyway," the man said. He spun me round to face him and lifted his sword onto my shoulder.

I had no time to think. My reaction was all instinct as I thrust the knife between his ribs.

Somehow, I did this with such force that he slammed against the wall. His limbs went limp as he slid to the floor, and my bloodied hand dropped the knife. He stared at me a moment as if not quite believing what had happened, then he went still, and his eyes glazed over. I had killed him. I had killed a man.

I had killed a man.

A loud scream jolted me out of my reverie. It had come from the last of our attackers, who was now lying on the floor with Cuan's sword in his stomach.

Cuan pulled his sword free and fell to his knees as if in prayer. His chest heaved.

I closed my eyes. I didn't want to see the blood anymore, and it was everywhere. Over the table, over the floor, over my hands. A minute or maybe more passed, the sudden silence contrasting with the ferocity of the attack. Then I felt a hand on my arm and Cuan hauled me to my feet. I hadn't even realised I had fallen to the floor.

"Isolde, look at me."

I forced myself to meet his stare. His thumb pressed against my chin, and he tilted my head sideways to examine the gash on my head. "Come, we need to go. There could be more of them."

Taking my hand in his, he pulled me through the forest. He wanted to run faster than I was able, and I seemed always on the verge of falling over, but he didn't slow. The shaking came back. Violently this time. Once we reached a river, he dragged me to a nearby alder tree. He sat against the trunk and pulled me down with him. Wrapping his cloak around us like a blanket, he breathed long and deep. The cocoon of his cloak allowed some heat to gather. But it wasn't enough. I couldn't stop shaking.

"Give me your hands," he whispered, his eyes now closed. I did as he asked. He folded my fingers in, so I made a fist, and then put them close to his chest. As heat radiated into my hands, I felt his heart beating hard and fast, though not as fast as mine. I had killed a man. *Killed him dead.*

Silence fell. Cuan rested his chin on my head, and I sank against him. I couldn't judge how quickly time passed, but my heavy eyes eventually closed, and a dark, dreamless slumber pulled me under.

Isolde

Kingdom of Ulaid

When I woke, my woollen cloak was wrapped around me. I reached out with my fingers to search for Cuan, only to find that he had gone.

The sun loomed high above the tree-line, blinding me every time the leaves parted with the wind. How long had I slept? From the height of the sun, I'd guess it was past midday, though I couldn't be sure from where I lay. I listened then, searching for any sounds that seemed out of place, but there was nothing. Just the rustling leaves, birdsong and the crash of the river water as it journeyed downstream.

Wincing, I pushed myself upright. My right temple throbbed, and the inside of my upper lip swelled over the gum. But there was something else within me that felt worse. Rolling over, I heaved, and a thick black liquid splattered onto the rock, and with this expulsion, my body began to shake.

I stared at the liquid, recoiling at the smell. It was just like on Rathlin. The black foul liquid in my mouth, the shaking, the fatigue.

You need training, Affraic had said when she noticed it. *To overuse our gift when we don't understand it is to risk ourselves. Do you understand?*

I didn't understand, but I knew somehow the witch gift that had awakened inside me was hurting me, and without the knowledge to control it, this gift would continue to do so. I wasn't sure how I'd used it yesterday, but I must have. Somehow, my gift had saved me from the men who'd wanted to kill Cuan. Or perhaps my witch-magic had caused the horse to rear and throw Scolaí from his seat.

If only I were at Seir Kieran. The other Descendants would know.

The bad taste in my mouth and throat deepened, and I felt as if the sour taste would make me vomit again if I didn't find a way to get rid of it. Pulling myself up, I limped to the riverbank. The water moved slowly on this side. Fallen branches and large rocks had created a secluded inlet which reduced the water flow to a trickle. It wouldn't be clean enough to drink, but it was good enough for washing my mouth. Crawling closer, I peered over the edge.

A strange reflection stared back at me. Someone not like myself at all. Blood-stained skin and hair. Swollen lips. Scared. Gaunt. Shaking.

I dipped my fingers into the river, the cool water balm to my aching hands, and scooped up enough water to swill in my mouth. The girl in the water staring back at me broke into fragments. Not wanting to see her again, I scrubbed at my face, then my hair, washing out the blood and dirt. But the washing away of the blood did not change what had happened.

Last night, I had killed a man.

I stopped moving as images of blood and knives filled my mind. I could see the man I'd killed so clearly. His words, his sneer, the look in his eyes when my knife pierced him, and then the look he gave me once he knew he was dying. Who was he? Where was he from?

A cough rang out. Tensing, I looked behind me. Cuan, sitting by an alder tree, waved at me. How long had he been there?

"You were too noisy," he said. "If anyone was looking for you, they'd have found you with ease."

I said nothing, but I knew he was right.

"Here." He held out a fistful of berries. "Take these, and let me see the cuts on your head and face."

"I'm fine."

He sighed, stood and folded the rest of the berries inside a bracken leaf. "Well, I can tell from here you don't look too bad." Striding forward, he thrust the folded leaf into my hand. "We need to go. We've to meet the others at the Bréifne border this afternoon."

"What about the bruidean?" I asked, finding my voice. "The dead bodies—"

"Eoghan is a friend. He knows what to do." Cuan's voice turned sharp, and it invited no more questions. "I've already invited the King of the Uí Echach Cobo to the Tailteann games and scouted the path ahead. It's clear, but if I tell you to hide or run, you must do it. If another ambush is waiting, it would be best if you weren't in the way this time."

I frowned. "I remember helping last night."

"I think it was I who helped you."

"You told one of them that I was a fuidir and that you didn't care if they killed me."

"If I'd said anything else he would have killed you instantly, and I couldn't reach you, in any case. I'd already given away my position to stop one of them from stabbing you."

"The position you got into because I hit one in the arm with my knife. You wouldn't have reached your shield if not for me."

He shrugged. "I'd have got to my shield, whether you did that or not."

"Then I'll not make the mistake of helping you next time."

"No, you won't. Because you won't be there. You'll be running or hiding."

Cuan grabbed his sword and set it over his shoulder. It was clean now, not a drop of blood on the pommel or fur scabbard. He wanted to go. But still, I did not move.

"Where's my knife?" I asked.

"In my bag."

"Can I have it?"

"No."

"Why?"

Cuan licked his lips, stared at me as if I was a source of great confusion. "You don't want to come with me, do you?"

I shook my head.

"If you can tell me which way Seir Kieran is, I'll let you go."

"It's not for you to let me or not let me. I'm my own person."

Cuan paused and stared, his pale eyes appraising me. "I would let you go... except... I remember the look on your face when you thought the men were there for you. What have you done that is so bad that you think people seek you out?"

"It's nothing to do with you."

"Were they the reason you left Rathlin?"

This time I didn't answer.

"Is your uncle really a monk at Seir Kieran?"

"Yes."

Cuan clicked his tongue, his interest in this conversation fading. "If someone is after you, being with warriors of the High King will help you. Besides, we'll be at Kells in less than a week, and you'll be a lot closer to Seir Kieran."

"And face a trial before the king? I'd rather not."

"Don't worry about that. The worst that will happen is that your uncle will have to pay a fine. Now come. We need to go, or we'll be late."

Shaking, I climbed up the riverbank. Now I was walking, it came upon me worse than ever. Even my teeth began to chatter with the force of it.

"Did you hit your head?" Cuan asked, reaching out to hold my arm.

"Yes. A little."

He tutted as he led me forward. "All this talk of you walking south alone and you can't even put one foot in front of the other. That knock to the head has driven the sense out of you. Moving this slow and wounded, the wolves would have you before the day was out."

Feeling in myself that I wouldn't get very far, shaking as I was, I followed. I hated that. Hated that I was so weak. Saying goodbye to my chance of escape, it was all I could do to keep my tears at bay.

Once we found Sleipnir at the edge of the forest, the journey south passed quickly, and soon we reached the Bréifne border.

"Cuan," Fearghus called out, as we approached him and Cathal. "You're late. Where's Scolaí?"

"His horse lost a shoe yesterday, so he returned to King Magnus' dun," Cuan replied, dismounting. "I'm surprised he isn't here already."

Fearghus held out his hand to help me down. His eyebrows creased when he saw the gash along my forehead.

"What happened to you?"

"She fell when Scolaí's horse reared up," Cuan said before I could speak. "Nothing serious."

I waited for him to follow on and tell Fearghus about the attack, or at least indicate that something more sinister had transpired. But there was nothing. Why didn't he want to tell his friends about the fight?

"Why don't you rest here?" Fearghus suggested. "Cathal and I can ride back a bit, see if we can spot Scolaí."

Cuan nodded and led Sleipnir to a nearby stream so he could drink.

Once Fearghus and Cathal were out of sight, I turned to Cuan. "Why didn't you tell him what happened?"

Cuan rubbed Sleipnir's side as he lowered his head to the water. "Because nobody knew where we were going except for Fearghus, Scolaí and Cathal. So, until I find out who betrayed me, I'm not telling anyone anything. Whoever it was knows I'm alive and the mercenaries they paid are dead. That's enough. Neither of us should speak of it again."

"But Fearghus wouldn't…"

"Let me tell you about Fearghus," Cuan said, breathing like he'd held in a laugh. "That's exactly something he'd do. He tells you stories and whispers compliments in your ear, but he's just like the rest of us. A warrior. If the king asked him to cut off your head, he'd do it the same as every other man under the king's command."

Heat rushed to my cheeks. I didn't like Cuan's words… but I understood, or at least I was beginning to. This dangerous land Broccan had warned me of, Cuan had lived in. The expressionless face, the long scar down the left side of his face, and his blood-red eye were proof of that. Still, I found this reality darker than I could have ever expected.

"How can you be friends with them if you think they knew what was going to happen to you?" I asked.

"They are my family, Isolde. Not my friends."

Turning his back on me, he removed Sleipnir's saddle and began to rub him down.

Still shaking, still feeling as if I might vomit, I pulled my cloak tight around my body and sat on a nearby rock.

A sudden coldness came over me as I tried to come to terms with what had happened and what was going to happen. Now we had regrouped, and I was shaking again, I knew my chances of escape had diminished.

But this was not the fear that truly haunted me.

It was the realisation that if Cuan had no friends, then neither did I.

I was completely alone.

And in danger.

The Fomorians were still out there, though I didn't know where. Yet, somehow, I sensed that they were moving closer. The smell of fire seemed to swirl around me, an invisible smoke dancing in the sunlight and over my skin.

Donnchad

Irish Sea

Ireland was already in view when I woke.
It was strange to see the southern coast after all these years. The journey to Rathlin had been turbulent, full of cliffs and rocks and an angry sea. The south was different. Calmer. Rugged rather than lost to chaos and wildness. So green it looked with the sunlight shining upon it. My heart beat harder within my chest. The blood in my veins felt warmer. Home. I was home.

Angelo looked over the sea, his golden eyes drinking in the view. I wondered if he remembered his time in this land. How old was he when we left? Seven? Yes. Seven.

"What do you think, Angelo?" I asked him. "Are you happy to see the land of your birth?"

Angelo nodded, a small smile creeping onto his lips.

I moved closer to him and set my hand on his shoulder. "One day we will go to Killaloe. When this land is ours again, we can go wherever we want."

Angelo's smile grew.

My son was not the only one looking at the land with wonder. The archers stood, standing on the tips of their toes to see beyond the heads of those standing in front of them. They'd spoken much of the stormy Irish Sea and of the fierce land beyond it. I wished I could hear their thoughts. Did they revile this land, desire it or fear it? They would be wise to fear it, I thought. Ireland did not like invading armies. The last time one had landed at Clontarf, by the end of the day, the beach was so filled with dead bodies that one could not see the sand.

The knights, I noted, did not look out to sea. Both Maurice de Prendergast and Robert FitzStephen sat cleaning their armour. The other knights did the same, meticulously polishing before we landed, even though everything they wore already gleamed in the morning sun. I'd noted their pride many times before now, but nothing displayed it more than this.

One of the knights prayed as he cleaned, reciting Latin words of scripture.

"You pray too much, Miles," one of the other knights said.

"I must," Miles answered. "It is an ungodly land we go to. Savages, these Irishmen are. More pagan than Christian. More pagan than the Moors I fought in Damascus."

"That is true from what I've heard," Robert said. "The Irish have many wives and swap them. I've heard of men setting aside their wives to marry their sisters-in-law or stepdaughters, and of men taking the wives of their brothers."

Another of the Norman knights, a quiet man called Meilyr, shrugged. "Diarmait was not so savage when he came to England."

"Oh, he's savage enough," Robert replied. "He had two women with him, did you not notice? A wife and a concubine. He is no true Christian, none of these men are. We must bring the word of Christ to them. Remember that. He guides us in all things."

This gossip continued, and I listened as they spoke of the savage ways of the Irish. It amused me, some of it. For these men were just as lustful of women as the Irish. Men had all the same vices and weaknesses the world over and I thought these Normans would know that, but as they spoke, their belief in their own superiority crept in. They believed this land would be theirs. They believed it as surely as they believed that the sun would rise in the morning. This would have diverted me more if it were not for the conviction in their voices – a sort of confidence that should not be ignored. Sitting down, I began to polish my own sword.

★

The ships came to rest at Bannow Island, just south of the Viking port of Wexford. Our ship landed first, though it didn't take long for Maurice's ship to catch up.

The Irish messenger, Riagáin, who had come to plead for our assistance at Chepstow, took one of the smaller rowboats and made his way to the mainland so he could tell Diarmait we had arrived. Robert tried to talk to him before he went, asking why we were on the island and not the mainland, but all Riagáin would say was that we should wait here.

The Normans looked at the mainland with more interest than they had on the ship. *What is so frightening that we cannot step foot upon it*, they asked. *Where is Diarmait? Why has he not come to greet us?*

The men wandered around the island, getting their bearings while they waited for the King of Leinster to arrive. But if he had not left his dun at Ferns, which I suspected he hadn't before our arrival was confirmed, we would have to wait until the following day to see him.

I gestured for the men to take out their tents. They stared at Robert, unsure whether to do as I said or not.

"You don't think he will come today?" Robert asked.

I shook my head. "It will take Riagáin until this evening to reach Ferns, which means Diarmait and his men won't be here until tomorrow. And believe me, the winds along this shore can be brutal. Even though it is summer, your men will feel the cold tonight if the tents do not go up."

"Why does Riagáin want us to stay on the island?" he asked. "Why does he not take us with him?"

"It is for his king's protection that you do not go with him. You have sworn no oaths yet, and you could think to take his dun for yourselves. It is for your own protection that you are not on the mainland," I said. "The Irish do not like foreign armies. Here you have the sea to protect you. On the land, an army of Diarmait's enemies might find you before Diarmait does. An enemy army might see you as a threat and decide to slit your throats while you slept."

Jaw set, Robert considered the mainland once more, then gestured for the men to put up their tents.

It was late afternoon on the following day when Diarmait's army came into view. Five hundred, all on horseback, the men dressed in their finest armour. It was a war party my father would have been proud of. Almost equal in number to the Anglo-Norman army, they were a fierce lot. The stoic restraint of the Normans was entirely absent in the Irish, who wore their emotions for all to see. It was almost as if I had gone back in time, and I was a young man once more. The weapons were the same. The armour, too. Some of them wore bull hide instead of chain-mail.

I watched the greeting party as they climbed into two rowboats and were rowed to the island. These were the best warriors of Leinster and no doubt some of them were the descendants of Máelmórda. If he were here, he might have found entertainment in discerning what or if any family resemblances lingered upon their features.

King Diarmait himself did not come over to the island. That didn't surprise me. What king would put himself in the way of a foreign army when he was not sure of their true intentions? He was being cautious and keeping his distance while he let his younger kinsmen do the work for him.

"Donn." Robert beckoned me over as the Irishmen came closer. "The man at the front of the boat, I know him. He's Diarmait's son, Domhnall. He came with his father to visit Strongbow when they were in England."

I followed the line of his gaze. Ah yes. I could see something of Máelmórda in this one, but a wilder version. Harder. In a strange way, he reminded me of Murchad.

"Is he known as Diarmait's heir?" I asked. "If so, I wonder

Domhnall allows his father to say he will pass the kingship over to Richard de Clare when he marries Ava."

Robert shrugged. "He's illegitimate. I don't suppose who the next king is matters to him."

I drew in a deep breath. Robert tightened his grip on his sword, the armour on his shoulders clinking as he did so. "Tell me your thoughts, Donn. I am paying you generously to tell me of these people. Look around us. Maurice and I have forty knights between us, and less than six hundred archers and foot soldiers combined. To have a chance at taking this land, I must understand what is going on within these Irish families. I do not trust Riagáin to tell us."

I nodded, thinking about how best to convey my knowledge without overcomplicating it. "In Ireland, men can have many wives. When you were speaking with your men earlier, you mentioned King Diarmait had a wife and a concubine, but this is not true. In Irish law, King Diarmait has two wives. Mór is the first wife. Sadbh is the second. They both have legal standing, and all of their children are legitimate."

Robert's nose wrinkled, and I could tell he found this deviation from Christian doctrine disgusting. Having multiple wives somehow was worse than having multiple lovers.

"Be that as it may," he said, "I do believe that this man was born out of wedlock. The two women you speak of, neither of them are the mother of Domhnall. That is what Hervey was told, in any case."

"Then I will endeavour to find out the truth of it, but it still doesn't matter to the Irish. If he's been brought up as a natural son and is a great warrior, the clan may still choose him to be the next king of Leinster. Illegitimacy isn't the bar to leadership in Ireland that it is in England. Indeed, the kingship doesn't even have to pass from father to son. It can pass to any man who is related to a king within five generations. Many of the men here in this army have the potential to be the next King of Leinster. Remember that. Strongbow's claim to kingship is a threat to all of them."

"You think they mean to trick us?"

"They undoubtedly mean to, though they will use you and your men first. That doesn't mean you have to fall for their tricks. King Diarmait has not come because he is afraid of you. You can work this to your advantage."

Robert stared at me for a moment, then turned to watch the two rowboats coming toward the island.

"They will ask you to swear oaths of friendship to them," I said to Robert. "They will swear oaths back, but you must remember that the strength of their oaths will fade over time for them. Even if they do not fade for you."

When Domhnall arrived, the oath-taking began. Only after Robert and Maurice swore on the Bible to fight for King Diarmait and do him no harm was it announced that they could sail to the mainland to swear these vows again to King Diarmait.

The Normans, having already packed away their tents, readied themselves and rowed across. This time, they took everything out of the ships that had sailed us over the Irish Sea. Their goods, their food, the knights' horses as well as three hunting dogs, and with this done, those ships sailed away. This army was in Ireland to stay now. There was no going back.

It was only once all the Normans had crossed over to the mainland that finally King Diarmait appeared. The old king stared at the Norman and Flemish knights, smiled at them, shook their hands and kissed their cheeks. The oaths that had been sworn to Domhnall were repeated and prayers were said to bind them to their word.

Diarmait stood the moment the prayers were over and mounted his horse.

"We go to war," was all he said, and quickly he rode north.

The knights mounted their own horses and followed. The foot soldiers and archers ran behind. Having no horses yet, Angelo and I joined the back of the army. The Irishmen had brought spare horses, but these were given to the lead archers. Though Robert needed me more than any archer, the hierarchy within the army was adhered to.

"Where are we going?" the foot soldiers asked each other as we ran into the forest.

Where indeed? Who was the first of Diarmait's enemies that he wanted us to destroy? I kept running, knowing that soon we would find out.

Isolde

The road to Kells

"Come on," Fearghus said. "If we go now, we'll be at Kells before midday."

I readied myself quickly, glad that after two days of shaking and permanent exhaustion, I had finally woken up feeling well.

"You can ride with me today, Isolde," Cathal said. "Don't worry, we won't be going too fast. The ground is too soft for that."

Holding out his hand, he helped me up, and as soon as everyone was ready, we made our way along the southern path.

"What events will you enter at the games, Cuan?" Fearghus asked after a while. "We all know Scolaí's up for the boxing, and that young Cathal fancies himself at the horse racing. What about you?"

"The running events and sword-fighting," Cuan answered. "But if you're entering those, I'll have strong competition."

"True," Fearghus said. "I've yet to meet a man better with his sword than me."

Cuan smiled at this. "We shall see how we fare if we face each other then. I must warn you – no one has ever beaten me with the sword either."

Fearghus chuckled and rubbed his hands together.

Cathal shifted his weight behind me. "King Ruaidrí says he'll use these games as a method of selecting his fianna. I wonder how many men he'll choose."

"Let's hope he doesn't apply the same rules as Fionn MacCumhaill," Fearghus said, "or else no one will make it."

Scolaí snorted. "On what account?"

"You, young pup, will fall down on rule number two. You won't even need to bother picking up your sword or spear. You'll be out before those contests begin."

Cathal laughed. Scolaí rolled his eyes.

"What rules did Fionn MacCumhaill have to join the fianna?" I asked.

Fearghus appraised me for a moment. "You don't know?"

"No. I've heard many tales of Fionn MacCumhaill, but never ones about how he selected his warriors."

"Well, the first thing you must know is there have always been rules for joining a king's fianna. The first." Fearghus held his forefinger out. "No officer of the fianna shall accept any dowry from his wife. Instead, he should choose her for her accomplishments and virtue. The second." He unfurled a second finger. "And this is where my good friend Scolaí falls down, is that no member shall insult a woman."

"Isn't this a rule all wise men should keep?" I asked.

Cathal sniggered, and I even saw a hint of a smile from Cuan.

"Third," Fearghus continued, gaining momentum. "No member shall ever deny a person food or drink, and fourth, all members of the fianna must swear allegiance to the commander of the fianna." Fearghus held up all four fingers in front of him. "Now, when Fionn MacCumhaill came to choosing his own fianna, he had no issue with these first four rules. They are good rules. It was the fifth rule Fionn didn't feel was challenging enough. This rule was no member shall turn his back on or flee from nine fianna champions." Fearghus paused for dramatic effect. "He decided, therefore, to write four new rules to take its place.

"The first of his new rules was that no man shall be admitted until, standing knee-deep in a pit, he can protect himself with the use of a shield and a hazel spear, without receiving so much as a scratch from the attack of nine warriors hurling their nine spears at him."

I raised my eyebrows. This couldn't be true. Surely, this tale had grown more exaggerated with every telling until it was all but impossible to achieve. I would have rolled my eyes, save for the seriousness of Fearghus' expression.

"The second new rule was no man could be admitted until he has been chased through a forest by a host of fianna, who are fully intent on wounding him, and escapes capture and injury."

Cathal sighed loudly and shook his head, and an expression of complete sorrow moved over his face. "I'll never be able to pass that one."

"The third of Fionn's new rules," Fearghus continued, "was no member should be admitted unless he was able to jump over a branch as high as Fionn's forehead and stoop under one as low as his knee, without delaying his speed. And the last of the new rules was no man should be admitted unless he could master the twelve books of poetry."

"Poetry?" I laughed. "Now I see why you don't think any of you will make it."

"Do we not seem learned men, Isolde?" Cathal chuckled. "My brother will be disappointed. He's spent a fortune on my education."

"Has he?" Scolaí said. "You'd never know."

Cathal tutted but took this insult with good humour.

"What competitions will you enter, Isolde?" Fearghus asked. "Are you a great singer or poet?"

"I'm not entering any competitions," I answered, my smile retreating. I couldn't think of anything worse.

"Well, if you don't want to participate, you can merely enjoy watching the festival. The games are a sight to behold, Isolde. Every warrior, singer and craftsman in the whole of Ireland competes to see who is best at their chosen skill. Thousands attended last year and the year before that. I expect more again will come this year. The plains of Kells will be filled from top to bottom with tents."

I tried to imagine this large gathering of people. Broccan had always warned me against such things. There was danger in large groups, he'd said. Tempers can flare. Arguments are started.

"Why?" I asked. "Why do they all come?"

"For many reasons," Cathal answered. "As well as the games, the kings pass new laws, and afterward, we celebrate the memory of Tailtu, the mother of Lugh of the Tuatha Dé Danann. The feasts and parties are legendary."

"You celebrate the Tuatha Dé Danann?" I asked. "My cousin told me stories of them, but he said no one believed in them anymore."

"Ah, well, we do not worship them anymore. That is true," Cathal said. "But they are the stories of our ancestors, and they still inspire us to greatness. The monks and priests can be displeased all they want, but when it comes to it, they attend the feasts and celebrations too."

Fearghus exhaled loudly and pulled his horse to a stop. "No more explanations are required, Cathal." He pointed at a hill in the distance. "We are almost there."

Guards greeted us a little further along the path. Here we all dismounted and the five of us walked up the hill, leading the horses by their reins. On cresting the summit, I discovered a large, flat plain stretching out ahead of us for miles. Hundreds of tents dotted the land just as Fearghus had told me, with thousands of men and women standing around the small campfires in between them.

There were so many people it made my head spin. All of them talking and laughing and smiling. Completely absent was the animosity and tension that Broccan had warned me of, and I knew then why the people came. To not be alone. When Móirne had looked out toward the mainland, this was what she had wanted. Something bigger and fuller than the emptiness of life on a small island. This thought, however, only made me yearn for my home. For the peace. For Broccan. Strange as it was, I felt lonelier here than ever before. The people, even the land itself, flat and treeless, was a stranger to me.

"Where are we going?" I asked Cathal as he and Cuan moved ahead of me.

"To the king's feasting hall, of course," he said. "Come. I'm starving and you need to speak to him in any case."

I had not forgotten this. Scolaí hadn't let me, though somehow I'd convinced myself that speaking with the king was not something to fear. Now I was here, I couldn't help but feel anxious. Cuan had been silent the whole morning. Was that a sign that he had lied to me about not having to worry?

In silence, I followed the men. Fearghus left to take the horses to their paddock while Cathal ran on ahead to speak with his brother, leaving me in the company of Cuan and Scolaí. I didn't look at either of them, preferring instead to examine the feasting hall in the distance. If the bruidean had been twice the size of our ráth, this was twice as big again. There was no outer wall, either, just one building made of wood. It looked freshly made, the wood pale and rough, rather than darkened with age and damp. A huge number of guards stood outside, as well as people entering and leaving, meaning our progress to the doors was slow.

"Cuan," one of the guards said, smiling. "You've made it. Just in time too."

Cuan nodded. "How has today been?"

"Fine," the guard answered. "Discussions of new laws and Mass aren't quite the same as the games. Don't tell the priests I said that though."

"Oh, I won't. I'm as keen to—"

"Scolaí. Cuan." Cathal came out of the fortress and gestured for us to come inside. "Isolde, my brother wishes to speak with you now."

Cuan followed Cathal, nodding a farewell to the guard while Scolaí pushed me inside. Eager to walk in on my own account, I sped up. Inside, I found a hall full of people, drinking and eating, laughing and talking. In the corner, musicians played various pipes and instruments, though their tune was indecipherable over the din. Most guests sat on the benches that ran up the hall while others stood to talk with friends, and of course, there were many serving girls running back and forth with food and drink. The men

I'd travelled with did not linger in this section of the hall. It was the long table at the back of the room that held their attention, and slowly we pushed our way through the crowd.

Twenty men sat at this long table, their silk tunics and thick fur cloaks shining against the beacons lining the walls. In the middle sat a tall, muscular man with a thin face and glossy red beard. He wore a golden crown and necklace, and his fur cloak was pinned at the shoulder with a large golden brooch.

The other men's faces were unknown to me, until I came to old King Magnus, who sat on the second chair from the end. A half-smile played on his lips as he noticed me, and he began to use his knife to pick out food from between his teeth. He whispered to the man beside him, a short, grey-haired man with a patch over his right eye, who promptly turned to look in my direction.

Scolaí pushed me forward. At first, only King Magnus and his friend paid us any attention, but one by one, the rest of the men at the table stared. The man with the golden crown and necklace was the last to turn his gaze our way, but when he did, everyone else stopped speaking.

"What have we here, Scolaí? You got yourself a woman at last?" the one-eyed man beside King Magnus teased.

Scolaí thrust me forward again, his nose upturned. He didn't answer the question, and instead bowed low to the man wearing the golden crown. "Good evening, High King Ruaidrí. This is Isolde. The spy we found in Ulaid."

The High King straightened, his already bright eyes flashing. He held up his hand. The music stopped, and the room fell quiet. "So, this is the girl with feet so quick it took four of my kinsmen to catch up with her. If she were a man, I'd make her one of my fianna!"

Several of the men at the table burst out laughing, the High King included.

I smiled uncertainly, not liking the laughter any more than Scolaí's scowl. It was too loud. Too boisterous. The warning Broccan had given me suddenly rang true and the hairs on my arms stood on end. There might not be danger in all crowds, but there was in this one.

"Cuan," the High King said, not taking his eyes from my face. "Come here."

Cuan tilted his head and walked toward the king. "Yes, uncle."

The High King appraised Cuan, then went quiet for a moment. "I am sure you must be hungry, Isolde. Please come and sit at the table with me. You too, Cuan. Let's talk without so much ceremony."

A serving girl set two chairs beside the king, while Cuan and I walked around the back of the table. Scolaí, while not invited to sit, stepped closer so he could listen. As soon as I took my seat, food and drink were set down in front of me, and the king gestured for me to eat. Talk and laughter slowly filled the room again, but I still felt the attention of the hall upon me. The discomfort from so much interest was like hundreds of spider legs crawling over my skin, and I tried my best not to shudder when I looked at the king.

"Isolde." The High King gestured to his left. "This is the Bishop of Armagh, and my brehon, Tóla Ó Conchúir." The two men bowed their heads at the mention of their names, and I nodded back.

"When Cathal arrived, he told us all about your journey," King Ruaidrí said. "Answer me this. Are you a woman of the Ulaid as you claim? Or are you a spy for poor King Diarmait? If you tell the truth, I shall not be cross."

"I'm not a spy, King Ruaidrí. I'm from Rathlin Island. It's an island north of Ulaid."

The High King leaned back into his chair and began to turn the gold and silver rings on his right hand. "In my experience, pretty young girls like you don't walk around unprotected. Nor do they dress in boy's clothes, wear armour and carry knives."

"There was a fire on the island. My cousin, who looked after me, did not… was not able to… When I realised that he wasn't alive, I wore all I could take with me, knowing that I wouldn't return."

"Have you no kin or friends in Ulaid who would've looked after you?" the bishop asked.

"No."

The High King shook his head. "I don't believe that. There must be someone who'd have taken you in. Which clan do you hail from?"

"I have no clan. My cousin only ever mentioned my uncle called Colmon, who is a monk at Seir Kieran. There is no one else."

"And so you travelled south," the king mused. "What do you want from this Brother Colmon? What help do you believe your cousin can give you?"

The High King's grey eyes were still now, suspicion in every expression, every gesture. Panic was building inside me, but I could not let it take me over. And why should I? I had done nothing wrong... but I quickly brushed that thought aside, for it was the thought of Isolde of Rathlin Island. Too naïve. Too assuming. The sense of injustice that I'd held within me since Scolaí and his friends had bound my wrists was still within me, but I did not trust in fairness anymore. These men were not Broccan who was patient and devoted to the truth. They were guided by other things, other emotions. All I could do was try my best and hope that keeping me prisoner was not in their interests, for it was their world I was in now. Their hall. Their warriors. Their eyes.

"I don't know, King Ruaidrí. All I know is that he is my family, and I want to be with him rather than strangers who I do not know and who do not know me."

Running his hand over his beard, the High King then clasped his hands together. "Your cousin from Rathlin intrigues me. He raised you by himself, did he?"

"Yes."

"It strikes me as unusual that he would want to take on such a task in isolation."

"He worked his land in the day, and in the evening, he made up stories and sang songs. It was a simple life. He seldom spoke of his past, but he was happy on the island. He did not like large gatherings of people, I know that much."

The king glanced at the brehon and the bishop. The bishop shrugged. "I've heard of Rathlin Island. There was a great Viking raid there. Years ago."

"True," the brehon confirmed. "The pagans burned it to the ground, and they took the people as slaves."

"Ah, you'll have no luck here, Cuan!" King Ruaidrí said, grinning. "Isolde won't favour a Viking like you."

"You're Viking, Cuan?" I asked, glad the focus had moved away from myself.

"Great Norse blood runs through his veins," King Ruaidrí answered for him. "His mother was a sister of King Godred, Viking King of the Isles. And King Godred tells anyone who will listen that he and his family are the descendants of Brian Boru, Sitric Silkbeard, Ivar the Boneless, and the famous Ragnar Lodbrok."

Cuan's face remained impassive as the king relayed this information. He simply picked up his cup of wine and drank from it. That was his strategy. His way of coping with unwanted attention.

The High King's smile faded. Pressing his forefinger to his lips, he pushed his plate away. He was thinking. Deciding. I bit down on my tongue and tried to calm my breathing. Part of me wanted to blurt out more about my life on Rathlin or to speak more of Broccan, but from the way everyone waited for the king to speak with bated breath, I didn't think that would be welcome. Reaching for the cup of wine that had been placed beside my plate, I took a small drink. If polite disinterest and quiet worked for Cuan, perhaps it would work for me.

"Scolaí," King Ruaidrí said. "Ask King Magnus to join us."

Scolaí's lips twitched as he bowed, and a minute later the old king came to stand beside King Ruaidrí.

"Well, Magnus, what did you think of Isolde's tale?"

"It's hard to know for sure, but my men did say there was a fire on the island. She tells the truth on that account. They also said there was a man who came over from the island to trade from time to time. A loner with scars down one side of his face."

"That's Broccan!" I said. "That's my cousin."

"Aye," King Magnus said. "That was the name they gave him."

"I see." King Ruaidrí smiled. "There. I knew we'd resolve this matter quickly. You are free to go, Isolde."

Scolaí glared. "But, my king, I've more to say on this matter."

"She's no spy, Scolaí," King Ruaidrí said. "King Magnus will have to find someone else's tongue to cut out." He leaned forward to catch the King of Ulaid's eye as he walked back to his seat. "What made you accuse her of spying is beyond me, Magnus."

King Magnus shrugged. "Scolaí put the idea into my head."

Relief flooded through me as the interest of both kings waned. I could have laughed or smiled with joy, only I knew from the way that Scolaí's skin paled that he was not done yet. The king's mind could be easily swayed perhaps, and so I kept my head lowered and began to pick at the food on my plate.

Scolaí's eyes, still full of disbelief, darted back and forth between the two kings. "She was violent, King Ruaidrí, and I worried about the welfare of King Magnus' granddaughters."

"Do you hear that, Magnus?" the one-eyed man said. "Scolaí's concerned about your granddaughters. If you don't have them engaged before the marriage fair, you may have an elopement on your hands."

King Magnus could only laugh as he lowered himself into his chair. "Scolaí, you ambitious boy! Perhaps I should cut out your tongue instead."

The outbreak of laughter which followed indicated the threat was insincere. Even so, Scolaí's cheeks flushed red. "But she spoke to the Norman man in the church in his own language. She took a message from him."

"If you were sure this man was delivering messages to a spy, why did you not try to find him?"

"We did try. He got away."

The one-eyed king snorted. "That is a poor excuse, Scolaí. I thought you were made of sterner stuff."

King Ruaidrí nodded. "As it happens, my men apprehended another spy trying to send messages to the Northern O'Neill kings. It seems King Diarmait is trying to get them on his side. I'm sure, given you didn't find this one, that he made his way to one of the Ó'Neill forts in order to spread Diarmait's lies and schemes."

"I apologise, King Tigernán," Scolaí replied. "The cunning are always the hardest to pin down."

Scolaí spoke his last remark while looking at me, hoping, I supposed, to imply that I was cunning too. I didn't react. Not one bit.

"What about my claim, King Ruaidrí?" Scolaí asked, quickly composing himself. "Regarding the injury to my arm when she tried to escape."

"Oh, yes," the brehon, Tóla, leaned forward. "Tell me the details again."

Scolaí's shoulders tensed as he stepped forward, but he spoke quickly. Eager, I thought, to tell his story and have the eyes of the kings upon him. "She walked past us in the forest. We called for her to stop, but she ran away. I caught her, and she stabbed me with a knife which drew blood from my arm."

"Have you healed?" Tóla asked.

"Yes," Scolaí said, "but there's a scar."

"Did you lose any wealth because of this attack?"

"No, but that's not the point. She attacked a warrior of the High King."

Tóla licked his lips. "Did she know that's what you were? Did you tell her when you asked her to stop?"

"No," Cuan answered before Scolaí could. "No one said. We assumed she'd know."

Tóla turned to me. "Did you truly not know they were soldiers of the High King? Be honest now. I will know if you lie."

"I did not know," I replied. "When I saw them at the edge of the forest, they frightened me, and I was alone."

"Why did you not tell her, Scolaí?" the bishop asked.

"She was wearing boy's clothes and armour. We thought he would know."

"Oh, yes. How unusual," Tóla said. "Can I see the knife?"

"I have it," Cuan said, and he took it out of his belt and handed it to the brehon who rolled it over in his hand.

I hated that it was being passed around. It was my mother's blade, given to me by Broccan. Aside from the small silver pendant, it was my only link to her.

"Odd, yes, but safer for a woman travelling alone," Tóla said as he pressed his finger to the tip, flinching at the sharpness. "I suppose I can see the sense in it." He closed his eyes for a second or two, the lines in his jaw slackening as he thought. When he opened them, he took a deep breath. "I think, in this case, a woman may protect her honour, and as you hadn't told her who you were, she committed no crime in defending herself."

Scolaí's eyes widened.

"That sounds sensible," the High King said, before Scolaí formed any coherent argument. "And since you've brought Isolde here against her will, she can stay at the games as my guest."

Scolaí spluttered. "But she ran away, King Ruaidrí. How would someone from Rathlin Island know Latin and the Frankish language?"

"My cousin taught me these languages."

The High King sighed. "If her only crime was to speak Latin and run away from you and Cuan, I don't blame her. I'll consider the time she spent in your company punishment enough for any wrongdoings."

This produced a loud burst of laughter from King Magnus and the one-eyed King Tigernán, and Scolaí bowed to show he accepted the king's decision, then walked out of the hall.

"So, Isolde. What shall I do with you?" the High King said, swirling his cup.

The relief that I had just allowed to rise up, ebbed away. I didn't want him to do anything with me except let me go.

"If you could show me the way to Seir Kieran, that is all I would ask from you."

"No, no," he said, shaking his head. "It's too dangerous right now. You can stay with my kinswomen until the roads to Leinster are safer."

The High King turned to Cuan. "Nephew, find Isolde lodgings. Try Blinne first and see if she's any room in her tent. Isolde is my guest, and she should be treated as such." He smiled at me and raised his cup. "You are both free to go for now."

I nodded and held out my hand to take Fragarach back from the brehon.

"No, I don't think so," the king said. "There is no need for you to have a weapon here, Isolde. I shall keep it safe for you, how about that."

Given that this wasn't a question, I nodded and left the feasting hall with Cuan. It was hard to push through the crowd, and as soon as I was outside, I sped up, desperate to get away from the thick crowd of people gathered outside the fort. Everything inside me hurt. My stomach. My chest. My head.

"Free at last," Cuan said. "I told you."

"I'm not free though, am I?" I snapped. "Tell me, am I truly a guest or a hostage?"

Cuan pulled my arm to slow me down. "You're a hostage."

"Why? Why won't he let me go?"

"Because you didn't convince him. It is odd that you speak Latin and Frankish. Aside from a daughter of a king, you won't find many women knowing how to speak those languages. He'll be watching you now. Waiting to see if anyone suspicious tries to talk to you while you are at the games."

"If he thinks I'm a spy, why didn't he just say so?"

"That wouldn't be useful to him. He'd much rather lure his enemies here and find out who you're talking to."

"And what secrets could I possibly reveal to anyone? Fearghus likes to tell stories? Scolaí hates me? That somebody despises you so much they paid four men to kill you?"

He studied my face for a second, his expression softening. "It's not me who is accusing you of spying. If you do nothing to provoke his suspicions, you will not stay in his mind for long. Then you will be able to leave. Eat. Drink. Have fun at the games." He pointed then to a tent a little further along the pathway. "That's Blinne's tent. She should have room for you."

He rapped the entrance, and a plump middle-aged woman came out. He spoke to her for a few seconds and then she waved me over.

"Hello, Isolde. I'm Blinne," the lady said as the two of us moved inside. "Please, take my granddaughter's bed."

"Are you sure?" I asked, trying not to let any anger enter my voice, for she did not deserve it. "Won't she need it?"

Blinne shook her head. "Not tonight. My granddaughter is to be married tomorrow. She's spending the night with her cousins. If you don't mind, I was going to visit them. I'll be back soon. Please help yourself to food and drink."

As soon as the entrance flap fell back, I exhaled and rubbed my hands through my hair.

Lying on the bed, I pulled one of Blinne's furs over me and listened to the rowdy cheers of the crowd outside. It didn't take long for the noise to fade. It wasn't even nighttime yet, but I didn't care. My body was exhausted, drained of all desire to speak, and so I retreated to a place of silence and darkness. A place that, for a while, no one else could reach.

Donnchad

Wexford

The walls of Wexford were much improved from the last time I was here. One hundred years ago, Wexford and Waterford lived very much in the shadow of Dublin.

No longer, it seemed.

When Diarmait had ordered his men to march here, I thought it was merely for the symbolism of holding a port. The Wexford of my memory was so small that I had no expectation of a battle, but rather a quick negotiation that the Wexford Vikings would quickly concede to.

Now I was here, I doubted that would happen. Wexford was twice the size it had been before. The trenches were deep; the wooden walls were high and sharpened at the edges, and no part of it was given to rot or damage. Even with the combined army of the Leinster Irish and Normans, now at over one thousand, I did not think we stood a chance.

The Norman knights eyed the city with interest. I guessed part of the reason Diarmait brought them here was because it would be familiar. Something worth taking. A city rather than a dun, for I had no doubt that King Diarmait's dun would be a disappointment to these Norman men. A dun, made in the old way, was nothing compared to the stone castles I'd visited in Bristol and Chepstow. It also dawned on me that if land was promised to these Anglo-Normans, the Irishmen fighting for Diarmait would have an easier time conceding territory they did not control.

So, yes, now I was here, I could see the reasoning behind it.

Common sense, however, was all very well and good… but only if the plan had a chance of working.

The men dismounted a cautious distance from the city. Some of Robert's men discussed setting up their tents while others spoke of hunting for food. I stretched my legs, then sat against a tree trunk beside Angelo. It didn't take long for Riagáin to walk over to the knights.

He spoke to Robert and Hervey first. He was excitable now, speaking fast while pointing at the city with his hands.

"What does he say?" Maurice asked, hurrying over to hear the conversation.

Hervey shrugged. "I understand his French less than his Irish. I think he wants us to attack, but I can't make out where or when."

"Donn," Robert shouted. "Come here. Tell us what Riagáin says."

Riagáin repeated his words to me, speaking even quicker than he had to Hervey.

"King Diarmait wants you to attack the city," I said to Robert. "He says you can choose which of your men will become the new overlord here."

Robert eyed Maurice and the two of them passed a knowing look. "I and my brother Gerald are to get the first of the spoils," Robert said. "Then Hervey. Strongbow's orders."

Maurice, thin-lipped, gave a curt nod of his head. Honour, what a terrible thing it was. For it made a man accept the word of another without complaint. Gerald, a man who'd never set foot on this land, was destined to control it before Maurice, a knight who had gathered two hundred of his men to fight. And Hervey came before him too, even though he'd no men with him at all. That was curious and I suspected this meant that Hervey had come here as Strongbow's eyes and ears rather than as a mere knight.

Robert leaned forward as if to dismount. "Let us make camp—"

"You don't have time. The attack is to start now." I pointed at the Irish, who were already moving into their ranks.

"How can they attack now?" Maurice spluttered. "They aren't ready. They have no siege—"

Whatever Maurice was about to say was drowned out by a roar from Domhnall and the Irishmen. They raised their spears in the air, while the Vikings shouted insults back from across the wall.

"What is wrong with them?" Riagáin asked me, confused by the anger in Maurice's voice.

"They say they aren't ready."

Riagáin frowned. "If they want to win the land, they must fight. King Diarmait has made that clear, and we cannot wait here all day. The Vikings will only call more kin to their aid if we do that, just like they did at Clontarf. A quick attack is best. Tell Robert and Maurice that."

I passed this message on to Robert, Maurice, Meilyr and Hervey. They gave each other grim looks but nonetheless began to rally their men. Smiling, I took out my sword. At last, we were at war. The first war since I'd taken in my new gift, and I was keen to see what I could do.

Walking toward my son, who was still sitting by the tree, I waved him over to me. "It's time to fight, Angelo. You stay with me. We will attack with the archers, and whatever you do, don't try to climb those walls."

Angelo took out his sword.

"You understand, don't you," I spoke softly. "You must only pass yourself. Do not put yourself in danger for these men."

Angelo pointed at my chest.

"I am different. I have the warrior gift now and intend to see what I can do, but even I have no intention of putting my life at risk. I will only ever do that if I am fighting for us."

As I expected, the attack didn't go well. The Wexford Vikings had gathered plenty of rocks to throw down on those foolish enough to attempt climbing over the wall, and, of course, on top of the wall, the Vikings were waiting with swords and axes to cut us down.

The Norman archers fired, but not knowing the layout of the city they were less effective than they'd hoped, and by the end of the day, we had lost over twenty men with twice as many injured, while the Wexford warriors had lost only one as far as I could tell. Once night fell and our attack waned, the Wexford men began to laugh and call us cowards.

Even worse, I'd been presented with no opportunity to use my gift. I was stronger, yes, I felt that when I swung my sword. I was quicker too. But with our enemies safe behind the walls, I could not test myself.

As soon as Diarmait called for a retreat, Robert called off his attack too and recalled his men into the forest. "Cut down the trees," he said to his archers and foot soldiers. "We need ladders. Lots of them."

Tired after a day of battle, the men did not complain and followed these orders. I watched them as they worked. Efficient and organised, the foot soldiers, archers and knights worked in unison while Robert spoke with Meilyr and Maurice about which section of the wall they wanted to take the following day. The Norman army worked through the night, taking turns to rest, and by morning, enough ladders had been built for another attack. I wasn't the only Irishman to be curious. In the dead of night, I noticed Domhnall come over and watch too.

Siege warfare was not something we knew about in Ireland. Why would we? The kings came out of their duns to fight, and they were so full of pride that if you declared a war, they couldn't bear the shame of hiding behind their walls. No, out they came. They would even let their enemies know the day and the place where they wanted to fight and let the opposing side ready their troops before committing themselves to battle. This style of warfare was a rarity. It was not so in the other countries I'd been to.

In Rome, oh Rome, the people there delighted in pulling down the homes of their rivals. In secret. In the dead of night. Knives in backs. Poison in drinks. Even the greatest of emperors died in such ways. When I lived there, the Orsini family built the most mighty machine that could throw stones at the tower of another, and they did this often, laughing while the children of their enemies lay dead in the street. It seemed that no matter how strong you made your building, there was always someone who could contrive to take it down.

To these Normans, who'd spent their lives fighting those in the stone forts of Damascus and Jerusalem, these wooden spikes along the Wexford walls were nothing. All they needed was time to build their ladders, and soon the city would be theirs.

While they worked, I leaned back against one of the trees and closed my eyes. Angelo was nowhere to be found. He'd snuck off into the woods after the battle, but I let him be. Now there was no stray arrow that could pierce him, he was safe enough, though what he wanted to do in the dark of the forest was beyond me.

Taking out the knife of mortality, I ran my fingers along the blade. My mother had wanted him to have a gift, but I didn't see how that would work. I wished often that Angelo had not been made the way he was. His mute silence was a hindrance. The men noticed his strangeness, some of them edged away from him when he walked past, while others looked at him in pity. I'd even heard some pray that God would give him the gift of speech. I tried not to let this discourage me. Angelo was strong. He did what I told him, but never could he assist me in the way that I hoped. For the first time since I'd left Chepstow, I thought of Cecile. Now her father was not here to watch her every move, she would see me. Want me. What children we might make.

"You are not getting ready to fight?"

I opened my eyes to find Robert staring at me, eyebrows raised.

"Why not?" he asked. "Are you injured?"

"I'm not injured, but I'm not fighting. Neither are you."

"What do you mean?"

"You will find out what I mean soon enough."

And so he did. No sooner had the archers lined up, fresh arrows readied, behind a line of foot soldiers holding their ladders, than the gates of Wexford opened. The King of Wexford and his kin rode out.

Robert gave me a wry glance. "Negotiating already?"

I nodded.

"I thought the Irish and Irish Vikings liked to fight. So far, I've only seen so-called warriors hiding behind their walls, and now they cannot even take a second day of a siege."

"Why would these men fight?" I asked him. "They pay King Ruaidrí Ó Conchúir tribute now. If they concede to Diarmait, they will pay him their tribute. It doesn't matter to them who they serve. Yesterday was amusement. That's all."

"But they have sworn vows to Ruaidrí. They will break them so easily?"

"I told you once before, oaths are broken with ease in this country. An oath sworn to Ruaidrí two years ago... Why, they'll barely even consider it."

Robert stared at the riders coming in our direction and motioned that I should follow him over to where King Diarmait and his son Domhnall stood. I did as he asked and walked behind him as he rode his destrier to the grouping. Maurice, Meilyr and Hervey joined him.

The Viking king was tall and flaxen, as many of their kind were. He smiled as he approached, bowed his head to Diarmait and asked what oaths Diarmait would have him swear.

Diarmait rode forward. This was the first time I had seen him so close. He did not smile back at the Wexford king. He glared at him, his eyes filled with disgust.

"Oaths of loyalty," he said in a low voice. "You will pay me your tributes and you will fight for me. There can be no more switching sides. I am your king and your only king. When I become High King, those who betray me will suffer greatly. This is your last chance to ensure you are spared my retribution."

The grin fell from the Wexford king's face, though I could not say he appeared afraid. "I will swear my oaths to you now, King Diarmait. I will swear any oath that you wish."

"Good. Now I want you to meet the Normans who fought with me. You will accept the knight known as Robert FitzStephen and his brother, Gerald, who isn't here yet, as your overlords. They will rule this city on my behalf. A man known as Hervey de Montmorency will be overlord on your farming territories. I also want four of your men to hold as surety."

The Wexford king nodded and four of the men who had ridden out with him urged their horses forward until they joined with the Leinster army.

"And I will call up your men to fight for me."

The Wexford king agreed to this.

"Now."

This caused a stir among the Wexford Vikings. "You go to war now?" the king asked, brow furrowed.

"Yes." This time it was Domhnall who spoke. "We go to Osraige. You have two hours to ready your men and then we ride out."

The Wexford king might not have surrendered if he thought this was something Diarmait desired, but it was too late now. Out in the open, his own life at risk as well as those of the four kinsmen who had just crossed over into the Leinster army, he had no choice but to agree. Reluctantly, he swore his vows so he could return to the city and call up his men.

"What did they say?" Robert asked.

"The Wexford Vikings have sworn their oaths to King Diarmait, and Diarmait's taken four of the members of the Wexford royal family as hostages to hold them to their word. He's also called up the army of Wexford. Apparently, we are going to fight again. We leave in two hours."

"Why?"

"I do not know. I suppose if you find out what the King of Osraige did to King Diarmait, you will have your answer."

I was about to suggest that I speak to Riagáin or even ask some of the warriors of the Leinster army, but was stopped by the realisation that Domhnall, son of Diarmait, was riding toward us.

"The King of Wexford has sworn his oaths," he said.

I translated.

Robert nodded.

"The city of Wexford now belongs to you and your brother as my father agreed, though my father still claims kingship over the land. The farming lands around Wexford have also been granted to another of Strongbow's men, Hervey, I believe you said."

Robert smiled when I translated this and he thanked Domhnall for the bequeathment of the city and land upon him, his brother and Hervey. I wondered how long it would take for him to realise that the gift of Wexford was meaningless. The Wexford Vikings would operate their city as they wished and send their tribute to whichever king demanded it. They would not heed these Normans nor give them their gold. Robert did not truly own this land, nor did he govern it. In England, perhaps they were used to this sort of hierarchy. Barons and knights and earls and kings. But in Ireland, there were only kings. This gift was empty and devoid of any true meaning… and now we rode to Osraige.

Diarmait was certainly determined to work this new army he'd obtained, while I was sure that once Robert realised how worthless Diarmait's offerings were, he would revolt. How long it would take to reach that point was the only question.

"What shall we do with the ladders?" Meilyr asked Robert.

"Burn them," came Robert's reply.

The men repeated this order, and as soon as everything was gathered, they were set alight. I turned to watch the fire, mesmerised by its dance. This fire, however, was more beautiful than most. Angelo stood beside it, reaching out with his gift to make it burn brighter. The old words of caution came to my lips, thinking to tell him not to use his gift where the Descendants might notice. I let those words die.

We did not need to be cautious anymore.

If anything, I wanted the Descendants to come. I was a Fomorian, cupbearer and warrior, and I had their knife in my possession. A knife that could take any of their gifts and make them my own.

Isolde

Kells

I woke the next day to a flurry of activity. Blinne and one of her daughters were getting dressed and talking excitedly about her granddaughter's wedding, while finishing off the embroidery on a new shawl.

Not wanting to appear rude, I got dressed too and helped them prepare the breakfast.

"Where is the wedding?" I asked as I poured out a bowl of honied barley oats and milk for each of them.

"At the mound of the buying," Blinne said. "It's the hill on the far side of the plain. There will be many brides there today, though none will be as beautiful as my Saraid."

I listened to them talk about the wedding fair, and on hearing their conversation, I believed I had stumbled upon the real reason why so many people came. While Fearghus and Cathal had been excited about the competitions, and I initially thought people came for companionship, it appeared the real reason people travelled so far was to find suitable matches for their children.

"You should come and watch the wedding ceremony this evening," Blinne said. "It happens just before sunset, and as long as the rain stays away, it's very beautiful to watch all the brides walk up the hill to say their vows and then walk back down with their new husbands at their side."

"It sounds wonderful. Thank you for inviting me."

"What are you going to do before then? Are you going to watch the games?" Blinne asked.

"Yes. I think so."

"There will be lots of competitions today. They've built a stand for the ladies of the royal families so that they can see over the plain. I'm sure, as a guest of the king, you'll be allowed there."

I thanked Blinne for her advice and smiled goodbye as she and her daughter left.

As soon as they were gone, my smile disappeared, and a deep sense of unease spread through me. Whatever reasons other people had for being here – to win competitions, friendship or marriage – none of those were mine. I was here because I was told I must stay... but I couldn't. I had to find a way to leave. Taking a deep breath, I tried desperately to keep the building panic at bay.

I tried to think of Broccan and what he would do in this situation, but that didn't help. He'd have left by now. I knew that for certain. He'd have slipped off in the middle of the night, and his warrior speed and strength would ensure no one could stop him. Indeed, Broccan would never have been caught in the first place. He'd already be at Seir Kieran by now.

Next, I thought of Affraic. What would she do?

She was wise. Patient. Careful. Slow to give her thoughts. That's what I needed to be like. I was new here. Therefore, of interest. I just had to make myself as inconspicuous as possible over the next few days and blend into the background until the High King forgot about me. I knew this was for the best, but it didn't make it any easier to accept.

I'd been reacting since I'd left Rathlin. Like a stick on the tide, I'd been pushed around. I'd been sick too. Shaking and exhausted after fleeing Rathlin and again after the fight at the bruidean. I needed to take control of myself and of my gift. I wasn't sure how to do the latter... that was the problem. I knew it came in times of fear and anger. Therefore, to keep it away over the next few days I needed to remain calm. I needed to take this time to understand my surroundings and the people I was with. Despite this being the land I was born into, I felt as if I didn't know it, nor the people. In many ways, I was a stranger.

On Rathlin Island, Broccan had told me the legends of old.

He'd told me stories of kings and their magnificent halls and brave warriors. When I looked out over the sea, that's what I thought awaited and it had daunted me. Now I was here, those stories dimmed in my mind. It was not as shining. Not as glorious. It had also dawned on me the stories of his life were from a time when my mother and father were alive. That was over one hundred and fifty years ago, and Ireland had changed. It was rougher now. Harsher. Harder. It was this that had created a feeling of otherness.

I had to close this gap, and I would. Already I felt myself becoming harsher and harder too, and I was not afraid of walking around the games alone. I didn't like the king, no, but I did not fear him.

It was the Fomorians alone who scared me now. Their golden eyes and fire were forever burned into my memory, and it was this and only this that haunted my dreams and the quiet moments when my mind wandered.

"Come on, Isolde," I whispered as I made my way outside. "It's time to move." I could not cower away and hide in this tent anymore. Squinting in the sunlight, I walked toward the wooden stand at the edge of the plain.

There were already hundreds of women sitting there. All of them wearing fine clothes and many jewels. Gold, silver and jet. Some of the girls had used berries to die their nails and eyebrows, while others had woven the summer flowers into their hair.

I didn't belong here wearing my old shirt and trousers, but still, I walked into the stand, trying to hide my poor clothing with the fabric of Broccan's cloak.

One of the women recognised me from the hall last night and waved me over to her. "The queen has heard all about you," she said, smiling. "She told me that if you came here, I should bring you to her." The woman didn't wait for a reply and led me deeper and higher into the stands.

The queen, even though we had not met, needed no introduction. She wore an embroidered dress made of a thick red fabric I had never seen before. Her fingers were covered in rings, and her wrists with bracelets. None of the other ladies, though well-dressed, could compare to her, but for all the ostentation, she had a kind face, and she smiled as I approached.

"Queen Gráinne, this is Isolde," the woman said. "The girl from Rathlin."

"Good morning, Isolde," the queen said. "I hoped you would come here. How did you sleep?"

"I slept well, Queen Gráinne."

"Do you wish to sit with us? The running competition is about to start."

"Thank you," I replied, surprised that she had offered. "You are very kind."

I sat where she pointed, a seat on the stand below hers with a good view of the plain. From here, I could see most of the competitions and the numbers of people gathered around them to watch. Thousands and thousands. It was a sight I never could have imagined.

A young woman sitting beside the queen grinned as a loud roar passed over the crowd. "What competition was that for, Mother?" she asked.

The queen looked out over the plain. "I don't know, Róisín. Oh, wait. There. The horse racing is about to start."

Róisín stood, eyes sparkling. "Yes. I see it now."

It turned out the Tailteann games was a spectacular affair. Even Fearghus and Cathal's descriptions hadn't done it justice. Thousands of men and women competed in a multitude of events, from chariot racing to storytelling. The competition was fierce, made more so by the rumour circulating that the High King would choose his fianna from among the winners. Queen Gráinne and Róisín commented often on the suitability of candidates. Only those who astounded won their approval. The other ladies were no less interested, and between the food and drink that the serving girls brought and the competitions, there was no need to leave the stand.

Watching the spectators walking around the plain interested me, too. The older men and women seemed to be viewing the young men who competed with a keen eye. It seemed this evening's wedding ceremony was in the forefront of their minds, not the fighting or running. It made me think of Moncha, King Magnus' granddaughter, and I hoped she had avoided being promised to an old king with no teeth. Then my thoughts ran to the beautiful girl wearing the golden orbs in her hair. Fearghus had told me she was to be married to King Tigernán at the games. He was the old one-eyed king who had sat at King Ruaidrí's table last night. No wonder she hadn't smiled that night at King Magnus' feast.

Only once the sun faded did the games finish, and the victorious made their way to the king's fort to celebrate. The crowds thinned, but those who stayed congregated in front of our stand. A huge ring formed, twice as big as any previous ones, and stood ten men deep the entire way round.

"Ah, Isolde," Queen Gráinne said. "You're in for a treat. The sword-fighting final is my favourite contest to watch."

"Mine too," Róisín added as she stood to get a better view.

King Ruaidrí himself approached the crowd, and the low hum of excitement began to build. The men and women parted for him to pass so he could stand at the front. Another man of a similar age to Cuan walked in his wake. Long red hair, the same colour as the king's, reached his elbows, and he shook the hands of the men next to him.

"Who's fighting?" Róisín asked no one in particular as her head bobbed up and down, her eyes scanning the faces in front of us.

"Look," the queen said, pointing. "Fearghus is one."

I examined the ring with renewed interest. Fearghus strode to the centre, holding a sword and a long wooden shield. He beat at it with his fist and the crowd roared.

From the other side of the ring, a second man entered. A large black raven decorated the shield he carried, and he spun it round with his fingers before gripping it tight. He turned, and a pair of ice-blue eyes stared at me for a second.

"It's Cuan," Róisín said.

"Yes," the queen replied, her back stiffening as she shifted her weight to see him better.

I leaned forward to get a better view too. Cuan and Fearghus had spoken of this competition during our travels, yet I had never expected to see it. Fearghus had spoken of it almost in jest. It was strange to see him looking so serious now.

"Who will win?" Róisín asked her mother.

The queen shrugged. "I've never seen Cuan fight before, but it's hard to look past Fearghus. He won last year and the year before that."

"What a shame Conchobar can't compete in the sword-fighting," Róisín whispered as she looked at the man with the long red hair standing beside her father. "He was so excited about it, too."

"He won the race," the queen whispered back. "It's only fair others are given a chance to win the other competitions. If your brother won everything, how would your father pick his fianna?"

A clash of metal rang out.

The fight had started. Everyone in the crowd silenced as Fearghus's sword bore down against Cuan's shield. Cuan was the taller of the two, but Fearghus was broader and used his weight to press forward. I could see why Fearghus was the queen's favourite. He was strong and fierce, and skilful with the blade.

For a moment, I thought Cuan would fall under the pressure of Fearghus' weight. Instead, he pivoted and thrust his shield against Fearghus' left side.

Fearghus laughed as he jumped back, but the laugh was short-lived as he moved into position. They edged closer, circling around each other. Round and round they went. The space between them grew smaller.

Fearghus charged. His sword crashed into Cuan's while he positioned his shield upward to protect his chest. Cuan parried the strike and spun away, hitting Fearghus on the shoulder with the pommel of his sword.

Cuan returned to the centre of the circle and waited for Fearghus to regain his footing, but this gesture only incensed his opponent.

Fearghus charged again. Cuan ran forward to meet him, and their swords collided. The fight quickened now, and their swords repeatedly connected, each man trying to wear the other down. Fearghus rained down strike after strike on Cuan, while Cuan blocked and deflected and then lunged forward at a speed Fearghus couldn't match.

Cuan was the first to bleed as a blow from Fearghus' shield landed against his nose, but there was no doubt Fearghus was beginning to slow. This was dangerous. Broccan had always told me this, and it was why he had trained me so hard. A tired warrior is a dead warrior.

Fearghus must have known this too, knew that he had to win soon, or it was over, because he suddenly sprinted, swinging his sword overhead. At the last second, Cuan shifted to his right, and the momentum of Fearghus' sword dragged him down, and his blade hit the mud. Cuan spun and pressed his sword against the back of Fearghus' neck.

Everything was still. The spectators clapped, slow at first, and then fast, like a downpour of heavy rain. I stood and clapped, too. It was a good fight. I wondered then if Broccan had ever entered these competitions when he was younger. He had told me that he'd had to repress his gift when fighting with the mortals, so they did not know of it. Perhaps that would have taken the joy of competition from him, but I thought he would have enjoyed watching it all the same.

Fearghus and Cuan embraced as they put down their swords and another man lifted Cuan's hand into the air, declaring him the victor. The crowd cheered and whooped, and Cuan laughed as he shook hands with those closest to him. He made his way to the High King, who stood in front of our bench. The king stared at Cuan in the same way he did last night. Smiling with his mouth but not his eyes. Why was that? What was the cause of the distance between them?

"Congratulations, nephew," the High King said, patting Cuan on the shoulder.

The young redheaded man beside the king reached out to shake Cuan's hand. "I hope, cousin," he said, "you're not too tired for the spear-throwing tomorrow."

"No, Conchobar. I'll be rested by then."

"He's half-Viking," the man standing behind Conchobar said. "When Cuan loses, he'll tell everyone you had an unfair advantage."

"If he says it, it won't be true," Conchobar replied. "While Cuan's been hosted by the northern kings all month, I've been working with my father to ensure these Normans stay away from our land. If anyone has a claim to tiredness, it is me."

"You have me there, Conchobar. And you are right, you have been working hard," Cuan said. "Don't think that means I'll have any sympathy for you though."

"I never would expect sympathy from you," Conchobar answered, the lightness in his voice evaporating. "I'll see you tomorrow, cousin, and well done on your victory."

Cuan stood back so Conchobar could pass, his expression as still as stone. I couldn't help but stare at Cuan as his uncle and cousin walked away. Cuan had not told me much about himself, but he was clearly an outsider. He was an Ó Conchúir, yes, but he was not a true part of the clan. Why was that? What had he done?

"Are you coming to the fort, Isolde?" the queen asked as she and Róisín stepped down from the stand. "You can if you wish, though I would come sooner if you want a seat inside. Once the wedding celebration is over, it will be too full."

"Oh," I said. "I told Blinne I would go and watch the wedding ceremony."

"Then please do, and enjoy yourself," the queen said. "Be careful, though, that no man tries to carry you up the hill. That happened last year, you know."

She left with her daughter then, the two of them laughing over the incident last year and how terrible it would be if it had happened to them.

I sat until the other women moved from the stands, then I

walked toward the mound of the buying that Blinne had spoken of that morning.

Blinne was right. There were hundreds of people gathering there, now that the sun was setting, and more and more were coming from the campsite. Not just those about to be married, but their families, too. It was easy to see who the brides were. They wore their finest dresses and jewellery. Those who had no gold or gems wore headdresses made of wildflowers. Blinne's granddaughter, Saraid, wore such an adornment, grinning from ear to ear as she waited to be called up the hill.

While one or two of the young girls seemed hesitant, most of the women congregating at the foot of the hill were like Saraid, smiling and laughing, and as soon as the king's brehon called them, they made their way upward, grins upon their faces.

I liked this.

Móirne had decided to be married. She had carried this hope for a new life inside of her too. I had not understood then. I'd only seen the uncertainty of it all. My life had been so easy. I'd been so loved and cared for by Broccan that I had never sought it out. Now I was here, I could feel the anticipation, the excitement that Móirne must have felt, and I understood her better because of it.

In the past few weeks, I'd fallen into despair. I had seen so much violence and unkindness. Endured so much loss. Here, however, there was joy, and as the women reached the top of the hill, I found myself smiling. Amid all the chaos and uncertainty, I was glad to find a small piece of hope.

"Isolde!"

I turned to find Dáirinn, King Magnus' granddaughter, walking toward me.

"Evening, Dáirinn," I said. "How are you?"

"I am well. I'm here to see my sister, Nuala, marry King Tigernán. You didn't happen to see her walk up the hill?"

"Oh, no. I was watching Saraid. I'm staying with her grandmother, Blinne… but I'm sure your sister looks very beautiful."

"Oh, she does. We're going to the fort to celebrate once they walk back down, but first I wanted to give you this." She handed over a leather parcel that she'd been holding. "It's your dress. The one I gave you at the dun. You left so quickly you forgot to take it with you."

"Oh." I blushed as I took the dress. "But I have nothing to give you in return."

Dáirinn shook her head. "No, it is not for you to give us anything. You were our guest, and this is our gift to you."

Shouts from her other sisters rang out behind her, and I saw Moncha waving her hand to get Dáirinn's attention.

"Thank you for this, Dáirinn. Enjoy yourself tonight."

Dáirinn grinned, then made her way back to her sisters who were staring at the hill, watching for Nuala. The newly married couples were holding hands now, bound in cloth, and beginning to return to their families.

Wrapping my hand over the parcel, I walked back to Blinne's tent and sat on one of the logs outside. The campfires had been lit now, and the fortress was filled with people dancing and celebrating the weddings or else the competitions.

The people around me, those not invited inside, danced and sang too. Their laughter was not diminished because they danced under the stars rather than inside a wooden fort. I watched them, accepted a drink, and slowly began to talk. First to Blinne. Then to her daughter and granddaughter. Then their friends.

The heaviness inside my heart lifted as we spoke, and a smile crept onto my face. Touching my lips, I took a sip of the ale I'd been given, and brushed away the tears sliding down my cheeks, unable to explain to myself how, even after everything I'd endured, life could sometimes be so beautiful.

Donnchad

Kingdom of Osraige

"Do they understand what I want?" Domhnall stared at me, impatient, though trying to hide it.

We'd been riding south for days, through endless forest and then through the mountain passes. Everyone was exhausted and tempers were fraying. Last night, the Norman army had camped away from the Leinster warriors and Wexford Vikings, and had set up patrols around their campsite. Whatever trust had been gained during the attack on the walls of Wexford had dissipated entirely.

"The Leinster warriors will be at the front of the army," I answered. "You want the Anglo-Norman men in the centre. The Wexford Vikings will bring up the rear."

Domhnall nodded, but stared at the men behind me, none of whom were ready to move.

"Your messenger said that King Pátraic of Osraige is waiting for us on the plain ahead and that he has five thousand men with him," I said. "Hervey's Irish isn't good, but he understood that."

Domhnall gave me a wry smile. "We can defeat them."

"But why would you want to fight like this? You will lose a lot of men."

"What concern is that of yours?" Domhnall stepped closer to me, chest out. "What's your name again? Donn? Is that even a name? And what are you? Norman or Irish?"

"I'm both."

"You don't look like both. You look like one of us. What a traitorous wretch you must be. A fuidir, no doubt?" Domhnall laughed when I did not contradict him. "Well, whatever you claim to be, your opinion is meaningless. Now tell Robert and Maurice that we are riding onward, and if they want any more land, they need to follow us or else we will leave them here. And tell them this: my father has forbidden the shipmasters of Wexford to sail them home. They are stuck here whether they like it or not. So, they can either fight like they promised, or they can spend the night in the forest which has a curse upon it."

I translated this to Robert, who passed it on to Meilyr and Maurice. I hung back this time and offered no advice. They gave each other grave looks, mulled over their options, but I could tell from their strained conversations that they knew there were no real options. They had to go onward and fight, for to leave now would only render all their work so far pointless.

Another reason for my silence was that I wanted to watch what the Normans would do in an open battle. Reputation was one thing, but I needed to see them in action. What was it about them that made them such a formidable force? It could be that their reputation hung upon the names of their fathers and grandfathers, and if so, they were useless to me. Better to find out now, rather than later.

"Five thousand is too much," Meilyr said to Robert. "And they will have the high ground."

Robert licked his lips. "We will use the archers to kill as many as we can before we ride out. Then we must push through the openings in their shield walls."

I looked over at the horses the Norman and Flemish knights had brought with them. *Destriers,* they called them. Mostly stallions. They were larger than the horses we used here. Bulkier. As well as saddles and reins, these horses wore armour on their chests and flanks. It meant they covered less ground than the Irish horses and tired more quickly. To me it seemed madness to slow them down in this way, but that the Normans won their battles with their heavy cavalry was no secret.

"Come, Angelo," I whispered.

My son walked over to me, eyes staring at the oak trees towering above us. He did not look like a man about to head into battle, unless one looked at the new weapon hanging over his shoulder.

"Where did you get this?" I touched the bow. It was thicker and longer than any I'd seen before. More powerful.

Angelo pressed a finger against his throat.

"This belonged to one of the dead archers?"

He nodded.

"Do the other archers know you have this?"

He nodded again and pointed at one of the leaders. I glanced behind my son and looked over at the group of archers gathered there. One of them gestured toward Angelo and said something that made the others laugh.

The men here did not like Angelo, not the Irish and not the Norman, and while giving my son a weapon might seem like kindness, it was not. The man who'd told the joke laughed again, petting one of Maurice de Prendergast's hunting dogs that seemed to favour him. "Down, Bruce," he said. "Easy now."

Angelo, however, seemed oblivious to the fact the men were laughing at him as he examined the bow between his fingers.

Pushing thoughts of my son and his place in this world from my mind, I began to mull over what the Normans' strategy might be and how these archers would be of any value. The Irish had archers, but never a significant number. Spears were usually favoured over the bow and arrow, and the sword was king. If not a sword, then an axe. To me, it seemed odd to have so many archers within an army, and their presence at Wexford had made little difference. What would they do when the warriors of Osraige came at them, swinging their swords? They'd be as sheep for the slaughter. Still, for them to be here, and hold such value with the Norman army, there had to be a reason. I just hadn't worked it out yet.

"If you wish to fight with them, Angelo, go ahead. Just remember to be careful. Do not risk your life for these men. Retreat into the forest if you must."

Angelo nodded.

"And do not let them belittle you either. That's important. Do you understand?"

Once again, my son gave a nod, then made his way over to the archers.

I would have to speak to him more later. Find a way to make him understand. When we had lived in Paris and Rome, we had kept to ourselves. That he was not good at socialising with other men hadn't seemed important, but now it was. One could not lead if men did not like you.

Once Angelo was in position with the archers, I lined up with the Norman foot soldiers, waiting to be called. It seemed that the Leinster riders were going out first, then their warriors on foot, followed by the Norman archers and foot soldiers. The Wexford Vikings moved into line behind us. The Norman knights remained at the back.

We marched out to the plain. The sight ahead of us was worse than I expected. Not only did the Osraige men have the high ground, but they had also dug trenches along the bottom of the hill so that the Normans could not ride their horses toward them.

Robert rode to the edge of the forest, pushing past the Leinster horsemen, who had stayed within the safety of the alder trees. "Loose," he shouted.

The Norman archers marched to the forest's edge and shot into the sky. Their arrows flew upward, hissing in the air as they glided toward the hill. The arrows, flying higher and faster than I expected, hit the Osraige warriors. Screams came thick and fast. The Osraige had the high ground, yes, but they had no shelter, and these Norman longbows would do their damage.

"Shields," I heard one of the Osraige leaders shout. Their men moved into a new formation, holding their shields over their heads.

Another round of arrows was loosed. Some of the Osraige warriors fell, but not as many as last time. So tightly packed together, it meant they could protect themselves well if they knew a volley was coming.

The soldiers beside me began to look at their commanders,

itching to fight rather than wait in the forest. That's when screams sounded out. Hundreds of Osraige men on horseback rode out from behind the hill, but rather than ride to us, they disappeared into the forest.

"They are going to ride until they get behind us and then drive us out," Domhnall shouted. "Men of Leinster, we must fight now. We must fight to avenge the blinding of our prince."

Ah, so the reason for the rush to fight the Osraige was now clear. It was a blood feud rather than a fight for territory. It was as well the Normans did not know this, otherwise they might not have agreed to come.

Domhnall, sword raised over his head, left the safety of the forest and rode toward the hill. Toward the trenches. His men followed.

"They are mad," Robert said to Meilyr.

"What shall we do?" Maurice asked.

"Do as I said before," Robert replied. "We must try to breach the trenches. Find gaps in their shield-wall. Antagonise them. Then we will retreat across the plain. Have Miles ready his flag. Rally on my call."

Meilyr and Maurice nodded and passed the strategy to the other knights, though I had not understood everything Robert had meant. What flag? Rally to where?

Robert rode forward and gestured for the Norman foot soldiers to join the fray. That was me. As we charged out onto the plain, we met with the back line of the Leinster warriors, but quickly, the Normans edged forward. Their armour, helmets and riveted chain-mail were superior to the Leinster men's. The Norman foot soldiers took some of the long Irish spears from the Leinster men and launched them at the Osraige warriors who stood on the other side of the trench. The Osraige threw their spears too but landed fewer than usual, unable to pierce the Norman chain-mail. However, chain-mail did not cover the whole of the body, and the Osraige spearmen were still able to find eyes and necks and armpits. The Norman soldiers began to fall.

All in all, this was a dirty way of fighting. Hills and trenches. Our spears pierced the Osraige men. Their spears pieced ours. But this would only ever suit the army with the greatest numbers. Today that was Osraige.

Arrows flew overhead. Now that the Osraige warriors had begun to fight, their shields protected their chests and on this third volley, the arrows did serious damage. Men on the hill tumbled forward, choking on their own blood as their bodies fell into the trenches. As more bodies fell, the trenches filled.

This was enough to cause some of the Osraige warriors to charge over the corpses of their fallen kin to push our line back. By moving the fight closer to our men, they prevented our archers from risking another volley, for fear of hitting their own. This suited the Osraige warriors… but it suited me most of all.

Sword at the ready, I moved into the crowd of Osraige warriors sprinting toward me and drew on my warrior gift, moving faster than I'd ever moved before. The warriors fell at my feet. One, two, three. Ten. Twenty. All unable to block or parry my strikes or see where the next attack was coming from.

"Retreat!" Robert shouted out over the fray.

I ran back, not wanting to be caught among an enemy army alone, and moved into a group of Norman foot soldiers.

"Retreat!" Robert roared again.

We all hurried. Exhausted and covered in blood, we did as commanded, and the Osraige warriors followed. The lower half of the hill emptied as the warriors there gave us chase and soon the plain was full.

"Rally to me!" Robert shouted another command from the far edge of the plain, and the knights turned their horses.

The foot soldiers turned too, moving so that gaps were left open for the horses to charge through.

Now the Osraige men were out of formation and away from the safety of their trenches, they were vulnerable. Half of the knights charged, using their horses to knock these Osraige warriors over. These horses, trained in battle, caused devastation, and the Osraige warriors scrambled frantically to cross back over their trenches, while the Norman foot soldiers and Wexford Vikings sliced and stabbed at them from behind.

It was the Osraige leaders who now called for a retreat.

I stood back as this happened. Watched. Listened to the Norman knights call their commands. Another knight, the one called Miles, rode out of the forest, to the other side of the plain, waving a flag. This flag prompted the archers to follow him and assemble over there. The Osraige warriors, still desperately trying to reach the hill, didn't notice the movement of the archers. They didn't watch as the archers nocked their longbows and aimed at the trees.

How clever. They were waiting for the Osraige horsemen who, at this very moment, were riding toward us, thinking they were going to charge into our flank.

As the fighting thickened by the trenches, the retreating Osraige men fell. At least ten of them for every three of us. The Leinster men fought hard in the thick of battle, using their swords and spears to bring down their foes. This was where they excelled. The Norman foot soldiers fought well, but they did not have the Irish passion for this type of combat. The Norman knights, however, were deadly. Using their horses to push forward, standing upright on their stirrups, they sliced and stabbed and hacked their way through the Osraige retreat.

"Loose!"

A volley of arrows flew toward the forest, catching nearly all of the Osraige horsemen who had just ridden out from the cover of the trees.

The Osraige men on the hill blew their horns. *Retreat*, they called. *Retreat.*

Chaos began in earnest. The Osraige horses, pierced with arrows, crashed into the horses behind them. Rearing and thrashing, throwing their riders from their seats and trampling them. Some of the horsemen were able to ride back into the forest while those thrown from their saddles could only try to make it over the trench and climb the hill with the other footmen. The archers turned their attention to them now. Death rained down from on high. Fewer and fewer made it to the safety of their army, and the ground around the trench was covered, two or three deep in some places, with the dead. Five thousand was now less than two thousand and the Osraige commanders, who had watched the fight from the hill, had tears in their eyes as they watched this onslaught. As the last of their men reached them, they disappeared, retreating into the safety of the forests behind them.

We had won.

After the battle, Diarmait and his men moved over their dead enemies and cut away their ears and noses, while the Wexford Vikings cut their heads clean off. Some of these heads were collected and set together in a pile.

Meilyr blessed himself upon seeing this. "What are they doing?"

"The land here is cursed," I said. "A geis is upon it, and these men believe the dead will haunt them if they do not cut away their ears and noses."

It was old, this superstition that the Leinster men had, but it was more than this that fuelled these acts. There was cruelty there too. There was a desire to please. For King Diarmait himself laughed on seeing one of the heads in the Wexford pile. It must have been someone high up in the Osraige clan. Perhaps even the man responsible for taking the eyes of his son. For Diarmait pulled this head away from the rest of the wall and sliced away the man's nose and ears himself.

Domhnall had already mounted his horse at this point and shouted at his men. They rode then toward a dun in the distance, though Domhnall stalled a moment to call out something to me.

"Tell the Normans that the dun belongs to one of the kings of Osraige, and he keeps much of his gold there. The Normans can take the spoils alongside our men if they wish. We will stay there tonight and march to Ferns tomorrow."

Robert gave my translated message to his men and watched his archers and footmen run to the dun. Neither he nor any of his knights moved.

"You don't want any of the spoils for yourself?" I asked him. "It is a generous lord who gives so much away to his men."

"It is not a blind craving for gold that has brought us here, Donn. We do not come here as pirates or thieves. We have come here to restore the fortunes of King Diarmait, yes, but we also come for the gift of land and cities. It seems to me that these many kingdoms of your land should someday be reduced to one, and perhaps the sovereignty over the whole kingdom will stand upon our shoulders."

"You would have Strongbow be King of Ireland?"

"Aye, I would." He stared at the dead bodies lying on the grass, men with their ears and eyes cut away from them. "I knew this was a savage land, but it is a godless one, too. I would remedy that. Not for myself, but for the people living here. I would have them step out of the darkness and into the light."

He moved to talk to his knights then and left me to stand alone.

That night, we slept in the shadow of the dun. Screams could be heard from the forest. Shields banged and clashed.

"What is this cursed place we have come to?" Hervey said, kneeling in prayer. Many of the archers and footmen fled the sound and hid in large groups in the forest, but the knights prayed or else stood with their swords drawn.

I hid in the forest with Angelo, watching how the men reacted. The noises, of course, were from the Osraige survivors. They had lost the battle, but they wanted to put fear into the Normans and Leinster men. It was the wind that gave their cries a ghostly veil. The wind itself seemed to moan as it passed through the tall trees, which in turn creaked and rustled. So loud it was that it felt as if an army moved toward us with death upon its lips.

It put fear into many of the men's hearts, but not these knights'.

Certainly not Robert's. I felt it, the power in this man's conviction. In how this conviction inspired the men who fought for him. They were united by it.

The Irish, for all they could fight and for all their superior numbers, didn't have this cohesion. They were too split. Their loyalties too divided.

I realised then that this Ireland I had returned to was ripe for the taking. I could see the wars that were about to unfold. The bodies that would line the fields. The kings who would fight among themselves rather than save their people.

I smiled at this.

These people of Ireland. These Anglo-Normans, too. All of them would be mine to subdue.

In the end.

Isolde

Kells

I *fell to my knees.*
My stomach throbbed and as I looked down, blood poured from the open wound there.

All around me were the ruins of a great building. The walls of the inner houses were burning still, the thatch and wood scattered over the ground. The outer walls, made of stone, were collapsed and destroyed too.

I looked to my side, wiping the liquid running from my mouth. Not the red of blood, no, but black. Thick. So thick it covered my teeth and tongue. The foul taste clung to the back of my throat, and I tried to spit it out, though to no avail. That's when I saw the dead body lying beside me. Long brown hair covered the grass, but I could not make out her face, for it was turned away from me and a thick layer of blood had pooled under her head.

What had happened here? I couldn't comprehend it. As I scanned the grounds, I saw many bodies lying on the grass. Many of them women and children. All dead.

"You did this."

Lying on the grass beside me was a man with black skin and white hair. His grey eyes stared at me. A sword pierced his chest and blood seeped from his body onto the grass.

"No... No, Colmon. How could I do this?" I crawled over to him, one hand over my wound so that I could move. I expected more blood to pour from my stomach, but none came now. I stopped crawling, prised the fabric open only to find that the skin had already knitted over. The wound, gone.

As I reached this man, Colmon, I tentatively reached for the sword.

"Don't," he said. "It is too late."

"I don't understand." I sobbed then. Sobbed to see him like this. "Who did this to us?"

"You. It is you who did this, Isolde. Look at the dead lying on the grass. It is all you. I told you that you must learn to control your gift, and you did not listen."

"I am sorry, Colmon. I'm sorry. Please let me save you. Please let me try."

He took my hand in his and shook his head as tears fell from his eyes and down his cheeks. "It is over, Isolde. Your strength has left you and we have failed. They will come for you now. You should run."

"I can't…" I wiped the tears spilling from my own eyes, too many to catch. "I cannot… what if I do this again?"

Colmon closed his eyes and as he did so, he turned his head from me. With this final effort, his last breath left him, and I had no answer to my question.

I woke up. Panting. Sweating. The dream had felt so terrible. So real. For a moment, everything felt strangely unfocused, as if I were underwater and drowning, only for all my senses to sharpen at the same time.

Throwing my legs out of the bed, I put on my shawl. Vomit was already swirling in my stomach, and as soon as I made it outside, I heaved. The vomit, full of the foul black liquid from my dreams, splattered on the grass.

What was wrong with me? I didn't know, but I needed to. This nightmare… it had to be my mind's way of telling me what I needed to do. The Colmon who I had dreamed of, he was a Descendant, a powerful one, though Broccan had told me he'd never woken after the attack on Fennit Island. My dream was showing me that all this waiting and pretending had to end. I had to find the other Descendants. I needed them to teach me control.

Quickly, I ran away from the tent. The campsite was quiet tonight. After a week of games and festivities, everyone was readying themselves for the last day tomorrow. I was grateful for this, at least. Grateful that nobody could see me shaking and sweating, and I ran past the tents to the edge of the plain.

But my strength didn't last for long, and I fell to the ground. Shaking and shivering, I couldn't even bring myself to stand. How could I escape now when I was like this?

The wind picked up as I stared out at the forest in the distance. I could almost hear the rustling of the leaves as the breeze blew against them. I was so close. No one was here, no one was watching me. If I could just get up, if I could....

Are you listening, child?

That voice again. The voice I'd heard on Rathlin thinking it was Móirne, and again when I'd been captured.

You must sing your song. Can't you hear the sadness within your words? Are you listening?

"Yes," I whispered. "I'm listening, though I don't understand."

My arms gave way, and I collapsed onto the grass, fatigue swimming at the edges of my mind. Inside the darkness, I saw Colmon's face again. *It is over*, he said to me. *It is over.*

"Isolde. What's wrong? Why are you here?"

Someone picked me up. I didn't know how long I'd been lying on the grass, nor could I answer them. My head throbbed, and the shaking, I couldn't stop, though I was not afraid. The vision, though, continued to play over and over, and this time I saw flashes of something else. The man, Colmon, I saw fire swirling around him as he fought with his spear. And I saw another in the distance. A man carrying a sword that was on fire. He was screaming my name. *Isolde*, he shouted. *Isolde.*

"My friend, I'm glad I found you."

It was a stranger who spoke, and a dull thud followed. Opening my eyes, I peeked through a gap in the blankets that someone had placed over my body. I was in a tent, not Blinne's. I moved a little more, until I saw who had spoken. Cuan, with his arms wrapped around a man I didn't know, came into view.

"How are you, Bjorn?" Cuan said. "I've missed you. How is Brenna?"

"I'm good. Brenna too."

Cuan pulled out of the hug and sat on the furs spread over the floor. "I heard Vikings died when the Normans attacked Wexford. I prayed it wasn't you or your family."

Bjorn clicked his tongue against his cheek. "It was only one of us who died, so don't be worrying. The gods still favour me. They don't call me to Valhalla yet."

"Still haven't converted, then?" Cuan asked.

Bjorn snorted. "Never."

They laughed and Bjorn sat. I closed my eyes and stayed still. This was a private conversation, I realised. I should move or cough or do something to alert them that I had woken. But I didn't. I wanted to listen. The Cuan who spoke with such affection aroused my interest.

Bjorn settled opposite his friend, and as I opened my eyes for a moment, I could just about make out his face. He had a rounded chin and snub nose, and his head was completely shaved aside from a thin line in the middle of his scalp where his black hair was long and braided. "I worry about you with these Irishmen," he said. "They are a treacherous lot. I know you're half-Irish yourself, but it is us you should be with."

"You're probably right," Cuan replied, his tone moving back toward the disinterested one I knew so well.

"Tell me, truthfully," Bjorn said. "Why didn't you stay in the Isles with your uncle? You helped Godred win back his kingship. He would've rewarded your loyalty with more than gold."

Cuan grunted. "I hear he rewarded you. You have a new ship."

"She's a beauty, yes... but you didn't answer my question."

Cuan hesitated. "My cousins Ragnall and Olaf are already eyeing their father's throne. I don't want to be there when they start to fight each other for it. My presence would only complicate matters."

Bjorn tutted. "But don't you have a similar situation here? If you're not careful, your cousin Conchobar will blind or kill you. By the look of that scar, he's already tried."

"This is my home, Bjorn. It's right that I am here."

"Then why do you still fight with your raven shield? Why do you wear your hair in our style? You cannot shed your true skin no matter how much you might want to."

Any desire I had to stop this conversation vanished. This man thought Cuan's cousin had tried to blind him? The one who had spoken to him after the fight against Fearghus? I had noted the tension between them, yes, but this was a serious accusation to make. Even stranger, Cuan did not deny it.

Bjorn sighed. "I see I can't persuade you to return home. Even though I can tell you're not happy."

"Don't worry, Bjorn," Cuan said after a moment. "I'm happy enough."

"We are brothers of the shield-wall, you and I," Bjorn replied. "I don't want you to die in this cursed land away from your friends."

Cuan brushed the gold arm-rings that decorated his forearm, making them clink as they hit each other. "Death doesn't scare me."

"That's what worries me. You won't tell me why you are here, and it is your business, but don't do anything foolish. Please."

Cuan didn't respond to this and reached into his bag. He took out a water skin and two cups. "Enough about me," he said, pouring liquid from the skin into the cups. "What's your news? I'm assuming there is a good reason you've crept into my tent in the middle of the night."

"I've come to warn you of King Diarmait's plans." Bjorn lowered his voice. "You know about Wexford, yes, but he's already attacked Osraige, and it is said the Normans won a great victory for him there. More Normans are coming too. The six hundred who arrived are just the start. No matter what oaths Diarmait swears during the negotiations, he doesn't mean it."

"The Normans aren't leaving now that Diarmait has Leinster again?"

Bjorn shook his head. "No. More are coming in the spring with a Welsh lord called Richard de Clare. Strongbow is what his men call him. Diarmait has promised Strongbow his daughter, Ava, in marriage, and the kingship of Leinster once he dies."

Cuan shook his head. "The kingship cannot pass through the daughter. Everyone knows that."

"In Ireland, that's true, but not in England. That's how I also know that these Normans are coming for land, and they don't intend to play by the rules of the Irish. Diarmait knows this and invited them all the same. Land is not his goal anymore. It's revenge."

"The negotiations between my uncle and King Diarmait have been going on for weeks. He's finally offered good hostages. His youngest son and his grandson are among them. Surely, he wouldn't put them at risk?"

"I think Diarmait is desperate enough that he'll do anything."

Cuan nodded. "Thanks for your words, Bjorn. They're welcome." This time, Cuan's voice was quiet. Thoughtful.

War was coming. Broccan had always warned me of the mortal wars. That they took years, sometimes decades to fester, and then the violence suddenly boiled over. I had to get to Seir Kieran before this happened.

Bjorn stared at Cuan, his expression darkening. "Use them as you wish, but it's not your uncle's throne I'm worried about. It's you. Next year, if they have any sense, Norman eyes will turn to Dublin."

"I had considered that myself. Asculv has too."

Bjorn clasped his friend's arm and then stood. "I'd better go then. One of my kin came to give a message to your uncle. I'd better be ready to leave with him, otherwise your uncle's men will start asking questions about where I've been."

Cuan and Bjorn moved to the door of the tent. Cuan watched for a while, then gave Bjorn a nod that all was clear, and quickly Bjorn left.

"Did you hear all that?" Cuan pulled the blankets away from my face.

Trying to push my body up, I nodded. "I didn't mean to. I woke and you were talking."

"What happened to you? You were on the grass. Shaking again."

"I don't know. I got lost, I think."

Cuan wrapped his hands around my arms and pulled me up. "Try not to get lost again, especially so close to the boundary of the camp. You might not see the guards, but they are watching you. I thought you understood that."

Trying to steady my balance, I closed my eyes and nodded. "Yes. I remember. Thank you for helping me."

"You can repay me by not repeating what you heard."

"That's hard for a spy to promise."

Cuan smiled a little.

"Are you going to tell your uncle what your friend told you?"

"Oh, my uncle already knows most of what he said. He's been sending messages back and forth to Diarmait, all throughout the games. Negotiations have been underway for months."

"Do you think there will be a war?"

"Maybe. That is why you must be more careful. No more running away," Cuan said, tying his cloak over his shoulders. A beautiful new brooch was there now. Twisted into a beautiful network of knots.

"I don't—"

"Isolde, listen. Leinster is now full of Norman knights and warriors. Some kings are fighting for Diarmait and some against. Now my uncle joins the fray. Leinster is dangerous. The most dangerous place in the whole of Ireland. You would be a fool to try to reach Seir Kieran... and you are still being watched. You should go back to Blinne's tent now before she wakes and notices you are gone."

Unsteady on my feet, I leaned against one of the wooden posts.

I was still shaking, but not as bad as before. I could not promise Cuan what he wanted to hear, so I simply nodded. Cuan frowned.

"You have a new brooch," I said. The words tumbled out awkwardly, so obviously trying to change the flow of conversation.

"My uncle made me one of his fianna. This is what he gave all those he chose."

"Oh."

"And I wasn't the only one who received a gift."

"Really?"

"You did. Dáirinn gave you a dress, I hear. You should wear it."

A sudden rush of heat flooded my cheeks.

"What I mean is, those who wish to fall from notice would do well to blend in. Dressed in men's clothes, you stand out. A dress would help."

Rather than cause less embarrassment, this explanation only made me blush all the more. "Like the way you still have your raven shield?" I glanced over at it. "A Viking emblem, isn't it?"

Cuan gave a small smile. "Come on. It's time for you to go. If the messengers have been, I want to hear what's been said in the fort." He moved to the door of the tent and peered out. "Go now, and hurry."

Anxious to get away, I crept outside, moving softly along the tents, and tiptoed into Blinne's tent to the sound of her snoring.

Her daughter, however, opened her eyes.

"Where were you?" she asked.

"I wasn't feeling very well," I said, holding my stomach. "I had to go outside."

"That's the ale," she mumbled. "I drank too much of it, too. Best to sleep it off."

I nodded and lay down on the bed and pulled my fur right around my body. I was shaking harder again, shaking and thinking of too many things at once.

The dream. The words of warning from Bjorn. Cuan telling me that Leinster was not safe. Everything was laced with danger and treachery, and no matter what I did, I could not get away from it.

Closing my eyes, I tried to sleep, but the darkness behind my eyes was filled with the faces of others. Of Broccan. Of Affraic. Colmon. Móirne. Cuan. Leaves blew along the ground, rustled against the tent, and a voice spoke to me.

Are you listening, child? Do you hear the sadness inside your song?

Isolde

Kells

I woke the next morning with a smile on my face. Despite the nightmare and the strange run-in with Cuan, I had much to be grateful for.

Today, the Tailteann games were over.

I had done nothing suspicious. Spoken to no strangers of anything regarding wars or kings or invasions. King Ruaidrí would surely let me go. Why would he not? With all the commotion of the games, I must have fallen from his mind enough that he would give me Fragarach and let me go on my way.

The shaking and sickness from last night gone, I walked outside with a spring in my step. One of Blinne's daughters was making breakfast, and I offered to stir the pot over the fire while she fetched more barley oats for the morning broth.

It was a fine morning, and before long there was laughter in the air as the children woke and began to run around with their friends.

"Careful by the fire," I said as a young girl came too close and I used my hand to swing her around.

"Sorry, Isolde," she said, giggling as she jumped over a log and disappeared into her tent.

Her exuberance made me smile, and I found myself realising that while I hadn't wanted to be here, there had been something pleasant about life at the games. Within the chaos that so many people together brought, I had found companionship with those camping around Blinne's tent. People waved at me. They knew my name. Offered me their food and drink. Generosity existed still, though it seemed those with the least were the ones who offered the most.

The morning continued in much the same way as the previous ones, aside from the fact that people were beginning to pack away their tents. Blinne had mentioned yesterday that one of her sons was coming to help take hers down and that I should gather my belongings.

That won't take me long, I had replied, for all I had was the leather parcel that Dáirinn had given me the night of the wedding fair. The blue dress still lay inside, untouched. It was too fine for me, I told myself, and yet Cuan's words played in my mind. If I wore it, I would fit in. Be accepted.

I wasn't so sure what to think about that. The people here accepted me well enough. They didn't seem to care what I did or didn't wear. And now that I was about to travel again, there was no point in getting the beautiful fabric dirty, which no doubt I would do in a campsite such as this.

"How's the breakfast coming on?" Blinne said as she came out of her tent. "How about—"

A loud horn interrupted her. It rang out loud and clear. Not just one horn, but several.

"What's that?" I asked.

Others came out of their tents on hearing it, and the men made their way toward the feasting hall as the horns continued to sound.

"May God have mercy on us," Blinne said, blessing herself.

Blinne's daughter, who had rushed over with the barley oats, shook her head as she put them into the pot. "'Tis a bad business, all this with King Diarmaid. I wish it was not so. Saraid's husband will be called up, and there will be no end of tears."

I cast my eye toward the feasting hall. Men were pouring inside. Men from all over the plain.

Blinne tutted. "King Ruaidrí lured us here with talk of games and weddings. When really, he meant to summon our men to war. He's a crafty one. Just like his father."

"A war with Leinster?" I asked.

"Who else?" she replied.

I remembered what Cuan and his friend had discussed last night. Yes, Bjorn had thought war inevitable, too, even when Cuan had said there were negotiations ongoing. Perhaps whatever message Bjorn's people had brought last night had roused the king into making a decision.

Blinne and her daughter went about their business and once the broth was ready, called people over to share it. They themselves seemed uninterested in eating though, and glanced constantly at the fort, waiting for someone to return to tell them what was happening. I was no different. I ate, but found my eyes trained on the feasting hall, too.

It didn't take long for the men to reappear.

As they had poured into the feasting hall, they poured out.

"We are going to Ferns," a man shouted over to his wife. "We leave now."

"To fight?" Blinne asked.

"To take hostages, but if Diarmait won't hand them over, then yes, we fight."

All around me, people began to talk and plan. Such noise filled the air. It was almost as if the games were still on. Feeling out of place, I moved away from the tents and over to the feasting hall. If the king was riding to war, he'd want rid of me. If I could just get Fragarach back, then I would be on my way.

Deciding that I had to act, I walked into the feasting hall.

The king, his sons, and Cathal and Cuan stood about the top table. The other kings, too. Huddled around. I didn't dare go there... but in the corner were the kings' wives and daughters. Queen Gráinne was there, as well as Nuala, King Tigernán's new wife.

Summoning my courage, I walked up to them.

"Oh, Isolde," the queen said. "I should have sent someone to fetch you. The horns frightened you, I am sure."

I smiled, not sure if her words were politeness or not. *Why should the queen be thinking of me at a time like this?*

"Yes, they did, which made me think…" I began. "That with the men riding out, it's time for me to leave. I wanted to ask the king for my knife. It belonged to my mother. I cannot leave without it."

"Now is not a good time to leave, Isolde," the queen replied, her eyebrows rising. "The women of the Ó Conchúir clan are going to wait here for the men to return. King Ruaidrí said that you should stay with us."

"Are you sure he wouldn't rather I be on my way?"

"Not at all, Isolde. You are our guest. Your place is here. I couldn't possibly let you rove into Leinster, where it's so dangerous. What sort of host would that make me if I were to let you run toward danger?"

There was generosity in her offer, but also a command. I was to stay. That was it. I felt as if the air was being pushed out of my lungs and struggled to get another breath. I hated this. Hated being trapped.

Unable to control my emotions, I walked away. Perhaps it was rude to turn and not say goodbye, but I couldn't help it. It felt as if the walls of the feasting hall were pressing down on me. I had to leave. I couldn't stay any longer. *But how could I leave Fragarach?* It was my mother's. A gift of the Tuatha Dé Danann.

"Isolde," Cuan came out of the feasting hall with a group of other men, all walking toward their tents or else the stables.

"What?" Quickly, I wiped the tears from my face.

"Did the queen say you could stay here?"

"Yes." I rolled my eyes.

"That is good, Isolde."

"It isn't. I want to go."

"If you want to go, listen. We are riding to Ferns now to collect the hostages and agree on a peace. While we are gone, impress the queen. The king listens to her. If she says you are not a spy, he will let you go when he returns."

Wincing at all of this, I closed my eyes.

"And just like I said last night, don't be tempted to run. The queen will be left with many guards, all of whom will be bored and will love nothing more than to chase a runaway."

He gave a curt nod, then left to go to his tent, leaving me to go to Blinne's.

The men around Blinne's tent were still readying themselves to march. I sat on a log while they swarmed about me, the din rising as they bid farewell to their loved ones, and barked orders for spare clothing and weapons to be found.

But just as suddenly as the din rose, it fell away as the men left the campsite to join the warband that was gathering outside the feasting hall. Flags with the colours of Connacht flew alongside the ones of Ulaid, Bréifne and Dublin. There were thousands of men, and more were to join as they marched through Connacht, or so I'd heard the men say.

The horns sounded again, and the men began to leave, marching south-west along the forest path to Ferns.

I couldn't help but look for the men I had come to know. Fearghus, Cathal and Scolaí, riding toward the front of the line. Cuan, too, with his raven shield at his back, an outsider still.

Soon the only sound was that of tears as those left behind watched their loved ones march toward an uncertain future. Peace or war. Nobody knew which way it would fall.

"Peace," I whispered as Cuan disappeared into the forest. "Peace."

Donnchad

Ferns

After a storm, there is always a period of calm. A time of stillness. As if even the daemons of hell have exhausted their power.

After the ferocity of the battle in Osraige and the screams of the ghost army, the Normans had found a place of stillness.

Ferns was where King Diarmait's dun was situated, and it was here that the men who had survived the battle recovered. There were many wounds that needed to be tended. Many prayers that needed to be said. The Leinster–Norman alliance had won the battle against the Osraige, but they'd had fewer men to start with. Fewer men they could afford to lose. The tally of the dead Normans numbered into the hundreds now, with one or two more added every day, for not all who die in battle die on the battlefield.

Today, however, not even the great dun at Ferns could hold on to this stillness. A new storm brewed along the horizon, and it crept ever closer. I could feel it in the air. In the way the men held themselves. In what they said aloud and in what they kept within.

Keeping out of the fray for now, I watched the family of Diarmait closely as they went about their business. Looking for family resemblances had become a favourite pastime.

The daughter of Diarmait had a trace of us. Aoife, or Ava, as she called herself now, to ingratiate herself to the Norman to whom she'd been pledged. She had dark curls like my mother, uncle and myself, though her face was longer and with eyes of a deep green. The boys looked nothing like us at all. Not like their father, either. Two of Diarmait's wives lived in the dun and so it was easy to see which of the boys belonged to which, each of them favouring their maternal line. Domhnall, the eldest boy, was indeed bastard-born as the rumours had suggested. His mother did not live in the dun. No one spoke of her. When I asked, no one seemed to even remember her name.

It didn't seem to bother Domhnall that he was a bastard, nor had it impacted his standing within his clan. I'd watched men follow him into battle with my own eyes. Still, this man was something of a mystery to me. This unwavering loyalty to a father who seemed determined to throw away his whole kingdom. I couldn't account for it. Domhnall was clever. He'd shown that, when we had spoken before the battle. He'd made it clearer in the days since. Just as I had watched the Normans and their battle strategies, so had he. Why then would he follow his father's plan that put Ireland at such risk?

Could it be that he was planning on using the Anglo-Normans only to abandon them later?

I suspected that the answer was yes, though I couldn't see how it would turn out in Domhnall's favour. A man with so many enemies could ill afford to throw away his friends, and without the gift of fire at his fingertips, how did he propose wresting the land away from the Normans if they took it? Was he fool enough to think that the men who fought with him now would fight for him always? Perhaps. He was a mortal. Forty. That was still fairly young. When I was forty, I had felt that I might forever be king and that the whole of Ireland would fall under my sway. How wrong that dream had proven to be.

"Énna. Come on." Ava held her half-brother's hand as they walked out of their house. "If you remember the steps we counted yesterday, you can make it to the feasting hall without my help." Slowly, she let go of him and walked at his side. Her younger brother, Connor, followed, though kept half a step behind his siblings.

Ah, yes, these younger sons of Diarmait, they were curious. One blind. The other still a boy. The first crying in the endless dark. The second unable to look at his brother's wounds without tearing up. Soft, these children were. Soft as only those who've always known comfort can be, and yet somehow astute enough to be wary of the strangers around them.

A lack of love from their father might have been the cause. They watched him for traces of ill-temper and scurried away when he stormed across the dun. Diarmait certainly held no interest in their welfare. Perhaps that was the family trait that had trickled down from Máelmórda. My uncle had loved power. Having it. Holding it. He had not loved any of his progeny though, at least not until Cecile had come along, and then only because she had a power within her that increased his own standing in the eyes of my mother.

Angelo chose that moment to sit beside me, a bowl of porridge in hand. I took it from him with a word of thanks, while Angelo picked at a piece of barley bread. He glanced up at the three younger children of Diarmait and followed them as they walked to the feasting hall.

Of course, it made sense that he was interested. My son was not minded to enjoy the company of those younger than he, but I had told him that the Mac Murchadha's were his family, distant though the connection was. Since our arrival, he'd watched them all intently. So intently that I'd had to tell him to be more cautious. To stare at royalty when you were not royal was a bold move… and we couldn't afford to be bold just yet.

"If you like her," I whispered to him, noting his frequent glances at Ava, "you can have her when we rule this land. But remember what I said. Do not stare."

Angelo nodded and lowered his gaze. This was good, for Domhnall walked around the dun today beside his father. He watched all the newcomers, me and my son included. No, it would not do for Domhnall to note Angelo's interest in his sister. For if his father did not love Domhnall's half-siblings, Domhnall surely did. He gave his sister gifts, helped Énna learn his steps around the dun so he might move more freely, and comforted Connor when he cried. What the father lacked in affection, the son had in abundance.

The violence of the Osraige attack now made more sense to me. It turned out that Énna had been held as hostage in the Osraige dun when Diarmait was driven from Ireland, and had been blinded as a punishment when his father returned to his lands without permission. Domhnall's rage was perhaps justified for it was hard indeed to watch this young man stumble around the dun.

The horns sounded then. The warriors of Leinster began to gather.

Ah. King Ruaidrí and his men had finally arrived for the vow taking and hostage exchange. I wondered how many men the High King brought with him. Surely, he'd heard about the battle against Osraige and how we'd defeated their five thousand men. For him to come with less than eight thousand was folly. I suspected, however, that he would come with many more.

"Wait here, son. I'll be back soon. No matter what happens, don't go outside of the dun without me."

Angelo gave a sharp nod, occupied it seemed with watching the Leinster warriors readying themselves to meet with the Connacht contingent, while I made toward Robert's house. When I arrived, he was sitting inside with Maurice and Meilyr. His hunting dogs lay at his feet, but on my arrival, they ran outside.

"Ah, the very man," Robert said, gesturing for me to take the chair beside his.

I swerved to let the dogs pass, then sat. "How can I help?"

"We are worried about the negotiations and what they might mean," Maurice whispered.

"You worry there will be a fight?"

"A little. Not so much."

Robert unfurled a piece of paper. "This was delivered to us during the night, and we don't want to show Riagáin in case he tells Diarmait. Can we trust you to translate and keep what you learn a secret?"

I nodded.

Robert nodded at Maurice, who handed over the parchment. "You've given us good advice so far. I have faith that you will again."

Reading through the message, I smiled. "King Ruaidrí has written to you himself, asking you to leave Ireland in return for gold and silver and many other worthy gifts."

"Yes." Robert licked his lips. "Hervey was able to decipher that part of the message, and we gave our reply. No."

"Then it sounds like you have made up your mind." I handed back the message.

"Hervey overheard that King Diarmait has secretly agreed that we are to return to Wales as part of these negotiations. That means Diarmait intends to send us home with nothing."

"You wish now you had accepted King Ruaidrí's gifts? He would be able to offer you more than Diarmait, that is certain."

"No. Not that. We cannot leave. There is nothing for us in Wales and England." Robert gave a nervous laugh, his hand running down his chin. "Do you know before I came here, I had lived the last three years of my life in a dungeon at the mercy of Rhys ap Gruffudd? I'm too dangerous to be let free in Wales and England, you see. I've too many claims and the lords of England and Wales fear me. Rhys is my cousin, and still, he held me captive. I cannot live like that again, so when I say I am not here for gold and silver, it is the truth. Diarmait gave me Wexford. Even if he didn't mean it, I intend to hold him to his word."

"I haven't yet been offered any land," Maurice added. "And so, it is not Ruaidrí who concerns us. It is Diarmait. That he's agreed for us to return but not said so to us. Is it a ruse? If not, how does he plan on making us leave if he's forbidden the shipmasters in Wexford from bearing us home? You think he will reverse that order?"

He doesn't mean for you to stay or to go home, was the answer. *Now he has what he wants, he means for you to die. It will be your noses and ears he cuts away next.*

Should I say that to them? The three of them watched me and

I took a deep breath while I thought, trying to gauge their expressions. Was it advice they wanted, or were they testing me?

"There is no way of knowing what King Diarmait intends," I answered. "My opinion is that you are too dependent upon him. He has granted you land that he can very easily take away. Land he perhaps never really intended for you to control. Today, he wants you to ride out with him to show that you are a force the High King should fear. A force so fearful that King Ruaidrí must allow him to keep hold of the kingship of Leinster which only a few years ago he stripped away from him."

"So, he uses us. You think he will betray us once he gets what he wants?"

I rolled this question around. The answer was obvious to me. The real question now was if these Normans were useful to me or not. If not, I should simply let Diarmait and Domhnall kill them. Five hundred and twenty they numbered now. It was not large enough to match an organised force intent on winning, but their strategies had impressed me. If I guided them, they could wrest this land from the Irish. They could do all the work for me, and when I was ready, I would take it from them.

"Yes. I believe his heart is treacherous. I fear as soon as the Connacht forces retreat that he will slit your throats. There is, however, a solution to your problem."

All three men looked at me.

"You must take advantage of the disunity and rivalries that already exist in Ireland, and one of you should leave now, take your men with you, and swear loyalty to another king."

"To Ruaidrí?" Meilyr raised an eyebrow, pleased I thought with his own suggestion. I could see why an alliance with the High King would intrigue him. These men loved power, after all. Like wolves to sheep, they hungered for it.

"No. With so many of the northern kings answering his call, he doesn't need you. There is, however, another king who is much more desperate and one who you've already impressed."

"The King of Osraige?" Maurice clicked his tongue. "We killed thousands of his men. Surely, he'd sooner kill us than ask us to fight for him."

"Oh, he would take you and dance for joy. You destroyed his army. You have new tactics, new weapons. By taking you in, he would strengthen his warband. Having you at his side also means Diarmait will think twice about raiding into his territory again."

"That would only serve to turn Diarmait against those who remained all the quicker."

"Not at all. Domhnall saw your strengths too. They will not want to have no Norman fighters in their army when their closest enemy has hundreds. By splitting your army, you go from an inconvenience to a necessity and Diarmait will see the benefits of keeping you through the winter."

All three of them looked at me, hesitant. I could understand why. Telling them to split their forces when their numbers were already so few was a risk, and their minds were so full of loyalty and honour that they found it hard to accept that the King of Osraige would welcome them with open arms.

"You Irish," Robert muttered. "I cannot understand you. A contrary people, if ever there was."

"There are rules to our madness if you care to learn them, but do what you will. Stay here and gain no new lands or split and move on two fronts."

"You think we can win land if we fight for the King of Osraige?"

"No. If he gives you land in his own territory, his own men will rebel. If he lets you raid south into Munster, you will only unite another kingdom against you."

Maurice threw his head back and cursed under his breath. "Then why would one of us risk going there?"

"Because you will do some raiding for him, and when you leave, you will ride through his land until you reach Waterford. Meanwhile, whoever stays can talk to Diarmait about the biggest prize of all. Dublin."

"Diarmait gave us Wexford. You talk of Waterford and Dublin.

These are the three main ports of Ireland. You really think they are all obtainable?"

"Yes. The Irish do not own that land anymore. Not only will it stop them uniting against you, but they will be easier to take. Look at Wexford, you took that without—"

Robert snorted. "We are no more lords over Wexford than you are. You cannot rule a city if you do not live within it and control the flow of commerce, but Diarmait doesn't want us to go there. This threat, that he had forbidden the Wexford shipmasters from sailing us home, proves it. How can we rule a city if the people do not obey us?"

"Then if you want to take the ports, you will have to actually fight for them. That is why, if you split, one of you should go to Waterford as I said, and study it. Learn the layout. The one that stays should do the same for Dublin."

Robert and Maurice pondered my words.

"Why are you helping us?" Meilyr finally asked. "We want an honest answer this time."

I took a breath. Máelmórda had always been better at these sorts of conversations. His humour did much to assuage the suspicions of others.

But I was not like him. Never had been.

"I told you before that my mother was Irish. She had a difficult time here and does not remember this land with any fondness. I came at first because I wanted to see it for myself. What I have found is chaos. Greed. A complete disregard for life. There is adultery. There are slaves. It was not meant to be like this. There was a king many years ago, Brian Boru was his name, and he banned slavery. The kings of today would speak of him as a saint, and yet they do not follow his teachings. As my mother told me, I see a land that was founded on honour, but that honour has vanished. It needs to be restored, but I do not think it can be done by those who rule now. A new order is required. A new king. A new king who can light a fire and show his people the way."

Meilyr took his helmet into his hands and gently threw it back and forth between them. Deep in thought, he hummed.

Robert leaned forward and gave out a low laugh. "If only you were born a prince, Donn. You'd be formidable indeed. Ambition suits you."

"Alas, I am just a simple soldier," I replied, giving a quick smile.

The horns sounded again, and the three knights stood. "I suppose we'd better see what we are dealing with," Meilyr said.

They made their way outside, and just as I went to pass through the door, Robert stopped me. "Move as close to Diarmait as you can. I want to know what he says."

Nodding, I moved to the gates.

Along the walls of the dun, the Mac Murchadha family and warriors congregated, and I moved to stand alongside them. If Robert wanted me to listen to the Irish, I had to appear as one of them.

The feasting hall emptied, with the three hostages, the boys Connor, Caomhán and Olcán, coming out last. All three of them were dressed well, and no tears stained their faces today, even though I could smell the fear upon them. These were good choices as hostages. Connor, the last legitimate heir of King Diarmait, Caomhán, the eldest son of Domhnall, and Olcán, the grandson of Diarmait's foster brother. All young. Innocent. King Ruaidrí no doubt expected that the loss of such youth would bring Diarmait to heel. But the truth was, Diarmait was gambling that their youth and innocence would save them.

For when Diarmait betrayed Ruaidrí, as he surely would, Ruaidrí would have to decide whether to execute these boys who Diarmait had pledged his word on. The killing of men was hard enough. The killing of children was harder still.

I thought then of Murchad and Fódla's daughter, only just reaching womanhood and lying dead in the lough. A child of my enemy, I knew she had to die, but there was something wasteful in the killing of one so young. For these three boys, only fourteen or fifteen, with their plump cheeks and hairless chins, a cold death would be a hard thing for any man to place upon them.

"You will do what King Ruaidrí tells you," Diarmait said to the boys. "But remember, you are princes of Leinster. Do not shame me with your actions. Be strong. Be brave."

Diarmait moved to his younger son and rested a hand upon his shoulder. "You are to marry Róisín, daughter of King Ruaidrí. Her father says in two years, when she turns eighteen, but marry her sooner if you can."

The boy's eyes narrowed and Domhnall whispered something in the boy's ear which made him blush. I didn't hear what was whispered but knew what was said all the same. Put a baby in her belly. Force the father to allow the marriage. It was one thing to kill a hostage. Another to kill a son-in-law.

The boy nodded and mounted his horse, and the three of them rode out together to join King Ruaidrí and his army.

The army was impressive. Ten thousand. Made up of the warriors of Ulaid, Connacht, Bréifne, Dublin and Oriel. I didn't suppose all of them were warriors, but still, numbers were numbers and Ruaidrí's had completely overwhelmed Diarmait's.

While the priests moved toward the centre, the Bible and illumed gospels in their hands, I moved closer to Domhnall and Diarmait as Robert had instructed me to.

"Look at Tigernán," Domhnall sniggered. "He looks like he's about to shit himself."

"He probably is," his father replied. "And there is King Magnus at his side. He looks old, does he not?"

Domhnall nodded.

"Ah, look who is beside Asculv." Diarmait's voice rose a little, spittle forming at the side of his lips. "Cuan Ó Conchúir."

Domhnall nonchalantly turned his head to the right, his gaze sweeping over a young man with flaxen hair and a raven shield.

"Are you sure that's him?"

"Yes. I'm certain."

Domhnall licked his lips but from that moment on stared

resolutely ahead, listening with an intent focus as the priest read out the vows that were to be sworn.

Vows were boring. They hadn't changed since my time as king, and so instead, I amused myself by staring at this young man who had elicited such interest, wondering what he had done to deserve the attention of Diarmait.

Viking blood was in him, that was for sure, with his pale hair and eyes, but that aside, he was not remarkable and spoke not once the whole time I watched him. The man beside him was of more interest, the one-eyed king, Tigernán Ua Ruairc, who glared at Diarmait the whole time. He did indeed look like he was going to explode. Not with shit perhaps, but with rage. I didn't know who the king next to him was, but he was old, with long grey hair and a permanent sneer on his face. Then came Ruaidrí and one who I guessed must be his son. That meant the man to the left of his son must be Asculv, the King of Dublin. It had to be, even though his colouring was more Irish than Norse. The double axe at his side gave it away.

"Do you swear, King Diarmait," one of the priests said. "Do you swear to accept King Ruaidrí as your High King?"

King Diarmait rode forward and placed his hand on the Bible. "I do."

"Do you swear to pay the eraic in full to King Tigernán before the end of next year?"

"I do."

"Will you send away these foreigners you invited to our lands?"

King Diarmait smiled at this one and gave a curt nod of his head. "I will."

The dun moved back to normality once King Ruaidrí's army left. The warriors removed their armour. Fires were lit, and pots of food began to boil over them.

But I knew better than to expect the storm not to break, for Robert FitzStephen and Meilyr had not looked happy when I told them that King Diarmait had sworn to send them away, and neither had the other knights. The mood in the Anglo-Norman camp was subdued as a result and the usual nighttime festivities finished sooner than usual.

Later that evening, when the men made their way to their beds, I walked over to Robert's house and closed the door behind me.

"Well," Robert said by way of greeting. "Did Diarmait say anything else of interest?"

I shook my head. "He and his son insulted the kings outside his walls. That was all."

Robert nodded and took a bite of his food. "Tell me this, if our army was to split, when should we do it?"

"You need to let King Ruaidrí and the armies he's called up reach their home kingdoms first, so they do not return here once they realise you've deserted King Diarmait. However, you cannot wait too long, otherwise you will be caught out by the colder weather too. Diarmait also is a problem. He doesn't have the food here to feed you for long. Give it a week. Ten days at most."

Robert nodded again, though he kept his gaze focused on the ground. "Thank you, Donn. The others do not trust you, but you have been useful today. Honest. I will not forget it."

Giving a bow, I left his house, knowing in my heart that I had won my own victory this day, and that this was the start of my rebirth in Ireland. As I made my way to my bed, I glanced up at the stars and smiled.

Gormflaith

Chepstow

I walked along the grass outside the castle walls. It was pleasant out here. Quiet.

Carefully, I put on the glove David had given me. "Are you sure this will work?"

"I'm sure." David set a piece of raw meat onto the leather covering my hand. "Hold it out and whistle like I showed you. The bird will come. I've never seen a bird form an attachment so quickly before. You are going to put all the knights of Normandy to shame."

Smiling, I did as he said and searched the sky.

Olaf, poor Olaf, was still assisting me in my role of burgeoning falconer, all while having to watch David touch my hands and kiss them. He was behaving though, our tryst in the forest still enough to bring him to heel for now.

"There he is." David pointed up at the sky. "My, he's beautiful. Even nicer than Le Gros' peregrine falcon, though don't tell him I told you so."

I held out my hand, whistled and watched Olaf as he flew toward me and landed gently on the leather glove that shielded my arm from his talons.

"Well done, Olaf," I said as I stroked his neck. "How beautiful you are and how much I love you."

David clapped his hands and tethered Olaf to a rope once he took the piece of meat. "Wonderful, Olaf. A king of birds just like your namesake." He stroked Olaf on the chest, and I held in a breath, hoping Olaf was able to rein in his temper and not bite this new lover of mine. "Named after the king who brought Christianity to Norway. What a wonderful idea your mistress had in giving you this name."

"I'm sure I've had many good ideas in my lifetime."

"Have you?"

"I stopped to speak to you, didn't I?"

David, always amused by my teasing, put the hood over Olaf's head and we walked arm in arm toward the castle and then over to where the bird cages were kept.

Making sure Olaf had enough to eat and drink, I placed him in the cage and removed his hood. "Good boy, Olaf," I whispered, stroking his neck before I closed the cage door. "I shall be sure to visit you tonight."

I had no choice, was the truth. In the evenings, I helped old Ranulf with the birds, which I much preferred to the kitchens, but still, Olaf did not need to know that. It was much better for him to think that I was spending time in his company out of choice.

Now that Olaf's training was done for the day, David and I walked in silence to my bedroom as it was time to change for the evening meal. That was another thing about living with these knights. They had strange notions about being properly attired for every event. Different clothes for eating, praying, entertaining. Of course, Cecile and I were poor, and it wasn't usual for people such as us to frequent the hall of a lord, but David had insisted.

"I swear that bird looks bereft when you leave him," David said once we reached my bedroom door.

"I'm sure you are imagining it."

"Perhaps it's because I am bereft when I leave you. You are the sunshine, Alys. I am the grass beneath. Without you, I wilt away to nothing."

Moving just out of his reach, I gave a small smile. This chivalry these knights had, the rules they held themselves to, oh, they were delightful. Courtesy and the wooing of women was a serious business that had elicited sweet words, even poetry, from this man of mine.

"If I am the sun, I would have you be my Icarus. I desire that you fly closer to me."

"You would have me burn?"

I grinned. "Yes, I would. If it was me you burned for."

"Then you are a wicked creature, and I should stay well away from you."

"Perhaps you should."

David grabbed my hand and pressed it to his lips. "Alas, it is too late for me to fly away." Moving closer, he wrapped his arms around me and ran his hands up along my cheeks. I wanted him then. Like I had wanted no other in a long time. When I was younger and women spoke of love, they spoke of warriors. Of kings. What a foolish thing it was to think love came from men like those. It was this man, a knight, and a lowly one, who had somehow given my heart new life. And what had he done? Nothing but be kind.

I kissed him softly, then harder. Letting the passion of my body move to my lips and tongue.

It was he who pulled away first.

"Soon, my love," he whispered. "When we are married." He pressed something into my hand, bowed and walked away.

When I opened the door to my bedroom, Cecile was sitting by the fire. "Do you two have to pant so loudly when you kiss? It's disgusting."

"Yes, we must. I like to pant. So does he."

Cecile scowled and pulled at the thread of her embroidery.

"What's put you in such bad form?" I asked. "Was the cook mean to you again today?"

"No." She paused a moment, glanced my way, then refocused on her needlework. "How do you do that?"

"Do what?"

"Change your demeanour. With David, you are so sweet and charming."

"And with you, I'm what? Drab and miserable?"

"I don't mean that. It's just when you are with him, you appear so happy, so in love. I'm not sure I could pretend."

"That's because you are younger than I. You still yearn for something true."

She sighed, set down her work, and poked at the fire.

"Who is it?" I asked.

"Who is who?"

"Who has stolen your heart? It turns out you are the drab and miserable one. Not I."

She shook her head, her expression moving from sullen indignation to something much sweeter. "No one."

I moved closer and sat in the chair beside her. "Tell me."

She shook her head. "Really, there is no one. I'm just bored, that is all. Being a hostage at Chepstow is rather restrictive, and working in the kitchens is truly hateful. I can't wait until Donnchad proves himself so we can go to Ireland. I want to see it properly this time."

Cecile was a good liar. I'd give her that. Unfortunately for her, she was not as good as me… and now I was intrigued. Who could it be? Strongbow was gathering his men for an invasion, but those men rarely entered the castle. The foot soldiers and archers camped outside in tents now. Only Strongbow's kin and closest knights stayed in the castle, and I had not noticed Cecile forming any attachments with them.

I unfurled the linen binding that David had wrapped over his present, pretending to accept her answer. "Do you want to go to the market? David has just given me some silver coins. Perhaps a new ring or bracelet? Or even a new dress?"

Cecile shook her head. "No, you go on and buy something. It's your silver, after all."

I put on my shawl, then paused by the door. "How is your leg?"

"It feels stronger. The scar isn't too bad either. I was sure it would be much worse when I first woke up after taking the witch gift."

This was good. A tired and limping Cecile didn't have the same prospects as the girl I'd watched in Paris. If her leg was healed, then perhaps it was time to get her out of the kitchens. Before that, however, there was something else Cecile needed to master.

"Have you practised your gift today?"

She lowered her head, focusing more intently on her stitching. "Yes."

"And?"

"Nothing."

"Well, seeing as your leg is recovered, we shall walk out tomorrow and practise. Do not lose heart. It can take a while to learn."

Cecile nodded, though she didn't seem particularly annoyed by her continued failure to master the witch gift. What was wrong with her? If it was me, I'd be practising day and night. This ineptitude and carelessness made me want to slam her head against the wall. How could she not care? The witch gift was powerful, and yet here she was with a thread and needle as if she were a mortal, and fawning over one too.

Leaving our room before I did actually slam her head against the wall, I hurried to the market. If I was quick, I might find the jewellers still out with their wares. A new ring would be just the thing.

That night we dined. The hall was mostly empty. Only around thirty men and ten women. Strongbow sat beside two women who I'd discovered were his natural daughters. Beside them were some of his knights. David's cousin Le Gros was one of them. A few of the newer knights to arrive had brought their wives with them, but they kept to themselves.

It was a quiet affair. Certainly nothing like the feasts Amlav or even Sitric used to hold, but pleasant enough. The kitchen maids who I used to work with came around and served us, giving Cecile teasing looks, though it seemed already that they had forgotten I used to work with them.

Cecile sat beside me, not as ill-tempered as earlier, but by no means good company. She almost appeared pious, studiously staring at the cross hanging on one of the walls. If I could be bothered, I might have tried to converse, but I was still displeased by her lack of effort in practising her new gift. Keeping her on side was important for now, for I didn't know how things would stand with Donnchad when, or if, he returned, but that didn't mean I had to enjoy the dullness of her company.

"I think I'll go to bed soon, Cecile. An early night would do me good, though I must check on Olaf if—"

"How are you this evening, ladies?"

I turned to find Strongbow walking toward us.

"Very well, my lord," I answered, giving him my brightest smile.

"I am pleased to hear it. How are the rooms? Not too cold, I hope?"

"Not at all, my lord. Everything here is very pleasing."

"You are becoming quite the falconer, Alys. This eagle you found in the forest has formed a strong bond with you, I hear."

"Yes." I smiled even wider. "It was a lucky day that I found him."

"I shall come out to see you train him tomorrow. Perhaps I might be of assistance."

"It would be an honour, my lord, but I think David praises me too highly."

"No indeed. He does not lie. What about you… Cecile, is it? Will you come out tomorrow to see Alys' eagle fly?"

"I think I shall, yes," Cecile replied.

Strongbow gave a curt nod, then left us. I glanced at Cecile to see how she bore the news that she was to come outside and see me training Olaf… but she wasn't looking at me.

Rather, she was staring after Strongbow.

Even more surprising, at the end of the hall, he paused a moment by the door and stared at her.

Ah, now it was clear who the object of her affection was. Well done, Cecile, on capturing the attention of an earl, even if his title was a contested one. This could very well be useful, if she was able to keep it.

And with such an opportunity, it was time to act. I'd been whiling away my time, pleasant though it was with David, for too long. It was time to see what Donnchad was up to in Ireland. I'd tried dreaming of him many times since he'd left but had only been able to catch glimpses of him. He had been fighting, I knew that. Riding throughout Ireland with the Anglo-Norman lords, but he was quiet. I'd overheard nothing of interest in my dreams. But of course, I had another way to find out what was going on.

After our falconry session tomorrow, I'd tell Olaf to fly and find Donnchad. Olaf would get a view of the camp, where they were and who they were fighting for. From him, I would hear the truth rather than whatever lies and half-truths Donnchad was no doubt spewing at that very minute to further his pursuit of gaining the kingship of Ireland.

Isolde

Kells

I walked along the plain and watched the birds soar above me. Their song was beautiful this morning, though it still seemed strange to walk about the plain and be able to hear it. It was even stranger to walk and not come across anyone, when only ten days ago I would have had to push to get through the crowd. The animals enjoyed the people's absence, I thought. The hares and the sparrows and the badgers.

It wasn't only the animals that had returned. The land itself was healing, too. Now that the plain was almost empty, grass had begun to sprout through the churned soil and mud that so many visitors had left behind. Crouching down, I ran my hands over the new shoots coming through. Ants and other insects crawled around them today, more than yesterday. Laying my hand flat on the ground, a ladybird ran onto my palm, and I lifted her up, thinking to set her on a thicker patch of grass where she was less exposed.

It made me wonder what Rathlin might be like after the fire. Would new plants and trees already be growing? Or had the fire burned so hot and fierce that the land had died forever?

My heart ached on thinking this. I thought I might have got used to that feeling by now. That the emptiness might have begun to fade, and the pain heal. But no. If anything, the ache inside my chest had deepened these last few days.

Not wanting to dwell on these feelings, I stood and continued my walk along the plain, making my way toward the forest.

Going slowly, I turned to the side as if I were practising a dance.

Four of the queen's guards were following me this time. One in plain view, another staying a little further back, while two had already concealed themselves in the forest. Still, four was less than the five that had followed me for the first few days.

If only I had Fragarach, I could make a run for it.

Sighing at the situation I found myself in, I walked over to an apple tree and sat underneath it. The apples weren't ripe yet, but they would be soon. That hadn't stopped the birds from picking at them. An apple, small and hard, lay on the grass beside me and I picked it up.

"Messengers!" one of the men following me shouted. "Messengers from the king."

The sound of hooves hitting the hard ground followed, and a few moments later, four horses came into view. Cathal was at the front, Cuan at the back. The two men riding between them, I did not know. They all slowed their horses as they approached the plain, and Cathal waved as he saw me sitting by the tree.

"Greetings, Isolde."

"Good morning, Cathal."

I glanced behind them, noting the absence of the army they had left with.

"We rode on ahead to tell the queen that the king and his army returns," he explained.

"Everything went well, I hope?"

"Yes, it did. Just as my brother said it would." He turned to the two men riding behind him. "Come on," Cathal said. "I'm starving." He gave a wave of farewell as they galloped toward the feasting hall.

Smiling, I waved back, glad that he had returned with no ill-tidings. Cuan smiled but did not push his own horse into a run. It dawned on me then that I hadn't seen him smile before, not a proper smile anyway.

"It's the apple tree," I said to him.

"What is?"

"It's the apple tree that's making you smile."

"Is it? How so?"

"When Manannán Mac Lir left his home of Tír Tairngire, he appeared to the High King, Cormac Mac Airt, carrying a branch full of apples. When Manannán shook the branch, it made a musical sound that made Cormac forget all his sorrows. That is why people smile when they see an apple tree. They've heard the music, and for a brief moment, their troubles are gone."

"It is a good story, but perhaps I was merely amused by the sight of you, wearing your new dress and sitting in the mud. When I told you to fit in, this isn't what I meant."

"I can't help it, for I cannot sit in the tent all day." I glanced over at the plain. The women were already lighting the fires. It was time for me to return and offer to help. No doubt if the army was on their way here, a lot of food would need to be prepared.

"How long do you think it will take for everyone to return?"

"Not long. A few hours at most. Everyone is eager to feast here tonight and then go home."

That was good. That meant my time here was almost at an end. "And where is home for you, Cuan?"

"It is Connacht, but as it happens, I am going to Dublin tomorrow."

"That's in Leinster, isn't it? Perhaps I can travel south with you?"

Cuan bit his lip. "You're going to Athlone, or so I've heard."

"Which way is Athlone?"

"East. It's in Connacht."

"But I don't want to go to Connacht. I've to go to Seir Kieran."

"The king has decided otherwise."

"Why?" I shook my head. "What's it to him where I go?"

"Apparently, he means to gift you to one of the nunneries. You said that's what you wanted to do. He's even said he'll ensure you are placed into a good position."

Cuan stared at me. Not quite smiling, but still he looked as if what he'd just said was a good thing.

"But I don't want that… I don't want to be gifted to a nunnery. What… What does that even mean? Gifted."

"It means he is the High King, and he can do what he wants with his people."

I snorted. "It's almost as if he thinks people are slaves to command."

"Many of them are."

"What?"

"Look around you, Isolde? You think these men and women who've stayed behind are all the kin and friends of the king? The ones who are making the fires and serving the queen and her daughters."

"Yes... aren't they?"

"Of course not. It's the same at the monasteries and nunneries. Many there are slaves, too."

I frowned. Broccan had never told me this. The only time he had mentioned slaves was to tell me that when he was a boy, it was the Irish who were often taken. I couldn't quite believe what Cuan was telling me. The serving women were slaves? Monasteries kept slaves, too?

"Let me guess," Cuan said. "There were no slaves on Rathlin?"

"There weren't," I said, standing. "There shouldn't be slaves anywhere... I thought King Brian Boru banned slavery?"

"Brian Boru? He was king over one hundred and fifty years ago." Cuan's forehead furrowed. "Isolde, I don't understand you. You know so many of the languages of this world. Your swordwork is as good as any boy your age, and yet you don't seem to understand how the world works."

He was right. I didn't. Broccan had trained me in so many ways, but in other ways he'd shielded me too much. He had never expected not to be with me. He'd thought he'd be with me to protect me always.

Cuan rode away then, making his way into the queen's tent. An outbreak of cheers followed. Queen Gráinne and her daughter Róisín laughed at something, and the other women, the slaves, hurried out to start cooking up the stews and broths required to feed so many men.

"Isolde," Róisín shouted. "Come here! We've good news to share."

I made my way into the tent. The queen was talking with some of the older ladies, all of whom were in good humour. They had grown used to me over the last ten days, and begrudgingly, I had to admit, part of that was due to wearing Dáirinn's dress. Cuan was right. I blended in more wearing it, and the women spoke to me as a friend now rather than a curiosity. Sitting down, I listened to the conversation. Róisín was doing most of the talking, expressing her excitement about returning home, while others spoke of the hostages. Róisín didn't appear so keen to talk about this, nor about the prince who she was now engaged to.

"You will come to like him. I'm sure of it," the queen said, noticing her daughter's reticence. "He is from Leinster, but he'll likely be king of that province one day. We all hope that he will be a better man than his father, and as his wife, you can help make that so."

"He couldn't be any worse than King Diarmait, I suppose." Róisín shrugged, but I could sense the fear within her that she would not like her husband-to-be. She stared around the room, restless, until her gaze fell upon me. "Isolde," she said. "How about a story from you today?"

Sitting straighter, I plumped up my cushion. "I am not a good storyteller. It was my cousin who always told me stories."

"Then tell us one of the stories he told you. Come on. Please. We've been here for ten days now, and we've nothing left to say."

All of them stared at me, full of expectation. I didn't like that… except I found myself smiling unexpectedly at the thought of Broccan sitting by the fire. He would be wrapped up in his furs, head leaning backward against the chair, only moving occasionally to stoke the flames.

"Ah, I can see you've thought of something," the queen said. "What is it?"

"Broccan told me a story once about Fand of the Tuatha Dé Danann and Cú Chulainn. Do you know that one?"

The women in the tent shook their heads.

"No," Róisín said. "I've never heard of Fand."

"Fand and her sister Liban were witches of the Tuatha Dé Danann. They often travelled from the otherworld to our world disguised as birds and linked themselves with a golden chain so as not to become separated from each other. One day, Cú Chulainn saw them fly overhead. On seeing their beauty, he decided their feathers would make his wife, Emer, a wonderful gift.

"He cast two stones with his sling but missed both times. Cú Chulainn couldn't believe it, for he never missed with his sling. Not to be deterred, he aimed next with his spear. This spear was called Assail, and it held great magic within it, which meant the spear could never miss. This time Cú Chulainn struck one of the birds in the wing. Before he could cheer his success, a great weakness came upon him, and he fell to the ground. In a fevered state, he saw two women walk toward him, one wearing a green cloak, the other crimson. They smiled, but as they came closer, they whipped him with rods until he was near death."

The queen's eyes widened. "The great Cú Chulainn laid low by two women? You're making this up, Isolde."

"I'm not. Witches of the Tuatha Dé Danann are very powerful, and Cú Chulainn had angered them greatly."

"What did Cú Chulainn do?" Róisín asked.

"Nothing," I replied. "His friends, not able to see the women, asked him what was wrong, but Cú Chulainn was so weak he couldn't speak. His friends carried him home, and he lay on his deathbed for a year until a woman dressed in a green cloak knocked on his door.

"She said, 'My name is Liban, wife of Labraid of the quick sword. He's told me to tell you he will give you all you can wish for, if you will fight for him in a battle against his enemies.'"

"But he cannot fight," the queen answered. "They have cursed him."

"That is true," I replied. "And Cú Chulainn said the very same thing. Liban, however, stroked his hair and told him that she would break the curse if he agreed to fight for her husband.

"Cú Chulainn refused to decide until his wife Emer heard the proposition, for he trusted her advice. Emer thought about it for a while and decided he should fight to regain his health. The instant he agreed, he travelled to the otherworld with Liban and won a mighty victory against Labraid's enemies."

Róisín frowned. "Why did they need Cú Chulainn to fight for them? Didn't the Tuatha Dé Danann have their own warriors?"

"Yes, they did, but Cú Chulainn was the son of Lugh, the greatest of the Tuatha Dé Danann, for he was the only one of them to hold all the gifts. The son, Cú Chulainn, held only the warrior gift, but some say in this, he surpassed the skill of even his father."

"My father used to say that too," Blinne said. "That is why Cú Chulainn is so famous."

I listened as the women chatted, some agreeing with Blinne and me, while others spoke of other warriors whose fame eclipsed Cú Chulainn. I smiled as they argued, but I also began to think of this story in a new way. All these years, Broccan had been teaching me of my ancestors, and I had not known.

"What happened next?" the queen asked.

"Hmm, where was I?" I wrapped Broccan's cloak tighter around my shoulders.

"You were at the part where Cú Chulainn fought and won the battle."

"Ah, yes, Cú Chulainn won the battle for Labraid, and afterward Labraid invited Cú Chulainn to his house. It was here he saw Fand. She was dressed in a red dress and crimson cloak, and he recognised her as the other woman who, with Liban, had beaten him."

"And what did he do?" Blinne asked. "Was he angry?"

"No. Far from it. That night, he fell in love with her, for her beauty was beyond compare. Fand also fell in love with Cú Chulainn and left her husband, Manannán, the Tuatha Dé Danann god of the sea, to come to our world with Cú Chulainn when he returned. Here, their love for each other grew strong. However, Emer soon found out about her husband's new lover. One night, she brought a knife to Cú Chulainn's bedroom to kill Fand. Cú Chulainn woke as she approached and asked her to put down the knife. Emer did this but asked why he had dishonoured her so.

"Fand woke and, on seeing Emer's great pain, vowed to give up Cú Chulainn. In her misery, she called her husband, Manannán to cross the sea and find her. Once Cú Chulainn realised Fand had gone with Manannán, a great anger and sadness overcame him. He lived alone in the mountains for many months, so wretched with longing that he could no longer bear to be in the company of others.

"Friends of Cú Chulainn sent the Druids of Ulster to visit him, but so great was his rage they couldn't get near him. The druids believed there was no cure for such deep sadness, so they made him a potion of forgetfulness. From the moment he drank the potion, he no longer remembered Fand. The druids also gave a drink of forgetfulness to Emer, so she would forget her jealousy. That same night, Manannán shook his cloak between Cú Chulainn and Fand, casting a spell so they should never meet one another again, and so that the love between them would never be renewed."

The story ended there, and I found my cheek wet with tears. There was sadness within the story. The sadness of Emer, who loved her unfaithful husband, as well as the sadness of Cú Chulainn and Fand that their love could not be. But that was not why I didn't want the story to finish. It was that Broccan's voice had been so clear in my mind while I told it, and now it was gone. It was like losing him all over again.

When I looked at the queen, I noticed a trail of tears running down her cheeks.

"What a sad story for one so young to tell," she said. "It's almost as if I can feel your pain upon hearing it."

I wished I could wipe my tears away and laugh, but I couldn't. My grief was now like an open wound, there for all to see. More tears came.

"Isolde, what is wrong?" Queen Gráinne asked.

"When my cousin Broccan died, I felt as if I should die too. He's the only person I've ever loved, and he's the only person who loved me in return. What is left now that he's gone?"

"Do not say that, Isolde," the queen said, wiping away more tears that trickled down her face. "Life continues. You will love and be loved again."

"How can that be when you will not let me find my family?"

The queen flinched at this, though her tears kept falling.

"I have other family in Leinster that I cannot go to, and I don't know why."

"You are unusual, Isolde," the queen said. "You must see that."

"Yes, I suppose I am. My cousin did not teach me how to raise a family. I was taught to fight and survive. I've lived in a wild place where the passing of seasons and comings and goings of birds and animals were my entertainment. Now I've lived among you, I see that is strange, but is that enough for my freedom to be taken from me? You don't understand me and therefore any hopes I had for my future must be forfeit?"

The queen moved back to her cushions, though the tears continued to fall down her cheeks. "It's a hard lot to be a woman in this land, Isolde. So much expectation and so little power. So many consequences for those who stray. It is marriage or the convent for us; there is no other life. The offer my husband has given you, a position in Clonmacnoise, is a good one. More than a girl of your background could hope to achieve on her own."

"I know, and I am grateful that he would help me, but I do not wish to go there. Having lost my cousin, I wish to find someone else who knows him. I want to talk of him with someone who knows of whom I speak."

The queen wiped her tears but said nothing more. Slowly the conversation of others built up around the two of us. Life moved on.

★

That night, I sat in the fort and ate with those who had remained. Blinne, loud and joyful, spoke to her daughter, eagerly speaking of returning to their friends and family who had not been able to attend the games. Some of the warriors spoke of their harvests and their hopes that no storms blew in until it was done. Deciding I was empty of conversation, I got up and made my way to Blinne's tent.

My mind was a mess. What should I do? Wait until I reached the convent and escape from there? But what about Fragarach? How could I leave it behind? If only—

"Isolde." Cuan walked toward me. "Where are you going?"

"To bed. I need my sleep. We are leaving early in the morning."

"Yes. We are." From his pocket he pulled out Fragarach.

Quickly, I took it from his hand. "The king will let me keep it?"

"Yes. I don't know what you said to the queen, but she has just convinced him to let you go. If you still want to go to Seir Kieran, I leave for Dublin in the morning. From there, I'll find you transport for the rest of the way, if you wish."

"I do wish."

"Then be ready. We leave at dawn."

Smiling, I breathed in the fresh air and walked along the plain. The ladybirds were still crawling along the grass, more of them now than earlier, and I picked one of them up. Just as they had found their new home, so would I.

Donnchad

Ferns

"Where is Bruce?" Maurice de Prendergast came out of his house, searching for his hunting dog.

I raised my head, though didn't move to help like some of the archers did. They walked around the dun, calling his name and whistling.

Angelo, who lay beside me, poked the fire with a stick.

"Did you see the dog?" I asked.

He shook his head.

Neither had I, not for a few days anyway, but then so many dogs ran around the dun that I hadn't paid close attention. However, now the search was underway, I noted how odd it was that the Anglo-Normans roused themselves to look for this animal – the very same men who would leave behind an injured soldier without a second thought. Animals had a way of eliciting strong emotions in the hearts of men, I remembered. Those that were loyal, most of all. I had forgotten this, but yes, I remembered now. Remembered how my father had loved his dogs too.

"Bruce was here yesterday, my lord," said one of the archers. "I saw him running outside the ringfort." I recognised this man. He was the one who had given Angelo his new bow, then laughed at him when Angelo wasn't looking.

"Out with you then," Maurice said. "He must have gone into the forest. Don't come back without him." The archer and a few of his friends took another of the hunting dogs and ran out of the gate.

FitzStephen told some of his men to follow and help too. His voice was calm, but his cheeks flushed. I understood the cause of his anxiety. He wanted to leave. Ten days had passed and already tensions were building between the Leinster men and the Anglo-Norman army. Not that he had confided in me again, but Robert was a clever man, and I knew my words of advice would have taken hold. They couldn't remain at Ferns all winter as guests when they had nothing left to offer King Diarmait. No, they needed to advance their own position and the only way to do that was to split the army, as I had suggested.

"Get ready, Angelo. Do you hear me? Be ready."

My son did as I asked and began to get changed while I made my way toward Robert's house. The knights were eating their morning breakfast, a bigger one than usual. Another sign that they meant to make a move.

"Is everything well, my lord?" I asked Robert.

"Yes, Donn. All is well."

His words were curt and dismissive, so I did not linger by the house and instead walked over to the cooking fire.

It was while I was here that the commotion from outside began to build.

It was the archers. They all came through the gates, carrying Bruce on a makeshift stretcher… or at least what remained of him. The lower half of his body was missing and the skin around his face and legs was peeled away.

"Wolves must have got him, my lord," one of the archers said, his eyes wet with tears.

Maurice examined the remains, then turned. "Bury him outside. Now. Deep enough that the wolves cannot get the rest of him."

The archers carrying Bruce did this, but a taut silence remained among the rest of the Anglo-Normans as Maurice wiped his forehead with his sleeve.

"Men!" Maurice raised his hand. "The men who sailed with me, we are leaving. Ready your things."

Robert shook his head. "Do not do this. I know you are upset, but do not act hastily."

"This isn't about my dog, and you know it. You promised I would have land, and still there is none for me," Maurice snapped. "I won't have it! Philip," he nodded at the man standing beside him. "Ready the horses. Tell the men we're leaving as soon as possible."

Robert argued with Maurice, reasoning at the start and then shouting. He hadn't broken his word. There would be more land to win next year. This was not the time to fall out.

The argument was well done. The words rehearsed, yes, but spoken with passion.

I wasn't the only one to listen as the row unfolded. Domhnall stood very still by the doors of the feasting hall and watched as Robert and Maurice shouted at each other. He might have stayed that way but for the speed at which Maurice's knights, archers and soldiers moved into formation, their armour and weapons ready.

"I came here for land," Maurice roared as he mounted his horse. "You and your brother, who isn't even here yet, are intent on keeping it for yourself. I lost men at Wexford and Osraige. Where is my land?"

"All in good time, Maurice," Robert said. "Please don't go. Let's talk about this."

"I'm sick of talking!" Maurice kicked his horse, and it bolted forward, galloping out of the dun. Maurice's men followed, and as they left, I noted that they took the path to Osraige.

Robert, red-faced, glared at the men leaving. Meilyr and Miles came to his side and whispered in his ear.

"Men," Robert shouted. "Ready yourselves. We are leaving too."

Domhnall now sprang into action and took Robert by the arm. Riagáin, on Domhnall's behalf, began to ask Robert questions. *Where had Maurice gone? What had caused the falling out? Why did Robert now want to leave, too?*

The quality of Riagáin's French had improved since our arrival, enough that his questions could be understood. Robert, however, didn't answer them right away and called for one of his men to ready his horse.

"We have not enough land," he told Riagáin once this was done.

"You have not kept your promises, and so Maurice rides to Osraige to fight for the king there. We are going home."

"No, do not go," Domhnall said, his voice trying not to show signs of the desperation that had found its way to his eyes. "My father is King of Leinster now. We can provide more land in the spring. You have my word."

Riagáin translated this. Twice.

Only then did Robert stop. "Ask him what land he offers."

"What do you want?" Riagáin asked, not bothering to translate yet.

"Dublin. And I want it now."

Riagáin translated for Domhnall, who stood still as he absorbed the sudden change of events and this new demand. Diarmait came out then, staring curiously at the knights on horseback.

"Half of them have gone, Father. Maurice and his men. To Osraige," Domhnall said. "Robert FitzStephen will only stay if we give him Dublin now."

"If they want to ride to Dublin, let's go. I would love nothing more than to see that smug smile fall from Asculv's lips."

"Are you sure, Father? We had thought to deal with Dublin next year."

"Plans can change, my son. If these Normans can take Dublin, let them have it for all I care. It is more likely that they will lose all their men in the attempt, but that is their choice. If by some miracle of God, they do take it, we can argue over how high the tributes are to be later."

Domhnall clenched his jaw. He knew. He knew how hard it would be to get anyone out of Dublin once they held it. But he also saw, as I had, that his father could not afford to let Robert and his men leave while half of the Anglo-Norman army planned to pledge themselves to his enemy.

"Tell Robert this," Diarmait said to Riagáin. "Tell him that it is unlikely that we can take Dublin this close to winter, but we will ride there if he wishes. Perhaps Asculv can be persuaded to change allegiance to us."

Riagáin translated.

"How will that serve us?" Robert asked.

"It means next year we will return to Dublin. If they've sworn their oaths to us, they will open their gates. Then you can take it. Next year, I swear it, one way or another, Dublin will be yours."

Robert nodded and held out his hand for Domhnall to shake. "We ride out tomorrow. Tell your men to be ready."

Domhnall agreed, and the orders to ride out the following morning were given. Smiling, I made my way to my tent and sharpened my sword.

Robert found me that night. He handed me a cup of wine. It was from Diarmait's store and so I knew before tasting that it would be poor fare. Another trait Diarmait must have inherited from Máelmórda. My uncle had notoriously kept a poor hall when he was King of Leinster, though perhaps I could sympathise with Diarmait. Being at war for so many years must have drained his wealth. Poor wine was the least of his worries.

"Your plan is now in motion," Robert said.

I nodded. "The argument between yourself and Maurice was a stroke of genius."

"Just because we keep to our vows does not mean we are not schooled in the games of war."

"Did Maurice go to Osraige?"

"He will see what can be taken there, but he doesn't intend to stay for long. Once he's spoken to the King of Osraige, he plans to ride to Waterford, assess it, and then go home, as you advised. When we are done with Dublin, I'd like you to meet him and return to Wales with him. That way you can answer whatever Strongbow's questions are about the Irish."

"You think Strongbow will come here?"

Robert took a sip of his wine, then set the cup down. "Maurice intends to convince him, and he rarely fails." Robert patted my leg and stood. "I'll let you sleep now. We go to war tomorrow. It's best to be ready."

I smiled and raised the glass of wine to show that I appreciated his gesture.

"Now," Robert said, "I just need to raise a toast to whoever it was who killed Maurice's dog. It couldn't have happened at a better time."

This caught my attention. "You don't think it was wolves?"

Robert snorted. "It was not a wolf. The dog's stomach was gone, but not his heart or lungs. And the skin on his face was sliced away with a knife, not teeth." He took another sip of his drink and shrugged. "A vicious man, whoever it was. Probably did it to scare us. But all it did was provide Maurice with an opportunity to start the argument we had planned."

He disappeared then into the shadows of the dun.

I lay down, happy with the events of the day. We were moving toward Dublin again, and this was the beginning, the true beginning of my rise to power.

For if Robert was schooled in the art of war, I was born to it.

Isolde

Dublin

After three days of travelling, we finally reached Dublin. Encased by a twenty-foot-high stone wall, the city was obscured from sight until we reached the end of the forest path, and from there, all I could see was the blue mass of sea that stretched from the walls to the horizon. The sea. How I had missed it. Gulls soared in the wind, squawking and diving for fish. The view was so like Rathlin that I could have imagined I was there, save for the smell. It wasn't seaweed and salt that filled the air around Dublin. No, it was something I'd never smelled before. Fragrant and sweet, but then sometimes the breeze could blow, and a deeper scent would catch my nose and make me sneeze.

A large gate in the wall was the only entrance on this side of the city, and I watched it as we came closer. Made of iron nails and thick wooden planks, it opened for King Asculv's returning army, then closed behind us.

The city itself was a strange sight. The remote countryside we'd travelled through had been scattered with ráths, miles apart. Even the tents along the plain of Kells had been spread out so people could move between them. In Dublin, the houses seemed to be built on top of each other. Children shuffled between them, or ran around in packs, their shrieks drowned out by the constant hum that thousands of people living together make.

As the train of horses continued along the path that led deeper into Dublin, homes made way for stalls. Here the smoke of the burning turf blended with the heady scents I'd noted from outside the walls. Furs and silk tunics hung on wooden stands, while whale bones, dried herbs and spices, tusks and jewellery adorned the tables.

"You've never seen anywhere like this, have you?" Cuan said as he pushed his horse over to mine.

"No. I haven't."

Cuan pointed to a large wooden building set apart from the other houses around it. A tower rose from the centre of the structure, topped with an iron cross. Men worked all along the front of it and had set up a scaffold near the window above the entrance. "That's Christ Church. My great-great-uncle, Sitric Silkbeard, who was King of Dublin for many years, built it when he converted to Christianity."

"What are they doing to it?"

He pointed to a large panel that lay in a wagon outside the church door. It was a strange material, shiny and clear, though in some places it was filled with colour. Blues, oranges, reds and yellows. "They call it glass. The tradesmen in Frankia have worked out how to put colour inside of it. They use it for church windows over there."

"It's beautiful."

"It is, especially when the light shines through. Though I don't know if a wooden church will hold the weight of it. The Frankish churches are made of stone, and the stone holds the glass tight. But Asculv's determined to try."

I glanced at the church again, but it was Cuan's face that fascinated me. His smile was wider, eyes brighter than I'd ever seen them. It was the expression of a man returning home, his caution momentarily forgotten.

"Cuan! Cuan!" A boy of about thirteen or fourteen ran toward us. Fluffy wisps scattered his chin, and his voice shifted as he shouted. "Cuan, you're back!"

"I am, Håkon! How are you?" Cuan leaned down to pull Håkon into a hug as he reached him, then ruffled his hair. "My, you look just like your father."

"Really?"

"Really." He looked Håkon over again and set his hand on his shoulder. "Now, tell me the truth. How are you getting on? I hope you've been working hard."

Håkon nodded. "Vígi says I'm the best he's seen with a sword in a long time."

Cuan raised an eyebrow and gave Håkon some words of encouragement, promising to watch him train the next day. Håkon ran off with a wide grin and disappeared into the swarm of people.

"A friend?" I asked.

"Yes. His father took me under his wing when I first fought for my uncle Godred. He died a few years ago."

"So, now you're looking after his son?"

Cuan's gaze lingered on the direction Håkon had run for a moment. "As much as I can, which isn't much, considering I'm seldom here."

Our horses continued to walk through the city without any guidance, and one by one, the Viking soldiers who'd accompanied us drifted away to greet their waiting families. Soon, only Cuan and I were left with King Asculv and members of his household guard.

"Where's your house?" I asked.

"I don't have one."

"Then where are you going? Where am I going, more to the point?"

I stared around the city again. There seemed to be so many people compared to the number of houses. Where did people like me with no kin or friends stay?

"I'm staying in Asculv's fort as a guest. I'm a nephew of two kings, you know." A hint of a smile crossed Cuan's lips. "It comes in handy, occasionally... when no one is trying to kill me because of it."

I snorted. "Did you just tell a joke?"

Cuan laughed by way of reply and pointed to a large building just ahead of us. "There's the fort. Once there, I'll have someone ready a house for you. There are usually a few kept vacant beside Saint Aodhan's church for guests of the king."

Cuan dismounted and gave his horse to one of the stable boys who came over. I did the same and removed Broccan's bag from my horse, my hands feeling for Fragarach through the fabric.

Now on my own two feet, I couldn't help but stare at the stalls. People shouted out their wares: *Bracelets! Bread! Dresses! Shawls!* So much gold and silver was on display, I couldn't believe it. Earrings, arm-rings and hair pieces. Gems. Golden orbs and combs made of whale bone. Slinging my bag over my back, I moved along the stalls, my legs grateful to be moving once again.

"Who is that for?" Cuan called to the blacksmith, his eye catching one of the swords that hung there.

"Eric Kolsson," the blacksmith replied. "He came into Dublin last night."

Cuan's face brightened at the name, and he turned to gaze at the longphort.

"Another friend?" I asked.

"Not quite," Cuan answered. "He's a friend of my uncle's. A trader. A rich one, as you can see." He tilted his head toward the sword and pointed at some of the gems inlaid into the pommel. The blacksmith, on seeing my interest, lifted the sword and twisted it around to show me more of his craftsmanship. As well as gems, I noted the gold woven into the grip and the silver engraving down the blade.

"Would you not want such a sword for yourself?" I asked Cuan.

"Me? Never. My sword was my grandfather's sword, and it was made by a master forger. No one knows how to make swords like this anymore, but they do not break, and they never wear away, no matter how often you sharpen them." He took out his sword to show me. The blade was wide, though the cross-guard was wider, and the edges razor-sharp. An eye was engraved on the pommel, but apart from that, it was plain.

Cuan said a goodbye to the blacksmith, and once again, he

stared down at the longphort. "I need to speak with Eric before I go to the fort."

Intrigued by the longships that I'd only ever seen from a distance, I walked with Cuan to the end of the market. Here, the stone walls encasing the city stopped between the edge of the river and the beach. Large earthen trenches piled with spiked wooden posts guarded this part of the city instead, and a thin wooden pathway allowed people to move between the market and docked ships.

Cuan pointed out Eric's ship, which was anchored at the far end of the port. It was the biggest of all the ships, with a sternpost carved into the shape of a two-headed sea monster. Hundreds of people crowded the wooden walkway opposite the ship – so many that I couldn't make out what was being unloaded.

Cuan and I continued along the pathway but didn't get far before a young man sitting in one of the docked row boats shouted at us. He leaped onto the pathway and wrapped Cuan into a bear hug.

"Hálfdan," Cuan replied, his mouth dropping open. "I didn't know you were here. I thought you were still on the Isle of Man."

Hálfdan took a step back, running a hand over his clean-shaven scalp. "No, I've been here for a while now, trading along the coast. Up to Ulaid and back to Dublin. It's nothing fancy but I am my own man for a change."

Cuan grinned. "Will you come to the feast tonight?"

"I'm not often invited to the fort."

"You are tonight," Cuan said. "I insist."

Hálfdan nodded, stared at me, then turned his attention back to his friend. "Who is this?"

"This is Isolde. She is travelling to the nunnery at Seir Kieran. Do you know of any ships travelling that way?"

"There are always a few going," Hálfdan said. "Not as many since the Leinster raids into Osraige, though. I can ask around for you."

"Please. I would appreciate it."

Hálfdan placed his hand on Cuan's shoulder and gripped it hard. "If only Bjorn were here, it would be like old times."

The smile half slipped from Cuan's face. "Come and find me later at the fort. We'll feast and talk, and you can tell me how you convinced Godred to let you go."

"Alright." Hálfdan jumped back into his boat and shifted a barrel of fish closer to the edge. "I assume, since you didn't know I was here, that you're looking for Eric? He's got himself a good haul this time. He'll be in fine form."

Cuan glanced at the imposing longship. "Then I'd better speak to him before Asculv's taxes put him in an ill-humour."

"Off you go," Hálfdan said. "You'd best be quick. The auction is about to start."

Auction? What did that mean? I'd not heard that word before. Slowly, Cuan and I made our way closer to Eric's ship, the walkway now too full of people to move with any speed. Edging through, I reached the ship, noting that the group of men and women I'd spotted in the distance were now lined up. Ropes bound their ankles together.

"Why are they tied up?" I asked Cuan.

"They're slaves. The auction's about to start."

That word again, but still I didn't know what it meant.

My frown deepened as the silent row of bodies shivered, huddling together as the sea-wind blew through their thin shifts.

The men standing on the longphort began to raise their hands, each time to show they were willing to offer more money than the person before. The young men and women fetched the highest prices, the older children too. Suddenly, a loud wail sounded out over the crowd, carried by the wind. A girl, not much younger than me, cried as she was dragged away. She begged the man who'd bought her to let her go, but he shook his head and exchanged money with a black-haired man sitting at a wooden table.

My lips trembled, and I struggled to not let the tears welling inside spill over, but nobody else appeared the least bit bothered by the girl's pleas. How could that be? How could everyone here be so heartless?

"Cuan." I gave him the silver pendant from around my neck. "Buy her."

Cuan stared at the silver and then me. "That's not enough to buy a slave, Isolde. Even if it was, I could not afford to keep her."

"I don't want you to keep her. I want her to be free."

"I cannot," Cuan said. "That's the King of Osraige's man who has bought her."

"Who?"

"One of the Irish kings. She's been bought to tend to his cattle. It isn't so bad. Probably no different to the life she would have lived in Northumbria before her parents sold her."

"Her parents sold her?"

"Most likely."

I shook my head in disbelief at the event unfolding around me. Slaves, sold by their parents or else captured along the coast. Sold and bought by men for gold. Everything about it was disgusting, and I turned to leave.

"Where are you going?" Cuan called, pulling my arm.

I pushed his hand away and continued to walk back along the longphort.

"Cuan," one of the men from the ship called out. "We meet again." The man strolled over to Cuan, grinning widely. This, I guessed, was Eric. Cuan gave me another look, but as the man approached, he turned and offered him his hand. I left them to it. Whatever Cuan had to talk to him about, I didn't want to know.

I made my way over to the beach and sat on one of the rocks. The view out to sea was similar, yes, but Dublin was a very different place to Rathlin. We were poor there. I could see that now. No jewels or gems. No silk dresses. We lived simply. We grew our own food and tended to our own cattle. It wasn't well kept and there were no feasts to attend, and yet I would gladly live like that always if it meant I was free and everyone else on the island was free too.

"What's wrong, Isolde?"

I hadn't heard anyone approach, but I knew who it was. Cuan's voice was soft, unexpectedly so. As I turned, he took a step closer, but I edged back, and he stopped.

"You don't understand," I said. "You're the nephew of two kings. How could you?"

Cuan lowered his head, his face a mask. He'd been brought up by Vikings, so these slave auctions were probably a normal part of life for him. He'd also lived with the Irish kings who bought the slaves. My sentiments must sound strange to him. *The woman's life would probably be no different*, he had said, but that wasn't true. It would be forever changed by her enslavement. How could he not see that?

"I forgot Rathlin Island was raided by Vikings," he said after a few seconds. "I should have known the auction would upset you. Please, I apologise. Let me take you to the house Asculv has provided for you."

Holding back a sigh, for I was too exhausted to argue, I brushed my hair from my face and followed him back into the city.

As Cuan had guessed, the house I'd been given was close to a small church built next to the wall on the north-east side of Dublin. It was small, but better constructed than the other houses closer to the beach. A small fire was lit in the centre of the room and a bed lay behind it.

"This is a hateful place, Cuan," I said, now I had gathered my thoughts. "How can you like it here? The girl was crying and begging to be let go, and nobody else even noticed it. How can that be?"

"It is a hard life for many, Isolde. I do not deny it, but you were wrong earlier. I have known hardship myself, and I do pity those on the ships."

"You? A relation of two kings? What could you know of hardship?"

"From where I sit, there is one of us who has had an easy

life, and it's not me. This cousin of yours, he shielded you from all the harsh realities of life. Took you somewhere far enough away that you could not see all the ills of this world. I was not so lucky."

"What do you mean?"

"When I was a boy, I lived like a prince and probably had the life you imagined. It was expected that my father would become King of Connacht, but when my grandfather died, my uncle, Ruaidrí, was made king instead. My mother and I fled to Dublin, and then to the Isle of Man. Her brother Godred is king there."

My hand dropped away from my face, and I stared at him. "Why? Why did you have to leave your home?"

"My father planned to have Ruaidrí killed in revenge for stealing the kingship, and my mother was scared I'd be killed in retaliation."

He rubbed the rough stubble on his chin, eyes lost in thought. "My mother's brother is King of the Isles, and she knew we'd be safe with him. And we were safe from Ruaidrí, but my mother died almost as soon as we arrived. My uncle Godred kept me, but he has sons of his own, and many other nephews and cousins, so from that moment, I had to grow up and learn to fend for myself. I lived with the men of his household. With the slaves, too. In truth, as warriors, we were treated much the same. All of us were expendable. All of us conditioned to fight for Godred the second he wanted it."

The ball in my chest unravelled ever so slightly. It seemed life was unfair to so many, and though Cuan had borne the brunt of my anger, it was not he who had upset me. He did not bring the slaves here, nor did he buy them. And yet he had spoken to Eric as if they were friends, even though I could tell he didn't like him. Why? *Why did he do that?*

"What are you doing in Dublin, Cuan?"

"Passing a message on to Godred from Ruaidrí. It seems one of my uncles wants the help of another and I am the link between them."

"That's why you were sent here… but it's not really why you are here."

Cuan shrugged and walked to the door. "There is a feast at the fort tonight, which you can attend. If you don't wish to go, I'll have food brought over to you. I'll also organise your passage to Seir Keiran for tomorrow."

"So many secrets, Cuan. I don't know how you can carry them all."

"Me?" Cuan closed the door. "You speak to me of secrets?"

"Yes."

"If I am a liar, so are you."

"No, I'm not."

"Well, you don't want to be a nun, that's for certain."

"What makes you so sure of that?"

"Because in the whole time I've known you, I've never seen you pray. Not once."

Arguing was futile. If I protested, I'd have to lie, and he'd see through it. So, I didn't answer at first. Being quiet was safe. Safer for me. Safer for him, too.

"Tell me this, Cuan," I said. "If you could have anything, what would it be?"

"Control over my own life."

"Why?"

"Because if I had control, I could do as I wished. I would be free."

"Aren't you free now?"

"No. You saw those slaves earlier and wept because they have no freedom, but who does have true freedom? We all must swear our vows and serve our masters. Happiness is only for those at the very top. For the kings."

I shook my head. "You could be happy if you wished to be."

"That's not true. You've seen for yourself that there are those who wish to kill me. How can I have anything – wife, children, friends? If these people who want me dead succeeded, and I had a family, what would become of them?"

I said nothing to this. There was nothing to say. There was so much wrong that I couldn't begin to understand how and why that was, and yet how strange it was that danger was so prevalent for all. Not just the poor but for the rich too. Cuan seemed to live his life on the edge of a blade. I met his gaze and saw he was looking back at me. For once, his expression was open.

"Why are they trying to kill you, Cuan?"

He tensed, the openness fading, and his fingers reached for the handle of the door. But I could not stop now.

"Like you said, I was at the bruidean. I saw them. Heard them."

He nodded. "Yes. There are people who want to kill me. Or blind me. It is the way my life is for now. I can say no more."

I didn't push him any further, for I suspected what the issue might be. Broccan had told me once of a king being blinded so another man could take his place. The blinding of a man barred him from kingship. This custom came from the Tuatha Dé Danann but had become a part of the laws of the mortals too.

Cuan exhaled, seeming to catch that I was studying the scar along his face and the redness of his eye. Pushing against the door, he paused. "You should attend the feast tonight, Isolde. Make sure to eat well. Tomorrow will be the start of another long journey."

Once Cuan left, I moved away from the fire and climbed onto the bed, using the fur there to cover my body so I could warm up. Cuan was a mystery indeed, and it was thoughts of his reactions that filled my mind. His happiness when entering Dublin. The change in him once he realised Eric was here. The way he kept himself apart from his family in Connacht while he had so many friends in Dublin. Biting my lip, I shook these thoughts from my mind. Cuan was not mine to think of. Instead, I thought of tomorrow and my journey to Seir Kieran.

I dozed for an hour or two, and when I woke, I woke slowly. The near constant shroud of fear and confusion seemed to have faded a little. My head hurt less. My stomach was not so tied up in knots.

Not that I was safe. *I wasn't.* The Fomorians could be anywhere – I always had to remember that – but at least in Dublin I could run if I wished. There was no king keeping my possessions from me. No one I had to impress, and soon I would be at Seir Kieran.

Pushing aside my blanket, I readied myself for the feast, my stomach rumbling at the thought of eating. Using the water basin beside my bed, I washed quickly. I had not the time to clean my clothes, but found I did not care. There was no one at the feast who I wished to impress. I could simply be myself, eat the food, smile a little, and then return here.

As soon as I was ready, I walked to the fort. The doors were wide open, and I looked at them with interest as I passed through. Intricate engravings of sea beasts and dragons covered the dark wood, and I ran my fingers along them, reading the story told in the pictures. A warrior who sailed into the seas had been beset by a mighty storm and dragged into the depths by a monster with tentacles. The warrior fought the beast to the death and made his way to Valhalla, only to find the beast had followed him there.

I couldn't linger, however, to see what happened next. The fort was too busy, and the people behind me were pushing to make their way inside.

Taking a seat, I helped myself to the food on the table. The feast was much as I expected. Not as busy as the fort at Kells, but more chaotic. Fish and meat were carried on platters and shared around the tables by the female slaves of Asculv. I felt odd being served by them and wished I could free these women, but how could I when I had nothing to give them and no way of helping them return home? *How could I fix something that was so broken?* For it wasn't just Dublin, it was all of Ireland. There were slaves at the fort at Kells, Cuan had told me. I just hadn't noticed, that was all. I had been too naïve to see what was in front of me.

Eating quickly, I thanked the serving girl for the food and made my way outside. Cuan had wanted me to come, so as not to appear ungrateful, I guessed, but the Dublin king was not watching me. *No one was.* I was the least interesting person here, and so I left without even a nod or word of farewell. I didn't care if that meant I was rude or not, and seeing as Cuan was not even at the feast himself, I cared even less.

Rushing toward my house, I opened the door.

Cuan was sitting at the table.

"What are you doing here?" I asked, closing the door behind me.

"I need the use of your house. Sorry, I should have asked. I thought you'd be at the feast."

"I was." Taking off my cloak, I put more sticks on the fire as I mulled over the meaning of his presence. Was this why Cuan was so insistent that I go to the fort? Had he secretly wanted to use the house he had found for me? Such an obvious deceit wasn't like him... and yet, from the way he held himself so rigid, I knew that was what he'd done. Why? Why would he—

Someone knocked on the door, and without waiting for an answer, two men came inside. One was an older man. Older than King Ruaidrí, though not as old as King Magnus, for he was well-built and still had dark hair mixed in with the grey. At his side was another man, bowed over with a grey woollen cloak covering his body.

"Son." The man, still concealed by the hood of his cloak, stretched out his arms.

"Father."

Cuan moved forward and pulled his father into an embrace. Withered fingers rubbed over Cuan's face, lingering on the scar for a moment longer than anywhere else. I watched as the hooded man shuffled closer to his son, unable to avoid the terrible scars that surrounded his eye sockets and the gaping hole where his eyes should be.

This was Cuan's father? I found myself lost for words. Cuan had mentioned him earlier, but not that he was coming to Dublin. Not that he was blind. *Not that he was meeting him in secret.*

Isolde

Dublin

Carefully, Cuan guided his father to the chair and lit another candle on the bedside table, the light illuminating his father's profile. Swollen features sharpened, contorted by the flickering flame. The blackness of his eye sockets seemed so deep. So painful.

"Who is this, Cuan?" the blind man asked. "I was expecting you to be alone."

Cuan nodded. "This is Isolde, and we are in her house. Isolde, this is my father, Bardán Ó Conchúir, and his cousin, Osán."

Osán gave a curt nod while Bardán held out his hands in my direction.

I placed my hands into his, and Bardán squeezed them between his finger and thumb.

"These are not the hands of a princess," he said. "The skin is too rough."

"You're right. I'm no princess."

"Then why are you in the company of my son? You are his slave?"

"No. Not a princess and not a slave. I'm a friend, that is all. I'll leave you now."

Picking up my cloak, I nodded a goodbye to Cuan, noting the pale pallor of his face. *I'd seen less fear in him when four men sought his death at the bruidean.*

"No," Cuan said, "we can talk in Norse. It's too late for you to be out alone, and it will be noted if you return to the feasting hall."

He waved his hand toward the back of the room, indicating

that I should sit on the bed – the coldness of his voice was at odds with the heat in his cheeks.

I contemplated walking out, but I couldn't bring myself to do it. There was something wrong here, so instead, I moved to the back of the house like he said and set my bag on the bed beside me, feeling for Fragarach between the leather.

The man Osán grunted. "I'll keep watch outside, but don't be long, Bardán. Asculv's men are watching your son. They will notice if he doesn't go to the feast soon."

Cuan nodded and sat in silence until Osán left and closed the door behind him.

"Do you still want it?" Bardán asked, speaking in the Norse language Broccan had taught me.

"I don't know," Cuan replied in Norse.

"How is it you don't know?" his father asked. "Never in my wildest dreams would I have believed that Dublin might be so easily taken. And you insult me by saying you don't know."

"It was never your wish for me to be King of Dublin."

"No. It wasn't. It was your mother's. But perhaps she was right and being King of Dublin *is* the first step. Sitric Silkbeard was King of Dublin once and so very nearly did he have the whole of Ireland at his feet."

Cuan rubbed his hands over his lips while I took out some thread Blinne had given me to mend a hole in my cloak. I had to at least pretend that I was not listening in, but I could not believe what Bardán had said. Cuan wanted to be King of Dublin? *Could that be true?*

"You divorced my mother for saying I should be King of Dublin," Cuan finally said.

"No, I divorced her for disobeying me and taking you away. A different thing altogether." Cuan tutted and his father gave a low, rasping laugh. "You're brave, Cuan. A good warrior from what I hear, but to be king you must be more than that, and to take a kingdom you must be more again."

The chair creaked as Bardán sat back, though Cuan didn't move.

I tried to look at Cuan's face, but I couldn't catch the fullness of it in the dim candlelight. From this angle, his expression appeared to change, first sullen, but then curious. A flicker of anger... then that disappeared, too.

"Tell me, son," Bardán said, his tone softer than before. "What is your name?"

"My name?" Cuan repeated. His voice rose with uncertainty. "My name is Cuan Ó Conchúir."

"No, " his father replied. "It's Cuan the Viking, Cuan the raven, Cuan the berserker. If your mother had done as I told her and stayed put in Connacht, you'd still have the name you were born with."

"She did what she thought was best when she took me to the Isles. At least I'm alive."

"Pah! Ruaidrí might have blinded me, but he wouldn't have killed a boy. I told your mother this. To stay put. Instead, your mother stole you from me, and now you are a child of two worlds and the warriors of Connacht do not know you as they should."

There was such venom in Bardán's words, but there was truth to them too. Cuan was part of the Ó Conchúir family. He feasted with his uncle and sat at his table, but for all that, Ruaidrí and his family were suspicious of him. One of them had even tried to have him blinded. This was the truth. Cuan was an outsider. Like me... and his father knew it.

Another silence lingered. Cuan was the first to break it. "Say I did want to take Dublin. How should I do it?"

"You'll need to fight," Bardán said, the harsh edge in his voice easing. "And you'll need gold and silver. It would be best if you didn't borrow from your uncle Godred. You could try Eric, or raid monasteries in Leinster." Bardán cracked his swollen fingers as he rubbed his hands together. "War can be a great time for those willing to exploit the chaos it brings."

I tensed, then immediately pulled the cloak higher up onto the bed, trying to even my breathing as I continued to sew. Who was this strange man who sat in my house? *A man who had almost been a king*. He was evil. A man filled with greed and anger, and that did not shock me for Broccan had told me many in this world were like this. It was Cuan who surprised me. *Who was he?* I thought I knew him, or at least knew him a little… but perhaps that wasn't true.

"You're convinced this war with Diarmait Mac Murchadha is about to start?" Cuan asked.

"Yes. I told you the Normans haven't sailed back to Wales. They're here for land, and Dublin will fall with Asculv as king. He's too craven to fend them off. Dublin needs a warrior in charge to stand a chance."

"But if I fight Asculv and become king here, your brother won't be happy. I thought you wanted me to stay in his favour?"

Bardán snorted. "Ruaidrí won't like it, but he'll accept it. Better you as King of Dublin than some Norman outsider. Fool him. Make him believe you are loyal, and then, when the time is right, take back the Kingdom of Connacht with the army of Dublin at your side."

Cuan leaned forward. "It won't be easy to regain his trust. I've sworn many vows to become part of his fianna, many of which I'll have to break to make myself king. I wish that wasn't so."

"Hush now, boy," Bardán chided. "Breaking your word to a man who has broken his so many times should give no cause for concern."

Cuan's voice rose. "But it does concern me."

"Then you're a fool, and you'll end up like me. My father named me his heir on his deathbed. I could have killed Ruaidrí many times over but didn't, because he swore an oath of loyalty to me. I understood what his ambitions were, but he was my brother, and I believed him. Mercy cost me everything. My eyes. The kingship. My wife. My son."

The next silence lingered for so long that I thought Bardán had fallen asleep. I kept sewing, pulling the fabric in and out, pretending that I could not understand their words, but inside, my heart pounded.

"What about your friend?" Bardán said at last.

Cuan shuffled, his cloak rustling against the hilt of his sword.

"I don't like that she knows I was here. What if she tells someone?"

Once again, I picked at thread, tying off the final strands.

"She won't tell anyone anything. You should have seen her when we found her – a starving wretch, wearing nothing but rags. Now she is on her way to family because I've helped her. She'll do what I tell her to."

His father sniffed. "It would be better to kill her."

I bit my lip. The hole was mended now, and I took out my knife to cut the woollen thread that was left over. I did not, however, put Fragarach back in the bag. I kept it by my side.

"That's not necessary," Cuan said.

"She knows we've met in secret. If Asculv or Ruaidrí were to discover this, they'd grow suspicious, and all your hard work will be for nothing."

"She won't tell," Cuan insisted. "She wants to become a nun. A vow of silence is enough."

Bardán cracked his knuckles. "A nun's vow of silence is almost as final as death, but not quite. I think I must insist upon it. If you find the task too disagreeable, I can arrange for Osán to do it."

Cuan cleared his throat. "No. I'll do it. Keep your hound on his leash."

Tears didn't come. A sudden coldness came instead. I couldn't believe what Cuan was saying, though there was a realisation that came with his words. *I did not know him at all. I never had.*

"Good," Bardán croaked. "Now I must leave you. Good luck, my son. Speak to Eric tonight at the feast. Be ready to fight the Normans next year when they try to take the city. If you can get rid of Asculv and be the one seen to defend Dublin, the city will be yours."

Cuan knocked on the outside wall three times, and moments later, Osán came in.

"A monk at Saint Aodhan's is waiting for us," he whispered to

Bardán. "He will open their gate that leads onto the river if we are quick." They walked out then, their footsteps growing fainter and fainter.

"I know you understood all that, Isolde," Cuan's voice was slow, resigned. He didn't move from where he sat.

I stood and tightened my grip on Fragarach. "If you want to kill me, why do you wait? Get it over with." I held Fragarach out, pointing it at his throat. "Kill me now if that is your wish."

"I do not wish to kill you, but if I hadn't said that I did, my father would have sent Osán to do it."

I held Fragarach steady. *If you point Fragarach at the throat of another, they cannot lie.* That was what Broccan had said. Did I believe that? I didn't know if I dared.

"You don't believe me," Cuan said, reading my mind.

His knuckles were white from gripping the edge of the table, and his face was held tight. Too tight. Like it would fall apart if he let go.

"When I think of you, Cuan, I don't think you would kill me… but then, when other people talk about you and to you, I realise I don't know you at all."

He rubbed his face with his hands, then placed them on his knees. When he next looked at me, his countenance had changed. Impassive and calm. He unsheathed his sword and set it down on the table. "I'll make you a promise."

"A promise?"

"Do you see the marking of the eye on my sword?"

My eyes darted to the silver etching on the centre of the hilt. "Yes."

"My mother told me it was a symbol of Odin. She loved Odin because he gave up one of his eyes for the gift of wisdom. He watches us with the one eye he has left and sees everything, understands everything. I swear to you and to Odin that I will take you to Seir Kieran." His thumb rubbed the eye and then he sliced the blade along the palm of his hand. "And I promise that I will not hurt you."

Blood dripped along his wrist and onto the sword. It snaked down the hilt, passing over the silver eye as if it were a tear.

"And after you get me to Seir Kieran, what are you going to do, Cuan? Are you going to do what your father wants? Try to be King of Dublin. Try to become the King of Connacht."

"I've promised him I will. I promised to take back what was taken from him."

"You can't live a life for someone else, Cuan. You can't fight Asculv and King Ruaidrí for a cause you don't believe in."

His eyes found mine, flashing darkly in the candlelight. "What do you know of belief, Isolde? You have none."

"I know plenty about belief."

Cuan shook his head. "When I was a boy, my father was a beast of a man. Six feet tall with a chest nearly as wide. He was the best father a boy could have. It destroyed me when I saw him blinded, to see him lying on the ground, his eyes removed from his body. His energy seeped out of him that day, leaving behind only bitterness and rage. The man I loved was gone. I vowed that day to avenge him. So, I'm not doing this to be a king myself. I don't care about that. But I will keep my promise, and before I die, King Ruaidrí will know what betrayal feels like."

I held my breath. "Are you going to kill him?"

"Yes."

I stared into his eyes. The bloodshot redness overpowered the pale blue of his iris tonight. "You will die, Cuan. You know that, don't you?"

He gave me a slow smile and stood, making his way to the door. "We'll all die one day, Isolde. That's the only certainty there is. All we can hope for is some choice in the manner of our death. And I chose mine some time ago."

Confusion filled me as he closed the door. *Rage. Revenge.* Cuan was filled with these emotions. I couldn't understand it, and yet, Broccan had been the same. Just like Cuan, he'd buried these destructive feelings deep down. Was this what the world of men was? A place devoid of joy and hope? A place of danger and despair?

This realisation should make me want to run away, and yet I could not. Something powerful pounded in my chest that I did not understand. Something that made me want to stay. Something that made me want to exist within this mortal realm. To make it become a place where I could always run, never slow down, and always be free.

I woke to the sound of horns and bells ringing. Over and over, they sounded. People were beginning to shout too. I hadn't even realised I had fallen asleep, for my mind had dwelled on Cuan's conversation with his father until the dawn.

Knowing instinctively that the noise was a warning, I packed my dress into Broccan's bag, put on my bull-hide armour underneath my old shirt and placed Fragarach into my cloak pocket. Pulling on my trousers and cloak, I tied back my hair then walked outside and followed the people who were hurrying toward the fort. The fort, however, was emptying. Even the warriors who guarded it were running outside and pointing at the walls.

Asculv came out behind his men, his wife and daughter at his side. Cuan followed.

"What is it, Asculv?" a trader shouted.

"We're under attack," Asculv replied.

"From whom?" the same trader asked.

"Who else could it be but King Diarmait of Leinster and his Norman knights." Asculv spat on the ground and stared at Cuan. "I told your uncle this would happen, but he wouldn't listen."

The space around the fort continued to fill with Asculv's guards and kinsmen, as well as the traders and local fishermen. Asculv, seeming to sense that the people were waiting for him to say something, scanned the Dublin walls and banged his fist on the wooden palisade. "Cuan, go to the gatemen. Tell them, until further notice, the gates are to be sealed. I want more men at each post. No one is to come in or out. Tell the monks too. Even their gate is to close."

Cuan ran to the stables to get Sleipnir, and Håkon, his young friend, bounded after him.

"Arm yourselves!" King Asculv shouted to the men in the crowd. "Let's show Leinster we're ready to fight." The warriors roared in agreement and rushed away, spreading the order across the city.

I stood rooted to the spot as people pushed past me. Asculv had ordered the guards to lock the gates, and I'd no idea how long for. What if there was a siege? It could last for days. Weeks or months, even. I needed to get out. Now.

My gaze moved to Saint Aodhan's church. Last night Cuan's father and Osán had left through a gate there. By the river, or so Osán had said. It was this gate that Asculv had just ordered sealed, which meant I didn't have long to get out.

The paralysis gripping me fell away and I began to run. I needed to reach Seir Kieran, and the church gate was my only chance of leaving before the city was locked. Cloaked by the chaos, I ran past the church. The monks and priests were still inside praying. The noise of the horns and bells hadn't drawn them out yet, and their gate – if it could be called that, for it was more like a gap in the lower portion of the wall – was still open. It wasn't big, but large enough that one or two people could fit through. A huge boulder sat close to it, which I assumed was rolled over to block the gap during times of invasion.

I pressed my body tight against the grey stone wall, peering out beyond to see if any of the Norman or Leinster warriors were close. All was quiet, the only movement coming from the small river just ahead of me that flowed close to the walls. Even better, the forest to my left was only a hundred feet away. If I could make it there without being seen, I would get away.

Taking a deep breath, I ran.

I ran so fast, the ground seemed to blur beneath me. Adrenaline pumped through me, and I refused to look to the side until I had reached the trees. Even when shielded by the forest, I kept going.

Running and running deeper into the forest. It was only when my lungs began to ache that I stopped and squatted behind a large oak tree to catch my breath. I had to go north. North until I was beyond where the army could be gathering and then cut west. From there—

A branch snapped. Leaves rustled. A deer perhaps?

I peeked around the tree.

The blood drained from my face. Cuan, riding on Sleipnir, was about one hundred feet away, his eyes following my tracks. Why was he here? To bring me back? Or to kill me as his father wished?

"Isolde," he called. "I know you can hear me."

I ran. Fast.

The densely packed trees suited my small frame, but his footsteps thudded behind mine. A fallen trunk blocked my path, and the seconds I took to readjust my course were all he needed. Leaping forward, he pinned me against a tree.

"Get back inside the city." His hand grabbed hold of my arm, and his eyes burned and flashed, though his skin paled above his cheeks. "An army, thousands strong, is marching this way! What are you thinking?"

"I have to get to Seir Kieran. You know this."

"Finding an uncle you've never met is worth risking your life?" His jaw tensed and his fingers tightened around my arm.

I pushed him back with all my might, so hard that he let go. "Cuan, I can't go back with you." I took out my knife and held it straight at him. "Do you understand me? I'm not going back."

"King Diarmait and two thousand of his fighting men are riding around Dublin. What do you think they will do if they find you?"

I shook my head. How could I make him see?

"Remember the attack in the bruidean?" he said. "You killed that man when you had to, but you were too slow to do it. You're not a killer, and to survive out here, that's what you need to be."

"I have to go, Cuan," I answered, my voice turning hoarse with the emotion creeping up my throat. "You should return to the city.

Your father told you this would happen. Isn't this your chance to work against Asculv and take Dublin?"

Cuan raised his eyes and tilted his head to the right. For a moment I thought he was about to speak, but then I heard it too. A low hissing, accompanied by an all too familiar smell.

"Fire," Cuan said. "They've set fire to the woods."

I looked upward. Black clouds of smoke rose into the sky. Just like on Rathlin. Memories of the sky, orange and black with the flames, came to me. The Fomorians... were they here? Was this them? *It was.* I didn't know how, but I could sense them. But why? Why were they here? Did they know I was alive? Had they come for me?

"Quick," Cuan shouted. "The forest will be alight in no time at all."

Without wasting another second, we sprinted to Sleipnir.

Cuan hauled me up behind him, and we galloped through the woods. Sweat poured down my neck, and when I glanced behind, the fire was already close. Flames leaped across the branches, spreading from tree to tree. If I had doubted the Fomorians were here before, I knew it now.

Cuan drove Sleipnir onward as fast as he could, weaving us between the trees and low-hanging branches that threatened to dismount us. The smoke thickened, the air disappearing as the fire consumed it. Suddenly, the trees were less dense, and flashes of blue appeared between the trunks. The river. My back burned with the heat, and I closed my eyes, urging Sleipnir to get there before the fire caught us.

Sleipnir burst out of the forest and rode down the riverbank and into the water. It was narrow here, less than two hundred feet, and he swam across to the other side. Once there, we watched the fire in silence for a moment as it surged along the trees, moving toward the city, licking the leaves and branches as it danced closer and closer to the walls.

"Will the city catch?"

Cuan shook his head, but didn't look convinced. "The forest was cleared around the walls to prevent a fire from spreading, but I've never seen a fire like this before. Look how high the flames are."

It was Fomorian fire. That was why it acted like this. And just like on Rathlin, it would destroy everything in its path.

Anger. Rage. Hatred. These emotions built up inside of me. I walked along the riverbank, moving away from the city, but my legs suddenly gave way, and I fell to the ground. My body felt as if it were on fire. That the fire was burning inside of me.

"Isolde, what's wrong?" Cuan came over to me. "Do not worry, Isolde. Look. A storm is coming. It will put out the fire before it does too much damage." He pointed upward at the blackening sky. Not one filled with only smoke, but with clouds that multiplied before our eyes. Thunder rumbled in the distance.

It was me. I had summoned the storm, just as I had on Rathlin.

My arms shook. My legs, too. Falling onto my hands, I threw up, the foul liquid inside my mouth turning the soil black.

Cuan helped me up. "Come on. Onto Sleipnir. I know somewhere close by where we can shelter until the storm passes."

Cuan rode Sleipnir hard, pushing him away from Dublin, the fire and the storm. The further from Dublin we got, the thicker the forest became, though Cuan kept Sleipnir always in sight of the river. After a while, Cuan veered Sleipnir further in.

"Where are we going?" I asked.

Cuan didn't answer, for the rain had started to pour now, but soon it became obvious. The ground was rocky here and up ahead, I could make out a cave.

"Smugglers hide their goods here sometimes," he said. "When they cannot afford to pay Asculv his taxes for docking at the longphort. We'll be safe here until the fire burns out and the storm passes over." Cuan dismounted, helped me down, and led Sleipnir inside the cave as the rain thundered down.

Stumbling after them, I cleaned out my mouth with a puddle

of rainwater that had gathered on the rocks, then made my way to the back of the cave. It was dry there at least, but the shaking had taken my whole body over again and I could not get warm.

"What's wrong, Isolde? I've found you shaking like this twice before. Does it happen often?"

"Not often, no."

"Is it the fire? Did it frighten you because of what happened on Rathlin?"

I nodded, for what else could I say?

Sitting beside me, he wrapped his cloak around the two of us. The heat from his body did a little to help, but still I continued to shake. I knew why this was happening, of course. It wasn't the fire. It was the storm. Somehow, I had summoned it, and because I'd used my gift without understanding, my body was reacting.

"Do you truly want to be a nun, Isolde?" Cuan's voice was soft as he asked his question. Without judgement. "I still don't believe that you do."

"You don't need to believe me."

"I know… but I want you to know that Seir Kieran isn't safe anymore. King Diarmait will raid it next year to pay for his war."

"If you don't raid it first."

Cuan stilled. I almost regretted it, for he hadn't agreed to do it… and yet, he had said he would see his father's plan through.

Cuan pressed his lips into a thin line. "Did you ever hear about Mór, the Abbess of Kildare?" He shook his head. "No, of course you didn't. Your cousin taught you nothing of the real world."

Sighing, I pulled my knees up to my chest. "Tell me."

"About thirty years ago, the Abbess of Kildare Abbey died. At that time, Diarmait Mac Murchadha's cousin Albe was gaining support, and many thought he'd be a better king than Diarmait. To show his strength, Albe placed his own sister, Mór, in the abbey and ensured the nuns elected her abbess instead of Sadb, who was Diarmait's cousin."

"What did Diarmait do?" I asked, interested despite myself.

"The rules of the church only allow virgins to become an abbess, so he had his men attack the abbey and rape Mór."

"Diarmait ordered the rape of an abbess?"

"Yes," Cuan replied. "That is Diarmait. That's what he does. Anything to get his way, he will do it. Sadb became the abbess, just as King Diarmait wanted, and nothing stopped Mór being raped. Not her name, not her vows, and not the silver cross hanging from her neck."

The story was awful, but I was not surprised either, at least not like I would have been when I lived on Rathlin. I had learned in these last few months that people did awful things to each other for power.

Still shaking, I wrapped my arms tighter around my legs. "I'm still going to Seir Kieran, Cuan."

"I know."

"What will you do?"

"I have to return to Dublin."

I nodded, not wanting to say what was on my mind. That it was his father who wanted him to go back, and then when he returned to Dublin, he would be expected to wrest control from Asculv and make himself king. I couldn't see this resulting in anything but Cuan's death… but Cuan knew that. I'd told him as much last night and he told me he didn't care if he died. Tears formed in my eyes, and I pressed them against my knees. I didn't want him to see me cry.

"Then if we're parting, Cuan, why don't you tell me the truth? Does any part of you want to be king?"

"I will never be king. You're no fool, Isolde. You see me for what I am. Just another man who is paid to fight. There's nothing great about me. You've noticed that very quickly. So will others."

I turned to face him. "You didn't answer my question. Thinking you cannot become king isn't the same as not wanting it. Do you want it?"

Cuan's teeth ground together, and he said nothing. A sudden

hollowness consumed me as I dwelled on what his silence might mean. Did he want power? Was that the reason he was going through with his father's plan? *Deep down he desired it, too?*

"No. I don't."

"Then why do what your father wants? You talk of me being in danger, but it is you whose life is most at risk."

Instead of answering me, he inched closer. Something unreadable flashed in his eyes, and his thumb touched my chin. Slowly, he leaned down, and softly, his lips brushed against mine.

"Sorry," he said, moving away. "I shouldn't have done that."

"Then why did you?"

"Because I love you."

Heat rushed up my neck and into my cheeks. "You love me?"

"Yes. Even though I've tried not to." He ran his hands through his hair. "What I mean is, I don't want to love someone I can't be with, who I'd put in harm's way. But you see, I can't help it."

I stared in silence, trying to digest what he'd said, but my inability to speak drained the light from his eyes.

He sat up. "Sorry. I shouldn't have told you when I know you don't feel the same way. I'll go and check on Sleipnir."

Without thinking, I reached for his hand. "No. Don't go." Placing my hand into his, I took in his eyes, his scar, his lips. "Don't leave."

His hand moved to the side of my face and brushed against my cheek. I wanted to kiss him, but I held myself back. I couldn't let him love me. I couldn't let desire take me over like this. "I am going to Seir Kieran and there are plenty of other women, Cuan. Many of them could make you happy."

"That's not true. What if… What if there was a way we could be together. Some place where you would be safe?"

I shook my head. I couldn't be with him, and I couldn't tell him why. It was impossible… but my arguments faded away as he moved closer, his hand trailing down my neck.

He kissed me then. Gently. Slowly.

And I kissed him back.

A small voice in the back of my head told me I should stop this, but it wasn't in me to do anything different. I was lost. Lost to the feel of him against me. My mind went blank of everything except him.

My heart ruled my body now, and I could not escape it.

Donnchad

The road to Dublin

We rode to Dublin with all haste.

Speed was of the essence when taking a city by surprise, and Robert, even though he'd accepted it would be difficult to take Dublin this late in the year, still held out hope that he could entice the Dubliners into open battle.

They would not do this, no matter how hard he wished it, for the Dubliners would not be so foolish as to leave their walls. Reputations could be a curse as well as a blessing, and I had no doubt the cavalry charge at Osraige was known throughout the whole of Ireland by now.

Diarmait's suggestion was the more obtainable by far. Our presence might convince the Dubliners we meant to form a siege. That would inconvenience them, their traders more so, who would no longer be able to sell their slaves to the Irish kings. Asculv, therefore, might decide to transfer his vows of allegiance to Leinster. These vows would be instantly broken, of course, but it would give the Dubliners time to build up their reserves and call King Ruaidrí and King Godred of the Isles to their aid. On our side, these insincere vows would give Diarmait some much needed gold and silver while also providing the Normans with an opportunity to appraise the city they wanted to invade next year.

So we rode and rode fast, Robert thinking it would be best that the city was not ordered when we arrived. Disorganisation is the key to fear, Robert had said, and we wanted to strike that feeling deep into their hearts.

Fear, however, could be achieved through many methods. We

burned the Dubliners' fields and grain stores as we rode, and the Leinster warriors herded the Dubliners' cattle west where their shepherds and cowherders would drive them toward Ferns.

Angelo took great delight in this, watching the untamed fire destroy. He wanted to reach out with his gift, but I told him instead to use it to rein in the fire. To make the fire spread along the path of his choosing rather than allow it to move out of control.

He did as I asked, struggling a little more than I would have liked, but still, it was good for him to practise his gift. I was sure by the end of this campaign he would have more chances to use it. When we were fleeing from Broccan, I had been scared to let him use his fire often, in case it drew Broccan to us. Now we had no need to worry about a Descendant warrior, it was time for us to become more comfortable in the use of our gift. To be proud of it.

"Come on," Domhnall shouted as the fire roared around us. "Dublin is not far. Let them see us before the smoke."

The rallying call galvanised the men on horseback, and we galloped to the crest of the hill.

I followed, only pulling my horse to a stop once Dublin came into view. The men behind me talked as they examined the city – the Norman knights already beginning to assess the walls and fortifications while they waited for the men on foot to catch up.

I could not be so calm. Dublin, oh, it surprised me. Gone were the wooden walls. It was now made entirely of stone. Three times as big as when Sitric was king. Sprawling and formidable, this was not the Dublin of my youth, nor even of my old age. It had evolved perhaps more than any other part of Ireland.

For an hour, I think, I stared at it. Remembering all that had come before. I remembered Sitric standing on the walls while Clontarf was underway. Edysis dancing in the fort. I remembered my mother plotting. Tomas, the druid Descendant, showing me the scrolls he had taken from Fennit Island before we destroyed it. Now that time was gone. Those faces and names lost to history. Lost to everyone apart from me and my mother.

Rousing though it was, I could not lose myself to memory forever, and once the foot soldiers caught up, we made our way to the city. On approaching the gates, the army moved into formation and the foot soldiers began to cut down the surrounding trees. *Ladders. More and more ladders*, Robert shouted. This time Domhnall did not object. He rode over to our army with his father, and the two of them watched the way the siege weapons were constructed with obvious interest.

"Set the forest along the north side of the city on fire," Robert ordered. "Do it quickly."

Five of his men ran to carry out this command, and Angelo followed them.

I could see what Robert was doing. He still wanted to draw the Dublin Vikings out. He still hoped for his battle, and the only chance of this was by filling them with so much rage that common sense abandoned them.

The Dubliners would not be so reckless, but I said nothing. I simply watched Angelo. Watched as the flames grew. Black smoke billowed into the air and flames spread down the line of the trees the whole way to the beach.

The screams started then, rising into the air with the smoke, and I found myself wishing that the Dubliners would come out to face us, after all. With my warrior gift at my fingers, I longed to destroy Dublin. I imagined Sitric looking down on me from his place in heaven. What would he make of his little brother fighting against his city? Those sniggering grandchildren of his, they were all dead now too. They had lost their city not long after Sitric's death. I hoped if I took this city, they would be watching too.

Alas, common sense won, and it didn't take long for the city gates to open and a messenger to ride out.

"Come on," Robert said to me, disappointment clear on his features. "I want to know what they say."

Quickly, we rode over to where Diarmait and his men had gathered. The approaching horseman stopped some distance away.

"I have a message from King Asculv of Dublin," the messenger shouted. "I will tell it to you, King Diarmait, but know that I have come in peace."

Diarmait nodded, and his men, ever so slightly, lowered their weapons.

"Asculv does not wish to fight. He will swear oaths of allegiance to you today which will accept you as his overlord and pay you tribute. He says, however, that it is too late in the year to fight and will not give you his army until next year. He offers two hostages instead."

"Very well," Diarmait said. "Tell him to come out and swear his oaths, and then we will be away."

I translated this all to Robert as the messenger rode back to the walls.

"It is just the same as Wexford," he muttered.

"Not quite the same. Asculv has not pledged his army, and I would guess the hostages he offers are low-ranking men who he doesn't care about."

"It's even worse then."

"It's still a submission, and with that comes opportunity."

Robert stared up at the stone walls. "Why submit at all though? They could have held us off. The air is getting colder, so we cannot stay here long, and they have food coming in and out from the port. They will not thirst or starve."

I stared at Robert. "They won't mean any of the vows they swear today. Over the winter, they will call on their allies in the Isles as well as King Ruaidrí. This is stalling the inevitable, that is all. From their perspective, why should they be the ones to fight and put their men at risk when King Ruaidrí and King Tigernán are not here?"

"Pride is why they should fight. Honour."

"Look," Meilyr said, pointing up at the sky. "A storm. A bad one. We should shelter in the forest until it blows over."

Robert looked upward, his face reading the storm as if it were an omen of things to come. Reluctantly, he followed Meilyr to the forest, and from there, he watched the rain pour down and the fire in the forests die out alongside his dream of taking the city.

I sheltered behind the trees as the storm battered the walls of Dublin and thought of many things. My life. My failings. What I wanted. How to get it. What needed to be said and done. Resolute, I watched as the storm raged and then blew itself out. Robert lost no time in calling his army back to the gates.

It didn't take long for Asculv and his men to ride out. The Dublin king looked agitated, and did not smile as the Wexford king had. He and his men pulled to a stop a little way from Diarmait and Domhnall. "I submit to you, King Diarmait, and I will swear my vows."

"You swear that I am your king?" Diarmait asked.

"I do."

"You will pay your tributes to me?"

"I will."

"Including thirty ounces of gold which I shall take with me today."

"Agreed."

The boy holding the heavy Bible, face so solemn, dropped his shaking arms quickly once the final vow had been sworn, while Asculv gestured to his men to bring over a wooden chest which was filled with gold.

Diarmait rode a little closer to Asculv as he examined the goods held within. His fingers brushed over a golden cross, and then he whispered something into Asculv's ear.

The men around them could not hear, but with my warrior gift, I could.

"Is Cuan Ó Conchúir inside these walls? I saw him with you at Ferns."

"He is here," Asculv replied, his eyes wary.

"I want him too. That is part of my price for leaving."

"The blood feud? Still?" Asculv pressed his lips together. "Cuan has pledged himself to Ruaidrí now. He was made part of his fianna. Killing Cuan will only antagonise the High King."

"I don't suppose Ruaidrí will overly mourn a nephew who challenges his own son… but leave that to me. Bring Cuan out, and then we will go."

Asculv turned to the man next to him and they rode away. The gates of the city closed behind them.

We waited there for a good time. I could see Robert staring over at me, wondering what it was that delayed us. Finally, the messenger returned with two men at his side. "These are the hostages as agreed, but the man you seek is no longer in the city, King Diarmait."

Diarmait raised his eyebrows. "You're a liar."

"No," the messenger said. "It is the truth. He left just before the gates were closed. His horse left marks along the river path. If I were Cuan, I'd already be riding toward Connacht. If you really wanted him, you could send your men out to follow him, but that is as much as we can help you, I'm afraid. Now, we have given you your gold and our vows. King Asculv asks that you leave."

The messenger turned his horse and rode back to the gates.

Domhnall gazed over at his father. "Will I ride out to find him?"

Diarmait nodded.

With the negotiations over, Diarmait and his army rode back up the hill and toward the path that led to Ferns. The men cheered as they rode. So did the foot soldiers, though it would be a long journey home. Thirty ounces of gold was a great victory and would see them well-fed over the winter.

However, at the crest of the hill, Robert pulled his men to a stop. "Hold your positions," he said.

"Why? What are we doing?" Hervey asked.

"Waiting."

And wait we did. Eventually, Domhnall realised that the Normans hadn't followed them and rode back to us.

"Come, friend," Domhnall said to Robert. "We have taken much gold from the city which we will share with you. Come to Ferns and feast with us. Next year, I promise you, we will go to war with Dublin and win it outright."

I translated.

"No." Robert leaned forward and tightened his grip on his horse's reins. "I am overlord of Wexford, and I mean to go there."

Domhnall didn't react once I translated this for him. How could he? He could not forbid Robert from going, though he knew as well as me that the vows the Wexford king had made were meaningless. I suppose he hoped that with the winter coming, Robert would retire to Ferns and be content with plans to raid Dublin next year. But Domhnall, for all he was clever, underestimated Robert's ambition.

"Very well," Domhnall said. "Ride to Wexford. They will welcome you into their city."

Robert smiled. "Thank you, Domhnall, and if you need us for any reason, do come and find us, and we will come to your aid once more."

Domhnall stared at me as I told him Robert's words. "I hope you give our words to each other honestly," he said.

"I do."

"Well, you should know that I do not trust you. Not you and not that brother of yours."

I smiled and bowed my head.

All politeness, Domhnall gave a curt nod, then rode away. I watched after him for a moment, noting how he rode off with a group of men and made toward the river path, rather than following after his father and the rest of the Leinster army.

"What was all that about?" Robert asked.

"Oh, he just wanted to make sure I'd passed on the messages correctly, which I assured him I had."

Robert clicked his tongue and turned his horse around, everything about him, his posture, his expression, completely at ease.

"What do you plan to do at Wexford?" I asked him. It was

impolite to ask, but I couldn't help it. Wexford wouldn't want them in the city. Surely, he must know that.

Robert didn't reply right away. Instead, he pushed his horse into a gallop. "Follow me and find out, Donn."

His army followed, leaving me and Angelo a little behind with the archers who followed on foot.

Angelo nodded at Robert, then at Dublin.

"We follow Robert," I said. "For now."

Isolde

The forest outside Dublin

A noise from outside the cave caught my ear. "Do you hear that?"

Cuan unwrapped his arm from around my waist and stood. Taking up his sword, he leaned against the outer edge of the cave and crept toward the entrance.

"Cuan," hissed a voice. "Can you hear me?"

Cuan stretched his hand out of the cave and pulled inside a slim young man. "Håkon," he said, embracing him. "You shouldn't have come. It's dangerous to be outside the city walls. Even more so with an army at the gates."

"I had to," Håkon said. "I remembered you told me about these caves and prayed you'd made it here."

"Why? What's wrong?"

Håkon's fists clenched. "Asculv didn't fight. He negotiated instead and pledged allegiance to King Diarmait."

Cuan nodded and patted his friend on the shoulder. "He's buying time, that's all. I know it seems a strange thing to do, but Asculv will send a message to King Godred and King Ruaidrí so they can move against Diarmait in the spring. Asculv doesn't mean to keep his word."

"If you say so," Håkon replied, though he didn't look convinced.

Cuan sheathed his sword. "Is it safe for us to return yet?"

"No. That's what I came to tell you. King Diarmait asked for you during the negotiations."

"For me? As a hostage?"

"I don't think so," Håkon replied. "I was asked to hold the Bible when the kings swore their vows, and I overheard them talking. King Diarmait wanted Asculv to hand you over. It was asked after they'd spoken of hostages. I think... I think it was meant to be a secret."

"Asculv agreed, I suppose?"

Håkon's silence confirmed the answer.

"Thanks, Håkon," Cuan said after a pause. "Thank you for finding me. Your father would be proud."

The tips of Håkon's ears turned pink, even though he shrugged the compliment away. I felt for Håkon. Orphaned and alone. I was impressed that despite these hardships, he held such courage within him.

"What will you do, Cuan?" he asked. "Go to King Ruaidrí?"

"Yes. It is the safest place for me now."

Håkon's smile fell. "Then it will be a while before I see you again."

"Maybe. Maybe not." Cuan pressed his hand tight around Håkon's shoulder. "I need you to listen to me, friend. If Diarmait has moved against King Ruaidrí so soon after swearing oaths to him, there will be war next year. That means I will see you soon, though the reason will not be a good one. Do you hear me? You are old enough for Asculv to send you out to fight now." Cuan slid one of the silver rings he wore from his thumb and handed it over to Håkon. "Give this to Vígi. It's enough for a chain-mail shirt. Make sure he gives you a good sword, too. Tell him this is from me. Anything else you need, he's to give to you."

Håkon took the gift with a grin on his face. "I would be happy to fight against King Diarmait," he said with a sudden fierceness.

"I know you would." Cuan smiled, though there was a sadness behind it. "But do not be too quick to take up your sword, Håkon. It is the young who suffer most in war, and I promised your father I would look after you. Don't volunteer to fight. Only go if you are called up." Cuan sighed. "Look to Hálfdan and Vígi. They will keep you right."

Håkon moved the ring onto his thumb, though it was more than a little loose. "Hálfdan was given as a hostage."

"Was he?" Cuan bit his lip. "Then stay with Vígi. He was friends with your father, too."

"What about Hálfdan?" Håkon asked, his face clouding with worry. "If Asculv doesn't mean to keep his vows to King Diarmait, won't Diarmait kill him?"

"I've known Hálfdan since I was half your age. He has a way of getting out of difficult situations like no one else. Don't worry about him."

Håkon gave Cuan another embrace, before making his way into the forest.

Cuan and I followed him to the river. Now that the storm had passed, the sky was clear and blue. Even the dark smoke of the fire had disappeared. Cuan watched his young friend as he swam across to the opposite riverbank. Håkon gave us a small wave once he reached the other side, then ran toward the city.

"There you go, Isolde," Cuan said. "We cannot return to Dublin. You have your wish. In three days' time, you'll be in Seir Kieran... unless you'd rather come with me to Connacht."

I knew what he was asking. It wasn't just to go with him to Connacht. He wanted me to be with him. To stay with him.

I wanted that too.

All this time, I had not understood why Móirne or King Magnus' granddaughters had wanted to marry, and now I knew it wasn't marriage they had desired at all. It was love. Even for the chance of it, they were willing to gamble everything. They wanted to be kissed, as Cuan had kissed me. How strange that I, who hadn't even looked for love, should be the one to find it... and yet could not accept it.

With this realisation, my whole body clenched so tight that my stomach ached. "I have to go to Seir Kieran, Cuan. I need to stay with my uncle."

Cuan bit his lower lip and frowned, but he did not argue. He simply nodded and moved past me to fetch Sleipnir. When I next glimpsed his face, his expression was the same impassive one he'd worn so often when we first met. He was retreating to a safer place – a place where appearing not to care was the best protection.

"Then it's time to go." He led Sleipnir onto the river path and jumped up onto his saddle. Holding out his hand, he smiled. "Are you strong enough for me to ride fast?"

"Yes." I was not fully recovered, but no longer shaking. Quickly I took his hand, trying not to notice that my heartbeat quickened when his skin touched mine. He pulled me up behind him, and together we rode further into the forest.

It was only when the sun began to fall and the light fade, that Cuan pulled Sleipnir to a slow walk. The forest was thick here and wolves howled in the distance.

"There is an abandoned ráth up ahead," Cuan said, speaking for the first time since we left the cave. "We should rest there for a while and let Sleipnir eat and drink before we move on."

I agreed, and before long, we came out of the forest. The ráth ahead was situated close to a thicket of bushes and a river lay not too far beyond. It was a good place for a ráth, close to water and sheltered, but I could see scorch marks over the house walls. The outer wall had fallen away, too, leaving scattered stones over the grass. Someone had lived here once and perhaps had been happy. The fire marks hinted at a darker reason for their leaving.

"I've used this ráth before," Cuan said. "The walls were still intact at the back, and it was dry. Hopefully, the roof has not collapsed since then."

Walking inside, I did not expect much, given Cuan's warning. Thankfully, the walls were holding, and there was a firepit that could be used. The wind had blown in sticks and dried leaves, and I began to gather them.

"Light the fire if you can." Cuan picked up an old pot at the far side of the room. "I'll go to the river and fetch some water for Sleipnir and ourselves. This far downstream, we'll need to boil it."

I nodded.

Cuan paused by the door. "What you do next is your decision, Isolde." His voice was soft. "I... just... I don't understand why you need to go to Seir Kieran so badly. I understand you want to see your family after what happened, but I know you do not wish to be a nun. If it's because you're scared... if there are people trying to hurt you, I can take care of you." He stepped away. "That's all I wanted to say. It's your choice, but I wanted you to know that I would like to do that."

I would like that too, but how could it be? It couldn't. Together... together we were an impossible dream. My body had overruled my head before, in the cave... but this time I could not allow that to happen.

"You said yourself, Cuan, that your life is dangerous. How could you keep me safe with such violent days ahead of you?" I pushed myself to be harder. I had to. There was no other way. "Now, go to the river to fetch the water and do not make me promises you cannot keep."

He said nothing as he left and I lowered my gaze, for I couldn't bear to look at him.

What had I done?

Regret filled me instantly. I searched for a way for us to be together. Was it possible to make him understand who I really was? To do that, I would have to tell him the truth and I couldn't think how to explain that. I didn't even understand it myself. Could I ask him to wait for me? My mother had loved a mortal, after all. Was there a way for us to be together? No, was the answer I told myself. Not if Cuan had plans to make himself king. Not if a path of destruction lay ahead of him.

And even if he gave that up, I was the daughter *who would destroy fire*. Allowing Cuan to be with me would be more dangerous for him than anything his father had planned. And yet, I couldn't bear it. I couldn't bear that we should part in this way, or that once I was in Seir Keiran I would never see him again.

The sound of hooves at last provided relief, and I ran outside. I had to tell Cuan something. Tell him that I was not able to be with him, but that I wanted to.

"Cuan!" I shouted. "Please, let me explain."

As I ran past the broken ráth wall, I stopped. It wasn't Cuan coming toward me. It was Hálfdan.

"Isolde," he shouted, out of breath and flushed. "Where's Cuan?"

"He went to the river. Why? What are you doing here?" I shook my head, trying to focus on this strange turn of events. "I thought you were given as a hostage to Diarmait?"

"Yes, I was." Hálfdan scanned the grass to see in which direction Sleipnir's tracks led. His horse paced and panted, dancing from leg to leg as Hálfdan pulled at the reins.

"King Diarmait's son, Domhnall, is following your trail. I escaped and have ridden hard to find you, but they can't be far away." He held out his hand for me to take. "Come. We all need to leave now."

I grabbed his hand and let him hoist me up onto the saddle in front of him.

The horse took off, and we followed the deep hoof-prints Sleipnir had made in the sodden soil. Suddenly then, Hálfdan veered us toward a hill and left the tracks.

"You're going the wrong way," I said. "Cuan went to the river."

"No, I just saw him on top of the hill," Hálfdan said. "Didn't you?"

I searched the hilltop, but couldn't make anything out. The horse bolted onward, and my heart raced as we made our way up the steep incline. Hoof-marks flattened the grass here. Lots of them.

"Hálfdan," I whispered. "King Diarmait's men must be here too."

"Yes, I think you're right," he answered.

He drew his sword from his sheath and held it out so that the tip brushed against the grass. Then he raised his sword and pressed the flat side of the blade against my neck.

I gritted my teeth. "What are you doing?"

"Something I should've done a long time ago."

The horse charged onto the hilltop and then came to a stop. A group of fifteen warriors turned to inspect us.

"Hálfdan," a man called out. He had long, dark hair and dark eyes. "Is this the girl?"

"Yes, Domhnall. Though I see we don't need her."

The warriors parted and through the gap their bodies made, I saw a man kneeling on the grass. Blood-matted hair clung to his face and his shoulder hung forward, dislocated from the socket.

"Cuan," I shouted.

He glanced up, his right eye so swollen it had almost closed over.

"She was running out of the ráth," Hálfdan said, throwing me to the ground. "Begging for him to come back to her."

The black-haired man, Domhnall, circled me, his long sword pointed in my direction. "A lover's tiff, nothing could be sweeter."

Cuan raised his head, no trace of emotion on his face. Not even pain, though he had to be in agony. "I am taking her to the nunnery at Seir Kieran. Her uncle is a monk there, and she is to become a nun. Believe me, there is no love between us. Let her go."

"I'm not sure if I believe that," Domhnall said, pulling at my hair. The tip of his blade pressed against my skin. He lowered it slightly, moving it onto the fabric of my shirt and noting the bull-hide armour underneath.

"He's lying, Domhnall," Hálfdan cut in. "I've seen them together, and I know he loves her. I've seen it in his eyes."

Cuan spat. "The word of a traitor is less than worthless."

The Leinster men whispered for a few moments, then Domhnall nodded. "Let's hurry to Ferns. We will ride through the night." He glanced at Cuan, then nodded at the man beside him.

This man drew out his sword.

Cuan struggled, thrashing against his rope, causing it to rip the skin along his neck and wrist. Four of the Leinster men held him down while another two beat him.

"No, don't," Cuan said, his voice straining. "I'll help you. Whatever you want. Don't do it."

They were going to kill him. Throwing myself forward, I punched Hálfdan and somehow ripped his sword from his grasp. Swinging the sword, I ran to Cuan. But before I got anywhere close, someone charged me from behind and pinned me onto the grass. Struggling, I had almost pushed him away when another came and grabbed my arm.

I screamed as they wrenched the sword from my hand. The warrior with the sword was close to Cuan now. "No," I screamed. "Don't kill him."

The swordsman stared at me, almost a look of pity in his eyes. He walked past Cuan.

I realised then it was Domhnall who had grabbed my arm, for he pulled me onto my knees by the hair. "His sword is sharp," he whispered. "If you don't struggle, I promise it will be quick."

Of course. Cuan would never beg for his own life. He wasn't afraid of dying. He was pleading for me.

"Don't," Cuan shouted. "She's the niece of a monk of Seir Kieran. Ransom her. They'll pay you."

Cuan's eyes shone with hope, but I'd heard Domhnall's voice, and I knew that mercy was not a virtue at his disposal.

"Take my body to my uncle," I said, my voice trembling. "I wish for him to pray for my soul."

At least, if the Descendants saw my corpse, they would know I could no longer fulfil the prophecy. They would know I had failed.

"We cannot honour your request," Domhnall said. "I will have my own priests pray for your soul. I swear it."

The violence of my end was beyond comprehension. The men circled me. Wanting to watch the sword slice me open. Rage, oh, I'd felt that many times since leaving Rathlin. And I felt it now, too, though it wasn't only anger that filled me. It was disgust. Disgust that men such as these could hold life in their hands and give it no value. I was merely the grass beneath their feet. There to be destroyed. There to be trampled on.

Glancing upward, I saw a storm brewing. Clouds building. The physical manifestation of my wrath brought to life by the gift inside me.

The sharp edge of the sword touched my neck.

Tears of regret fell down my face. *It was too late.* I was going to die.

Domhnall pulled my head back and pressed his knee against my back.

Cuan shouted and screamed. Begged for them to let me go.

I closed my eyes, hoping that when I died, I would see him again.

A moment later, the sharp steel of the sword pressed against my throat. Blood gushed down my chest and poured onto the grass. The pain was beyond words, but as with Cuan's screams, it faded.

And then I felt nothing at all.

Donnchad

Hill of Carrig

I rode with Robert toward Wexford. He did not, however, ride into the city as I expected. Instead, he made for a hill two miles beyond it. It must have been the site of a dun once, for the land on top of the hill was flat, and the foundations of a stone wall were still apparent.

Even more surprising was the fact that another army was waiting for us there. It was made up of about one hundred archers and foot soldiers, with another forty men on horseback.

What had Robert been up to? I had thought him caught up in the whims of Diarmait and Domhnall, but perhaps this was not the case. Intrigued, I rode to the front, making sure to keep close to Robert.

Robert called out a greeting as he rode toward this new army. Bringing his horse to a sudden stop, he dismounted and opened his arms. One of the men on the hill opened his arms too, and they embraced.

"Gerald. Brother," Robert said. "It is good to see you."

"Yes," Gerald replied. "I was only too glad to come once I received your letter." He took off his helmet and grinned. I would have known then that these two were brothers even if they had not greeted each other in this way. They were so alike. Gerald's dark hair was even shorn short in the same fashion as Robert's.

Robert examined the hill. Raising his hand over his eyes to block out the early autumn sun, he gazed toward Wexford. "Is this the best site? It's a little far from the city."

"It is the best place, believe me. We've scouted around for days.

The locals call it the Hill of Carrig and say a fort used to be here. It gives us a good view of Wexford, too."

"Did you go to the gates and introduce yourself?" Robert asked.

Gerald laughed. "I did. As you suspected, they did not greet me with the new titles that Diarmait gave us. Very quickly, I decided it would be best to leave. They know we are here, but so far, they have left us alone."

"Very well." Robert walked around the hilltop, his fingers pulling at the long grass. "Men," he said, holding up his arm to command their attention. "This is where I mean to build our first castle."

I smiled, surprised but also intrigued by this plan. This far outside the city, a castle wouldn't hold much value. However, by building their own fortification, it made Robert less dependent on Diarmait, as I had told him he needed to be. It also meant they could sleep safely and would have their own home to winter in.

Gerald nodded, deferring to his brother, and began to organise the men. They were to collect stone and fell trees. It would not be a grand castle, Robert said, for they didn't have any master builders, but still it was to be good enough to withhold an attack.

As Gerald gave his orders and rallied the men, Robert gestured for Meilyr and Miles to come to him. Pretending to dig up stones along with the other men, I used my warrior gift to listen to what was being said. "Tomorrow, I want you both to leave here and meet Maurice at Waterford. Meilyr, you are to report here once you've spoken with him. Miles, you are to sail to Wales with Maurice. Hervey will stay with me. Tell Strongbow, nay beg him, to come. This land is ripe for the taking. I'm convinced of it now."

Miles and Meilyr nodded.

He turned then, noticed me, and beckoned me over.

"Take Donn to Wales with you," Robert said to Miles. "He can help you plan the invasion. And tell Strongbow that Donn has done as he promised. I therefore recommend that David can marry Donn's sister, if he still wishes. What was her name again?"

"Alys." Bowing low, I was all too happy to show him my delight, for this was good news. By marrying my sister to a knight, it would elevate my position in this army.

"When do we leave?" I asked.

"Tomorrow," Miles said. "At first light."

That night we slept in tents. The wind howled and the temperatures plummeted, and I was sure the Normans realised that holding out over this next winter would be hard. The summer had ended, and the nip in the air was a sign of things to come. They needed to build their castle, or at least some portion of it, quickly, so the winter frosts did not sap their strength. They would also need to convince Wexford to sell them food, so they didn't starve to death… but these concerns were not for me. I was returning to Chepstow. Returning to my mother and Cecile.

Now that Máelmórda was gone, everything was different. Angelo did as I bid him, and Cecile and Mother would learn to do the same. This *learning*, however, would not be easy. *Nothing was easy where Mother was concerned.*

She had complained to me often that Máelmórda did not love her. Did not care for her. But the truth was, he had done both, in his own way. He certainly would never go against her in my favour. He had protected her and allowed her to remain as head of the family for too long. That had been fine during our exile, but now we were back in Ireland, things had to change. When I returned, my mother needed to understand that our ambitions had to centre around me. Not her.

I did not sleep well that night, and I was all too glad when the dawn arrived.

"Angelo." I shook my son awake. "We are going with Meilyr and Miles to Waterford. We are returning to Wales."

Angelo shook his head and pointed at the ground.

"You want to stay?"

Angelo nodded, then pointed at his ears and eyes.

It made sense that he should stay and observe the men here, and yet Angelo would find it difficult without me. The other men did not like him. They did not trust him, and he would be the sole man with Irish blood on this hill. Being the only outsider was a dangerous thing to be in an army of this size. When ill-fortune fell, which no doubt it would, he would be blamed.

And yet, Angelo was a survivor. He'd roamed the streets of Paris and Rome and always come home. Perhaps it was time to trust him, and indeed, with his fire-magic improving, who could hurt him?

The Descendants of the Tuatha Dé Danann was a whisper that came to my mind. What if there were others? There might be, though I was sure there were no more warriors… but perhaps, if there were more, it was best that they revealed themselves before I returned with my mother and Cecile.

This was a hard thought for a father to have. To think of my son and to believe his death would be preferable to that of my cousin's. It was an easy thought for a king to have, though. Cecile was my future. With fire-magic in her blood, our children would have Fomorian fire too, and hopefully, one of them would be fit to rule. As much as I loved Angelo, it was not him. Too slow of mind, he could never be king.

"Very well, Angelo," I said. "You can stay. I'll be back in the spring. Stay safe. Keep your gift hidden, unless it's absolutely necessary."

Angelo nodded and handed over my cloak. Putting it on, I felt for the outline of the Descendant knife, took up my sword and left.

It was time to go. Time to help launch an invasion that would change my life forever.

Isolde

The road to Seir Kieran

Cuan kneeled on the ground. A thick rope tied him to a wooden post, while the men around him laughed and jeered. Some threw stones at his head. He didn't look up. There was no point. His right eye was swollen shut and blood poured down his face from a gash on his forehead.

"I prayed that my enemies would face their judgement," an old man said from the shadows. "First God sent me an army. Then he gave me you."

The old man moved forward until he stood in the sunlight. A thin white beard blew in the wind, but he was unmoved by it, frail though he seemed. The man beside him, a man with long, dark hair, handed the old man a knife.

"Domhnall," the old man said. "I thank you for bringing me such a gift. What a son you are."

Domhnall bowed as his father took the knife from him, his face as solemn as if he'd been blessed by the Pope himself.

The old man walked over to Cuan and sat on a chair that had been placed beside him. "Cuan Ó Conchúir, I am King Diarmait of Leinster, and you are at my home of Ferns. You must wonder why you are here. An unfairness, I think, and I shall enlighten you. You are a man with the blood of kings in your veins. Brian Boru, Sitric Silkbeard, Tairdelbach Ó Conchúir. Ivar the Boneless. Brought up by Godred, King of the Isles. Now part of the High King's fianna. You might think you know kings, but I want you to understand that my father was the greatest king that Leinster has ever known. Greatness, as it does with all men, lends itself to jealousy, and it was your great-grandfather, Domhnall Gerrlámhach, *who envied him the most. He invited my father to Dublin. Pretended to be his friend. Then, once he took the life from my father, Domhnall Gerrlámhach buried him alongside the body of a dog."*

Cuan didn't move. Didn't speak… but he was listening.

"Énna, my older brother, and I made a vow that day, even though the two of us were still boys. That we would kill these men who had shamed our father's body so. In due course, Énna became King of Leinster and then also became King of Dublin. He took power from the men who killed my father by force, but this was not enough. On hearing that Énna meant to kill him, your grandfather fled to Wexford. So cowardly. So craven. My brother was neither of those things, and he went after Domhnall Gerrlámhach."

The old man, King Diarmait, leaned forward a moment as if his strength had left him. *"Domhnall Gerrlámhach killed my brother. Stabbed him in the back."*

The crowd around King Diarmait turned quiet, almost transfixed, as they listened to him tell his story. *"My brother, who had everything, risked so much to keep his vow. Imagine how sad I was to learn that Domhnall Gerrlámhach died in his bed, my vow unfulfilled.*

"But my promise of revenge did not leave me, and so I decided to transfer it to Domhnall Gerrlámhach's progeny. He had one son, born from the great-granddaughter of Godfrey Sitricsson, the son of Sitric Silkbeard. You are the last, Cuan Ó Conchúir. The last man alive sprung from the seed of Domhnall Gerrlámhach and his wife, and now you are mine."

King Diarmait stepped closer to Cuan and ran the blade down his face. *"I promised myself that I would kill the heir of Domhnall Gerrlámhach and bury his body with a dog. But that, I feel, is too kind. They did not give my father an easy death, and I do not intend to give you one."*

He pointed to the top of the post that Cuan was tied to where a symbol of an eagle, stained red, was engraved into the wood. *"The blood eagle,"* the old king muttered. *"The blood eagle, yes. It is fitting that you should die this way. In the way of your own people who still blight this land."*

★

When I woke, everything was still. No shouting. No screaming. Just silence.

Lifting my head, I rubbed my eyes. It was not yet morning, but the sky was shades of grey and dark blue rather than black. Birds flew above me, swarming back and forth. It was the start of the day for them, catching their food before they followed their brothers and sisters south for the winter.

I pushed myself up, and it was only with this motion that I realised how wet I was. Not even wet. Soaked through. Looking down, I could see the red bloodstains over my shirt. My trousers, however, were not covered in blood, but in water… as if I'd lain out in a torrential rainstorm.

A rainstorm?

A memory of clouds looming above me, multiplying, came to me. Then the man with a sword and it cutting me open.

My hands rushed to my throat. There was no cut. No wound at all.

But it had happened. The memory of violence was sharp now. I remembered it. Remembered Cuan shouting as the man with the sword approached me.

I was dead. I had to be.

"Aoife!" I shouted for my sister, thinking she must be coming to take me to the otherworld. Standing, I searched the land for signs of her. "Aoife?"

Where was she?

With this movement, an all too familiar feeling of sickness washed over me, and I vomited on the grass. Shaking, I bent down and used my arm to hold myself upright, but even that was a struggle.

What was happening to me? If I was dead, why did I feel this way? Wasn't the otherworld a place of peace? Where were my mother and father? Where was Broccan? Affraic?

It was all wrong. Peace. There was no peace in my heart. I felt hollowed out. As if everything good within me had been removed and only despair and grief remained. A dream had come to me. A story to explain the grief. It came in flashes. Glimpses. An old man stood beside Cuan with a knife in his hand. Diarmait, he had called himself. King of Leinster. Cuan had kneeled, bruised and cut, at his feet.

The pain was too much. Pain like this would be too much for anyone to bear. "Help me!" I sobbed as I crawled forward on the grass. "Please. Someone help me."

No one answered my plea. It was only the wind that moved. So cold it was that my fingers and toes ached.

I wasn't dead, was I? Somehow, despite a man opening my throat, I was alive.

Are you listening, child?

The wind blew harder around me. Those strange words I'd heard once before came to me. The voice I'd heard during the fire of Rathlin and when I was encamped at Kells.

"What do you want?" I shouted. "What must I do?"

You must not linger. Go to the water. You cannot trust it. Do not listen. Go. Find the eagle.

The wind blew again, and I made my way down the hill to the river. To the water. Washing out the foul taste from my mouth, I spat it back out. I was thirsty, but the water was not clean enough to drink, so I took a step away. What was I supposed to do now?

The shaking took hold as I looked around me and I wrapped my wet, blood-soaked cloak around my body. I was sick of this. The way my body reacted after using my gift. I'd summoned three storms since I'd left Dublin, and it was destroying me. I felt inside myself that I was not well. That my strength had gone. My gift was killing me.

Or was it saving me?

Slowly, I felt my neck. Felt the lack of a scar.

I assumed I had the witch gift... that was what Affraic had told me... but how then was I alive? And my dreams. Were they dreams? Or were they visions as my aunt Rónnat had?

The sound of hooves sounded out, and I spun around, reaching for Fragarach from my belt.

"Sleipnir."

The horse came to a stop a little further upstream, and I held out my hands. "It's me, Sleipnir. Isolde."

The horse slowly walked toward me until his nose touched my hand.

"Good boy, Sleipnir. Good boy."

Sleipnir, so powerful and strong, snorted and touched my hand with his nose again. He was in good condition, even my bag was still tied to the saddle. Somehow, he'd avoided capture.

The wind blew up around me, though the voice had gone, and I thought about what to do. Seir Kieran wasn't too far away. That was where I was supposed to go… but the wind had told me to find the eagle. The eagle of my dream, the one engraved on the wooden post, was with Cuan. At Ferns.

"Will we look for him, Sleipnir?"

The horse snorted and didn't move as I climbed onto his back. The wind blew up around me, pushing my hair in the direction of the southern path.

"Come on, Sleipnir. Let's go."

Gormflaith

Chepstow

Olaf soared above a ship, then perched on the top of the mast. I looked down. One hundred and fifty weary men sat along the benches and floor. Some closed their eyes, hoping to find sleep, others kept their eyes to the east as they cleaned their swords and armour.

From this vantage point, I saw my son sitting beside one of the knights who had left with him. Maurice de Prendergast. Yes, that was his name, but they did not speak.

On the other side of the ship, a Norman warrior leaned over the side, vomiting, while his friend, who was re-feathering his arrows, sat close to him.

"How long do you think it will be till we reach home?" the man said, once he finished retching. "I pray to God that Maurice never asks us to return to that godforsaken place."

"Oh, we'll be back," said his friend as he trimmed the feathers with his knife. "Wexford didn't want to fight us. Apparently, neither did Dublin. For all the Irish say they love to fight, they haven't wanted to against us."

"What about Osraige?"

"It wasn't so very bad... aside from the way they remove the noses and ears of the dead."

"Battles like those are usually a game of numbers," the sick man said. "We got lucky. Next time, they will be better prepared. Then it will be our noses and ears that will be cut away and our bodies left out to rot. Strongbow needs to add his men to the fight, otherwise there is no hope of keeping the land we were given, but I don't think I'll go, either way. I'm done."

The two men continued their conversation, agreeing and disagreeing on whether Strongbow would ever go to Ireland, and if so, how many knights he would call into his service.

"What do you think, Donn? Do my men speak the truth? Will the land Robert was given be taken back unless Strongbow invades next year?" I moved my attention to the other side of the ship. Back to my son and Maurice.

"I do not know, Maurice," my son replied.

"You gave Robert good advice. That is true. But if anything, our incursion into Ireland has been more difficult than I expected. Not because of the fighting, for there was little enough of that, but because of the people. The men of Ireland are a bigger mystery to me than those I fought in Damascus."

"Men are not so great a mystery. What motivates us is the only thing perhaps that differs. The Muslims of Damascus, they are religious, are they not? They worship Allah as devoutly as you worship God."

Maurice wrinkled his nose. Donnchad had to be careful here. I knew from my time in Chepstow that the religious fervour of these Norman knights was unparalleled. Holier than the cardinals I'd met in Rome. To a man like Maurice who had fought in the Crusades, anything that sounded like Donnchad admired the followers of Islam would be as good as heresy.

"What I meant to say is," Donnchad said, perhaps sensing this himself, "is the men of Ireland do not worship celestial beings. Their conversion is weak, as I told you once before. It was why King Donnchad of Munster once went to the Pope to ask for his help in bringing true Christianity to Ireland. The Irish... they have not taken Jesus and the doctrine of Rome into their hearts. They still, if I am honest, follow the old ways. That is why you do not understand them. It is the land they worship. Their customs. Not God."

"What do you want, Donn?" Maurice stared at my son, his shoulders relaxing. But there was danger flashing in his eyes. Distrust in his voice.

"I came to Ireland to see it for myself. I do not deny that was my primary motive, but I also came for the same reason as many of your men. For an honest payment."

Maurice scratched the overgrown stubble on his chin. "No, Donn. There is more. You said men are not so different, and that is true. Over the course of my life, I've met many. I know what men are and how to read what is in their hearts. Something other than payment motivates you."

Donnchad's lips twitched, and he paused to take a breath. "My father was a trader, but a poor one. He is dead now, as is my older brother. I have a sister, Alys, to care for. Angelo, my younger brother. And a cousin, Cecile."

"I thought the women at Chepstow were both sisters."

"We call Cecile our sister because my father took her in when she was young, but she's actually the daughter of his cousin."

"I see."

"I've loved Cecile for many years, but cannot ask her to marry me when my standing is so poor. I have nothing to give her. If you were to take Ireland…" He stuttered to a stop, pausing as if to appear bashful.

"Go on," Maurice said.

"You will need men to help you run your holdings. Any such position would suit me. Anything at all where I felt I could provide for my family and have children of my own."

Maurice relaxed and leaned back against the mast. "Marriage is a noble pursuit. I cannot fault it, and I am sure it is something I or Robert can arrange if we were to be successful." Now it was his turn to pause. "But success does depend on Strongbow. My men are right. You'd better hope he's still of a mind to be a part of this."

"You think he won't?"

"He wants to come to Ireland, but King Henry watches Strongbow, and Strongbow has sworn many vows to him. If Strongbow feels coming here will break any of them, he will stay in Wales, no matter how it pains him. But enough for now. We are nearly home. I don't know about you, but I need to wash and shave and eat before I can think of Ireland anymore."

★

I woke out of my dream, still sitting on my chair by the fire. What an interesting one it had been.

So, my son was planning to make Cecile his wife. I knew that he wanted her and would one day make this move, but the fact he fabricated this lie meant he wanted her now *and* believed he needed the Normans to further our interests in Ireland. Incest certainly would not work for these pious Christians, and so Donnchad was correcting our story. They were not brother and sister, but cousins – as they were in truth.

Poor Cecile.

Her love for Strongbow, no matter how useful, could no longer be allowed to flourish. With Máelmórda gone, my son had taken it upon himself to lead our small band of Fomorians, and for now, I'd have to allow that. At least I had to appear to allow it… all the while ensuring that Cecile and Angelo, when it came to it, would answer to me. That would be difficult but not impossible.

Cecile came into the room a short while later. Smiling. Windswept.

"Morning," she said. "I thought I'd go for a walk while the weather was nice."

"Did you go alone?"

"Yes."

What a pretty little liar she was. "Strongbow wasn't with you?"

"Oh," she stopped. "I spoke to him a little. He was out walking, too."

"Was he?" I grinned. "How convenient."

"Gormflaith… what are you insinuating?"

"I'm not insinuating anything. I know you and Strongbow have formed an attachment. Sadly, it must come to an end. Donnchad is coming home. Apparently with the intent of marrying you."

"Donnchad doesn't want to marry me."

"Yes, he does. Do you not want to marry him?"

This question finally granted me Cecile's full attention. She set down her cloak and looked at me, searching for traces in my expression that I might be joking.

"No. I don't."

"Then why did you go to Rathlin with him? Máelmórda only followed because of you. Now he's dead."

This wiped the smile from Cecile's face. "You blame me?"

"Blame is for fools. The past is the past and cannot be undone. Now we must look to the future."

"I will not be Donnchad's wife. I don't want it."

"Sit, Cecile." I tapped the cushion of the chair opposite mine. "Let me tell you some truths."

Cecile, struggling to control her emotions, reluctantly sat, her eyes burning when she stared at me as if this situation was my doing.

"In my life, there have been two women in my care. The first was Gytha. A daughter of my first husband. Oh, she was stupid, Cecile. Even worse than stupid, she was dull. And even worse than that, she was so very plain."

Cecile huffed as she pulled a fur blanket over her legs, but I knew she was listening.

"Her father ignored her, and she was no match for her husband. Useless and almost barren, she was dead only a few years after she married him."

Cecile sniffed, holding back her tears for now. "Who was the second?"

"She was my granddaughter Edysis, and she was the opposite of Gytha in every way. Beautiful. Full of spirit. Clever. When Edysis was in the feasting hall, everyone watched her. She laughed so loudly you could hear her from outside."

"I've never heard you talk about her before. What happened?"

"She died young too. That's the problem when everyone notices you. They want you. Put ideas in your head. Use you. Her father, my first son, Sitric, could not say no to her. He let her dress as a shieldmaiden and even bought her a fine sword. She stood out too much. He may as well have put a noose around her neck."

"So that is it. I am beautiful and I stand out too much? Just because Edysis couldn't survive this world, doesn't mean that I will fail too."

"You can't endure the harshness of this life. I know that well enough."

Cecile's eyes narrowed. "Just because you're a washed-up old hag and centuries old doesn't make everything you say right. Strongbow likes me. I can tell."

"And what do you suppose Donnchad will do to him when he realises that you love him so much? Let you marry him? Welcome him into our family?"

"It's nothing to do with Donnchad."

"Then you did not listen to what I told you about Gytha and Edysis."

"I did listen," she snapped. "Two women in your care both died young. Don't worry. I've no intention of being in your care or dying."

"You are not young anymore, Cecile. Not in mortal years, anyhow. You look twenty, but in truth, you're almost forty. If you were to walk along the river and speak to the washerwomen, you'd see women your age, wrinkled and dried-up from the sun, and call them washed-up old hags too."

"I am a Fomorian, just like you."

"Barely." I gave her a scathing look. "You can scarce tame a fire, and the witch gift you took… You can't so much as move a blade of grass. I half suspect the gift didn't go into you at all."

She frowned at this. Hugged herself tight. "Strongbow is an earl. Donnchad wouldn't dare hurt him."

"Oh, my darling niece, you do not know your cousin. For power, he killed his father, nephew, and stabbed me in the stomach. If he is willing to kill a High King, you can bet on the fact he will kill an earl. Especially an earl who is only a lord according to the king."

"But I don't like Donnchad that way." Cecile stormed away from the chair, running her hands through her hair. She knew what must happen, or at least she was beginning to.

"I've envied your freedom, Cecile. You may as well be a child still, for your father did not want you to grow up. He wanted you to look at him with doltish adoration always. He followed you, you know, when you went out with your friends in Paris."

"I know he did. He loved me. He looked after me."

"In some strange way, I suppose he did. But he's not here anymore, and you are alone now. You're about to learn how hard being alone can be."

"I hate you."

I shrugged and closed my eyes. "That is a foolish thing to say. It is not I who wants to marry you. Save your hate for someone else."

"Please."

This word came out like a whimper, and when I opened my eyes, I found Cecile on her knees.

"Please talk to him for me."

"Oh? You want me now, this washed-up old hag?"

"Keep your son away from me."

"And why would I do that?"

"Because I don't love him."

"Ah, then this is your final lesson." I reached forward and touched her chin with my thumb and forefinger. "Only the most fortunate among us get to marry those we love. I've hated almost all my husbands. A few were tolerable. There is no love in this life for women like us. That is what you need to understand. That is why you need to learn to hide who you really are, and that I can teach you."

Cecile, tears now streaming down her cheeks, shook her head.

"Gytha stood out because she could not perform the duties expected of a wife. Edysis stood out because she burned too brightly. You must not stand out as they did. You must marry and breed. Then maybe one day, if you are very lucky, you can move on."

"How stupid do you think I am?" Cecile snapped. "I understand that is possible when you marry a mortal, but if you make me take Donnchad as my husband, that can never be. He will always be at my side."

"That is where you are wrong. Donnchad will win the kingship. We will let him. Then, when he least suspects it, you, Cecile, living in the shadows, shall take it from him. And I shall help you. You shall be queen. Then you can have whoever it is you want."

Cecile wiped her cheeks and stared, her large golden eyes widening.

There, she had her desires, too.

I knew them as I knew my own.

She tried to push it down and walked away from me. She was soft, Cecile. And Donnchad would punish her if she didn't go to him. *Let him*, I thought. Let his ambition and hate drive her into my arms. That would accomplish more than anything I might say.

I could have told her another truth. *My truth*. But now was not the time for honesty. Instead, I let my mind drift. I let myself remember that the worst day of my life had not been Donnchad plunging a knife into my stomach, or even the day my father had married me off to Amlav, old and decrepit as he was. It was the day I realised Olaf had betrayed me.

It was hard to think of Olaf in that way now. The love potion had ruined him as much as the scars Svein had given his flesh. But once, I had loved him. I had loved him and even bore him a son. Unmarried, I had placed our giftless son into Sitric's son's crib and removed my own grandson so the switch could be made. Godfrey, Sitric had called my baby. Even the naming of my son had been taken from me. And what had Olaf been doing while I had been loving him and giving him a child? He had left me alone and deceived me. Putting his own needs ahead of mine and taking the prize of queenship from me in the process.

That was the day that I realised love was worthless. Even sweet David, for all his poetry and gifts, meant nothing to me.

For who wanted love when they could be a queen?

Isolde

The road to Ferns

The wind guided me as I journeyed south. I didn't know how or why it was helping me, but I trusted it. *Find the eagle*, the voice on the wind had said. *Find Cuan* was what it had meant.

By the end of the following day, the wind finally blew itself out. The air became so still, so clear there was almost a heaviness to it. Pulling Sleipnir to a stop, I gazed along the path ahead of me until my eyes met with a hill in the distance. A great dun was built there, surrounded by a tall stone wall. This was it. *Ferns*.

"Stay here, Sleipnir." I dismounted and tied his reins to a low-hanging branch at the edge of the forest. The sun had nearly set, and it wouldn't take long for darkness to follow. An idea forming, the only one I could think of, I took the dress out of my bag and removed the blood-stained shirt and trousers from my body. Cuan was right about one thing. I stood out in my trousers and shirt, and even if I used my cloak and shawl to hide my hair, the fact my clothes were blood-soaked would surely attract unwanted attention. But that left another question. What would a girl, alone, be doing walking to Ferns? What could I say that would induce the guards to allow me inside?

Well, if Scolaí had believed I was a spy, perhaps I could pretend to be one this time.

Dressed in Dáirinn's blue dress and using my shawl to cover my hair, I walked to the dun. There were plenty of people walking around, cleaning, cooking, washing clothes. The guards, though, there were so many of them. As I approached, I felt their eyes upon me. More and more of them. It was frightening to be watched by so many, but I could not show my fear. I was a spy, after all. A messenger. I belonged here.

"*J'ai un message des Normands,*" I said to one of the guards at the gate. *I have a message from the Normans.*

The man looked me up and down, then motioned for another of the guards to approach. "Go and find Riagáin. Tell him that FitzStephen has sent a messenger."

I stood there, head lowered and holding my scarf tight. If any of the Leinster men who'd watched me die recognised me... well, there was no telling what they'd do. My disguise might be good enough from a distance, but up close, they would see my eyes, the shape of my face. A ghost, they might think me, come back to haunt them for the taking of my life. That would certainly cause a commotion, one that I could do without.

While I waited, I took a step inside the gate. I moved slowly. Appeared docile. Those few steps were enough to allow me a view of the dun grounds, of the tall wooden post inside, and of the man tied to it. I could hardly make Cuan out, for he was on his knees and slumped over. This surprised me. I'd expected Cuan to be looking for any chance of escape, or at least to be watching his enemies.

Quickly, though, I had to turn my attention away from him. The warrior returned, this time with another man at his side. Cheeks flushed, this man, Riagáin, they'd called him, appeared in good form, though his smile faded slightly once he reached me.

"*Oui?*" *Yes?*

"I have a message from the Normans," I said to him in Anglo-Norman French. "More men are coming. They will land at the harbour of the woman." I repeated the message the spy in the church had told me, thinking at least this would have a ring of truth about it.

"*Combien?*" he asked. *How many?* I had no idea how to reply. I didn't want to say so much that it sounded ridiculous or alarming. What was reasonable for an army? I thought back to Dublin and how many men had sailed on some of the ships by the longphort. Two ships, maybe.

"Three hundred," I replied.

"The Normans left in a hurry. What do they want with so many new soldiers? Is this a threat? Or is it... friendship?"

"Friendship."

Riagáin sniffed and spat on the ground. "They sent you all this way to tell me this?"

I nodded, smiling as sweetly as I could. "Friendship is important."

"Very well," he replied. "I will write a message for you to take back with you. Do you want some food while you wait? Would you like to rest?"

"A little food and drink would be kind, but I will leave once you've prepared your message."

"As you wish."

Riagáin walked back into the feasting hall, the suspicious look on his face already fading. Did he believe me? I doubted it, despite the lack of questioning. Perhaps, like King Ruaidrí, the Leinster king would not act quickly, but rather wait and watch who I spoke to. It didn't matter in any case. The guard at the gates gestured that I go toward the cooking fires, and I meant to be gone soon. Long before any reply could be concocted and written down.

One of the serving women handed me a bowl of stew. I took a mouthful, thanked her, and walked toward the feasting hall. Quite a number of men had gathered by the doors, some of them pointing at Cuan and talking of what was to come. *Blood eagle. Blood eagle. Blood eagle.*

Now that I was close enough to see him, slowly I lifted my gaze.

I swallowed my gasp, my tears, and pushed down all my emotions. I couldn't let the people here see it, but on the inside, my heart ripped open.

They had taken both his eyes.

Hollowed out and streaming with blood, they had done to him what Ruaidrí had done to his father. Slumped forward, Cuan shook. He was alive. Awake... though gone somewhere else in his mind. Of course he wasn't trying to escape. He was simply waiting to die.

Why did people have so much hate inside them that they would want to do such terrible things to another? Why was death not enough for those intent on killing? Why did they have to ruin and destroy the body first?

Whatever it was, this darkness inside the heart of man, I couldn't let this happen. I had to get Cuan out of here. Out of this terrible place.

Staring up at the sky, I watched the stars shimmering. I had summoned a storm before. Hailstones so large that it prevented a Fomorian from killing me. It had not come for long – and not long enough to save Affraic – but it had helped us for a while. I had been all rage then. So full of anger that the Fomorians had come to Rathlin Island and destroyed it. Now my rage was cold. Cold because the rage came from grief and an inconsolable sadness.

Affraic's words of warning rumbled in my mind. *To overuse our gift when we don't understand it is to risk ourselves. Do you understand?*

I did understand, but I didn't care if this storm hurt me. I didn't care if I vomited and shivered and shook. My gift would do this for me, no matter the cost to myself.

With this vow sworn, I pictured the storm I wanted to conjure… and the clouds came. Dark. Seeping across the moonlit sky like a deepening bruise. Then came the rain. Fog this time too, and then the hail. The people standing outside rushed into the feasting hall. Even the warriors who guarded the gates. The hail came down like arrows. Those slow to reach the safety of the feasting hall screamed as the stones sliced their skin. The downpour quickened, until the air was like a waterfall, obscuring Cuan behind its veil.

Now alone, I picked up a discarded wooden shield and ran toward Cuan, disappearing into the fog and hail.

"Cuan." Sliding to a stop beside him, I held the shield above our heads, glad the post had shielded him from the hailstones so far. "It's Isolde."

Cuan didn't move. His clothes clung to him like a second skin and thick clumps of his hair had matted over his face. Perhaps he couldn't hear me. I shook his arm. "Cuan. It's me."

Cuan jumped as if woken from a deep sleep. "Isolde?" His teeth chattered, and he shook his head. "Have you come from the afterlife to take me with you?"

"I'm not dead, Cuan." I took his hand into mine, kissed it, and pressed it against my cheek.

"You are. I saw them cut your throat."

"I'm alive, Cuan." I leaned closer. "Feel the heat of my face and strength in my hand."

Cuan's fingers moved to touch my face and brushed through my hair. Moving downward, they touched my lips. "How?"

"I do not know. All I know is that I've come to save you."

Cuan stilled, the sound of his breath drowned out by the hail pounding the ground beside us. "Isolde, if you're not a ghost, you must leave before they find you."

"No. You're coming with me."

He turned his face away. "They will catch us. I cannot see. Go." Even though he had little strength within him, he pushed my hand away from his.

Searching, I felt for the rope that tied him to the post, took out Fragarach, and cut through it.

"Come on."

But Cuan didn't move.

How could I make him understand that I would not leave without him?

"I love you, Cuan," I said. "I didn't tell you before... I don't think I even understood it myself, but I do." Pressing my body against his, I rested my head under his chin. There was a war going on inside him. He'd already accepted death. Hope had to be remembered. Not just for him. For me, too. "Please. Please try, Cuan. Come with me. I can't go without you. I can't lose you. Please."

"All right, Isolde," he said, his hand finding mine. "I'd rather die seeking freedom with you than kneeling at Diarmait Mac Murchadha's feet."

I hauled him up, glad to find he still had some strength in his legs, and I wrapped my cloak around the two of us to shield our heads from the hailstones. The two of us staggered to the gate, trying our best to find our footing through the storm. I could not use the shield anymore, and even the thick fur of my cloak did not protect us completely, but we kept moving, nonetheless. Moving toward freedom.

Making our way through the deserted gate, I led Cuan down the hill and to the forest where I'd hidden Sleipnir. The hail had stopped here, though I could see the clouds I'd summoned still swarming around the dun. I pushed Cuan up onto Sleipnir, then climbed up myself, making sure his hands were around my waist before I urged Sleipnir into a gallop.

We rode for an hour, but with every minute that passed, Cuan slumped lower behind me. The rain had stopped long ago, but he shivered violently, and I knew he'd fall from Sleipnir if he grew any weaker. We needed to rest.

Desperately, I looked about for signs of shelter. There. In the distance, the shape of a ráth and rising smoke caught my eye, and I steered Sleipnir toward it.

"Help," I shouted as Sleipnir came to a stop just outside the earth wall. A man and a young girl stumbled outside in alarm. The man looked set to shout at me until he saw the wounds over Cuan's face, after which he ran away from the ráth with his daughter.

Cuan slid down, using me as a crutch. Barely able to stand, he allowed me to navigate him inside. His hands were like ice and his whole body trembled. If he could just get some warmth by the fire and some water, we could leave and start riding again.

"We haven't travelled far enough," he said. "They'll be here soon."

"We've had a decent head start." I lay him on a bed close to the fire and threw a couple of sticks into the flames. "You just need to drink some water and warm up. Then we'll go."

Cuan shook his head. "I won't make it, Isolde. You must leave and save yourself. I've spent the last day believing you were dead. The pain here," he said, touching his chest, "was worse than the pain when they took my eyes. If I die, knowing you got away, I'll die happy. Please go."

I lay beside him, trying to coax heat into his body, but the shivering continued. I realised then it wasn't just he who shivered. It was me too. My strength was also fading. The foul taste was surging into my mouth. I'd be sick soon and then I'd be almost useless. I couldn't let that happen. *I refused to let it happen.* Standing, I searched the house for a dry cloak. Perhaps another tunic. Anything to warm Cuan up.

Howls and barks rang out in the distance. Far away still, but not for long. Shuddering, I moved back over to Cuan. "Come on. We need to go."

"No, Isolde." Firmly, Cuan pushed me back. "Put my sword in my hand and leave. Once they have me, they won't worry about looking for anyone else. Take Sleipnir and ride to Seir Kieran."

I argued, but no matter how hard I tried to pull him, he kept trying to make me leave. Begging. Pleading. Pushing me away. The barking outside grew louder, as did the shouts of the men with them.

"I'm not leaving without you, Cuan."

"Why?" He reached out and his hand brushed against my face. "Why won't you ever do what I tell you, Isolde?"

I fell into his outstretched arms. "Because I don't want to leave you. I love you." It was true. I couldn't leave. I couldn't leave behind another person I loved to die.

"Cuan Ó Conchúir," a deep voice shouted from outside. "Come out and face me." The voice was low and harsh. Full of venom.

"Is that King Diarmait?" I whispered into Cuan's ear.

"Yes."

"Your uncle was very cunning sending a girl to save you," King Diarmait continued. "Cowardly, but clever. I'll give him that. I will send him her head as well as yours. But know this – if you both come out now, I will offer you a quick death. If you force us to come in and drag you out, you will suffer."

Reaching out with my gift, I tried to summon the rain. Pain pulsed throughout me, black liquid surged into my mouth, and I vomited on the ground. Something dripped from my nose too, trailing over my lips and chin. I wiped it away. Blood smeared my hand.

I was spent. Unable to control my gift, I had nothing left.

Cuan pushed himself up, though I wasn't sure how he found the strength. In his right hand, he clasped hold of his sword. "No," he whispered, trembling. "Not like this."

"Cuan." I reached out to hold him, then recoiled. He was scalding hot. Boiling to the touch.

A man rushed into the house then, sword swinging, ready to strike Cuan.

Cuan held out his left hand and fire flew out from it. The Leinster warrior who had come in was thrown outside the house by the force of the fire, and like water flooding over a riverbed, the fire climbed the walls and spread over the thatch.

Cuan ran outside. The fire was not only on his hands but over his arms and skin. The fire seemed to be a part of him. Half consuming, half escaping his body.

I couldn't understand what was happening. Shielding myself from the flames, I could only watch as he left the house. Screaming, he opened his arms, and more fire came from him. It spread along the ground, along the walls and soared into the sky.

The men who had chased us were riding away. Their dogs too. Whimpering and crying as they ran. The fire was no longer consuming the house but spreading out over the grass and rushing toward them. Hurrying outside, I watched this fire and noted the dead bodies lying on the ground. Burnt and blackened.

"Cuan. Stop!" I threw myself against him, pushing him to the ground. "What... What have you done?"

Shaking and shivering, the fire left him, and when I reached for his hand, Cuan's skin was cool. As if there had never been a fire at all.

"Cuan. How did you do that?"

"I don't know. My mother..." He rolled over and black vomit spewed from his mouth onto the ground.

He had fire-magic. He was a Fomorian.

The screams of the men in the distance rose into the air with the wind. They were gone for now but could come back. I had to get us out of here.

"Sleipnir!"

I shouted and shouted, but Cuan's horse was nowhere to be seen.

Dragging Cuan up and onto his feet, together we staggered toward the trees in the distance.

Weak as we were, we found strength from somewhere as we clung to each other. Moving deep into the forest, I did not care for the howls of the wolves nor for the creaking of the old trees as we passed. We just had to keep moving for as long as we were able.

Only once I became so tired I couldn't keep going, did we stop. My stomach churned and a terrible smell filled the air... the smell of burning flesh. Using the last of my strength, I guided Cuan and set him against the tree trunk. Taking my cloak, I sat beside him. He shook, not with the cold, for he was not cold, but with pain. He put his head into his hands, covering over the bloodied sockets where his eyes had once been. Wrapping my arms around him, I held him, wishing that we could go back in time. Wishing that we could go back to the cave where we held each other. When I did not know he was Fomorian, and his eyes had not been taken.

Isolde

The forests of Leinster

"Isolde."

I woke to Cuan nudging my side. "Isolde, you need to get up."

Rousing myself from my sleep, I opened my eyes and turned to face him.

Cuan was sitting up, his hands running over his face. "Isolde. My eyes. Look! I can see."

I stared at him, moving to sit up straighter. His pale blue eyes stared back. Even the blood-red of his left eye was gone. He was... healed.

Gently, he ran his fingers over his eyes, feeling them, then rubbing at the blood dried into the skin of his cheeks. The blood from when his eyes had been taken.

"What are you, Isolde?" he said. "I saw you die... saw the knife slice open your neck... and the storm... and now this."

I stilled, for I knew what I was. A Descendant of the Tuatha Dé Danann. *A daughter who would conquer fire.* But what was my gift? I didn't know anymore.

"I'm not the only one who has kept things secret," I said, running my hands through my hair. Limp it was, wet and cold, just like my skin. "You're a Fomorian."

"Why do you call me that? What does it mean?"

"You've never heard of them from the old legends?"

Cuan frowned, thinking. "They were the enemies of the old gods, weren't they? I can't remember. It's been a long time since I heard those stories."

"Yes. They were the enemies of the Tuatha Dé Danann. They had fire-magic, like you do. When the men attacked us, the fire came out of your hands and spread over the ground."

Cuan kneeled back onto the heels of his feet and stared at his hands, looking for traces of the power he'd unleashed.

"You said something about your mother when it happened. Did she have fire-magic too?"

Cuan nodded. "When Ruaidrí came for my father, she set the dun on fire to try to save him. She told me it was a curse within our family and that it comes out when we lose control of our emotions. It kills us in the end. My mother made it to twenty-six. Her mother died at twenty. I thought, I hoped, I had it under control."

"There were others before your grandmother?"

Cuan nodded. "My great-great-grandfather said he was the first. He was a grandson of Sitric Silkbeard, but he said it must come from the north, for he knew no other in his family with it. His father, Godfrey, didn't have it. Neither did Sitric. But he said he had an aunt called Freya, who knew of the old Norse gods. She said their magic was powerful and that this could be a gift from Odin. Why? What do you know of it?"

"I've met others like you."

Cuan's eyes widened, the hint of a smile at his lips.

"It was they who burned Rathlin Island and killed my cousin. You see, I am descended from the Tuatha Dé Danann, and my kind and the Fomorians have been at war with each other for centuries. That is why the Fomorians searched for me. They want me dead."

The smile faded and Cuan came closer to me. "I would never hurt you."

Nodding, my chin trembled. I could feel my heart ache. I knew he wouldn't hurt me. The fire had come out of his hands because he had wanted to save me. His love for me was true, and yet, this fire-magic that he had… it could only come between us.

"I know, Cuan, but you cannot come with me to Seir Kieran now. The others like me… they won't understand. They will only see you as an enemy." I tried to stand, then sank to my knees.

The black liquid surged up into my mouth, but blood too. I felt it seeping from the corners of my eyes and my nose. The shaking and shivering started again too, but worse this time. Worse than ever before and my eyes closed. I felt myself drifting away.

"What's wrong, Isolde?" Cuan rushed over and held me tight.

"I've used too much of my gift."

Cuan wrapped his cloak around me. "You need a healer. Hold on."

I had no choice but to lie in his arms. I couldn't speak. My body surged with pain, and I drifted away to somewhere dark and silent – somewhere even my dreams could not find me.

Broccan

Kingdom of Ulaid

When I opened my eyes, my legs would not move. No matter how I focused, I could not lift or turn them. Not even an inch. The memory of pain flooded through me, though I did not feel it now.

"Morning, Broccan."

A woman came into view. Smiling, she touched my cheek. To see Senna surprised me more than anything, for I had not laid eyes on her since my mother had died. A witch Descendant, she had decided not to come with me to Rathlin or to live with the others at Seir Kieran. I had not heard from her in so long, I had thought that she must have perished in the wilderness that had become her home.

"Senna?" I said, though I struggled to give voice to my questions. *What had happened? Where was I? Why was my mind so blank?*

"Your mother spoke to me on the wind and told me where to find you, Broccan. I turned myself into a seal and pulled you from the rocks. We are in Ulaid now. I found a cave along the beach."

"What?" I closed my eyes, trying to think. Flashes of fire came to me. Máelmórda. Donnchad. They had come to the island. They had set it on fire.

"I've used my potions to keep you asleep until the pain faded. You screamed so much at the start. Screamed until your voice went hoarse. The burns over your body. They are bad."

"Where is..." Already I felt my grasp on consciousness slipping away. "Where is Isolde?"

"I do not know, Broccan. She had already left the island when I tried to find her."

Trying once again to move, I attempted to push my body up. I had to get to Isolde. While I'd been sleeping, she'd been alone, but once again, I struggled to find my strength. My arms moved, though to do so brought on waves of pain… but my legs, they still wouldn't do what I wanted. "What's wrong with me?"

"You broke your back when you fell from the cliff."

"Can you take me to Seir Kieran? Siobhan will be able to heal me. Then I can search for Isolde."

Senna frowned as she looked me over. "As soon as you are strong enough, I will take you."

"I am strong enough," I said, lying back on the ground. Sweat poured from my skin. My heart raced. "Take me to Siobhan. Please."

"You will not like what I have to do," Senna said. "I cannot move you as you are. I'll have to change you into another form."

"Do it," I said. "Change me. As long as I get to Isolde, I do not care."

Isolde

Seir Kieran

When I opened my eyes, I found myself in a room with walls made of stone. Everything was grey. I moved slowly, tentatively, but the pain I expected didn't come. The shivering and shaking. The foul taste. The smell of burning flesh. All of it was gone.

Where was I? Where was Cuan?

I sat up and looked around me. I was alone and dressed in a clean woollen leine. Who had dressed me in this? And who had washed me?

Standing, I rushed to the door, terrified that King Diarmait had found Cuan and me, and that I was locked inside. To my relief, the door opened.

"Oh," a voice said. "You're awake."

I peered outside to find a stone corridor, and a woman walking toward me. Dressed in a plain woollen dress, she appeared not much older than me and had long, dark brown hair that hung to her hips. Her face was familiar, though. I'd seen it somewhere before.

"I'm Báine," she said, smiling.

"Affraic's daughter?"

"Yes."

"You look like her. Very much so."

"You look like your mother, too." Báine's smile didn't waver, but her eyes hardened as she said this. "Where is my mother? I've been looking for you. For months. Broccan too."

"I am sorry, Báine." The wind seemed to empty from my lungs. After all these months wishing I could be with someone who knew Broccan, I now wished I could be anywhere else but here. The telling of my story would be an arduous task, and I didn't feel up to it just yet, though I couldn't remain silent either. Báine deserved to know what had happened to Affraic. "The Fomorians found us on Rathlin. Your mother and Broccan both died trying to save me."

Báine's chin quivered, but she nodded her head. "I feared as much when I saw the island. I just hoped that somehow, she'd managed to get away in time."

Báine placed her hand gently on my shoulder. "You have much to tell us, I see, but all in good time. The others will want to hear your story, too, and you must make sure you are well enough. You were half-dead when you arrived here. Siobhan, our healer, has been with you for three days and nights now. She says your wounds, both inside and out, were great."

"I've been sleeping for three days?"

"At least. A man left you here. He told one of the monks that he found you in the forest."

"Is that man here?"

"No. He left as soon as Siobhan came out to tend to your wounds. Why? Was he a friend of yours?"

I didn't know why, but I didn't want to say what he was. Was that strange to think this? This was supposed to be my place of refuge. A place where I would be looked after and sheltered, but it didn't feel that way yet. What if they asked me questions about Cuan? He was a Fomorian. An enemy of the Descendants. What if they wanted to hurt him?

"No. Not a friend."

"Come," she said. "I can introduce you to the others, and you must be hungry."

"I am, but there is someone I want to meet first. Colmon."

"Colmon?" Báine's forehead furrowed, but she led me along the stone corridor without argument. "He's inside this room," she said as we reached the final door. "What did Broccan tell you about him?"

"Just that he had trained him."

"Did he tell you he hadn't woken since the battle at Fennit Island?"

"Yes. I know it seems strange that I want to see him before all others, but I just wanted to hold his hand for a while. To let him know that I am here."

Báine opened the door, appearing to understand this sentiment. "I will bring the others to you then. Take a seat. There is no rush."

Slowly, I walked into Colmon's room, listening to the fading sound of Báine's steps as she made her way back along the corridor. Colmon was lying on a bed. His slow breaths were now the only thing I could hear.

As my hand moved to hold his, tears fell down my cheeks. I'd spent the last few months with my emotions held in so tight. I hadn't let myself cry or linger in my sadness over what happened on Rathlin, but now, that was all I could think of. Broccan was meant to be here with me. He was the one who was supposed to introduce me to everyone. I detested the empty space beside me. But there wasn't just one empty space. There were three. Broccan. Affraic. And Cuan.

I tightened my grip on Colmon's hand. It was cold. Stiff. As if he were dead, after all. With my other hand, I touched one of his braids, feeling the white strands intertwined with the grey and black. I knew this face. I knew it well.

There was no doubt this was the man from my dream. The one where I had destroyed everything. He'd been awake, though. *Dying.* With a sword in his stomach. He had spoken to me. *It is you who did this, Isolde. Look at the dead lying on the grass. It is all you. I told you that you must learn to control your gift, and you did not listen.*

Was this a dream or a vision? I had thought it a dream at the time.

But it couldn't be a dream, could it? It had to be a vision, for how else could I have conjured his likeness so well. The dream of Cuan too. The knowing of where he was and what was happening to him at Ferns.

"Wake up," I said. "Wake up, Colmon."

Nothing.

"Colmon. Wake up."

Still, he didn't move.

I hated this. Hated this place. Hated that Broccan was not with me. Hated that Cuan was gone. Hated that the safety I was supposed to feel here would never come.

Releasing Colmon's hand, I walked toward the door. My heart pounded and my throat tightened so that I felt as if I could hardly breathe. The sickness came back too, I could feel it swelling inside my stomach. What was wrong with me? Why was I always like this?

"Isolde?"

I turned just as Colmon's eyes fluttered open.

"Colmon?" I rushed to his side.

The man on the bed took my hand this time. It was so warm as it wrapped around mine.

"You have arrived," he said, smiling. "I am glad, for I have been waiting a long time for you."

EPILOGUE

Angelo

Kingdom of Leinster

It was late, and the forest ahead of me was quiet. The birds did not sing around me, they never had, and the larger animals had the sense to keep away.

It was nice, however, to finally be alone.

My father had left me at the Norman camp close to Wexford, but I had not stayed there for long. Months of building a fortress was not something that interested me. It was Ferns that intrigued. I enjoyed it there. Enjoyed watching my distant cousins and their ineptitude, but I also wanted to explore this land. To know it better. My Fomorian blood kept me warm, and so the winter winds that frightened the mortals did not worry me.

Taking out my father's knife, I spun it around in my hand. *The Descendants' knife.*

I wondered how long it would take for him to realise it was gone. Perhaps Gormflaith would demand it back, and only then would he know that I had switched our cloaks before he left.

It was as well I had it. A man and his daughter had told me the most peculiar story when I had stopped at their ráth to ask for food and water. They had told me a story of the escape of Cuan Ó Conchúir from Ferns and a girl with red hair who had saved him by conjuring a storm. *A hailstorm.*

When they described the girl, I knew who it was. *Isolde, daughter of Fódla.* She was not dead, after all.

I also listened to what was said about Cuan. They told me a tale of fire. Fire that had poured from his hands and chased the Leinster warriors away. It had destroyed their ráth, they told me. The king himself had his men build them a new one in exchange for their silence.

You are not being so silent now, I had said to him.

It is so strange a story, I cannot imagine anyone will believe it. Even you might think me gone mad, the man replied.

I laughed then and shook my head as I ate this man's bread.

Who is Cuan Ó Conchúir, I asked him next.

He's the nephew of King Ruaidrí, the man replied, *and through his mother, he's a descendant of Sitric Silkbeard and his son Godfrey. Vikings.*

The man spoke of some sort of blood feud that had compelled Diarmait to capture him, though the particulars of that had bored me. It was the bloodline that I had listened to. Both Sitric and Godfrey were Gormflaith's mortal sons. Gormflaith spoke of Sitric often, but I'd overheard her speak of Godfrey to Máelmórda only once. A secret child with no magic she'd had with Olaf back when she had loved him.

Somehow, our gift had skipped a generation.

I didn't know it could do that, but I tucked that information away. To be pulled out another day.

I wished the man and his daughter good health, noting how different people were when I spoke to them. Spoke with them. It was something I seldom did, and never with my family. But sometimes, when it was important, I used my words.

This was the thing about not speaking. When not engaged in conversation, it enabled you to listen. To see what others were too distracted to see for themselves. However, there were downsides. I could not deny that.

Silence was a death to some. I could see the discomfort when people realised I had no reply to give them. That warm smile of introduction fading as quickly as a wave receding from the shore.

What was wrong with me, they would ask? Mute? Cursed? *Disturbed?*

I had always found this reaction to be wrong. Why such fear of a man with no words?

Marcus Aurelius once said, *the happiness of your life depends upon the quality of your thoughts.* Why then did we not live in thoughts? What was the urge to speak always, to chatter like a bird in an eternal morning? It was the animal within us longing for contact, longing to judge and be judged, like a dog sniffing the faeces of another.

I would not be judged by anyone. Not these knights with their thick armour. Not by my grandmother, who lived in a half world of fire and dreams. Not even by my father, who had killed Máelmórda but did not think I knew.

I mulled over these thoughts, but did not dwell on them. There was something important that I needed to do while my father was away. A gift of my own. *It was what I craved most of all.*

I would have one at any cost.

Now I had a lead, and I wanted the girl, Isolde. I wanted her gift. I didn't know what it was... but the power to be dead and then alive... it was something I wanted more than anything. And I would have it.

When they escaped, they rode south, the man had said.

And so south I would go.

Standing, I stared at the bodies of the old man and his daughter, then made my way into the forest. I should not have killed them, but it had been all too easy. Easier than the dog at Ferns who had struggled and fought to free himself. Besides, the man had already proved that he could not be silent, and I could not have rumours spreading of a tall, thin man roaming the lands asking questions about a girl with red hair.

Historical Note

A new era has begun.

We've moved on from the events of Clontarf and we've said goodbye to King Brian and Killaloe. As you will have realised, this book is set around one hundred and fifty years after the events of *The Land of the Living and the Dead*. What has happened in the interim, you might ask?

If we look at Munster first, it is interesting to know that to begin with, after Clontarf, Brian's son Donnchad held the kingship. Tensions, however, grew between Donnchad and his half-brother Tadc, and it is thought that Donnchad ordered the killing of Tadc in 1023. Finally, in 1063, Tadc's son, Toirdelbach (Toir as I've called him in my novel) finally ousted him. It is noted by Irish historian Geoffrey Keating that Donnchad then went to Rome to plead with the Pope to help him re-take his kingdom. The answer was no, but this meeting is significant for reasons that will become clear as the trilogy continues.

It is also important to note that the legacy of Brian Boru and Clontarf impacted all of Ireland, not only Munster.

As I have explained in previous historical notes and interviews, Brian Boru broke the old order of kingship in Ireland, and it never recovered. What I mean by this is that a king of Munster holding the high kingship was unusual, as for centuries this title had resided with the Ó'Neill kings. In showing that a new family could hold the high kingship, Brian had laid the foundations for future kings of Connacht, Leinster and Munster to try taking this title. A new rung had appeared on the ladder of ambition, so to speak – and soon kings from all over Ireland rushed to grab hold of it.

Initially, the heirs of Brian tried to retain the high kingship, but given the number of Munster kings, heirs and military leaders who had died during Clontarf, this proved to be difficult. Toirdelbach (the son of Tadc) and his own son Muirchertach did try: Muirchertach especially had a good go, however he was unable to bring the Kingdom of the Northern Ó'Neills or the Kingdom of Ulaid to heel.

The next real contender for the high kingship was Toirdelbach O'Conchúir of Connacht. However, he too failed to gain the submission of all the kings in Ireland. It was his son, Ruaidrí, who eventually succeeded in 1166, and he was then able to call himself the first high king without opposition since Brian Boru.

The Viking kingdoms of Ireland diminish in power over this time, too. Trade continued to flourish, but the Irish kings became better at controlling the ports, and as we enter the mid-twelfth century, the Dublin, Wexford and Waterford kings are either related to the Irish kings or under their control.

We also enter into a time of renewed religious conflict. Not between differing religions, but over what Christianity means to the Irish.

Ireland had once been *'the land of saints and scholars'*. By the twelfth century, this thought was no more. In fact, monks who visited Ireland were beginning to comment that it was a godless and barbaric country. The practice of divorce and of having more than one wife were lamented in particular. The setting aside of wives had become commonplace, and the marrying of stepmothers and stepdaughters also raised eyebrows. It is also evident that some kings in Ireland wanted to improve ties with Rome and the wider Christian church, while others wanted to pull away.

By the time we get to the mid-twelfth century, and the build-up to the Anglo-Norman invasion, Ireland really has become a land of contradictions. In some ways, despite all these dynastic struggles and religious conflict, Ireland had changed very little since the tenth century. Indeed, the new high king, Ruaidrí O'Conchúir, brought back the Tailteann Games, an ancient festival (akin to the Olympics), perhaps wishing to draw on the traditions of old to cement his position. It is also noted that stone buildings were being constructed, but not at the rate they are in England or Europe. People still live in scattered raths, they still live off their livestock, and the land is relatively unfarmed compared to Europe, which is also noted by the monks and priests who come to visit.

While this lack of change may seem tranquil, in my opinion, all was not well. Ireland at this time feels more vicious than before. The practice of kings blinding rivals or blinding hostages has become widespread... but it is not just kings blinding strangers from rival clans. Kings blind their own sons, and brothers are blinding brothers.

Slaves are also thought to have been common in Ireland at this time, with the Irish kings still buying them from the Viking ports, despite the fact this practice had mostly ceased in England. It is a strange thing to note that a country, after enduring such hardship with their own people being taken in previous centuries, had begun to utilise the slave trade in such a way. The slavery in Ireland is so widespread that the language had its own word for a female slave which indicated a unit of currency.

But it was not just blinding and slavery that were giving Ireland a bad reputation. In another infamous account (which I re-tell in my story), King Diarmait had the abbess of Kildare, Mór, raped so that he could have his own cousin instilled as the abbess (as not being a virgin disbarred a woman from holding the position of abbess). The kings appear to have become bloodthirsty and, seemingly, there was nothing that was out of bounds in the pursuit of power.

And it is this viciousness that really sets off a chain of events that changed Ireland forever. This event being the kidnapping of

Derbhfhorgaill Ua Ruairc, wife of King Tigernán of Bréifne, by King Diarmait Mac Murchadha of Leinster.

Derbhfhorgaill is depicted as a Helen of Troy character by the Anglo-Norse chronicler, Gerald of Wales. As Helen brought Greece and Troy to war through love and desire, Derbhfhorgaill brought the kingdoms of Bréifne and Leinster against each other. Modern historians disagree with this claim and feel that Derbhfhorgaill might have left her husband willingly at the behest of her brother.

Either way, Tigernán was outraged that his wife was taken. He was even more outraged when she was returned without any honour price being paid. The new high king, Ruaidrí, who was friends with Tigernán, eventually ousted Diarmait from Ireland. Diarmait, with his last unmarried daughter at his side, went to Henry II of England to beg for help in retaking his lands. While Henry II was disinclined to help, an Anglo-Norman lord called Richard de Clare (Strongbow) decided to aid the down-on-his-luck king, especially with the promise of a new bride and land in Ireland.

Thus begins the second era of the Gael Song.

The events in this book are accurate to what we know of this time. I have perhaps embellished the motivations of the Anglo-Normans a little more. Our main source of this time, Gerald of Wales, is Anglo-Norman, and extremely biased to his own side. In his writings the Anglo-Normans are always just and chivalrous, while the Irish are always treacherous. I've tried to get more into the heads of our key protagonists by studying their cultures and what their motivations might have truly been.

If you wish to read more about this time in Irish history to see what you think, I suggest the following books:

The Conquest of Ireland by Giraldus Cambrensis (translated and edited by Thomas Forester, revisions by Thomas Wright)

A New History of Ireland II: Medieval Ireland 1169-1534, edited by Art Cosgrave
The War of the Irish Kings by David Willis McCullough
Strongbow: The Norman Invasion of Ireland by Conor Kostick

Shauna Lawless
May 2025

Acknowledgements

So here we are. Era One of Gael Song is over and we are onto Era Two. It has really been the most fabulous few years – I've enjoyed every minute of my publication journey with Head of Zeus. To say it is beyond my wildest dreams is true because so many things have happened that I wouldn't have imagined four years ago.

A huge thanks must be given, as always, to my husband, Gerard. To my three sons, Darragh, Shay and Finan, for their jokes, laughter and hugs. To my Mum and Dad who are always there for chats, ice-cream and conversation.

Ed Wilson, my lovely agent, thank you so much for everything you have done for me.

Greg Rees, my editor, and the constant in my Gael Song journey – thank you for everything. It's been quite the journey getting four novels and three novellas out into the world. I'm sure I'm not even aware of half of what goes on to get these books onto shelves, but I know you and the rest of the Head of Zeus team work tirelessly to get them there.

And finally, a huge hug for my critique group and beta readers. You have got me through the hard times, spotted a deluge of typos, and made me laugh when I need it most. I'm very lucky to have you all in my life.

About the Author

SHAUNA LAWLESS is an avid reader of Irish mythology, folklore and history, which inspired Gael Song, her historical fantasy series set in turbulent medieval Ireland. Her critically acclaimed novel, *The Children of Gods and Fighting Men*, was nominated for Best Debut at the British Fantasy Awards. She lives in Northern Ireland with her family, where you can often find her writing or curled up with a good book.

Follow Shauna via her newsletter or at shaunalawless.com
Instagram: shauna_lawless_author

THE MYTHOLOGY. THE HISTORY. THE MAGIC.

Discover

GAEL SONG

from Shauna Lawless